KING
OF THE
ROAD

Books by Paul Hemphill

King of the Road
Me and the Boy
The Sixkiller Chronicles
Too Old to Cry
Long Gone
The Good Old Boys
The Nashville Sound

PAUL HEMPHILL

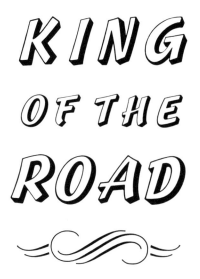

KING OF THE ROAD

Houghton Mifflin Company · Boston · 1989

Copyright © 1989 by Paul Hemphill
All rights reserved

For information about permission to reproduce selections from this book, write to Permissions, Houghton Mifflin Company, 2 Park Street, Boston, Massachusetts 02108.

Library of Congress Cataloging-in-Publication Data

Hemphill, Paul, date.
King of the road / Paul Hemphill.
    p. cm.
ISBN 0-395-49860-0
    I. Title.
PS3558.E4793K5 1989   89-32782
813'.54 — dc20   CIP

Printed in the United States of America

P 10 9 8 7 6 5 4 3 2 1

The author is grateful for permission to quote from the following:

"Do Not Go Gentle into That Good Night," from *The Poems of Dylan Thomas*. Copyright 1952 by Dylan Thomas. Reprinted by permission of New Directions Publishing Corporation and Dent Publishers.

"Six Days on the Road," by Earl Green and Carl Montgomery. Copyright © 1960, 1963 by Newkeys Music, Inc., and Tune Publishing Co. Used by permission. All rights reserved.

"I'm Movin' On," by Hank Snow. Copyright 1950 by Unichappell Music, Inc. (renewed). All rights reserved. Used by permission.

"There Stands the Glass," by Russ Hull, Mary Jean Shurtz, and A. Greisham. Copyright 1953 by Unichappell Music, Inc., and Jamie Music Publishing. Used by permission of Warner/Chappell Music, Inc. All rights reserved.

In memory of my father,
PAUL JAMES HEMPHILL, SR.,
the last trucker.

And for my mother,
VELMA NELSON HEMPHILL,
who waited up.

ICC is a-checkin' on down the line,
   Well, I'm a little overweight
   And my logbook's 'way behind;
But, nothin' bothers me tonight,
   I can dodge all the scales all right;
Six days on the road
   And I'm a-gonna make it home tonight . . .

        "Six Days on the Road"

And you, my father, there on the sad height,
Curse, bless, me now with your fierce tears, I pray.
Do not go gentle into that good night,
Rage, rage against the dying of the light . . .

        Dylan Thomas

KING
OF THE
ROAD

PROLOGUE

AT SUNDOWN, on the bleak warehouse fringes of the old soot-and-sweat factory towns where things are Made in America, sinewy tattooed men in cowboy boots and grease-stained windbreakers and baseball caps crunch across gravel lots, past heaps of discarded tires and engine blocks and the sad rusted carcasses of cannibalized trucks; the men clean-shaven, rested and ready to roll now as they approach the line of hulking behemoths silhouetted against the magenta sky. *Red sky at night, trucker's delight.* Guard dogs snarl, gophers shuffle, stray cats whine. There is the rhythmic *putt-putt-putt* of refrigeration units and, from a nearby railroad yard, the clanging of steel-on-steel as mulish diesels move boxcars into place.

For the drivers, leathery men better known as Buster and Smitty and Stick and Red, their chariots await. Macks, Whites, Freightliners, Peterbilts, Internationals, Kenworths. Big rigs, little rigs, new ones, old ones. Monstrous chrome diesels, for the salaried Teamsters, with sleeper cabs holding toilet and wash basin and bed. Scrawny little gasoline jobs with fifty-gallon tanks strapped to the sides, for the gritty independent owner-operators, their rigs' amenities not extending beyond an army-surplus wool blanket and a soiled lumpy pillow and a radio dangling from wires beneath the dash. Pet names crudely painted on the doors, in the manner of World War II B-17 bomber pilots: Bama Belle, Lucky Seven, Arkansas Traveler, Queen of Hearts. Chrome air horns and fanciful winged hood ornaments gleam beneath the wan lights of the lot, itself enclosed by barbed wire fencing, and attached to the trucks by wires and hoses serving as umbilicals are the trailers, the *raisons d'être*: huge wheeled silver warehouses filled to the top during the day, while the drivers sleep, with steel for Chicago and lumber for Miami and pipe for Dallas.

In such a place, in Birmingham, Alabama, a man and his boy walk past the line of fancier rigs until they reach a faded four-ton Dodge, almost hidden in a dark corner of the lot. Hand-painted in a florid scroll, just below the driver's-side window, there is the proud legend *Dixie Redball*; below that, in smaller letters, there is Jake Hawkins, Owner-Operator, and taped to the center of the door a posterboard advisory: Leased to Alabama Highway Express. While the boy settles into the shotgun seat the father rakes a kitchen match across the fender to relight his cigar and then, flashlight in hand, walks around the rig for a look-see: tires okay, air brake lines connected, fuel tanks full and cinched down, fifth-wheel secure, toolbox and oilcans stowed behind the cab, trailer locked and sealed.

Swinging up into the driver's seat, grinning to see the boy ogling the truck-stop pinup of Rita Hayworth in a negligee, he surveys the cluttered cab: work gloves, logbooks, coffee, cigars, cold biscuits, aviator glasses, blanket, pillow, road maps, clean clothes. Slacks and dress-up shirt, just in case. First aid kit and fire extinguisher and emergency flares and pint of booze, just in case.

Thumping the accelerator now, jiggling the throttle, checking the trailer through the rear-view mirror and the wide side ones, he winks at the boy and then fires the ignition. Contact. *Baramp-BamBam-Barrrooom-BomBom-Bbrrrrmmmmmppppp-Bbrrrrmmmmm.* Thunder and lightning. A growling lion, disturbed and angry, awakened from its sleep. Revving up the r.p.m.s. *Bbrrrmmmmmm, Bbrrrmmmmmm, Bbrrrmmmmmm.* A final rundown: radio, gauges, heater, air horns, brakes, steering, lights a-blaze. Engine purring at idle now, heat already rising through the floorboards, they wiggle down into their seats. Ready to roll.

Think you could drive this thing?

Aw, I don't know. Maybe when I'm older.

What Mama's afraid of.

Mama?

Said just before her and Sis let us out, said, Now I don't want him growin' up to be no truck driver. Know what I said to that?

No, sir.

Told her, It's good enough for me and I notice you ain't starvin'.

It's a mechanized army out there, a brotherhood on wheels, a caravan of wagoneers rolling across the new American landscape to feed the fancies of a nation glad to be rid of Hitler and the Japs. Rolling, rolling, rolling. Hauling stuff: steel, tires, washing machines, automobiles, dishwashers, clothing, tricycles, toasters, radios, furniture, and bathtubs. Hellbent and moving on — *Don't take a curve/At 60 per/We hate to lose/A customer/Burma Shave* — past junkyards and silos and See Rock City barns, racing over the old undulating macadam roads against Greyhounds, pickups, station wagons, the Santa Fe, and the moon and time itself.

In the cabs, riding high, every man a king. Grabbing gears,

blasting horns for little boys on country roads, beating trains to crossings, swooping down mountains at seventy miles an hour, standing on the running board to pee as the truck crawls up the other side. Whistling wind, singing tires, telephone poles zipping past, *stickety-stickety-stickety*, lonesome thoughts: Like for somebody to tell me when they're gonna make the farmers fence up their cows out here . . . goddamned women drivers, lookit that. Between them and the tourists and the speed traps, a man's got a better chance at night . . . I might pay about a hundred dollars for a cup of coffee and somebody to talk to right now.

And all across the dial, the truckers' radio shows. Clear-channel 50,000-watters like WCKY out of Cincinnati and WWL from New Orleans and WSM, the Opry station, out of Nashville. WHO Des Moines, WWVA Wheeling, KMOX St. Louis. Those 200,000-watt stations down in Mexico, the 'X' stations, like XERF, damned thing sounds like a local station far away as Minnesota. *That's one-thousand baby chicks, friends, sex not guaranteed*, like some old boy's gonna buy his chickens through the mail. Hell, they'll sell you Magic Prayer Cloths and Gro-Mo-Hair and their daughters if you like Messicans, probably even got autographed pictures of Jesus. Nothing but country: Hank Williams, Kitty Wells, Cowboy Copas, Little Jimmy Dickens, Roy Acuff. *Big eight-wheeler rollin' down the track/Means your true-lovin' daddy ain't comin' back/I'm movin' on/Don't you hear my song?* And if they ain't singing, they're selling: Martha White Self-Rising, Garrett Snuff, Prince Albert, Goo-Goo candy, records, harmonicas, truck seats, satin pillows that say Mama, gold Bibles with Jesus talking in red. *ICC is a-checkin' on down the line/Well, I'm a little overweight and my log book's 'way behind . . .*

A truck stop at two in the morning, east Tennessee, neon oasis blinking in the night. Moe's & Joe's: Eat-Gas-Showers-Bunks-Truckers Welcome. Gravel lot big as a football field, used to be planted in corn, now filled with rigs from everywhere. Baggett, Alabama Highway, Campbell 66 ("Humpin' to Please"),

Colonial Refrigerated. All squatting in the eerie shadows cast by spotlights on gawky pine poles. Curtains drawn on some, reefer units chugging on others, long lines at the pumps, a Truck Stop Annie going door to door (ten dollars for a dose of clap). Legs of a mechanic protruding from the opened snout of a disabled International out of Florida.

Inside the place, through double screen doors, a carnival: clattery floor fans about to take off, scarred linoleum floors, chrome coffee urn dull from grease, torn puke-green booths against the walls, a long red Formica counter with rickety spinning stools holding truckers who pop pills and slurp coffee and jostle for elbow room beneath sputtering fluorescent lights. Breakfast 24 Hrs., eggs and sausage and grits and biscuits and gravy, coffee hot and black and endless. Jukeboxes at every booth and every stool, pinball and shuffleboard and a ragged pool table in an alcove designated Recreation Center, revolving metal racks near the cash register below a poster saying If We Ain't Got It You Don't Need It: chewing tobacco, sunglasses, key chains, No Doz, picture postcards, aspirin, Murine, cigarette lighters that play "Dixie," glass figurines of a woman whose clothes disappear when you turn her upside down. And for serious shoppers, spread out on laundry tables against a far wall, a truckers' bazaar: cowboy hats, baseball caps, belt buckles, pinup calendars, plastic Jesuses, Rebel flags, bumper stickers (Dimmit Dammit, ⟨Passing Side/Suicide⟩, Insured by Smith & Wesson), steering-wheel knobs and squirrel tails and fuzzy dice.

Moneen, rawboned redhead smacking gum and bearing fly swatter, elbows her way toward the booth where the man and boy sit. She splats a fly dead in the center of the table, startling them and sending the salt shaker reeling. She says, Whatchyawnt?

Jesus. Took a lotta guts to do that, Moe.

Me or the fly? Everybody's gotta go sometimes.

Well, flies got rights, too.

Not in my place, they don't. Little nasties.

The man peers toward the plastic carousel on the counter and says, Kinda pie you got?

Sliced.

What's got a-hold o' you tonight, anyways?

Hell, Jake, you know what kinda pie we got. Same as last week.

Probably the same ones, too. It's like rotatin' tires, Moe. Looks like you could at least move the damned things around every now and then. Gimme the lemon icebox. One you made in high school Home Ec.

I'm gonna let that pass. This your boy? Looks just like you.

Ain't his fault. This here's Jake Jr. Sonny. First time out.

That's nice. You want the icebox, too, hon?

Y'all got hamburgers?

Honey, Joe *invented* hamburgers. All the way?

Yes'm. And a Coke, please.

At a round table in the middle of the room, six truckers sprawl under a cloud of smoke. Stirring coffee, rubbing bloodshot eyes, ogling Moneen. Having spoken only to themselves for the last 200 miles, they debate women, rigs, shortcuts, politics, weigh stations, weather, and chicken-fried steak: Know that steel bridge at the Brazos? . . . Was gonna buy me a GMC 'til I found out it stands for General Mess o' Crap . . . Kansas Skyscrapers . . . That ol' gal must take Ugly pills . . . Just seen ol' Ernest Tubb's bus headed back to Nashville . . . Truman, now, he'll straighten their yellow asses out in a hurry . . . Shakey-town . . . Call that U.S. 50 out west the Loneliest Road in America.

One of them grabs his check and eases away from the table. Sucking on a toothpick, tugging at his crotch, straightening his short-billed driver's cap, ambling toward the cash register, he stops by the booth where the man and the boy sit.

How you doin', Jake?

Fair to partly cloudy, Grady. Where you headed?
Choo-Choo Town. Runnin' empty. You?
Cumberland, then Rubber City.
Still got that run, huh?
Two years. Tire executive. Take the twine up, haul the tires back. How's it look up the line?
Had the scales out 'bout an hour ago, right past the Holston trestle. Might ought to check it out if you're heavy. Fog's bad. Maybe the boys packed up and went home by now. I don't know.
Well, much obliged.
Keep 'er in the road, good buddy.

Movin' on. *Little overweight and my logbook's 'way behind.* Trailer lit up like a roadhouse. Blowing smoke, changing gears, following the river and the tracks up into the black Appalachians. Old U.S. 11, an asphalt ribbon shimmering in the moonlight as it twists through mountain towns closed for the evening. Parking the rig just below the crest of a pass, leaving the boy half-asleep in the cab to go check out the Holston River bridge, the man trots back fifteen minutes later with news that the scales are closed, reaches for low gear and makes tracks: The boys don't take their work half as serious as me. Bristol, where it is Tennessee on one side of the street and Virginia on the other; Abingdon, Marion, Wytheville. Truckers blinking lights: once for Howdy, twice for The Boys, three times for Trouble. Pulaski, Radford, Christiansburg.

Damn fog's so bad you gotta get out and *feel* the signs for Roanoke.
Awwww.
I ever tell you 'bout the time I was overloaded with chickens?
No, sir.
The boys said, You're gon' have to take some of 'em off to make the limit. Had me a plan.

Uh-huh.

Got out the tire iron and started bangin' on the trailer. Chickens got airborne. Said, What's it weigh now, Cap'n?

Awwww. Didn't.

Listen, son, if you see me nodding I want you to pull that chain.

This one?

Works the air horn. Tends to wake me up.

Yes, sir.

That's providing you don't fall asleep yourself. How you holding up?

All right, I guess.

Tell you what — shifting down, squinting through the mirrors, setting the air brakes, turning on the blinkers — reckon we ought to pull up for a while.

A little two-pump gas station, wide gravel lot, set back under sweetgums and oaks, shut down for the night, only the blue and white Pure Oil sign illuminated. Engine shuddering to a stop, silence overwhelming. Steam rising from the hood of the truck. Smells of hot oil and simmering rubber and gravel. Pops and sighs from hot metal cooling down. Eerie.

How do we sleep?

Just curl up. You'll sleep, I promise.

How 'bout you?

I'm fine like this.

Sitting up? You want a pillow?

Biscuit, shot of whiskey, 'bout an hour of shut-eye and I'll be a new man. Think I was born like this. Get some rest, son. You don't want to miss the Shenandoah.

Part One
WHISKEY

1

IT WAS ONLY eight o'clock in the morning, but already they were flashing like trout in the pool below his window, about a dozen of them: bronze baby bachelors and tawny blondes, none older than twenty-five, cavorting before his weary eyes. "*Marco!*" came a bellow from one side of the kidney-shaped pool, the deep end where the hydrangea and azalea flourished. "*Polo!*" came a response from the opposite side, near the pavilion shading the Ping-Pong table and Coke machine, and suddenly the boys were belly-flopping into the pool and the girls were squealing as though something Olympian were on the line right there in Tallahassee. Fine, he thought as he turned from the window, but what kind of first name is Talmadge, and what do you *do*, actually?

Sonny Hawkins knew exactly who they were and what they did, and that had become reason enough for him to stay away from the pool except when they were away: grunting in the Nautilus room at Doak Campbell Stadium, typing press releases at the Florida Chamber of Commerce, hustling memberships at Osceola Country Club, hunkering over worn ledgers in the law library at Florida State University, covering the legislature for the *Democrat*. They were promising young men and women all, he a forty-five-year-old with a great future behind him, so he had resolved to keep his distance, to remain above the fray, be the mystery man in Apartment 213, in hopes that nobody would notice. He remembered a veteran minor-leaguer in Class D, spring training of '54, on a morning after Sonny had struck out all four times: "Drop the bat and grab your glove, kid, you don't want to overexpose yourself." Low profile. Stay under the radar.

Still feeling awkward in the pinstriped Dior pajamas his sister had given him for Christmas, the latest move in her relentless campaign to make him respectable, he shuffled across the burnt-orange shag carpet of his apartment. *Seminole Gardens, eff, pool, cable, A/C, nr FSU, 1-yr lease, adults, no pets.* There had been worse places in the years since he had left his wife and kids, the sort of hovels that cause faculty wives to confuse charm with hard times ("Isn't it just like it's *supposed* to be?"), but this one looked much better on paper than in person. Sixties Motel was the décor: cheap Mediterranean furniture, Murphy bed, kitchenette, walls hung with Greek fishing-village prints heavy on the avocado to match the orange carpet — a color scheme that oozed like bile right on out the door into the hallway — all of it so crammed into the tiny space that about all he could add was the trusty old whitewashed picnic table that had been his "desk" for nearly a decade, lugged in the back of his pickup as he followed the trail of "visiting lecturer" jobs across the South from one small college to another until, finally, Panhandle Community College.

Above the table, which held his vintage portable typewriter and the accouterments of the teacher and erstwhile writer (pencils, paper, dictionary, wire catchall basket), he had hung a cork bulletin board and a truck-stop calendar and a dozen family photographs, chief among them being an oil painting of his father, the retired Birmingham truck driver, a tortured Van Gogh vision in swirls of violet and black that was remarkable only because the friend who painted it had only met the old man once in passing. There was something else, but it was now out of sight: the manuscript for a novel he had begun ten years before, *Children of the Swamp*, about the removal of the Seminole Indians in the 1830s: dog-eared pages he now showed only to females lured to his web, having given up after eighteen rejections.

A Bloody would be nice, he thought, lighting his first Camel. *There stands the glass;/fill it, waiter, and go/while I'm lost in the glow/ of a happier day.* Webb Pierce, about 1950, one of the heroes of his youth. But there stood the chip, too, on the counter separating the kitchen and living areas, big as a silver dollar, evidence that Sonny had been true for three months solid. He picked it up and read the awkward slogans — Think Before You Drink, Easy Does It, One Day at a Time — and then flipped it into the "crystal" bowl on the counter, his former party-peanuts bowl, to rest among the dozen others he had collected in a fitful encounter with Alcoholics Anonymous that had flickered now for nearly two years.

This was the last day of classes before the summer break, and Sonny's only official duty was to make the final meeting with his Freshman English students at ten o'clock. Unofficially, though, there was something else, and he did *not* look forward to that: a faculty party, around dusk, at the home of Dudley Lyons, the dean of the college, an imperious man who wore bow ties and affected a British accent and still called Sonny "Buddy." He hated the prospects of catering to such a man, but as long as there was a possibility he might be invited back to teach in the fall he had little choice. In between, so the day wouldn't be a complete loss, there would be lunch at Garcia's with Leo Miranda, about the only faithful companion he had found in Tallahassee, a shaggy poet who had made his separate peace with the snug world of academia a dozen years earlier when he was only thirty.

For his final performance, he determined as he sat on a stool at the counter slurping Cheerios and sipping coffee, he would read poetry. He wasn't bad at all on his feet, probably something he had picked up from his old man on those long summertime trips in the truck when he was a kid, and entertaining the troops seemed to be a fit way to end the quarter. He would perform "Coy Mistress" and "Living in Sin" for Sherry, the lip-gloss queen, to give her something to think about; and "To an Athlete Dying Young" for Larvelle, the wide receiver trying to get himself eligible for the FSU Seminoles, just to watch him blink. Then, because he liked his kids and they seemed to like him, some silly farewells — *Don't call me, I'll call you* or, hey, *Zero pregnancies, now* — before freeing them, and himself, for the summer.

Showtime. Slipping into a Grateful Dead T-shirt and jeans and moccasins, arming the answering machine he had bought on a whim the week before, grabbing the red-bound poetry reader, Sonny slinked down the side stairwell to his red '67 Chevy pickup. Within ten minutes he had careened through the muggy streets of Tallahassee, made his way around the cluster of state office buildings aglow in the morning sun, passed the sleek FSU campus of magnolias and high-rises, reached the treeless "campus" of Panhandle, created a parking place beside the double-wide trailer that had been serving as a "temporary" classroom for three years, and found himself in the company of the eight students who had bothered to show up in their cutoffs and sandals and halters and T-shirts.

It went about the way he had expected: him sitting on the

edge of a metal desk beneath fluorescent lights and air conditioning, now and then bounding to his feet to startle the nodders, Sherry pretending to blush over "Coy Mistress," Larvelle frowning when "Athlete" was prefaced, the rest drowsily watching others toss Frisbees on the grass outside. He plowed ahead through Frost and Housman and Plath, pausing occasionally to demystify each poem, all the while glancing at his watch.

Then something happened. Looking for one more poem, a short one since time was running out, he found Dylan Thomas's "Do not go gentle": pithy, neat, nineteen lines. While students rattled pages, searching for the place, he tried to tell the story behind the poem in terms that a gaggle of college kids could appreciate. "Dylan Thomas's father had been pretty much a hell-raiser in his time," he began, "kind of a maverick, a protester, a militant. But then one day the old man just said to hell with it. Gave up the good fight. Took to his rocking chair." Nobody seemed very interested, but Sonny hardly noticed. "Thomas didn't know how much he really loved his father until it was almost too late to tell him" — *Hey, wait* — "so he wrote this poem for his father, the hero of his youth, and what he's saying is pretty simple: 'Give 'em hell, Pop. It ain't over 'til it's over.' So there you have it. 'Do not go gentle into that good night.'"

What's this? What's happening? Sonny eased off the desk, ostensibly so he could walk to the lectern for his grand finale, but in truth there was a catch in his throat. *An old-folks' home, for Christ's sake.* He began to read. "'Do not go gentle into that good night, Old age should burn and rave at close of day; Rage, rage against the dying of the light . . .'" *Old-maid teacher, never made it through Emily Dickinson without bawling.* "'. . . Wild men who caught and sang the sun in flight . . .'" *King of the Road.* "'. . . blaze like meteors and be gay . . .'" The students were leaning forward, suddenly rapt on a day that had held no promises. Sonny took a deep breath, sniffed, raked his hair, and managed the last stanza in a hoarse whisper: " 'And you, my father, there on the sad height' " — the bell rang, ending class, but nobody moved — " 'curse, bless, me now with your fierce tears, I pray. Do not go gentle into that good night. Rage . . . rage . . . against the dying . . . of the light.' "

At Garcia's, an earthy Cuban tavern downtown on East Tennessee known for its black bean soup and eclectic clientele, Sonny saw that Leo had beaten the Friday crowd of secretaries and FSU football coaches and state capitol drones to the favored front booth by the window and already had a beer. This combination, Garcia's and Leo Miranda, had made life tolerable for Sonny during his year in town: Garcia's not only because it was his kind of place, a democratic bar with dark wooden booths and TV sets stuck on ESPN, but also because Vincent Garcia and the boys cared enough that they would eighty-six him if he even *looked* like he wanted a drink; Leo because he knew something about everything, loved the English language more than tenure, was content to "do my jobs," and was about the only person Sonny knew who saw nothing embarrassing about having a novel rejected by eighteen publishers.

"Minor Regional Sage Takes Lunch," Leo said when Sonny slid into the booth.

"Maybe you're buying. Sage short $49.18."

"How so?"

"You know Lu-Ann, the Peanut Princess."

"Super-Tits."

"Bless 'em both. Presented me with a bill last night. Had it all written down: round trips from the trailer camp, baby-sitters, even the time she bought spaghetti fixings. Said grad school wasn't free."

"And you complied, my man?"

"Pussy ain't free, either. You wind up paying, one way or another. Wrote her a check, but where it says 'For' I put down 'Fucking, 23 Attempts.' "

One of the waiters placed a Perrier in front of Sonny without a word. "Thanks a bunch, pal," Sonny told him. The waiter didn't have to ask what they wanted for lunch.

"Friend of yours was asking about you this morning," Leon said. "Wanted to be sure 'Buddy' was going to be at his soirée."

"Dudley Do-Right."

"Any word about the fall?"

"Nothing. Ain't kissed enough ass yet, I guess."

"It'll happen. The kids love you."

"That doesn't seem to matter much."

"Hey, come on. You've got the old tour de force in the oven, and the paychecks run through August."

"Look, Leo. No more jokes about the goddamn book, okay?"

"I'm not kidding. Nobody's ever done a novel about the Seminole removal."

"It's easy to see why. Eighteen publishers can't be wrong. Why the hell do they always say 'alas'? 'Alas, *Children of the Swamp* doesn't fit our needs at this time.' Why don't they just say it sucks?"

"There's plenty more up there."

"I won't be bothering 'em anymore, Leo."

"Hey. What are you saying?"

"I'm dead meat. It's over."

"C'mon. Where's the spirit?"

"Dead and gone to teaching, pal. With all due respect, of course."

"Christ."

"Gentle into the night, Leo."

Lunch came, steaming bowls of black bean soup and hot chunks of greasy Cuban bread, and the two men attacked it while the place began to fill. A kid from the sports information office at FSU came by with a boxload of new eight-by-ten glossies of Seminole football players to replace the ones currently decorating the walls. Some guys at the bar booed when a soccer game came up on the TV sets, but soon they were rooting for

Chile. Heads turned when a pair of coeds walked in, breasts bursting from halter tops, enough to make a reedy middle-aged government type in a clip-on bow tie choke on his iced tea. Right behind them came three young blacks, obviously football players for FSU or Florida A&M, wearing cutoffs and sandals and mesh T-shirts cut high to reveal washboard stomachs and sunken navels. One of them was Larvelle, of the English class, who smiled and waved at Sonny.

"A funny thing happened this morning, Leo."

"They gang-raped you, out of thanks."

"Naw. Serious funny. Odd." After the waiter had cleared the table and taken orders to fetch another Perrier and beer, Sonny told of his barely making it through the poem. Leo, peeling the cellophane from a cigar, listened somberly. He had told Sonny once of *his* father, an irascible old Conch in Key West who used to get drunk with Hemingway; and how now, with gay boutiques all around him, he refused to budge even though offers for the old family cottage and its spit of sand were reaching six figures.

"So that's it," Leo said.

"What?"

"Why you've been fucked up lately. How's your old man doing?"

"Well, Leo, it's sort of taken a turn toward the Southern Gothic."

"They're still in the nursing home, I presume."

"Mama is, but he may not be long for it."

"Well, you can't rope a cowboy."

"Listen. I get a call from my sister last week, telling me the latest. The preacher that runs the place had her in for a chat. Preacher says, 'Miz Bradford, now we're not blind to the fact that some of our, ah, *residents* are in the habit of going to their rooms before the evening meal and having a, ah, *cock*tail.' I'm laughing like hell and I tell her, '*Cock*tail? My old man never had a *cocktail* in his whole life.' Know what he's been doing?

Brown-bagging it from the trunk of his car, right out there in front of God and Brother Boggs, just to gall the bastards."

"They run him, or what?"

"It gets complicated because of my mother."

"Alzheimer's, you said."

"Bad. Last time I was in Birmingham she started talking *of* me, *to* me, in the third person. 'My boy Sonny lives in Tallahassee, did you know that?' If she gets on the elevator alone, it's like Charlie on the MTA. But they ain't gonna put up with my old man's shit much longer. We're talking serious Christians here, and that includes my sister and the asshole she married. The old man wants to take Mama back home, but there ain't no way he can look after her and I don't think a private nurse would make it to daybreak."

Leo rolled his eyes and mumbled something about what a shame it was that their fathers hadn't met. He swilled the last of his beer to a head and swallowed it, a bit self-consciously, it seemed to Sonny, and said, "You think he's an alcoholic?"

"Hell, I don't know, Leo. Last time I was up there he circled around for a while before he sort of blurted out, 'Does it hurt?' He knew about me and AA. Said Mimosa Towers made him nervous so he'd been conducting a little experiment: couple of shots of whiskey before breakfast and he was okay. I told him I'd tried the same thing for ten goddamn years and I didn't think much of the idea. One thing that throws me off, though, and he won't let you forget it. He drove a truck three million miles 'without an accident chargeable to myself.' "

It was nearly three o'clock before Sonny got back to the apartment, after waiting for the paychecks to be released and then running by the Barnett Bank to make a deposit, and when he walked in he saw the message light blinking on the answering machine. He considered the possibilities — Lu-Ann was contrite, and figured she had overcharged; Robby, his wandering son, had another speeding ticket; Dudley Do-Right was calling off his party due to lack of interest; somewhere in the canyons of New York an editor had gone crazy over his novel — but when he flicked the switch he heard the voice of his sister, Phyllis, sounding grim.

She answered on the fifth ring, out of breath, and he said, "Dr. Hawkins here."

"Oh, *hey* there, Sonny? I was just going out the *door*." His sister spoke in italics and question marks and exclamations, and "door" came out as "doe-ah." Hollywood would love it, but it got on his nerves.

"I just got your message."

"An *answering* machine. I s'wanee!"

"Another small step for mankind. Catch you at a bad time?"

"Oh, heavens, *no!* I was leaving for the club to meet Penny. Penny Padgett?" — *Pe-ah-nee Pa-yuh-jit* — "Preacher Padgett's daughter? It's my tennis day."

"So. What's up?"

"Well, Sonny, it's about Daddy."

Oh, shit. "What now?"

"I didn't know how you'd take it, so I — "

"Take what? What's happened, Phyl?"

"Daddy's gone away, Sonny."

"Gone? What the hell?"

"Now wait, Sonny. Try to relax. I want you to understand. I know how you feel about Daddy."

"Okay, let's have it."

Phyllis was grim, all right. "I told you about the drinking, and how Brother Boggs said they couldn't have any more of that? Well, Saturday, Sonny. Oh, it was just awful. He and Mama were sitting there at breakfast, you know? The nice big dining room where they all eat? All of a sudden Daddy just went *crazy!* He stood up and knocked his orange juice all over Mama and the other ladies at the table, and he started yelling and saying just *terrible* things about the colored help and the food and Brother Boggs and the church and everything. Oh, Lord, Sonny. Our daddy. Just a second."

While Phyllis blew her nose, Sonny gazed at the painting of his father above the picnic table-*cum*-desk and imagined for a split second that the old man had winked the way he always did when he was pulling Mama's leg or getting ready to tell a whopper like how the watermelons in Texas "grow so fast the bottoms wear off before you can pick 'em."

"There, I'm back," said Phyllis. "Lordy me."

"Where's he now?"

"Please relax, Sonny. Let me finish. So before anybody could stop him he ran right out of the dining room and jumped in the car and drove off. I knew where he'd gone. He'd gone home to the basement. Well, just to make a long story short, that's where we found him the next morning. Oh, Sonny, he was drunk again and there was blood all over the place where I guess he fell down. And he started saying these ugly things again about everybody, you know? He even tried to fight Collier, and everybody knows how much Collier loves him."

"Right, bosom buddies," Sonny said.

"Well, Collier *tries*."

"This was Saturday? Phyl, it's Wednesday now. Why didn't you tell me sooner?"

"We didn't know if you would approve."

"Approve? If he loses it, he loses it."

"No, I mean approve of our *decision*."

"Decision."

"We took him away, Sonny, so he can get better."

"What, a hospital?"

"Well, yes, sort of. I mean, it's one of those recovery places, you know. Sonny, I'd hoped you of all people would understand, being in AA and all."

"You mean to tell me that y'all went and threw my father into a drunk tank? Not even seventy years old and you've got him playing checkers so he won't drink anymore? Jesus Christ — "

"Sonny, Brother Boggs thinks — "

"I don't give a good goddamn what that pious — "

"There wasn't anything else we could do." She was being cold and calm now. "We have to think about Mama now. If Daddy can't behave himself, he can't live there anymore. But Mama has to, you know? They've moved her out of their room and put her in the Health Care unit so they can take better care of her. It's real nice there, Sonny. Mama *loves* it."

"Where'd y'all lock him up?"

"Oh, Sonny, *please*." She was clearly disgusted.

"He's at DeSoto Springs, in Mississippi. Near Hattiesburg? It's a place called Piney Woods Recovery Center. He'll have to stay a month, but everything's paid for by Medicare. We drove him over there Monday and he really liked it. They've got shuffleboard, color TV, everything. Oh, Sonny, he's the center of attention. When we said goodbye to him he was playing pool and telling truck-driving stories. Daddy's the center of attention. Wouldn't you know it?"

"Can he have visitors?"

"Not until this weekend."

"How about phone calls?"

"Any time after noon tomorrow," Phyllis said. "What are you going to do, Sonny?"

"Quit looking at my navel, for starters."

"I don't understand you, Sonny."

"Me either, Sis."

Sonny wrote down all the information and told his sister he would drive to Birmingham in a day or so to check on things before driving on to Mississippi. He had intended to hang around the pool for a while that afternoon, maybe take a nap before suiting up for the ordeal at Dudley Lyons's that evening, but he didn't have the heart for it. He turned on the campus easy-listening radio station and, for the longest while, sprawled on the avocado sofa to contemplate the anguished painting of his father.

Dudley Lyons and his wife, Vivian, lived in a pretentious new subdivision where FSU deans and state government bosses were cloistered in an odd mixture of fake Disneyland palaces. Crowding against each other, on rolling land dotted with newly planted magnolias and water oaks and an occasional ill-advised palm, were low-slung Spanish adobe haciendas and cute Colonials and white-columned Taras and breezy flat-roofed glass Malibus. The Lyonses had chosen a neo–Tudor Castle: two-story, turrets, cathedral windows, fireplaces, lawns laid out for croquet, formal garden, pool; a fairly impressive layout, at first blush, until you noticed that the exposed beams were made of Styrofoam and that somebody had nailed a bronze marker to the mantel in the "great room" that read The Lyons Den.

"Forgot the apostrophe-ess, *eck-shly*." It was Leo, who had come up behind Sonny while a black waiter in a butler's uniform twisted a lime peel for his Perrier. Sonny had worn his seersucker suit and a bow tie.

"Misspelled 'din,' too," Sonny whispered. "Who the hell are all of these people?"

"Dudley giveth tenure and Dudley taketh away."

"Is there a particular place where they hold the ceremony? I mean, does he drop his drawers by the pool or what?"

"It's over. You kissed ass when you showed up. "See you even wore your 'cocksucker' suit."

"Wanted to be in uniform."

The crowd numbered nearly a hundred, more of them from FSU and state government than from the skeletal faculty of Panhandle Community College, and they spilled through the French doors onto the flagstone terrace and around the pool and onward to a manicured lawn where portable bars sat beside torchlights flickering black smoke at the edge of the treeline. Silver trays of hors d'oeuvres were being circulated by coeds in crisp servants' uniforms with sexy net stockings. Fireflies and bats darted in the twilight, and from somewhere came Beethoven. On the far side of the pool, surrounded by students and intent young instructors who hung on his every word, there lolled Dudley Lyons: teeth glistening, Miami tan, silver mane still wet from a swim, white ascot, double-breasted blue blazer with six gold buttons, white canvas trousers, white bucks. Sonny still couldn't figure out where the money had come from. Dean of a little community college in the scraggly Florida Panhandle?

Wanting to get it over as soon as possible, Sonny moved toward Dudley and his court with Leo at his side. They were halfway across the terrace when they ran smack into Vivian Lyons. She was done up in Laura Ashley this evening — lacy white collar, busy Scotch plaid high-waisted dress with billowy sleeves, cute patent-leather flats, June Allyson hairdo — all of it belying her sixty years. "Why, Leo!" she said. Thick-tongued. Into the sauce.

"Sonny and I were just commenting on what great parties you have, Mrs. Lyons," Leo said.

"Oh, posh. The dean and I just believe in having a little backyard fun on weekends."

"Tell that to the Black Panthers," Sonny muttered out the side of his mouth to Leo.

"I'm sorry?"

"Sonny was just remarking on your good taste, Mrs. Lyons."

"Oh, please, now, Leo. Vivian."

"Yes, ma'am."

"I remember when you were nothing but a student. You babysat for us one time, 'member? But, now, whom do we have here?"

"Sonny Hawkins, Mrs. Lyons. He's a well-known writer who's been a visiting lecturer at Panhandle this year. If we're lucky he'll decide to — "

"Oh, look, there's Senator Stovall and his wife," she said, waving across the pool to an aging couple. "Hawkins. Buddy Hawkins. Forgive me, but — "

"It's Sonny, ma'am."

"You write novels, I hope."

"Well, ma'am, I — "

"None of those *paperbacks*, now. *Novels*, you hear?"

Sonny and Leo were looking at each other with mouths open, hoping they had heard wrong from the wife of the dean of the college, and when they looked up they saw that she was weaving her way toward her husband. They fell in behind her, grabbing canapes from a silver tray as they wound through the crowd, and came upon Dudley Lyons as he was finishing a story about an encounter with a Cockney cabbie on a recent trip to London: ". . . 'if I do say so meself, guv'nah.' *Pygmalion* lives . . ." Strained laughter came from the four students huddled before him.

"Ah, Señor Miranda. ¿*Cómo está?*" Lyons waved his drink and stroked his ascot. The students parted for Leo and Sonny.

"*Muy bueno*, dean. Thanks for — "

"And Buddy. How's the book on the Seminoles?"

"Well, dean — "

"The boys in sports information cooperating?"

"Sports information?"

"FSU didn't even have football until 'forty-eight, you know. All-girls school until then."

"Seminole *Indians*, dean."

"Indians. You're writing about *Indians?*"

"Yes, sir. We talked about that when you hired me."

Flustered, Lyons reached over and tweaked Sonny's bow tie. "Nice suit," he said. "You *look* like a writer. Rumpled. Faulknerian. I'd say it's a Southern novelist's uniform."

"It's my cocksucker suit."

"I beg your pardon?"

"Cocksucker."

Leo Miranda froze and cut his eyes to Sonny, trying to discern what kind of look that was on his face: mean? mischievous? playful? Nearby guests, who had heard only the last words of the exchange, also froze. The air hung still between Sonny and Dudley Lyons until the dean cocked his head and said, through tight lips, "I see. Seersucker. Cocksucker."

"That's right. Cocksucker."

It wouldn't do to say the devil made him do it. Too complex for that. No, it was some primordial instinct that had been passed on to him — hellbent, blind to pragmatism, unyielding and, sooner or later, suicidal — the same black force that had been at once his father's most appealing strength and his great weakness. How many times had he heard the old man rage on, into the night, squinting through the windshield of those countless trucks, cursing anything that resembled authority? Government. The rich. Church. The Interstate Commerce Commission. Banks. General Motors. Country clubs. Politics. Insurance companies. They were all on his list; along with the Teamsters, who put a brick through his windshield from an overpass after he had tilted the vote nonunion at Alabama Highway Express, only to make him surer of his cause. His creed: *Only organization I believe in is my family; everybody else can go to hell.* The cost: everything but his pride, even that now being torn from his hands in his involuntary retirement.

They were right, Sonny thought: you may drink again, buddy-boy, but it'll never be the same. *The beer I had for breakfast tasted good so I had one more for dessert.* The neon lights of the package store on the south of Tallahassee were long gone from the rear-view mirror as Sonny, a bottle of Jax cold between his thighs, wrestled his pickup along the ribbony black potholed road leading to the backwaters of the Gulf. Moon down, stars up, salt air whipping through the cab, lovebugs giving their lives on the windshield, *took a lot of guts to do that.* Country, country, country; ah-hah: WWL, New Orleans, Merle Haggard, "Okie from Muskogee." Woodville, Wakulla, stop sign in the middle of nowhere to let old U.S. 98 pass, finally St. Marks, then on to where the oyster-shell road quits. *We like livin' right and bein' free.*

Shirt sleeves and pants legs rolled up, six-pack in hand, windows left down for the radio, Sonny pushed through the scrub and mounted a dune. The Gulf of Mexico, trashy in those parts, lapped against a narrow strip of beach made gritty by oyster shells and shrimp heads tossed from the pier at Posey's shoreside diner. Solitary gulls, sandpipers, and pelicans went about their business. There was the faint light of a lantern from a shrimp boat, bobbing alone like flotsam in the sultry breeze. There was none so alone, though, as he. *Wait up, Pop, wait up.*

2

SONNY'S HEAD felt like a cantaloupe when he finally peeled out of bed around ten o'clock the next morning, but that was the least of his concerns. Now his father had come roaring back into his life, like a tornado warning, and whatever angst he might have been experiencing lately regarding his own situation suddenly seemed inconsequential. It wasn't the nature of cowboys, he figured, to remain offstage for too long. Another way of putting it was to quote one of Jake's own homilies: "The fleas come with the dog."

Phyllis had given him a special coded number he could call at the recovery center in DeSoto Springs to find out about Jake's condition, but he knew that all they would tell him was that the patient was "resting comfortably" or "doing as well as could be expected" or something equally vague. He wanted to hear it from the horse's mouth, and the time difference between Tallahassee and Mississippi meant that he had three long hours to conjure up visions of how it must be for Jake to be cooped up in a church-financed institution dedicated to making him change his ways at the age of sixty-nine.

He certainly knew, from his own experience, what the seventy-two-hour delay was all about: thorough physical examinations to assess the damage and the threat of a seizure from alcoholic withdrawal. His seizure had come two years earlier, when he had gone a week without a drink for the first time in his adult life, and he didn't care to go through that again. (It had happened, fortunately, in the company of a friend who had coaxed him into AA, and when he awoke in the hospital the friend was there at his side to say, "Frankly, I kind of miss the workouts I got when I was having seizures. I don't get near the exercise I used to.") To guard against a recurrence, Sonny had held back one of the beers from the six-pack of the night before. *The old hair of the dog*, he thought, nursing the warm beer as he whiled away the morning.

What would he find when he finally talked with the old man? Perversely, he hoped to hear some guilt and remorse; even of a seizure, maybe, and of a warning that one more drink would kill him. Sonny wasn't particularly sold on these recovery centers or the psychiatrists and clergymen who tended to run them, not after several hundred AA meetings during which he learned that nobody ever quit drinking who didn't want to quit, but he could share Phyllis's hopes that something would happen at Piney Woods to at least make Jake be more discreet if and when he completed his stay and went back to Mama's side at the retirement home. What he didn't want to hear was that his father had gone to Mississippi for a vacation.

Promptly at noon, Mississippi time, Sonny dialed the number for the "patients' phone" in the hallway at Piney Woods. It was finally answered, on the tenth ring, by a whiskey-throated woman who could barely speak for laughing. "Just a sec," the woman said, letting out a squeal. It sounded to Sonny like he had reached a pool hall, not an alcoholic recovery center, what with the clacking of balls and general merriment in the background. He thought he heard somebody shout "Jake," but he wasn't sure.

"Who'd you want?" the woman said when she had composed herself.

"Jake Hawkins."

"He been here long enough to talk?"

"Three days. They said I could call at noon."

"Well, it's noon, all right."

"Look, this is Jacob Hawkins Junior. I'm calling to speak to my — "

"Good Lord. Sonny." She held her hand over the receiver and shouted something.

"He's okay, isn't he?" Sonny said.

"Honey, if he was any better I couldn't stand it."

"Who are you?"

"I'm Jolene." She had to leave the phone for a few seconds, merely giggling this time, clearing her throat when she returned. "Sonny, yo' daddy has taught this old girl more this week than she's learned in a lifetime."

"I'll bet."

Jolene dropped her voice. "Here's one. You know what you get when you cross Einstein with a hooker?"

"I give up," Sonny said.

"A fuckin' know-it-all." She was beside herself. It took another minute's wait for Jolene to compose herself. "He's got a million of 'em. But I guess you oughta know that by now."

"I'm familiar with his work, yes." When Jolene started howling again, Sonny knew he was going to enjoy his visit to Piney Woods.

"You coming to visit?" she said.

"That's my plan."

"Well, you better hurry up."

"How so?"

"Jake ain't long for this place. Nothin' wrong with Jake Hawk—. Oh, my God, he did it. He ran 'em on Reggie."

"Hey, what the hell?" Sonny said.

The receiver had been left to dangle against a wall. Sonny heard hoots and stomps and snorts and challenges until, finally, he heard his father answer the phone in a way that had been infuriating his mother for half a century: "Lum 'n' Abner's. Lum ain't here."

"You must be Abner, then."

"Hey, boy."

"Hi, Pop. How's it going?"

"Thought maybe I'd lost the touch. Got this nigger boy here name o' Reggie, just learned the old man can still run 'em at eight ball. Don't figure I'll be buying any more Cokes while I'm here."

"Let me guess," Sonny said. "First four days you shot left-handed."

"Story is, I was injured."

"You ought to be ashamed of yourself."

"Hell, boy, I could beat 'em all with *one* hand." Jake lowered his voice. "Truth is, they're all a bunch of drunks. Fella had a seizure when they hauled him in last night. Got stretched out like a tuning fork. Like to swallowed his tongue. I thought he was a Holy Roller at first."

"What're they saying about you, Pop?"

"I'm being held against my will. Everybody knows that."

"I mean the doctors. You had a checkup yet?"

"It's a wonder I got any blood left."

"Well, what'd they say?"

Sonny could hear the familiar sounds of a kitchen match being raked across a hard surface and the sucking noise: his father, lighting a cigar. "This young doctor that did the checking, he's from Jasper, right there where the old 'Frisco tracks cross 78; hell, I even know his daddy. Damned depot's one o' them fancy little restaurants now. Any rate, when the doc finished pokin' around he said he couldn't believe it. Said not only was I the oldest human being ever 'committed' around here — that's what I call it, 'committed' — said my liver's perfect."

"You're kidding me."

"I'd swear on a stack of Mama's Bibles."

"Christ, Pop, there's been a mistake."

"What I told the doctor. Said, 'Look, we all make mistakes.' He can't figure it out, either."

Sonny was perturbed. He had been advised when he was forty that if he didn't quit the boozing he wouldn't see forty-five. And now here was his father, who had drunk enough whiskey to fill Lake Michigan, and they were telling him he had a perfect liver. What was this, hysteria from Birmingham or a faulty test or what? Sonny had sat in enough AA meetings to have heard the same puzzle, usually delivered tearfully in a Why-Me-Lord? voice, about how some can drink better than others. The discussion leaders at these meetings always shot down such talk, of course, and Sonny always walked away not knowing exactly what to make of it. Maybe that was why he had such a colorful collection of chips in the crystal bowl now glinting in the sun from across the room.

"Son, this call's costing you a lot of money. Thought you had enough sense to call after nine at night. The damned phone company loves people like you."

"Forget that, Pop. I got worried about you."

"Reckon Phyllis and that Yankee sonofabitch she's married to told you about locking me up."

"Yeah, but that's not the way they put it."

"Well, you know damned well that's what it amounts to. It's a Methodist Conspiracy, boy. These preachers over here are on the phone every day to that bastard at Mimosa. I bet they call Boggs if I don't eat my peas."

"Come on, Pop, you're imagining things."

"No, I ain't. And they'll get you, too, if you don't watch the bastards. You don't believe that church stuff no more than I do. You and me are the same, boy."

"There's some truth to that, Pop."

Jake cleared his throat and said, "You talked to Mama lately?"

"I called her on her birthday last month, remember? At Mimosa."

"How'd she sound?"

"Christ, you were there. You answered the phone."

"Well, yeah, but I wanted to hear it from you. How'd your mama sound to you, son? Tell me the truth, now."

"Lost, Pop. I don't think she knew who I was."

"There you go. You see what I'm up against now, don't you?" Jake's voice cracked and he began to blubber into the phone. Sonny was embarrassed, and he choked a bit himself. "That's the only woman this old man ever loved. You know that. Lots of other drivers used to drive hard all night because they had women hid out in the next town. Not me. Not Jake Hawkins. Like they say, I didn't have to go out for no hamburgers, because I had me a prime steak right there at home. Yo' mama." Jake blew his nose. "Now the poor thing can't remember who I am half the time."

"I understand, Pop."

"No, you don't, son."

Sonny couldn't argue with that. He could sense, though, that for the time being Jake was much better off in Mississippi than at Mimosa Towers. The food was good ("They know how to cook in Mississippi, and they don't let niggers serve it"), there was Ping-Pong and a swimming pool and a mile-long nature trail ("Hell, I *ran* the damned thing, but my roommate, he's a doctor that lost his license and everything else, he had to go in a wheelchair"), and "There's a pretty good view of the old road I used to take when I hauled to New Orleans." Sonny could only hope that his father might impress the authorities in Birmingham by biting the bullet, riding it out, for the mandatory stay at Piney Woods.

Jake could have his first visitors after three o'clock Saturday afternoon, exactly five full days since his being dropped off by Phyllis and Collier, and Sonny said he would be there. His father seemed excited about the visit and, to his surprise, hadn't made a direct pitch to be kidnapped. "That Jolene, one that answered the phone," Jake said, "she's as good as Tammy Wynette, if you ask me. Old gal must've worked every fightin'-and-dancin' club in Mississippi before she starting drinking the profits. Me and her, we'll make some music for you."

"They got a piano there, huh?"

"Plays Hank Williams. Not that queer Liberace."

"Hoagy Carmichael, too, I bet."

"Yeah, except these young'uns ain't never heard of Hoagy."

"Well, I can tell you, *I* sure have."

"Reckon so," said Jake. "Look here, son, I hear tell they're hauling us off to a meeting that night. You might want to go along if you're still makin' those things."

"AA meeting?"

"Church in town. They probably want to show us off like it was a zoo or something."

"Sure. Why not."

"Undecided if I'm gonna go, myself, understand."

When Sonny said he would first go to Birmingham before driving on to Mississippi, Jake proceeded to rattle off convoluted directions for a shortcut to DeSoto Springs, one guaranteed to cut eight minutes off a five-hour drive along interstates. Sonny had learned years earlier to write it all down to keep the old man happy and then throw away the notes.

"What do you need, Pop? Clean underwear? Magazines? What can I bring you?"

"I'm 'bout out of cigars."
"The big El Productos, right?"
"Biggest they got."
"I'll bring you a box, then."
"Aw, naw, just a couple ought to do me."
"You always said they're cheaper by the box."
"Just be extra baggage for me when I leave," Jake said. "I ain't gonna be here long enough for a box."

3

LEO MIRANDA had talked to Sonny's answering machine all day Thursday after the conversation with Jake — "Come out, come out, wherever you are"; "Your FBI at peace and at war"; "Okay, Bielski, out with your hands up and no monkey business" — but Sonny had been in no mood to talk with anyone. On Friday morning, when he came trudging up the outside stairs from the laundromat with the clothes he would need, he found Leo in the apartment replaying his own messages.

"Pretty clever stuff, you ask me," said Leo.

"You missed your calling."

"I thought maybe you'd be interested in hearing about your future."

"That's the least of my worries right now." He dumped the basket of clothes on the unmade bed and invited Leo to sit on the sofa.

"At least Lyons knows your name now."

"Good?"

"Not good." Sonny had left the boss with egg on his face, and their "cocksucker" exchange was already the stuff of legend in a world that thrives on gossip. "Sonny," Leo said, "why?"

"Like father, like son, I reckon."

"I smell Birmingham."

"My old man needs me, Leo." He gave a capsule version of Jake's situation. "He's needed me for a long time, and I didn't know it."

"Yeah. I can say the same for myself."

"Maybe the stuff with Lyons will go away."

"I'll work on it. How long will you be gone?"

"A week, maybe," Sonny said. "It's going to be like trying to tame a mustang."

"Not a bad analogy."

"Not a bad mustang."

On the road again. By noon Friday, chain-smoking Camels, headed west out of Tallahassee with a hot breeze in his hair, suitcase on the floor of his pickup, Sonny had crossed the Apalachicola River at Chattahoochee. He took the shortcut north through the scraggly Florida Panhandle and drove on into the Wiregrass country of south Alabama, by-passing steamy Dothan, past undulating pastures dotted with Black Angus. There were plenty of pickups and logging trucks now, all with "Heart of Dixie" license plates. Ozark, Brundidge, Troy. After circling Montgomery and slicing through the neat peach orchards of central Alabama, he finally topped the ridge overlooking Jones Valley and saw the South's own City of Big Shoulders: Birmingham, The Magic City, Pittsburgh of the South.

Not really. Not anymore. Birmingham had changed radically since U.S. Steel, the Big Mule for nearly a century, had capitulated to the Japanese by shutting down the last of the steel mills in the southernmost valley of the Appalachians: chief among them TCI, Tennessee Coal & Iron, the bitch-goddess, daddy to generations of men who coughed and sweated through fiery nights of flying sparks and molten slag and white-hot sheets of steel. Now the plants lay rusting like white elephants asleep in the kudzu, tombstones to a way of life that once orchestrated life in gritty blue-collar communities with old-country mining-town names like Ensley and Fairfield and Bessemer. In place of the plants had risen the modern cluster of edifices housing the University of Alabama–Birmingham and the attached Medical Center, and the bottom line was this: 4,000 steelworkers had been replaced by 4,000 people who had gone to college and spoke without a Southern drawl and preferred opera over Opry.

Still, Sonny felt protective about his hometown. When he peaked Red Mountain at four o'clock in the afternoon, under the shadow of the statue of Vulcan, the Roman god of metallurgy, there was a catch in his throat as he observed Jones Valley laid out below. Civic pride dies hard. Sonny heard the words of his father, belligerent as usual about any sign of change: "The day there ain't no smoke in Birmingham is the day folks start starving." One thing his father always left out was the painful scenario, something that seemed to happen every year, when the steelworkers went out on strike: swarthy men in the prime of their lives, going from door to door, begging for odd jobs to make it through the summer.

That had happened often enough when Sonny was growing up in Roebuck Hills, on the eastern side of town abutting the municipal airport, to make a lasting impression. Although the neighborhood was across town from the mightier of the steel mills, the majority of the men could be seen at all hours, depending on which shift they worked, trudging down the hill to take the trolleys to the plants, and nine or ten hours later they would return, lungs choked with dust, lunch pails empty, nothing much to discuss with wives waiting on stone stoops in aprons.

This was in stark contrast to the arrival from work of Jake Hawkins, the independent long-haul trucker, who would top the hill around dusk every Friday after being on the road for a week, an adventurer home from the wars: old Dodge truck belching, air brakes hissing, horn shattering the tranquillity of the neighborhood, King of the Road, home before dark. The other fathers were good men, Sonny mused, but a big rig was something a kid could sink his teeth into.

As Sonny topped that same hill, three decades later, he saw that the neighborhood hadn't changed much on the surface. It was still marked as blue-collar by simple frame single-story houses, each with a chimney and a front porch, houses that had been steadily added onto by the men themselves as their families expanded. The yards were small but tidy, alive with azalea and hydrangea, and trees formed a canopy over most of the streets. He hadn't spent much time there since going off to college, but he had learned of the deaths and defections of those who had been neighbors. He had heard that the very last of them, Beulah and Monk Strickland, directly across the street, were shopping for a bungalow in the suburbs now that Monk had retired after forty years on the line at the TCI plant.

In the driveway of the Hawkinses' house was his father's getaway car, the five-year-old four-door Dodge hardtop, as good as the day it was bought. Except for the roar of a jet taking off from the airport, the streets were quiet, devoid of children now, as he walked to the front door. The key was under the doormat, where it had been for thirty-five years, and taped to the inside of the front door was a note from Phyllis, the good daughter, on lined composition notebook paper, in Palmer method script:

> Welcome home!! Coffee is fresh, but nothing else. Made up your old bed. Please call when you feel like it. Maybe lunch with Mama Sat.?

and a P.S.: "You want the piano?" Sonny closed the door of the house, musty and virtually unused for a year now, and flipped on lights and air conditioning before heading down the hallway toward his boyhood room. He was stopped in his tracks by the gallery of framed pictures, some of them going all the way back to the early 1930s, and there was a poignancy to them now.

In the hallway, stilled of joys and sorrows, a lifetime was on display: himself on his first bicycle, Phyllis like Shirley Temple, their parents as newlyweds perched on the running board of somebody else's A-Model roadster, his father standing tall beside his first truck in 1940; graduation pictures, wedding pictures, grandbaby pictures; his parents glowing on a cruise to Alaska; Sonny at twenty-three, crew-cut with clip-on bow tie, sports department of the Birmingham *News*; and Phyllis at thirteen, dressed in a leotard sequined by Mama, tap-dancing to the strains of "Stairway to the Stars" up a pedestal sawed and nailed together by Pop.

His room and his sister's had reached museum status, Sonny saw as he walked on to the end of the hall. Except for a sewing machine and an elaborate hooked rug of the Great Seal of the United States that Mama would never finish now, Phyllis's had gone practically untouched since the day she married Collier Bradford some twenty years before: antiqued furniture, a sampler above the bed (What Are Little Girls Made Of?), white leather Bible on one nightstand, a pink ceramic piggy bank on the other. And Sonny's was that of a skinny teenager lost in a gossamer dream of baseball: a bedspread imprinted with bats and balls and sliding base runners, a sampler of his own (What Are Little Boys Made Of?), an entire wall papered with color portraits torn from sports magazines, a Motorola that had caught many a crackling episode of Harry Caray's St. Louis Cardinals broadcasts over KMOX, hatrack in a corner (crafted by Pop in the basement) with a half-dozen authentic major-league baseball caps. Sonny tossed his things on the bed of his youth, not sure if he wanted to sleep there again.

If those rooms were reminders of the sweet days of baseball and tap-dancing and Pop's calamitous arrivals and Mama's cooking, their parents' bedroom was something else. Everywhere there was evidence that it was over for them; dust and clutter giving the look of a place that had been ransacked while the owners were away. The bed was cantilevered, out of deference to the illnesses that had preceded his mother's Alzheimer's, and there wasn't room left on any flat surface for so much as one more bottle of aspirin. When his parents moved to the retirement home they had left behind a pharmacy, and when Sonny poked into the medicine cabinet he saw a bottle of pills for his mother with a prescription that was fourteen years old.

There was a formal living room, a place that guests never seemed to be able to recall, and Sonny didn't care to linger in its suffocating tackiness. It was a room of uninviting furniture and chalk figurines and plastic flowers and vacation souvenirs, a room so sterile and unlikely that he wondered why they ever bothered to take the wrappings off the furniture when it arrived. "Today Is the First Day of the Rest of Your Life," he read on one of the plaques his mother was fond of tacking to the walls, and that ponderous message sent him scurrying to what had always been known, with quite good reason, as the "family room."

Sonny was stretched out where he had always felt most comfortable, on the sofa in the family room, beneath louvered windows that slanted the afternoon sun onto pine-paneled walls holding, among other things, a sconce where there reposed a tarnished trophy proclaiming Jake Hawkins as "Trucker of the Year, 1951." Directly across from him was the old black upright Baldwin piano, where his father had been thumping out the best of Hoagy Carmichael and Hank Williams for forty years to his own curious honky-tonk beat ("I'd be a sight better if the Injuns hadn't shot the Pony Express rider before he could bring me my left-hand lesson," he said, repeatedly, between chomps of his cigar), and he was imagining the clumsy beat of "Stardust" and "Your Cheatin' Heart" and his father's disclaimers about having grown up so far back in the hills of Tennessee that "Monday was always a day late," when he was startled by the phone on the kitchen wall.

"Well, hi there." Phyllis. "I didn't know if you'd tried to call. I've been with Mama all day."

"We ought to start with a bulldozer, Phyl."

"They saved everything, didn't they?"

"It's a museum. Ought to put it on a tour."

Phyllis said, "Sonny, I've heard about these professional house cleaners who come and do everything *for* you, you know? I was thinking that we could go through the personal things together while you're here. The family pictures and all? And then there's these people who do yard sales, and I — "

"Hey, Phyl, whoa. What if Pop doesn't make it? The man's gotta live somewhere."

"Well, Sonny, he'll just *have* to straighten up."

"It's not that simple. Believe me."

"Collier's giving me the hurry-up sign. I've got to fix dinner so we can get to a church meeting. Can you go by and see Mama tonight?"

"I'm tired, Phyl, and I'm going to drive to Mississippi tomorrow."

"You've talked to him?"

"*Him?*"

"Daddy, then."

"Yeah. He's having a ball."

"Oh, Sonny, that's *wonderful*. I'm so happy? That means he's getting well, then."

"I don't know, Sis. I'll call you when I get back."

He had been sitting at the round table in the kitchen, and when he hung up the phone he was struck again by the way ghosts of a previous life were in every cranny and on every wall of the house. It was at this same little Sears Roebuck dinette table, now scratched and sticky with sugar and syrup mishaps, that the four of them had sat around 'til many a midnight in marathon rounds of canasta when the family was a unit. There was the ubiquitous sampler, "Kissin' Don't Last, But Cookin' Do," and one of those phoney clocks with the numeral "5" at every hour and the legend, "House Rules, No Drinking 'Til 5." The kitchen, of course, was Mama's domain: organdy curtains, cornucopia wallpaper, fake red-brick linoleum flooring, canisters, chopping block, trivets, ladle rests, cookbooks collected over a forty-year period, a newspaper cartoon that had struck her fancy (Wife to husband as she sets the alarm: "What time do you want to start complaining in the morning?"), pots hanging from the ceiling, and unused modern gadgetry like the Cuisinart that had come to her too late. It had always been referred to by Evelyn Hawkins as "my kitchen," and nobody had ever thought of it otherwise.

The basement was his father's bailiwick. If there can be any such thing as an "office" for a man of the road, this was it: a dank haven where Jake could go to fix toys, figure taxes, stockpile canned goods, take naps, and dream dreams. Over the years it had become a warehouse for a born packrat, a place for a survivor of the Depression to, well, *keep* things. Sonny, aimlessly rummaging through the basement, marveled at how a person's private domain could so define his life. There were old tires, oilcans, tools, paint buckets, dead plants, bags of cement, two baseball gloves and a bat and a ball, the "Stairway to the Stars" pedestal, cardboard boxes holding every logbook he had ever filled out, busted radios, truck-stop "gimme" caps, and smelly clothes that had never quite made it to the washer and dryer that had always been Mama's only reason to visit the basement. And somewhere in all of that mess, to be sure, there were pint bottles of bourbon hidden like Easter eggs.

The clamminess of the basement drove Sonny outdoors into

the searing heat of late afternoon. Another jet thundered overhead. The yard had gone to hell, too, and not even the man Phyllis had hired to cut the grass could save it. Wilting fruit trees, vegetable garden, flower beds; all living things were returning to the wild. Still, as in the basement, there was evidence of his father's hands at work: the flagstone patio and open barbecue pit, up under the twin sweetgum trees, built one trip at a time with flagstones wrenched from mountain streams and shoved into trailers already overloaded with tires; the picnic table and benches Jake had fashioned, in the basement, rather than buy from Sears on credit; the See Rock City birdhouse he had made and hoisted on an eight-foot length of pipe.

And then Sonny saw something that took his breath away. Down there in the most distant corner of the lot where kudzu had at last conquered the rear fence, at rest beneath a makeshift roof of rippled green Fiberglas supported by four-by-fours, crouching in the gravel like a giant red frog too tired to jump, there she was: Dixie Redball IV, the last in a line of trusty Dodge trucks that had given purpose to Jake Hawkins's life.

"I s'wanee, Sonny, you're getting downright *puny.*" He had walked halfway down the slope leading to the truck when he heard the squawky voice of Beulah Strickland. She was coming toward him from around the side of the house, in sandals and a flowery cotton dress, carrying a brown paper bag. Several steps behind her, in sneakers and jeans and an unadorned white T-shirt, smiling and scratching his head, was her husband, Monk.

"Just lean and hungry like Pop," Sonny said.

"Call it what you want to, but I say you need one of my roast beef sandwiches."

"I'll admit it's pretty slim pickings in there."

"It's a shame, Sonny, a real shame about your mama and daddy. Reckon it'll happen to me and Monk soon enough. But here" — she presented him with the paper bag and smiled victoriously — "the minute I saw you through the curtains I told Monk, 'Monk, I'm fixing that boy a roast beef just like Evelyn would.' Got some iced tea in there, too."

After Sonny had whipped out a bandanna and dusted off the table and benches, they sat on the patio beneath the trees. Cicadas were beginning their chorus as he took the sandwich from its wax paper wrapping and unscrewed the cap of the Mason jar. He nodded, between bites and sips, while Beulah filled him in: Edna Riddle had been killed by a train and her husband Walter "died of a loneliness" soon after; dead or moved away were the Hoods, the Hackadays, the Rutners, the O'Briens; the Stricklands' own son, Rickey, was running a hardware store now, and their daughter, June, already had three children; and, yes, they were pretty close to selling their house. Monk Strickland sat mute and grinning, like hired help.

Sonny said, "When you move, will there be any of the old neighbors left?"

"Just Lee," she said. "Edna and Walter's boy."

"Lee? He was my best buddy. Where's he?"

"Up at the house. Moved back in when they died."

"Well, I'll be. What's he doing?"

"We don't hardly ever see him, Sonny, so I don't know." They looked toward the dark stone house on the hill. "Works at the post office is all we know. Just comes and goes."

Lee Riddle had completely dropped out of sight after the college years, and Sonny was intrigued by this vision of him, the most likely to succeed, being holed up alone in the old family homeplace. He was making a mental note to see him before returning to Tallahassee, when Beulah began to chatter again.

"Fifty thousand dollars for that old house," she was saying. "I can't believe it."

"You've been in it for what, thirty years?"

"Thirty-one. Bought the old thing for eight thousand dollars in nineteen fifty."

"It's inflation," Sonny said.

"I know. But there's niggers all around us now, and there's the airplanes all the time. Course, the jets don't bother Monk much anymore."

"How so?"

"I thought maybe your folks told you." She smiled at her husband, who merely grinned back. "Forty years that man gave to TCI, working the graveyard shift in that noisy old mill, and when he retired right ahead of the closing you had to shout for him to hear you."

"That's awful."

"That ain't all, either. He'd waited all his life to retire and play golf, and even Paul Harvey couldn't make up what happened next. The very first week of his retirement he was learning to hit balls down at the city course — the one in East Lake? — and I'll be dogged if he didn't get hit by one of 'em right between the eyes. Monk's near 'bout stone deaf now."

Monk rubbed his forehead, and when he spoke he shouted. "It ain't that bad. Maybe I wadn't cut out to be no golfer is all."

"Anyways," said Beulah, "retirement isn't what it's cut out to be. Your daddy sure knows about that."

"He been around the house?"

"Just last week. Monk saw him."

"Heard the truck fire up," said Monk. "She did, anyways."

"That truck right there?"

"Same one. Ol' Dixie Redball."

"I didn't know it would still run."

"Me, neither. Anyways, the wife pushed me out the door and I come over here to see about it and there was yo' daddy. Sittin' at the wheel, cigar in his mouth, pattin' the gas. Me and him had a beer or two."

"Hah. Three or four is more like it," said Beulah.

"Now that I'm *retarded*, the way Jake likes to put it, reckon I can handle a few. Seein' as how golf didn't work out."

"What'd Pop say?"

"Just talked about the old days when your mama was all right and he was driving. Pretty soon he got to crying. Reckon I can't blame him. Sonny, yo' daddy was a truck-drivin' fool."

It had been three years since Jake's last run, to pick up a load of tires in Texas, and Sonny remembered it well. He and Phyllis were putting together a golden wedding anniversary party for their parents, with all of the relatives and the old friends like Beulah and Monk invited, and when Sonny finally got Jake on the phone, at an air base in Amarillo, the old man said, "Tell Mama I'll be there when I get there. I got work to do." He made it back, though, and they were a stunning couple. Fifty years after winning a contest to be married on the stage of the Ritz Theater in Birmingham, Mama caused her friends great consternation by fitting into the same wedding dress. As for Pop, who played the piano and danced jigs and told outrageous stories, it was the last time Sonny had seen him truly happy.

4

SONNY HAD GIVEN some thought to making the trip to Mississippi in his father's cushy Dodge ("my touring car," the old man called it) in order to air it out and build up the battery, but he figured Jake would take that as a sign that he had come to spring him from Piney Woods. The road from Birmingham was all interstate, anyway, smooth and undulating through the sparsely populated forests of west Alabama and eastern Mississippi; and, besides, he had grown attached to his old pickup with all of its dents and idiosyncrasies and what Leo Miranda called "character." In that regard, he sensed an affinity with his father, who, in an era when most truckers would mortgage their soul for any of the awesome new diesel-powered Peterbilts or Freightliners or like monsters of the road, continued to "dance with the one that brung me": the reliable old gasoline-powered Dodges that had never let him down. Jake, he thought, was not unlike the stock-car mechanics he had once seen engage in a bloody tire-iron melee, right there in the pits at Daytona, over which was better: a Chevy or a Ford.

By quarter-of-three in the afternoon, having found a cheap motel room near the campus of the University of Southern Mississippi on the main drag in Hattiesburg and then driven back north on old U.S. 11 in search of the crossroads town of DeSoto Springs, Sonny came upon a sign quietly announcing Piney Woods Recovery Center. It was housed in a sleek one-story sandstone building, literally set in a patch of piney woods, looking out of place in a section of Mississippi characterized by sawmills and weedy fields and tarpaper shacks and kudzu. He was not surprised to see, as he took the circular driveway through the main gate, that there was a small parking area with few cars in it. No getaway cars.

The patients, he was told, were in a meeting that would end at three o'clock. Sonny told a middle-aged nurse at the desk that he had come to visit his father and then took a seat in the small waiting area, amid plastic plants and Scandinavian furnishings, waiting for the Muzak to begin. Instead, he heard a flurry of whispered exchanges on the other side of the nurses' station, and when he looked up he saw a young man step toward him with one hand extended and the other clutching a manila file.

"We're so glad you could come," the young man said. He was Bryan Peters, a theological student from Memphis, doing a summer internship at Piney Woods for the Campus Crusade for Christ: razor-cut hair, volleyball tan, good teeth, button-down shirt, Weejuns.

Sonny said, "I was hoping to see the doctor."

"No, sir. They're off on Saturdays. I'm a counselor."

"Is it true about the physical?"

"Pretty amazing, isn't it? He's not only the oldest person ever admitted here, he's in better shape than any of the sixteen patients we have now."

"What's he here for then?"

"On the recommendation from Mr. and Mrs. Bradford, primarily." Bryan Peters opened the file and began fingering sheets of paper. He seemed nervous. "That's your sister and your brother-in-law, correct?"

"Yeah." Sonny lit a Camel. "So. How's he doing?"

"Physically, he's fine. No withdrawal symptoms. Eating like a *horse*. The others love him."

"I'm sure. Give him three squares and an audience, the man's like a pig in slop."

"Yes, sir. That's exactly how he puts it."

"So what's the problem?"

Bryan Peters frowned. "He may like it *too* much."

"I got the same impression."

"He'll, like, break out singing in meetings."

"They're supposed to suffer, that it?"

"In a way. To be honest with you, it would help if he had a religious background. Your sister tells us you're in AA. So you know what I mean."

"I'm afraid so. The Jesus stuff gets to me, too. But look. Is he gonna make it here?"

"It's too early to tell. He's still angry, like they all are the first week. He's claiming he's being held here against his will when he ought to be at the side of his dying wife. And that's another thing. He's got all of the others believing his story. Frankly, Mr. Hawkins, we might have a problem on our hands."

Sonny stifled a grin. "Mutiny?"

"Maybe."

The patients' meeting had broken up while Sonny was talking to Peters, and when he didn't see Jake milling about the central lounge with the others, who were drinking Cokes and either starting up card games or settling down to watch game shows on the two large-screen television sets, he was told to check the courtyard. Sonny walked down a long corridor, past closed doors marked Counseling and First Aid and Therapy, until he reached a sliding glass door that opened onto a grassy courtyard where there were picnic tables, benches beneath striped beach umbrellas, horseshoes, and shuffleboard. He stood in the shadows of the portico, against the building, looking for his father.

There was a commotion at the shuffleboard, and Jake Hawkins was in the center of it: wearing cowboy boots and chartreuse wash-and-wear Sansabelt slacks and a plain white T-shirt and a green and white baseball cap promoting Poole Truck Line of Evergreen, Alabama, chewing on the stump of a cigar, holding a shuffleboard stick in his hand, baiting a young black man. That would be Reggie, Sonny deduced; the blonde had to be Jolene; and the man in the wheelchair could only be his father's roommate, the doctor who had lost it all.

"If you'd play left-handed, I might take you up on it," Reggie was saying.

"Double-or-nothing, how 'bout it?" said Jake.

"George Wallace sent you. Understand what I'm saying?"

"This ain't got nothing to do with politics, son. We got plenty of time to talk about that."

"I can't wait."

"Want to hear what you got to say about the nigger situation, anyway."

"How about just playing, Jake," Reggie said. "Maybe I'll learn something."

"Probably will," Jake said, and with that he drew back his stick and let fly. His puck was a blur as it zipped along the smooth concrete and slammed into the first of the three already inside the triangle at the other end, setting off a chain reaction that left all four of the pucks in the grass. Reggie just shook his head. Jolene let out the same hysterical wail that Sonny had heard over the phone when he had called while his father ran the table on Reggie at eight ball. The man in the wheelchair merely chuckled as he wheeled himself down to the other end. "How-*dee*, I'm just so glad to be *hyar*," Jake said in his Minnie Pearl-at-the-Opry imitation, breaking into a jig. "It got to where my boy wouldn't even *play* shuffleboard with me anymore."

"Bullshit," Sonny said, stepping out of the shadows, grinning, walking toward them. "It's a game for old farts."

"Damned if it ain't my driver, come to get me," said Jake.

"Lord, Jake," Jolene said, "is that Sonny?"

"If it ain't, there's been a hell of a mixup."

"Looks just like you."

"Well, the boy can't help it none." Jake dropped his stick, shifted his cigar, and met Sonny halfway. Sonny winced at the bone-crushing handshake his father gave him, as they both knew he would, and they smiled as though members of a secret society. Then they embraced.

Jake introduced his son to the others. Jolene, a wasted peroxide blonde who probably *had* worked every roadhouse in Mississippi, said she wanted to give Sonny a copy of her one and only album just for being Jake Hawkins's son. Reggie, a muscular nineteen-year-old from McComb, was a testimony to predominantly white Southern football factories: sent by Ole Miss to either get straight or forfeit his scholarship. Eminently sad, in comparison, was the doctor: Frank, a broken man of fifty whose only hope was that therapy might put his mind and his body together again.

"They're just a bunch of drunks," Jake said, winking at them, and from the way they smiled with good-natured resign Sonny could see that either his father had, indeed, "taken over the joint" or that Jolene and Reggie and Frank were, indeed, responding to the AA program. They were still clucking and shaking their heads when Jake walked away from the game to go inside.

The room Jake shared with Frank resembled a military bachelor officer's quarters, similar to the room his wife had at the retirement home in Birmingham in that it was divided into two identical halves, each with a single bed, a bureau, a nightstand with lamp, and a narrow closet. The two men shared hardy rust-colored indoor-outdoor carpeting, a spacious bath, walls painted institutional green and hung with bad paintings ranging from Mississippi River scenes to Jesus, a dresser topped by a mirror along the length of one wall, and a wide window revealing the piney woods around them. Immaculate, with only a Gideon Bible for reading material, the place looked as though the maids had cleaned it just in time for the next traveler.

"Not exactly home," Sonny said. They sat on the beds, facing each other, the Muzak coming from somewhere now, and suddenly, in this cold and spotless room without a single thing to mark it as Jake Hawkins's place — no piano to play, no audience to entertain, nothing to *do* — his father seemed as forlorn as an eagle in a cage.

"Bastards won't even let you put your stuff out. Everything's got to be *in* the drawers. Ain't got anything to speak of, anyway, seeing as how they took it when I got here."

"Money, Pop. Are you covered?"

"Medicare. Costs eight thousand and five hundred dollars a month. That'll show you what the government does with your taxes. Wasting it, in my case."

"What do you do with your time, Pop, besides hustle Reggie at pool and shuffleboard?"

"Horseshoes, too."

"Jesus. You don't take prisoners."

"That boy's okay, son. First time I ever talked much with a nigger. The way he grew up, it's a wonder he's still alive."

"You're learning something, anyway. I see they got TV. Do they let you read the papers?"

"The *Commercial-Appeal*'s in there somewhere, in the drawer with everything else. I'd have the crossword done by now if it wasn't for these stupid damn meetings they keep having."

"What was the one about this afternoon?"

"They showed us a movie about drunk driving."

"I've seen that one. Color? Lots of blood?"

"I walked out on it."

"Three million miles without an accident, right?"

"Why, hell, yeah. My record speaks for itself. It's the four-wheelers that cause all the wrecks, anyway. Everybody knows that. They had it in *Trucker* magazine. Women drivers in them little Jap cars, they're the worst ones of the lot." Jake raised his voice to a falsetto. " 'Oh, my Lord, that big dirty old truck back there's gonna run right over me. I better stop.' So she hits the brakes going sixty-five miles a goddamn hour and this poor sonofabitch behind her in a Peterbilt that's hauling eighty thousand pounds of ball bearings hits *his* brakes and starts shifting down but it's too damned late. Bye-bye, that's all she wrote. There's arms and legs and blood and ball-bearings scattered every which way. Next day, the papers are saying we got to get these trucks off the road before everybody gets killed. It ain't *truck* drivers, son, it's *women* drivers. You can look it up."

Sonny had heard it a million times, over the supper table and at loading docks and in truck stops at three o'clock in the morning, and he figured the old man's last words, from his deathbed with the family gathered around, wouldn't be about burial wishes or insurance policies or the Hereafter or how much he loved Mama; no, he would still be telling stories about the road. Sonny fluffed up the pillows on his father's bed and lay back against the headboard, settling in for the long haul. Jake spoke excitedly, in a rush, as though afraid that he might leave something unsaid before he died.

"I was always pretty good dealing with the boys at the scales. One time I was comin' out of California and I come up on some scales I thought was closed for the night. Well, you know me. Overloaded, behind in my logs, didn't have the right permit for what I was hauling, running late. When this old boy asked me for my records and said he had to weigh me, I got to talking my head off. Told him I wasn't really the driver, that the driver was back there in the sleeper passed out from drinking it up in San Diego and I was just helping out 'til he sobered up enough to drive. 'I ain't even got a driver's license, Cap'n,' what I told him. Hell, I didn't want 'em running no check on me or they might put me *under* the jail. Told him, 'I'm from Tennessee and I can't get back home fast enough. You got some crazy people out here in California.' I could see I had him. He was getting tired o' listening to me. When I told him, 'I wonder if you could show me how to shift gears on this thing,' that did it. 'Get the hell out of here,' he said, 'and don't come back.'"

Jake went on like that for nearly an hour, in an animated monologue where fact and fiction were of equal value, and Sonny tried to act as though he had never heard the stories before. Maybe this was the therapy his father really needed, he thought, as Jake rambled on about truck stops and icy roads and mountain passes and outwitting "the boys" and the truck graveyard at the bottom of the canyon on U.S. 160 — at the notorious Four Corners, the common boundary of Colorado, New Mexico, Utah, and Arizona — where lies many a young driver who didn't listen to the first lesson in pulling the mountains: "You go *down* a hill," said Jake, "in the same gear you went *up* it at."

When Sonny caught his father coming up for air he said, "Beulah and Monk told me you went by the house and cranked up Redball."

"That so. How they doing?"

"Same. Still trying to sell their place."

"Hell of a thing about Monk, ain't it?"

"Says he wasn't cut out for golf."

Jake said, "I was just curious about whether she'd still start. Lots of times I'd sit on the porch over there at that damned prison they had me and Mama in and I'd hear some old boy grabbing gears and it'd kinda get to me. I reckon that was one of those days, son, the night I went and cranked Redball. I've said it lots of times that your mama's the only woman this old man ever loved" — Jake's voice cracked again when he said it — "but something else I've always said, at least to myself, and that's if something was to happen to her what I'd do is just get myself a little apartment somewhere and start hauling again. I ain't nothing, son, if I can't drive."

"That's great, Pop, but you're going to be seventy in August. I mean, I understand, but — "

"Naw, I don't think you do. Phyllis sure don't."

"Oh, hey" — Sonny pulled a five-pack of El Productos from the thigh pocket of the fatigues he was wearing — "I almost forgot."

Jake took the cigars and inspected the wrapper.

"Two dollars thirteen cents?" he said. "You should o' gone to Robinette's. Dollar eighty-seven there."

"What the hell. It's only a quarter."

"Naw, it's twenty-six cents. You sound like that damned ex-wife of yours."

"Shit, Pop, come on, I don't need this."

"She near-'bout ruined you. Too bad you couldn't o' married somebody like your sister."

"Phyllis? The last I heard, she and Collier were 'sonsabitches.' "

Jake said, "*He's* the bastard, son."

"Since when? For years I've felt like I'd been replaced by some ass-kissing banker from Pennsylvania, of all places. What is it, the church stuff?"

"Naw, there's something else."

"What? Putting you in this place?"

"Better not say yet, son."

"What the hell, Pop. I never knew you to withhold information."

"I ain't saying 'til I'm sure."

Sonny was left to ponder this new turn of events when there was a clatter at the door and they looked up to see Frank wheeling himself into the room. Before he knew what had hit him, Sonny held in his hands a thick spiral notebook in which Frank had already written nearly one hundred pages, in a shaky longhand, of what would be an autobiography he was entitling, *Ashes to Ashes: The Story of Frank 'X'*. Sonny, feeling cornered, agreed to take it back to his motel room and give it a read. Dinner at Piney Woods was at six, guests not invited, so he would grab something to eat and then return at visiting hours. Maybe young Bryan Peters would let him go along with the group for the AA meeting that night in Hattiesburg. He wanted to go not so much for himself but to see how his father chose to comport himself.

Dinner, for Sonny, consisted of picking up a hamburger and fries and a shake at a McDonald's drive-through window and taking it back to the Tick-Tock Motel along Hattiesburg's neon strip. There he wolfed down the food and, as the television played the six o'clock news and truckers began to park their rigs out front in the gravel for a night's rest, skimmed through Frank's caterwauling confessional. It was a story he had heard many times, with only slight variations: an alcoholic father, medical school, a troubled marriage, loss of his son in a boating accident, drinking the sorrow away, access as a doctor to the wonderful world of drugs, loss of his license and everything else until, finally, finding the Lord at Piney Woods. Sonny appreciated the therapeutic value of writing, which seemed especially poignant in this case, and he felt a small debt to his father's roommate. He scribbled some notes in the margins, as he might for a student who lacked promise but at least was *trying*, and soon he was on his way back to Piney Woods.

In their room, at dusk, Frank sat in his wheelchair, frowning at the scrawls in the notebook, while Sonny perched on the edge of his bed and explained the suggestions he had made. Jake lit one of the new cigars, striking a kitchen match on the bedpost, and stood by quietly as the two talked.

". . . the main thing," Sonny was saying, "is stories. People want you to show 'em, not tell 'em."

"Yeah," said Frank, "but how can I show 'em what's going on in my head?"

"Easy. Don't just write that you were nervous; *show* us. Have yourself chain smoking, reaching for a bottle, going out for a walk; hell, punching out a wall or something. *Show* us, Frank, don't *tell* us."

"I remember details pretty well."

"Good. Use everything you got."

"People don't care about my life."

"Come on, Frank. If *you* care, *they*'ll care."

"You think I could get published?"

"Don't even think about that right now. The main thing is to get it off your chest."

"I've got some pretty good stories, you know."

"Tell 'em, Frank. Tell 'em."

Frank had to use the bathroom before it was time for the bus to leave for the AA meeting. Sonny watched him spin away in his wheelchair, and when he turned his head he saw that Jake was staring at him with a quizzical grin. "You know, son," he said, "that's the first time I ever heard you talk about what you do."

"Could be, you never asked," Sonny told him.

Jake sniffed. "Where'd you learn all that stuff?"

"By doing it, mainly."

"I could have gone to college if things had been different."

"You told me."

"One semester away, but I had to support Granny."

"I'm not so sure you missed anything, Pop."

"Shoot, boy, I could've been a doctor or something. Made a lot of money if I'd o' gone to college."

"You would've been miserable, and you know it."

"Probably."

Sonny said, "I've got this friend down in Tallahassee, a guy who writes poetry and teaches, and I was telling him the other day about you and me. I told him that you were probably the best teacher I ever had when it came to writing. It's the way you tell stories, you know? Nobody ever learned that in a classroom. And the other thing I told him was that I figure you're a hell of a lot better truck driver than I ever was at anything."

"Well, I'm much obliged for that," said Jake, "but I don't think I like hearing it. Sounds like a goddamn quitter to me."

"You don't understand, Pop."

"The hell I don't. I've almost quit myself."

"Come on. You never *thought* about quitting."

"There's a lot o' things a boy don't know." Jake relit his cigar and sat down on the bed. "I reckon you was about seventeen. That'd make me forty-two or thereabouts. Them was bad times, I tell you. Mama had the big-eyes for a new house over in Crestwood, that suburb where all her church friends were moving, and she kept asking me why I didn't get a job driving a Greyhound or something. Well, hell, the first time you look at somebody funny they'll call the company and get you fired. That was around the time I said I wouldn't join the Teamsters and they put the brick through my windshield and about when that mule stepped in front of me up in Virginia and damned near wrecked ol' Redball II. On top of that, you and Sis was both about to need money for college, so things was getting pretty hot in the kitchen. But, by God, I didn't quit."

"It ain't over 'til it's over, right?"

"Took the words right out of my mouth."

All of the patients at Piney Woods except two who had just checked in had agreed to go into town for the meeting of the local AA group, the HOPE Club (an acronym for Help Other

People Enjoy), and now they stood outside the recovery center waiting for Frank to be loaded first onto the shuttle bus, a little pink twenty-seat jitney with "Piney Woods Recovery Center" scrolled on its sides. Some of the veterans like Jolene and Reggie, who had been making the trip for nearly a month, seemed to be looking forward to it ("Last week," Reggie whispered to Sonny, who had been okayed to go along, "this dude told about bein' high on *Nyquil* for two years. Pharmacist. *Nyquil!*"). Others, first-timers like Frank and a sweet motherly sort named Wilma, had on their grim game-faces as they pondered going public. Jake had taken a seat directly behind the driver, young Bryan Peters himself, and was stoically chewing on his cigar and checking out the dials on the dashboard.

Fifteen minutes later, after a bumpy ride down U.S. 11 and through the narrow back streets of Hattiesburg, the jitney stopped in the gravel parking lot of the Bethel United Methodist Church, where they could hear the sounds of the choir rehearsing, and when the sliding door was jerked open they disembarked and were directed to the basement of the old stone church, Frank last, in his wheelchair, helped by Jake and Sonny. It was another steamy night, redolent with honeysuckle and privet, the moon now in its decline, fireflies dancing in the darkening sky. When the choir began to sing "Church in the Wildwood," Jolene joined them, in a pretty soprano, doing her June Carter Cash impersonation, as they filed down a short flight of stairs into the dank basement.

The group from Piney Woods was greeted with curious stares and polite nods from the locals, about two dozen of them, who had already helped themselves to the coffee and doughnuts laid out on a laundry table in an anteroom and now occupied the choicest metal folding chairs in the spacious room: concrete block walls painted battleship gray, warped linoleum floors, floor fans stirring the fetid air, framed samplers proclaiming the familiar AA slogans. Nervously passing another laundry table laden with literature — the "Big Book," *AA Today*, pocket-sized Bibles — the visitors shuffled to the rear of the room.

The meeting began when a bearded man in a three-piece suit, a professor of some sort from the university, stood behind a lectern and said, "Welcome to the regular weekend meeting of the HOPE group of Alcoholics Anonymous. My name is Noel, and I'm an alcoholic." The group chanted back, "Hi, Noel," and then there were the ritual readings: the Twelve Steps by a jittery teenaged boy named Terry, who said he was an alcoholic and a drug addict; the Twelve Traditions by an old black man, Harold, who boomed them out like a preacher; How It Works by a middle-aged housewife, Carolyn, her coiffed pink hair smelling of the beauty salon.

When the readings were done, Noel returned to the lectern and said, "We would like to welcome our visitors from Piney Woods as a group, and we hope that you will feel free to join in tonight's discussion. I understand that for some of you this is a first AA meeting, shall we say, out in the real world." There was laughter, led by Noel himself. "Beyond those, are there any other newcomers to the HOPE Club, or to Alcoholics Anonymous?" Sonny figured he might as well set an example for his father, so he stood and said, "I'm visiting from Tallahassee. My name is Sonny, and I'm an alcoholic." "Hi, Sonny." When he sat back down between Jolene and Jake, he was startled to find her patting his knee and his father wrapping an arm around his back in a clumsy hug.

Since nobody had a better idea, Noel said he thought the issue of "lowered expectations" might make a good topic for that evening. He started off by sketching the trail that had led to his addiction: a "good boy" growing up in a well-off family, pushed to be a superachiever, Yale education, dreams of being another Freud or Jung, failure to get tenure at Yale, drinking out of despair; now, at the age of forty, thankful to be alive and have a job heading up the Remedial Studies program at USM. For the next half-hour the HOPE regulars took turns pouring out their souls: a ruddy young farmer named Willy, clean-shaven and dressed in ironed overalls, said he couldn't read yet but his wife read the Twelve Steps and the Bible aloud to him every night before bedtime; the housewife, pink-haired Carolyn, said that Librium was no replacement for love; the skittery teenaged boy, Terry, amazed the older crowd with stories about drug traffic right there in Hattiesburg; the old black man, Harold, went off on a lyrical parable depicting whiskey as the devil and said his church was going to let him back in the pulpit if he stayed sober for a year; another fellow, in his seventies, had them in stitches with an elaborate story about a garden hose that he once hooked up to a giant vat of vodka buried beneath his roses.

The group from Piney Woods had sat quietly in the back of the room, wide-eyed but volunteering nothing, and with fifteen minutes remaining in the hour Noel pointed at Reggie and asked if he cared to say anything, and suggesting that maybe the others from the center, ranging from Reggie at one end to Jake at the other, would "speak up if you feel so disposed." Jake struck a match on the linoleum floor when Noel said that.

"Right, well, my name's Reggie and you name it, I've done it. Understand what I'm saying?" The people said, "Hi, Reggie," and he was off and running about drugs he had known in his time: moonshine whiskey and "speed" in the housing project, painkillers and steroids as a college football player, the heroin that had finally brought him to his knees. The next three from Piney Woods passed, on the grounds that they would just as soon listen, but Frank gladly gave a capsule version of his "autobiography" from his wheelchair; ending his spiel in a spasm of crying. Jolene supplied the theatrics of the evening: telling of being hypnotized by the singing of Patsy Cline as a kid listening to the Grand Ole Opry on a battery radio, giving a lively description of life in the raucous clubs of backwater Mississippi, describing her first guest appearance on the Opry and a subsequent week on the road with Ernest Tubb and the Texas Troubadors that she didn't remember too well, until, finally, wailing a confessional that she would make it "one day a time, with the help of you good people and the Lord who makes all things possible, thank you very much," ending with a dramatic *plop* as she fell back into her seat. Nearly everyone in the room turned to smile at Jolene for her pluck, and one soul even tried to get some applause going.

Sonny was next. Throughout the meeting, he had been weighing the options: simply proclaim his addiction and let it go at that or leave his father with something to think about? He dreaded this part of AA meetings, so much so that usually, if he intended to speak out at all, he raised his hand at the beginning and spouted something halfway "meaningful" so he could sit back and enjoy the rest of the hour; if, indeed, AA meetings could be called enjoyable. A glance at the clock on the wall showed that only five minutes remained. He heard an inward voice say, *Am I my father's keeper?* He also heard coughing and the shuffling of feet, and saw Noel staring at him. He finally stood up and said, "My name is Sonny, and I'm an alcoholic."

"Hi, Sonny," came the chorus of voices.

"Frankly, like most of you, I don't know exactly *where* my problems with whiskey got started."

"Damn bitch you married, that's where."

Jake had tilted his Poole Truck Line cap back on his head and leaned back in his chair and was staring up directly at Sonny when he said it. Every head in the room was turned their way, and Sonny thought he heard Jolene stifle a giggle. When he cut another glance down at Jake, he saw that now he was peering innocently toward some point on the far wall, looking angelic for a scrawny old codger wearing a gimme cap and chewing the stump of a cigar.

"Yes, go on," Noel said from the lectern.

"Right," Sonny said.

Jake muttered, "She'd drive anybody to drink."

This time Jolene couldn't contain herself. This time Sonny confronted his father. "Hey, Pop, knock it off, will you?"

"If you'd picked somebody like your mama it would o' been different."

"This is an AA meeting, for Christ's sake."

"Go ahead, son. I'm all ears."

"Thanks a bunch."

"You oughta send her a bill for damages."

Shit. Two minutes of rambling commentary was about all Sonny had in him. He heard his voice, but he felt somehow disconnected from it. ". . . sometimes, sure, I ask myself if Hemingway ever stood up in a room like this and said, 'My name's Ernie and I'm an alcoholic.' He probably should have, but . . . but, what the hell, here we are. I guess 'lowered expectations' is what's keeping me alive." Sonny shook his head and sat down. This time Jolene leaned over and kissed him on the cheek.

"This has been an interesting meeting," Noel said, looking at the clock. "Time for one more, if anybody's got anything to add before we pass out the chips." *One more?* There was only one person remaining, one person who had not spoken, and all heads in the room turned slowly toward this person with the cigar and the baseball cap who sat in the very last chair of the very last row. Throats cleared, fannies wiggled, lips pursed, and eyes widened as the spotlight narrowed on Jake. In the heavy silence, the floor fans sounded like 747s revving up for takeoff.

"You, sir?" said Noel.

Jake didn't bother to get up. Instead, he sat ramrod-straight in the chair and cleared his throat and took the cigar out of his mouth and tugged the cap tightly over his graying close-cropped hair and then, playing to the crowd, crossed his leathery arms. "My name is Jacob Eulysses Hawkins *Senior*," he said, in a booming voice that rang out like a cannon, "and I'm not guilty of a damned thing."

It was a grim ride back to Piney Woods. Jake's statement was, to use one of his favorite terms, like farting in church. Pandemonium had reigned in the airless basement for a full two minutes after he had said it — Jolene whooping, Reggie standing with both fists raised in victory, Frank laughing out loud for the first time since Sonny had met him, the locals treating it as comic relief from the tensions of their confessional — solemnity returning only when Noel banged his fist on the lectern and shouted that it was time to pass out the chips. All of the Piney Woods patients making their first meeting, except for Jake, of course, had made the trip up to the front of the room to accept the white chip announcing their surrender. It seemed to Sonny that the others had made their separate peace: they belonged there, Jake did not. On the ride back to the center, Jake again sat behind Bryan Peters and tried to talk transmissions and shortcuts; but Bryan, jerking the gearshift and rolling his eyes, refused the bait.

By nine-thirty, Jake and Sonny sat on a stone bench in the courtyard at Piney Woods. The inky blue Mississippi sky was alive with cicadas and fireflies and sweet summery smells and, somewhere in the distance, the mournful cry of a train. They hadn't spoken to each other since the outburst at the church, merely gravitating in silence toward the courtyard, and the silence didn't break until Jake struck a match on the bench and, relighting, pointed in the direction of the highway, U.S. 11, that ran past the center.

"See that underpass over there?" he said.

Sonny could make out the silhouette of an arched stone bridge supporting a railroad trestle. "That the Southern tracks?"

"Yeah." Jake hummed low. *I'm the train they call the City of New Orleans.* "Of a morning, before they start up the damn meetings,

I'll come out here and watch. Ain't nothing like a train whistle to make a man want to get up and go somewhere."

"The 'City of New Orleans' run by here?"

"Chicago to New Orleans."

"I'd like to ride that someday."

Jake stood up and walked to the fence separating Piney Woods from the highway, Sonny following, and together they hooked fingers in the chain link fence and observed the bridge. "Been forty years since me and that underpass met up," he said. "The war was about to start up then, and I was busier than a whore on payday. Come through here one day hauling one of them big storage tanks like they bury under gas stations, taking it on a flat-bed from Birmingham to the docks. Trouble was, there ain't but twelve-and-a-half foot of clearance. I was new then, and nobody'd bothered to tell me about that underpass. Letting air out of the tires wouldn't do no good. Wadn't no way I could go over the bank. Finally found me a dirt road through the woods that the army had made. Had to drive ten miles to make the ten feet to the other side of the bridge. Summer of 'forty-one, I think it was."

The irony was lost on neither of them. They stayed at the fence to watch the train, slowing on its journey through Hattiesburg, and then returned to the bench. Sonny heard the sliding glass door open and saw, framed in it, Jolene; who seemed on the brink of joining them, but instead gave a discreet little wave and slid the door closed.

"I'm being held against my will. You know that."

"You made it pretty obvious tonight."

Jake sneered. " 'Higher Power.' You know what *my* Higher Power is, don't you?"

"It ought to be Mama."

"Naw, it's the other way around. She's another reason I don't need to be here. I'm supposed to be home looking out after her, not here with a bunch of damn drunks."

"Pop, don't you understand? They're liable to kick both of you out of Mimosa if you don't stick it out here."

"They ain't gonna kick *her* out. That damn Collier and Phyllis, they'll see to that. Them and that preacher. They want *me* out, not your mama, and that suits the hell out of me."

"What are you gonna do, then? Observe visiting hours at Mimosa when you're sober enough to get in? Drink yourself to death at the house in between visits?" Sonny was exasperated. "Come on, Pop. 'The only woman this old man ever loved,' remember? Do it for Mama, Pop, do it for Mama."

"I been thinking about that Higher Power business while I been here, son."

"Doesn't sound like it to me."

"My Higher Power's sitting in the backyard."

"Hey, wait a minute."

"Dixie Redball Number Four."

"Are you crazy? You're almost seventy. You're retired."

"Re*tarded*. A man ain't re*tarded* until he thinks he is."

"Who'd give you a load at your age?"

"Charley Graddick would."

"The tire place?"

"Best friend I ever had."

"Forget it," Sonny said. "That's over, Pop. What's it been, three years? You weren't worth a damn for a week after that trip to Texas."

"Outdanced everybody at the anniversary party, didn't I?"

"Yeah, but that's dancing. This is driving."

"I know exactly what it is, son."

To Sonny's surprise, Jake didn't pressure him to storm Bryan Peters at the front desk and demand his father's immediate release. When the lights inside and outside of the building blinked three times — the signal, Jake said, for "cookies and milk before they put the babies to bed" — they arose and walked toward the parking lot to Sonny's pickup. Sonny said he had noticed a schedule on the bulletin board showing a full day of meetings, and since he wouldn't be able to visit Jake until after dinner the next night he would be driving back to Birmingham in the morning.

"Couple of things you could do for me when you get there," Jake said when they reached the truck.

"Whatever you say, Pop."

"Crank up the touring car, will you? Batteries need a workout."

"Got you covered."

"Guess you'll be seeing Mama."

"I plan to. Does she know you're here?"

"I don't know what they told her."

"Well, I'll play that one by ear."

"When you go over there, son" — here came the grin and wink Jake always flashed before pulling a leg — "how 'bout checking on my tomato plants."

"Tomato plants. Where?"

"Behind the building at Mimosa."

"What the hell did you do that for?"

"You know how I like vine-ripe tomatoes," Jake said. "You might call ol' Billy Potts over at Trussville and see if his septic tank's full yet."

"You're putting human *shit* on 'em?"

"Ain't nothing better for tomatoes," said Jake. "I got 'em planted back there where Boggs has got his goldfish pool and a Jesus statue. Might need watering, too. What I'd intended to do was rig up a hose so I could siphon from the pool. Like that fellow at the meeting said he did with the vodka in his rose garden." Sonny cranked the pickup and pretended to note the directions Jake was giving him to avoid Hattiesburg's church traffic the next morning. "And here's for gas money and the cigars you paid too much for," his father said, sticking a twenty-dollar bill through the window.

"Hey, it's my pleasure." Sonny tried to give it back.
"Naw, take it. I don't need money in this joint."
"This wouldn't be dirty money, would it?"
"I don't know what you're talking about."
"Money you made hustling Reggie."
"Naw, some old boy at the retirement home."
"What?"
"Horseshoes."
"You hustled somebody at the retirement home?"
"Retarded dentist. Rich as Roosevelt."
"Pop, you're crazy."
"Son," Jake said, shifting the cigar in his mouth, "that old fellow was dying of boredom 'til I came along."

5

THE LAST TIME Sonny had been to Mimosa Towers was at Christmas, when so many lights had been strung up that from the outside it looked like a honky-tonk, and he didn't particularly look forward to returning on Monday morning to visit his mother. The place wasn't so bad architecturally: twin four-story "towers" of brick and glass, perched on a knoll thick with mimosa trees and a flower bed shaped like a cross, sandwiched between the eight-lane Airport Boulevard and I-20, insulated against the outside world with air conditioning and carpeting and Muzak. All of that, plus relentless rounds of "crafts" and chapel services and bingo, meant a long waiting list of good Methodists waiting to die. And that was the rub. Dress it up as they might, Mimosa was no more than the last stop before the grave.

Dressed in a blazer and slacks to please Mama, he followed

the arrows to the Health Care unit where she had been moved. By eleven-fifteen the residents were gathering in quiet knots throughout the building for lunch in the spacious dining hall where his father had revolted a week earlier. The airy atrium lobby seemed to be the most popular place, with its greenery and sofas and walls hung with portraits of Methodist heroes ranging from John Wesley to a born-again steel baron who had financed the latest refurbishing. Plopped deep in the sofas, or parked in their wheelchairs, they waited: mostly snow-haired widows, canes and walkers at hand, murmuring to each other; the few men dazedly smoothing their bald heads and rolling their rheumy eyes as though plotting escape. The centerpiece of the lobby was the white baby grand piano, topped by an ornate brass candelabra, a distinguished Steinway begging to be played by, say, Liberace, but not, alas, by Jake Hawkins.

When the elevator doors opened at the fourth floor Sonny saw a long row of chairs lining the narrow corridor, all of them occupied by old women staring wordlessly at the blank opposite wall or talking to themselves or fidgeting with their brassiere straps while a nurse headed down the line with paper cups holding pills. All heads turned toward him and there was much clucking and smiling as he searched the faces and wasted bodies: opaque eyes, brittle hair, blotched skin, gnarled fingers, hospital wristbands, blue-veined arms tracked with needle bites.

There was a flurry toward the far end of the line. A woman in a frayed ivory robe and satin slippers, her silken hair and regal face bespeaking elegance in a previous life, had gotten out of her chair and was waving at Sonny. She pointed at the woman next to her, Evelyn Hawkins, cupping her chin and turning her face for him to see, and then looked back at him, beaming. Sonny walked toward his mother, slowly, to give her time to recognize him.

"Why, would you look?" his mother said, staying in her seat, pale eyes ten years older than at Christmas. Her hair looked well-attended, though, and she was dressed in a lime green pantsuit and brown sandals as though she had expected company.

"I thought maybe we could have lunch."

"Lord, I s'wanee. Just *look* at you."

"You still my girl?"

"When did you get back, honey?"

"Last night."

"I s'wan. How was Mississippi?"

"It was fine, Mama."

"Did the truck make it all right?"

The woman in the ivory robe offered him her seat and said, gently, "Evelyn, this is your boy. It's Sonny. Now y'all sit and talk. Lunch is in about ten minutes."

He knew he should announce his visits in advance; with a letter a week ahead of time, perhaps, and then a phone call just before his emergence at the elevator. Phyllis and Jake had warned him about the fluctuations in her mind, and he had even gone to the Medical Library at FSU one night to read up on Alzheimer's disease. Reading about it, though, did little to prepare him for the sight of his own mother becoming a vegetable.

"So what you been doing, Mama?"

"Lord, it's Sonny." She patted his knee.

"They keeping you busy?"

"Daddy's gone away."

"They told me about that."

"Sonny" — leaning toward him, conspiratorial whisper — "you remember the Ritz Theater?"

"I sure do. And the Alabama, where they have the organ."

"Not the Alabama. The Ritz. Your daddy and I were married at the Ritz. You remember?"

"Well, I *hope* I don't, Mama. You know?"

"Aw, *you*." She was giggling now, a little girl with a joke, eyes suddenly clear, familiar twinkle in her voice. "There was an ad in the newspaper and they wanted the perfect couple to be married right there on the stage at the Ritz between picture shows. Well, I told Daddy, 'I'm not going to kiss you in front of all those strangers,' but he told me times were bad and it was free. Rings and the preacher and everything. We even got the honeymoon suite at the Thomas Jefferson. Then we went to Chattanooga and rode the Incline."

Lunch was announced. When Sonny arose from the chair he found that his slacks were soaked, clammy, sticking to his skin. Urine. The woman in the ivory robe was incontinent, and had not an inkling. Tugging at his pants, trying to air them out, he took his mother's hand and walked her through the double French doors into the dining room.

Sunlight, fresh flowers, willow tree wallpaper, waxed floor, Formica tables. Amiable nurses, mostly young and black, wheeling carts like airline stewardesses, were bringing lunch on metal trays: meat loaf, steaming cabbage, carrots, English peas, apple sauce, easy to chew and digest. Evelyn Hawkins placed a linen napkin in her lap, observing the feast, and began dumping the contents of each bowl into a pile on her plate, humming to herself, content, stirring it all into a mushy casserole with her fork. Muzak again: Mantovani. "Enjoy your lunch, ladies," said a nurse. "Chapel service at two-thirty."

After lunch she wanted to show Sonny her room. Unlike the cluttered master bedroom back at the house, with so much space that it was easy to backslide on housekeeping, her cubicle here was manageable. There was a twin-sized hospital bed, a wide dresser, a color television set and rocker from home, a nightstand for her Bible and *The Upper Room*, and a small closet. It was, in effect, a motel room with a view of I-20 through a large picture window. There was no need to clutter the table tops here with medicine bottles and paraphernalia, because now there were nurses to take care of her around the clock. The top of the dresser here held a simple display of family photographs in gilt frames: of her four grandchildren, of her own mother, of herself and her husband in happier times.

Sonny had been too preoccupied with taking in the room, and trying to blot his pants dry with a towel, to notice that his mother now sat on the edge of her bed and daubed at her eyes with Kleenex.

"Mama." He moved to her side.

"Oh, Sonny. Why did I think you were Daddy?"

"The older I get, the more I look like him."

"Elleree Hunt came to see me and I didn't even know who she was. My best friend, and I didn't even know her." These moments of clarity startled Sonny more than when she was drifting. "Sometimes the same thing happens with Daddy. I'll ask *him* where *he* is. That must make him feel terrible."

"Mama, he understands. Everybody knows — "

"I know where he is, and I know why."

"You do?"

"He's my husband, isn't he?"

"I wasn't sure they'd told you."

"Phyllis is a sweet daughter, and I know she's doing what she thinks is right. But I know. A woman knows, about her husband."

"Well, Mama, how do you feel about it?"

"I'm really worried about your daddy, Sonny. I really am. He's lonesome as he can be."

Then she had gone under again, left him hanging, spinning off into a story of the time she had gone on a trip in the truck and saw the Gulf for the first time and they went skinny-dipping under the moon and something about a Ferris wheel and Louis Armstrong and an organ grinder's monkey breaking loose. He had escorted her to the main lobby and kissed her goodbye, leaving her with others awaiting the afternoon chapel service, and then had driven back to the house to get out of his sticky pants and into some jeans.

By midafternoon he was rolling the pickup into the driveway of his sister's house, a split level on an elevated cul-de-sac in a leafy subdivision called Smoke Rise. *Good,* he thought, seeing Phyllis's four-year-old Volvo in the carport, *she's here and the asshole isn't.* There was no love lost between Sonny Hawkins and Collier Bradford, and their connection to the former Phyllis Hawkins was all that had kept them from open warfare. Collier, a pale, aquiline Pennsylvanian named for his wealthy maternal grandfather, had dazzled Phyllis with his money when they met at the University of Alabama. Now he was, to Sonny, the most singularly smug individual he had ever encountered: on the surface a church deacon, successful banker, golf fanatic, and an ardent contributor to the football operation at Alabama; beneath that, though, Sonny found him to be a racist of the worst kind, meaning he had the power and money to deliver. Collier had built the house on a hill so he could "shoot down on 'em when they start coming." He had seen to the banishment of a preacher who gave a special Thanksgiving offering, earmarked for a "needy family in our midst," to a black family. Once, when Sonny in his previous life as a homeowner said he was going to low-key Christmas out of deference to the Orthodox Jews next door, Collier said not to worry: "Hymies *love* Christmas; Santa Claus makes their year." Sonny had watched with interest when the new black-majority city council revealed a systematic policy of denying home-improvement loans in black neighborhoods, even the more affluent ones, by Collier Bradford's bank, but the bank simply ignored it and the newspapers slept and Collier went back to playing golf.

Phyllis's position, in this and all matters, was that everybody should be "nice," her synonym for order and the status quo, and for her faithful years of service to Collier she had been rewarded with a "nice" life: a weekly allowance, country-club membership, vacations, plenty of time for her sorority and the Red Mountain United Methodist Church. Still, Collier was not only a severe man who ruled with an iron glove, punishing their children with a belt in the basement when they were young, he was also patently *dull*. One time, into the sauce, Sonny had asked Phyllis if she were truly happy; she merely said that Collier was "a good provider." Phyllis was just as much her mother's daughter as Sonny was his father's son. How, then, Sonny wondered as he stood on the Alabama Crimson Tide doormat and rang the doorbell, could his sister begin to understand him or their father?

She was in her tennis outfit, tanned and vibrant, wearing Ray-Ban sunglasses, when she opened the door. "Well, I s'wanee" — where in the *hell* did that saying come from? — "I thought it was Penny."

"Does Martina Navratilova know about this?"

"Who?"

"Never mind. Ponytail looks great."

"Well, thank you. Come on in. I've got a pot of coffee on if you want some."

"Phyl, it's hotter than Sloss Furnace out there. Iced tea, if you've got it."

His sister had a great shape, passed along from their mother, and he figured that she would also be able to show up at her golden wedding anniversary in the original gown. Another similarity, he noticed with a glance toward the dining room, was this thing for sewing: laid out on the banquet-sized table was a pattern (Butterick, like Mama) and a bolt of cloth and a portable Singer. She was a throwback to the fifties, the most committed "homemaker" he had seen since Mama's better days. He trailed along through the cool den to the bright bay-windowed kitchen for what he knew would be a great glass of iced tea. A nice one, anyway.

"So how are the kids?" said Phyllis, fishing for cubes in a

double-wide refrigerator covered with scraps of paper — Things To Do, PTA and Delta Zeta and church bulletins, messages for Collier — held up by magnetized bananas and apple cores.

"Same-old with Robby," he told her. "All he learned at Auburn was how to cut cards and cocaine."

"Will he go back?"

"Maybe later. Right now he's seeing America with some rock band. Driver and go-fer."

"Oh, Lord, Sonny. I'm so sorry."

"Typical male Hawkins behavior," Sonny told her. "But, hey, Michelle's in thick with the Lord."

"I already knew about the Campus Crusade."

"She got bored. All the guys looked like Pat Boone. Now she's on the Rio Grande, teaching English and Jesus."

"Mexicans?"

"Brown as the berries they pick."

"Aren't you worried?"

"Hey, that's my kind of church. I'm one of her sponsors. Is that deductible?"

Phyllis either let it pass or missed it entirely. Her kids were doing the same normal things, she said as they took their tall glasses of iced tea to the pine-paneled den. Collier Jr. was touring Europe with the patriotic chorale, "Up with People"; Courtney was counseling at the same church camp where they had gone as kids and would enter Randolph-Macon Woman's College in the fall.

But enough of that. The issue was their parents, and it came as no surprise to Sonny that the grapevine had carried the news of Jake's performance at the AA meeting on Saturday night. "Sonny," she said, "didn't you try to *stop* him?"

"Phyl, that's ridiculous. He's a grown man."

"Well, he doesn't *act* like it."

"What do you expect, a miracle?"

"I expect him to understand what's going to happen if he doesn't straighten up. He's got to quit, Sonny. It's that simple."

"It's not that simple."

"He's an alcoholic, isn't he?"

"He doesn't fit the usual profile."

"Well, just what *is* an alcoholic, anyway?"

"Me. Your brother. Somebody who drinks to celebrate and drinks to forget and drinks when he's undecided."

"That sounds more like Daddy to me."

"Phyl, listen. Pop did his share of cussing you and Collier and this Boggs, and he did some crying about Mama. But do you know what he talked about ninety percent of the time? Truckin'. Movin' on. Charley Graddick. Work, Sis. Work."

Her eyes widened. "Charley Graddick?"

"Says Charley's the best friend he's got."

"Lord. Daddy did some of his worst drinking down at that old tire place. Charley Graddick isn't Daddy's friend. He's his *drinking* buddy."

"Maybe so. Maybe not." Sonny told her about Jake's going by the house and cranking the truck. "His real best friend is his truck if you ask me."

"Humph. That old truck. Why doesn't he sell the thing? It's *tacky*. How will it look when we try to sell the house?"

"Whoa, Sis. First the piano. Now the truck."

"We have to *think* about these things, Sonny."

"That'd be like selling one of your kids, Phyl."

"I can't believe you said that."

"Just trying to make my point."

"Oohhh." She was frowning behind her dark glasses, fingering her ponytail. "I *s'wanee*, Sonny, I'm surprised at you. We were counting on you to talk Daddy into his senses. It's a wonder you didn't bring him home."

"It didn't come up. Honest. But you know as well as I that he's his own man."

"Sonny" — she was leaning forward on the sofa now, smiling earnestly, staying cool — "that's a nice place at Mimosa. Mama loves it. Didn't you see that?"

"I did. I hate to admit it, but I did."

"I mean, where else is she going to go?"

"My place or yours, huh?"

"Exactly."

"How about back to the house with Pop?"

"They've already tried that. A month ago."

"Nobody told me that."

"Oh, Lord, Sonny. Maybe Mama forgot. One morning about dawn Daddy sneaked her out and took her over to Channel 6 to be on the 'Country Boy Eddie Show.' That old hillbilly singer that Daddy loves? Well, that was bad enough. I mean, we didn't see the show because nobody we know would *dream* of watching it, but somebody said Mama didn't even know where she was and Daddy sat there saying these ugly things about Mimosa and Brother Boggs and how he might take her to the Grand Ole Opry."

"Christ. Sneaked her out?"

"Uh-huh. And then he took her home."

"This is too fast for me. How'd it go?"

"We went over there when nobody would answer the phone. Well, you just *know* Daddy was drunk. Mama hadn't had any of her pills all day and she was standing in the middle of the kitchen looking for something to cook when we got there."

"And?"

"Well, that's when Daddy started saying the ugly things to Collier. I thought they were going to fight. I didn't know Daddy felt that way about Collier."

"Whiskey does have a way of freeing the spirit, Phyl." Sonny couldn't wait to hear his father's version of this and was preparing to push Phyllis for more details about the "ugly things" that had passed between their father and her husband. But then she absently took off her sunglasses and he saw that both of her eyes were black.

When she saw Sonny staring, she quickly put the glasses back and blushed. "Oh, Lord," she said. "I forget."

"Phyl, what happened?"

"It was just a tennis accident."

"Looks like a mugging. You mean a girl isn't safe at old Vulcan Hills?"

"We were playing doubles. Penny and I. We tried to hit the ball at the same time. That's all. Really."

Even though the mechanics didn't seem right to Sonny, who reckoned it would have taken a hell of a shot across the nose to bring shiners like that, he let it go. "So after the shouting with Collier, what?"

Fidgety, Phyllis said, "We cleaned Daddy up and he took a nap, and then we took them back. Brother Boggs was real nice, Sonny. They're lucky he let them back in."

"And it was about a week later that he lost it and y'all exiled him to Mississippi."

"It's a nice place, Sonny. It's not 'exile.' "

"In a thousand AA meetings I've never heard a good word about those places or shrinks."

Phyllis said, "We've all about decided if Daddy doesn't straighten up he'll just have to take care of himself. Mama's right where she belongs."

"You mean you're ready to hang him out to dry like that?"

"If he doesn't stay for the whole month, Brother Boggs won't let him back. Mama can stay, but not Daddy."

"It'd be me and Pop, then."

"I guess so."

"Out of the Bible. 'Am I my father's keeper?' "

"The Bible says you *are*, Sonny."

"I never thought it'd come to this, you know."

"Nobody did."

"I mean, The Last Cowboy. King of the Road. Having his strings pulled by some preacher. Christamitey, Phyllis. You want his balls, too?"

At first she blushed, but then she swallowed hard and launched into a soliloquy that he didn't know was in her. "I know you love Daddy and you have a very special feeling about him. Y'all have fought each other a lot, and I always felt it was because you were just alike. But if you want to talk about cowboys, I'll tell you about cowboys. They're fine up there on the movie screen, Sonny, but they're pure hell to live with. They're selfish, they're childish, and they don't clean up after themselves. Mama and I are sick and tired of cleaning up Daddy's messes. He's not funny to us anymore, Sonny, so it's your turn."

The doorbell chimed the opening strains of the Alabama fight song, one of the few frivolities Collier Bradford allowed into his life, and Phyllis was back to being herself when she opened the door for Penny Padgett: Delta Zeta, tanned blonde, loose skin hinting of crash diets, trying too hard to be "cute" in a skimpy Gussie Moran lace-panties outfit.

"Was it a forehand, or a backhand?" Sonny asked after pleasantries about the heat and court times.

"Hunh?"

"The weapon has been established, but the M.O. is unclear."

Penny sensed a joke, but was flustered. "I knew your brother was different, Phyllis, but can you please tell me what in the world he's talking about?"

"The assault on my sister, madam."

"What?" Glances darted between the two women. Penny began to laugh uproariously. "Oh, my Lord, *that*," she said. "I must be about the clumsiest thing that ever picked up a tennis racquet. Why, I wouldn't even be playing if Phyllis hadn't practically dragged me. I'm bad enough at singles, and we just should have *known* something awful would happen if I got put right *next* to some — "

Phyllis cut her off. "Sonny, you've just *got* to have dinner with us at the club tonight. There'll be Collier and I, and Penny and Peck. Peck Padgett? He was at Auburn when you were?"

"It's Hawaiian Night," Penny said.

"Do you get lei-ed at the door?"

"You bet," said Penny. Sonny could swear she winked.

"Come by the house at seven," Phyllis said. "I hope you brought something nice to wear."

"Sis, I've got a suit that's been waiting to be worn at Collier's club."

The only thing Sonny could say about Hawaiian Night at the Vulcan Hills Country Club was that it could have been worse. The evening began portentously when he apparently walked in on the aftermath of a fight: when Phyllis got into Collier's Mercedes for the ride to the club she slammed the door with some fury, prompting him to get out from behind the wheel, walk slowly around the front of the car, his wingtips tapping on the paved driveway, open the door and gently close it, and then say to a shaken Phyllis, "Don't you ever slam *my* car door again." Sonny's sister, now in orange sunglasses, said she was sorry.

It would have been easy for Sonny to make a scene at the club — "Hawaiian" band led by a Don Ho look-alike, middle-aged Republicans drinking Mai Tais and dancing the cha-cha, some wearing sarongs and flowery shirts bought on the latest vacation to Honolulu — but he had been sombered by the visits with his parents. He had worn his seersucker suit and sworn that he would try not to embarrass his sister on her own turf, something that hadn't been easy to do at times. Penny Padgett, the preacher's daughter, got tipsy and put a clumsy move on him. All of the friends of "Collie" turned out to be silver-spoon racists, with first names like Townsend and Turner and Brock, who ignored their women and spoke of golf and Ronald Reagan and Alabama-Auburn football, one of them producing, at one point, a Xeroxed sheet listing Auburn's mythical football signees for the year: *Willie Ali Washington . . . 6-4, 250, RB, Memphis . . . Led state in rushing and burglaries . . . Has been clocked at 4.2 in 40-yard-dash with 25-inch TV . . . Lists IQ as 20-20, church preference as red brick.* Sonny let that pass, but he had a hard time restraining himself when one of Phyllis's sorority sisters began extolling her platform as a candidate for the county school board: for school prayer, the playing of "Dixie," a no-pass no-play rule for high-school sports (keep the niggers out); against sex education, *Catcher in the Rye*, skirts above the knee, and then, after all of that, she raved about the novels of Danielle Steel. Sonny felt he had been hurled backward in time to, say, 1957.

But he endured, and he felt comfortable enough to go back to the Bradfords' for coffee and pecan pie. They sat on the brick terrace off the kitchen, at a round redwood table, watching the fireflies and smelling the honeysuckle, talking about football and kids and the weather and Hawaii, everything casual and safe, no religion or politics, meandering right along without any trouble, until the issue of Jake came up.

"Alcoholic recovery isn't the only thing he needs," Collier said, leaning back and sniffing, always the sign that he was ready for combat.

"I'm not even sure he needs that," Sonny told him.

"He's a drunk. Anybody can see that."

"There's drinkers and then there's drunks."

Phyllis tried to cut in, but Collier simply raised his hand to stop her. "He's already got two strikes on him. The time he took Mrs. Hawkins out of Mimosa and the time he ruined breakfast for everybody. If he doesn't straighten up, he's gone and so's your mother. I can't ask Brother Boggs to give him any more chances. If you ask me, I think the man belongs in Bryce."

That did it. Bryce was the state mental institution, in Tuscaloosa. "You ignorant sonofabitch," Sonny said evenly, leveling his eyes at Collier, hearing Phyllis gasp.

"I'm sorry, but your father is crazy as a loon."

"Who says what's 'crazy'? What's the definition?"

"Well, he's about the stubbornest man I've ever known," said Collier, backing off.

"You don't know a goddamn thing about that man. I'd agree to 'confused,' but you ought to watch how you use 'crazy.' There's a big difference."

Collier said, "Where've you been all of these years?"

"What?"

"We've been right here, cleaning up his messes, and we haven't seen you around."

"Money doesn't come to me, I have to go get it. Just like Pop."

"You say I don't work for a living?"

"Bet your ass. First, you inherited it. Now you process other peoples' money."

"At least I've got something to show for it."

"Possessions, asshole. *Things*, like a wife and kids who don't jump 'til you bark. You said it all when you told Phyl, 'Don't you ever slam *my* car door again.'"

"I was just trying to make a point with her."

"Bingo. She apologized, didn't she?"

"I *s'wanee*, y'all" — Phyllis stood and began gathering cups and saucers and plates — "it's getting late. I bet the ten o'clock news is already over. Collier, you've got a breakfast meeting with Peck."

Collier calmly pushed away from the table and walked across the terrace, through the kitchen and den toward the bedroom, without saying another word. After Sonny had helped his sister carry the dishes to the kitchen, she followed him out the front door to his pickup.

"I'm sorry, Phyl. We just don't have anything in common."

"You're just worried about Daddy. It's okay."

"Don't you ever get to where — "

"Don't. Please don't."

"I mean, the sonofabitch — "

"He's my husband, Sonny, for better or for worse."

"Well, for your sake, I hope it gets better."

Sonny and Phyllis turned their heads toward the mournful cooing of an owl somewhere high in the trees behind the house. Sonny cut his eyes toward his sister, his sweet, rules-playing sister, and thought of the prices we all have to pay for what we want, how Collier had won her over, these twenty-odd years earlier, by actually proposing to her on one knee after showing Jake his financial statement. Sonny said, "He knows where to hurt, though, when he asks where I've been."

"You're not going to *do* anything, are you, Sonny?"

"Calling him an asshole helped."

"No, I mean about Daddy."

"I'm not going to go back and get him, if that's what you're saying. I don't know, I guess I'll hang around for a few more days. See Mama a few more times, call Pop over there. He's probably the loneliest man in America right now. I've told you how I feel about those places. You gotta *want* to quit."

"I just didn't know what else to do, Sonny."

"I know, Sis, I know."

"Our daddy" — Phyllis began to blubber, and Sonny pulled her head to his chest — "ending like this."

"Hey, Sis. In the words of the old man. It ain't over 'til it's over."

6

AT DAYBREAK Tuesday, having fallen asleep on the sofa in the family room while watching "The Tonight Show," Sonny was jolted awake by the first jet roaring away from the Birmingham airport and by the nasal braying of Country Boy Eddie. "Hee-haw! Hee-haw!" Country Boy was calling from Channel 6 on Red Mountain, on a barnlike set made of hay bales and horse collars and pitchforks, that being the signal to set a steel guitar player off and running with "Steel Guitar Rag" to welcome the dawn. The special guests that morning were some teenaged cloggers, the Sand Mountain Stompers, from the hill country near Scottsboro, and as they beat the boards to the music Country Boy did the silly jig that Jake Hawkins had adopted as his own.

Jake was a friend and neighbor of Country Boy, and their friendship was such that Jake was welcome to pop in on the show whenever he felt the urge. He had felt the urge often over the years, much to the chagrin of Phyllis and Mama, and once he had even talked Sonny into going along, during Sonny's stint as a sportswriter for the Birmingham *News*. That had been fun, if not a little quirky, Sonny thought as he now watched Country Boy, in a spangled red and yellow cowboy outfit and a bad blond toupee, sing an off-key version of "Sleepin' at the Foot of the Bed," but he winced to think that his father had dragged his mother down there in her condition. When Country Boy finished singing and announced that he would be appearing at noon that day in a new mall at Anniston, an hour up the road, Sonny wondered if the man ever slept. "Hee-haw, yourself," he said, just to hear a live voice, stepping into the kitchen to make some coffee for breakfast.

What to do? He had already scoured the basement in a vain search for the keys to Dixie Redball, now glistening with dew under its covering in the backyard, so there was no way he could sit in the cab to pretend it was 1948 and he was riding along to Akron and Cumberland with the old man while Hank Snow wavered in and out of WCKY with "I'm Movin' On." He intended to go up the hill for a visit with his boyhood pal Lee Riddle before returning to Tallahassee, to see what had gone wrong, but he wasn't sure he was ready to hear the answers right now. He had burned himself out with family the day before, and he needed a break from that. Maybe a leisurely drive around the city, to see the old haunts, to check out the "new" Birmingham that had evolved since the closing of the steel mills?

All it took was a pot of coffee and a long shower to bring Sonny's day into focus. There was only one thing to do, one place to go, and he had known it since Saturday night after the AA meeting in Hattiesburg when Jake had sat in the courtyard of Piney Woods and abruptly called to mind a name from the past. To hear the name again, especially when Sonny thought it had been consigned to the family's archives like an old snapshot, was both chilling and thrilling. Charley Graddick. Sonny would go and talk with Charley Graddick.

Charley Graddick & Sons Tire Company occupied a squat stone two-story fortress in a neglected area of town dominated by railroad sidings, loading docks, lumberyards, warehouses, and small foundries. Little had changed, outwardly, in the thirty years since Charley had bought a turn-of-the-century coffee warehouse and converted it into a place to recap tires; but Sonny knew that there was more to that building than met the eye. Charley, a high school dropout whose interest in tires had grown from his days as a wild-haired minor stock-car racing hero on dirt tracks all over the Deep South, had discovered that a fortune could be made in recycling tires, and by the age of sixty or thereabouts he had made that fortune in that sweaty underworld. This grim old building, barely visible for the mounds of used tires now recapped and stacked and awaiting shipment to points all over the globe, for use on heavy earth-moving equipment at open pit mines, on farms, and on highway projects, was headquarters for what had grown into a multimillion-dollar corporation with offices and warehouses in dozens of other cities and on two other continents.

Charley could be in Europe or Japan, for all Sonny knew, but at least he should be apprised of the latest on Jake. It had never occurred to Sonny until his father brought it up that Charley Graddick really might be his last True Believer. It was Charley who had cosigned the note for Dixie Redball IV in 1972, when Jake was sixty years old. It was Charley who kept the old man on the road at an age when no unionized truck line would touch him: flying him to air bases all over North America to inspect and bid on lots of tires, then dispatching him to pick them up and haul them back to Birmingham when he had won the bid for Graddick & Sons. It was for Charley, in fact, that Jake had been inspecting and loading tires at the air base in Amarillo and nearly missed his own golden wedding anniversary party. So, yes; if anybody deserved to know about Jake Hawkins's escape and recapture, as it were, it was Charley Graddick.

Chuck Graddick — Charles Jr., the oldest of the four sons — was on the phone at the long front counter, filling out an order sheet, when Sonny entered. He waved and pointed his finger toward the ceiling to signify that his father was, indeed, upstairs in his office. This was familiar territory to Sonny, who had learned that physical labor wasn't for him when he spent one of his college summers there moving tires around, and as he mounted the stairs it all came back to him: the incessant wheezing and clunking of the recapping machinery, the oppressive smell of searing rubber, the breath-sucking heat of the warehouse, the taste of bad whiskey shared with swarthy black laborers on break, the persistent ringing of phones, the swirl around the front counter of truckers impatiently waving pink order slips at the dispatchers, the sheer *sweat* of this world he had tried to forget.

Charley was on the phone, swiveling from side to side in a brown leather executive's chair, thumbing a suspender and wiggling his toes in the wingtip shoes he had hoisted on top of an expansive cherry desk. He was talking to somebody about meeting in London later in the week, and he winked and pointed to a box of cigars on the desk when Sonny came in. Cuban. Sonny took one.

". . . *Cats*," Charley was saying. "Figure we might as well get in a little culture while we're there. Then we'll go on to Munich . . . Naw, he's in Manila this week, but I 'spect to hear from him today or tomorrow. I never can get that time difference straight. Hell, I have to stop and remember it's a different time in *Atlanta* . . . Right. And let me know when that shipment leaves Bremerhaven, will you? . . ."

When Charley hung up the phone he stood and shook hands across the desk with Sonny and said, "Looking for a summer job, are you, son?"

"Hell, no. I want to go see *Cats* in London. Who was that?"

"My man in Holland."

"They know about this at Dixie Speedway? Stick Graddick, on the phone to Holland?"

They both sat and lit cigars simultaneously. Charley had virtually soundproofed his office, now paneled and soft-lighted and lined with bookcases holding dozens of athletic trophies won by his sons, and from there it was easy to forget the din and the stench of the warehouse. He said, "Sometimes I can't believe it, myself. Hell, it wasn't long ago I used to throw away tires when they got a little slick. Who would've thought it?"

"How many countries are you in now?"

"Thirty-four and counting. And China's about to open up. Look here" — Charley reached for a photo album and began flipping clear plastic sheets that held snapshots of him posing all over the world — "me getting a shoeshine in Tokyo. Damned shoeshine was five bucks. Me and the wife in Berlin there. Got one somewhere in here from a bullfight in Madrid. Guy tried to give my wife the bull's ear, but she fainted when she saw it. All of this because of a bunch of old tires." Charley closed the album and rocked back in his chair. "So what's up? Where you hanging out these days?"

"Tallahassee. Teaching."

"Good tire town. Lots of trucks."

"Logging trucks, mainly," Sonny said.

"Naw," said Charley. "You get a town that sits on highways like that, I-10 going one way and U.S. 27 the other, you got yourself a tire town. Your daddy ought to know about that."

"I guess so, Charley. Shame, I never asked him."

"Well, that's between you and him. I never did understand it, though."

"Understand what?"

"Hell, Sonny. You know what I'm talking about."

"Me and Pop."

"Sometimes I felt like I was put on this earth to hear him

bitch. You heard plenty of it yourself. 'I may not be nothin' but a truck driver, by God, but I notice they ain't starvin'.' He'd come down here and start to going on about your wife, or Phyllis's husband, or your mama wanting a new house. Hell, I didn't know anything about all of that. All I knew was, I had the best damn truck driver in the world working for me and I'd best keep him happy."

"I know, I know. I'm trying to do better by him now."

"Another one he had. 'He that tooteth not his own horn, the same shall not be tooteth.' "

"Yeah, yeah, Charley."

"Got pretty tired of the tootin' sometimes."

"Right, Charley."

"So. I guess you've come to see 'em. They doing all right over there? I stay too damned busy."

"There've been some changes, Charley."

When Charley heard about Jake and Mississippi, he slammed his palm on the desk and shot out of the chair as though he had sat on a tack. "Why the hell doesn't anybody tell me these things?" he bellowed.

"I didn't know until after it happened myself. You know Phyllis."

"Oh, forget that, Sonny. She's from another planet. I just wish, goddamnit, they'd understand how much I loved that man." Charley pursed his lips and tried to suppress a grin. "Say he was brown-bagging it at the retirement home?"

"In front of God and everybody."

"Well, we might've know it was gonna happen."

"Probably."

"They think he's turned alcoholic, you say."

"They're convinced of it."

"What do you think? You've had some experience."

"Hell, I don't know. He's a hell of a drinker. Everybody knows that."

Charley stopped to relight his cigar, then threw his feet up on the desk and rocked in his chair. "I might be wrong about this, but I don't think anybody knows your daddy as a man and a truck driver like I do. I don't think I ever saw anybody so wrapped up in what he does for a living. Without that truck Jake Hawkins ain't nothing. You ask me, he died the day he quit driving."

"He didn't have much choice, you know."

"Poor Evelyn. It sure came on fast, didn't it? I don't suppose she's any better, your mama."

"It gets worse every day."

"Shame he never had any hobbies, you know?"

"Phyllis has recommended the Lions Club."

"He'd be a 'tail-twister,' all right. Hah. Lions Club. She don't know a damned thing about him, does she?"

"Charley," Sonny said, "a couple of weeks ago Pop sneaked away and the neighbors heard him firing up the truck."

"Don't surprise me. Wonder he didn't bobtail it to Memphis or somewhere, looking for a load. Ol' Redball's still running, huh?"

"It starts, anyway."

"I'll be damned." Charley rolled the cigar in his mouth. He was smiling, as though he had gotten word that Ty Cobb had risen from the dead and gone four-for-four at Yankee Stadium just to show the bastards, and then he stood and told Sonny to follow him. "I want to show you something you might not know about your daddy."

Charley, who had been left with a limp from a wreck in his racing days, sidestepped down the stairs to the main floor of the warehouse, Sonny ambling behind him past a dozen glistening young black men busy recapping tires, and soon the two were standing in a distant corner of the lot in front of a dozen stacks of tires that had been sorted by size and type. Bees and mosquitoes swarmed over carcasses filled with stagnant rainwater. Forklifts were parked where they had last been used.

"Big mothers, aren't they?" Charley said. "Those are your two thousand-by-twenties."

"Where'd they come from?"

"Different air bases. All over."

"B-52 tires?"

"Used to be. Law says they got to throw 'em away after a hundred landings. Doesn't take a month to do that. That's the kind your daddy used to go bid on, and if we got 'em I'd rent a trailer and he'd hitch up Redball and go get the load. Now, if you win a bid you've got to take the whole shebang, duds and all. I'll never forget the time me and Jake went down together to bid on a big lot of mixed tires at Tyndall Air Force Base in Panama City. We won the bid, but there was about three hundred duds in there and we had twenty-four hours to haul the whole thing away. Well, to make a long story short, Jake got busy loading the good ones and I hired some old boy to haul away the duds and bury 'em in a sinkhole outside of Panama City."

"Nothing you can do with the duds?"

"Carcasses rotted out. Too far gone."

"But that's the deal. All, or nothing."

"Yeah," Charley said. "There's canyons all over the West where Jake Hawkins rolled duds all by himself. Well, what happened on those three hundred from Tyndall was, one day I read where all of a sudden there was a big demand for that size of tire. Somebody was paying two hundred dollars apiece for 'em, no matter what kind of shape they were in. I chartered me a plane and flew down to Panama City and rented a car and ran over to where we'd buried those tires. Guess what? Somebody had put a shopping center right on top of 'em. Sixty thousand dollars' worth of tires, buried under a K Mart."

"Pop handled these things himself?"

"He'd back the trailer up to the dock, and then he'd roll 'em into place. Said the way you got killed was working with somebody else. One man, alone, that was your daddy's way."

"Jesus. Those things must be four feet tall."

"The B-52 tires are, lemme see, fifty-two inches tall, seventeen inches wide, two hundred and fifty pounds each. But they're babies, compared to the ones over there."

Charley walked across the yard to a loading dock, the end of the production line, and motioned to a phalanx of monstrous tires. They were standing at attention on their new treads, perhaps two dozen of them, six rows deep, each as tall and as wide as a man.

"What the hell is this?"

"Earth-mover tires. Goodyear calls 'em the twenty-nine-point-five-by-twenty-nine. Thousand pounds each. Seventy-eight inches tall, twenty-seven wide."

"Where are they headed?"

"Nevada, when we get around to 'em. Mining outfit wants 'em."

"Don't tell me Pop handled these, too."

"Why, hell yeah."

"Come on, Charley. He's as scrawny as I am. Christ, if one of 'em fell on him — "

"Did, one time," Charley said.

"Tell me."

"I was in the office late one afternoon, getting ready to leave, and he kinda staggered in looking like a ghost. That wasn't more'n five years ago, when he was about sixty-five. We had a load going to Colorado. Anyway, I said, 'Jesus, Jake, looks like you could use a drink,' and he said, 'Don't mind if I do.' Maybe he'd got himself too tired or something, but one of 'em got to wobbling on him while he was trying to get it rolling to the front of the trailer. I don't know how the hell he kept from breaking his neck that day. Must have jumped through the hole. Ain't no telling how many other times that same thing happened out on the road somewhere and he didn't bother to tell anybody. To Jake, it was all in a day's work."

"Why'd he load 'em himself? You got fork lifts and plenty of help around here."

"Same reason he'd sleep in the truck instead of a motel. Same reason he'd eat hamburgers instead of T-bones. Same reason he'd drive around the scales in the middle of the night even if he was legal."

"Shit, Charley. Why?"

"Pride. There was a little orneriness mixed in there, and some of that old dog and new tricks stuff. But mainly it was pride."

It stung Sonny to be hearing this about his father from somebody else. "You know, Charley," he said as they walked toward the pickup, "I did my share of bitching, too, about his not understanding *me*. Seems to be a problem when somebody comes up out of the 'working class' and doesn't sweat for a living. He was always saying, 'You got a job yet, boy, or are you still teaching?' What the hell. Maybe it's been the same way for him, too. Mama always wanted him to do something 'respectable' like drive a bus, and it's like he spent his life trying to show her how wrong she was."

"Like I said, I'm familiar with all of that."

"I guess he used you like a priest over the years."

"Wouldn't put me in the priest category. But yeah, he had to have somebody to talk to. I always seemed to be handy."

Sonny said, "He brought up your name when I was in Mississippi, Charley."

"I shouldn't be surprised at that, I guess."

"It was more than a mention."

"Does he need money?"

"No. For the first time in his life, he's okay for money."

"I can't get him out of that place, Sonny."

"Nobody wants to do that. He belongs there."

"Tell you what. Give me the number over there and I'll — "

"He says you'd give him a load, Charley."

"Say what?"

"Said, 'Charley's the best friend I've got.' "

"That doesn't mean I'd give him a load."

"Maybe he's reaching," Sonny said. "He ought to know he's too old for this anymore."

They reached the pickup. Sonny slid into the cab and cranked the engine, and when he closed the door and began patting the accelerator, Charley leaned in. "There's a lot I don't know, Sonny, and I'd sure like to find out what's happening to your daddy. He's probably lonesome as hell, and that's got him talking crazy. But I'll tell you one thing: Jake Hawkins never drank until he'd finished his work. Maybe he's decided he isn't through working yet."

7

STRETCHED OUT on the sofa again on Wednesday afternoon, musing that more questions than answers had come forth in the week since he had read "Gentle" to his students in Tallahassee, Sonny was jarred from his reverie by the ringing of the phone. He figured it might be Phyllis, making sure he didn't forget their dinner that night with Mama at Mimosa Towers.

"Mr. Hawkins?"

"Hawkins Junior. Sonny."

"Oh, thank goodness. This is Bryan Peters, at Piney Woods Recovery Center."

"Oh, yes."

"How are you today?"

"So far, so good."

"I'd prayed you'd be there. There was no answer at Mrs. Bradford's house."

"She's probably playing tennis. What's up?"

"It's about your father."

"What now? He finally have a seizure, or what?"

"He's threatening to leave."

"There's nothing new about that, is there?"

"No. But this time he's standing here at the front desk with his suitcase. He wants his money so he can catch the bus."

Sonny heard muffled voices, what sounded like an argument, and then his father came on the line. "That's what happens when you give somebody a little power," he said, his voice almost presidential. "They took my money when I got thrown into this joint, and now they won't let me have it back."

"Pop, what the hell are you doing?"

"I'm getting out of here, boy."

"What about Mama? You got to think about Mama."

"Aw, hell, Mama's fine. You told me yourself."

"You know what they say at Mimosa, Pop. If you don't stick it out there, they might throw her out."

"Naw, the damn Methodists ain't *that* mean."

"We don't know that for sure."

"I've figured it out now. It's that Methodist Conspiracy. They *want* me to leave, boy, so they can have Mama all to theirselves."

"You're paranoid."

"Good word. Came up in a crossword the other day."

"That's amusing, Pop."

"Naw, it's a fancy word for crazy."

"Shit. Well, what'll you do when you get here?"

"I got plans, son, I got plans."

"So does Brother Boggs, I bet."

"Damnit, boy, are you gonna help me or not? The bus leaves at ten tonight and I want to be on it."

"Let me talk to that kid again, Pop."

Bryan Peters got back on the line. Jake had been at the front desk with his suitcase for three hours, he said, ever since finishing lunch, and his story about being held against his will had the other patients so convinced that the two who were completing their thirty days were offering to drive him to Birmingham when they checked out. "He was causing such a disturbance that we had to hold a group meeting for the others," Peters said in a whisper.

"I don't know what I can do," Sonny said.

"Families have gotten restraining orders before."

"What's the chances?"

"Not good. All you can do is try."

"You still think he needs to be there."

"Absolutely. Yes, sir. He's the toughest to crack that we've ever seen."

"Okay, I'll make some calls. Don't let him go yet if you can help it. Show him a movie or something."

"Law offices."

"I need to talk to Flip Hanes."

"May I say who's calling?"

"Tell him Hawkshaw."

"How do you spell that, sir?"

"Ah, shit. Tell him it's Sonny Hawkins."

"Are you a client, sir?"

"We're old pals. I got an emergency here. Come on, move it."

"Well, excuse *me*."

Muzak. Finally, J. Ellsworth Hanes. "If she's rich, white, and under sixteen, I can't help you. Hawk, what the hell's happening? Where are you? Where've you been?"

"To hell and back, Flip."

"How was the trip?"

"You didn't get my postcard?" It had been nearly twenty years since the day they had returned from a year in France during the Berlin crisis with the Alabama Air National Guard, but it seemed to Sonny that Flip Hanes hadn't lost a bit of the edge he had as the jocular judge advocate general for their hapless band of weekend warriors. "Flip, listen up," Sonny said. "I got a problem."

By the time Sonny had finished outlining the situation, Hanes was laughing hysterically. "Hell," he said, "I think your old man's probably right."

"I didn't ask for commentary, asshole. Can we keep him there?"

"What good do you think a restraining order would do if he doesn't *want* to stay?"

"I've got an obligation to try, Flip."

"Okay. I know this gal lawyer in Jackson. It's late in the day, but if she isn't out influencing a judge or something maybe I can check it out. I'll get back to you soon as I can."

Phyllis answered her phone, out of breath, on the eighth ring. Tennis with Penny Padgett.

"Her backhand improving?" Sonny said.

"Huh?"

"Forget it. Look, Phyl, something's come up."

"Oh, you can't have dinner with me and Mama."

"Worse. Pop's busting out of Piney Woods."

Momentary silence. A deep breath. Exasperated sigh. "I knew it. I just knew it. When you went over there, I told Collier — "

"Damnit, Phyl, listen." He told her the latest, and said he should keep the phone clear for Flip Hanes's call. "I don't think there's enough time," he said, "but it's worth a try. I guess."

"What do you mean, you 'guess'?"

"Phyl, he's a grown man."

"No, he's not. He's being a *child* about this."

"Maybe you could get Brother Boggs to call him."

"Sonny. Do you think that might work?"

"Don't be silly. I was just kidding."

"Oh, my Lord." She sounded terrified. "What's Collier going to say?"

*

"Hawkshaw, it's your erstwhile barrister here."
"The meter running already?"
"No charge for false starts."
"What, no deal?"
"The lovely Miz Counselor Deborah Farnelle Givens is convulsed in laughter over your predicament."
"I admit it's gotten a little Faulknerian, Flip, but I'd appreciate a little gravity."
"I can give it to you straight. The laws are damned tight about these restraining orders, even in Mississippi. I don't think I have to tell you why."
"Right. Senile old codger gets put away so the kids can get to the money."
"I know we aren't talking major estate here."
"A truck, Flip. A truck, a house, a piano."
"The principle's the same, though, understand?"
"I figured. Well. Much obliged."
"Miz Counselor Givens did ask a favor."
"Tell her to send me a bill."
"Naw, naw. No charge. She just wants to meet your old man."

"Piney Woods Recovery Center."
"Bryan Peters?"
"This is he."
"Sonny Hawkins."
"Oh, hi."
"Let him go."
"Just like that?"
"Just like that. There's no way to keep him."
"Brother Boggs will be very disappointed."
"*Let* Brother Boggs be disappointed."
"Your father's right here. Shall I put him on?"
"In a minute. First, I want you to promise me something. I want you to personally put him on that bus tonight. I think he said it leaves at ten."

"All right, sir."

"The last place he ought to be is in downtown Hattiesburg, wandering around after dark."

"I understand. Liquor stores."

"That, and he's liable to call the wrong guy 'nigger' and I'd never see my father alive again."

"But he gets along real well with Reggie."

"Reggie ain't a nigger anymore."

"I don't understand."

"Me neither. Let me talk to Pop."

Such sweetness. Such vindication. Such a patronizing victor. "*Hel*-lowww," said Jake, in the forgiving tone he had always used after winning an argument.

"You got all your stuff together?"

"What there is of it."

"Look, Pop, they've agreed to take you down to the bus station tonight."

"That's right white of 'em, son."

"You want me to tell Mama?"

"Why don't we just surprise her?"

"What time do you get to Birmingham?"

"About daybreak, I reckon."

"I'll meet you at the station, then."

"I'd be much obliged for that, son. Unless they've moved it, it's down there near Woodrow Wilson Park. Where Bull Connor hosed the niggers."

"I know where the damned station is, Pop."

"I'll be the one smoking the cigar. You can't hardly miss me."

== *Part Two* ==

REDBALL

8

AT THE DOWNTOWN bus station, a block from where the Commissioner of Public Safety had once fought blacks with water cannons and police dogs, Sonny parked his father's Dodge at the curb and fumbled for change to feed the parking meter. It was the hour before dawn, already muggy, and the city had barely begun to stir. Streetlights showed the way as garbage trucks and city buses made their early rounds. In an alley beside the depot, a man slept against a steel dumpster while a woman with a grocery cart picked through its contents. Parked at the loading zone were two cabs, their radios crackling, their drivers drinking coffee. Somewhere, a train cried.

Inside, dodging a man pushing a broom along the pitted linoleum floor, Sonny made sure that Jake's bus was on time before getting coffee and doughnuts from a machine and then moving on to one of the hard bucket chairs. Two burr-headed teenagers in army khakis, working the pinball machines, were doubtless headed to Columbus, Georgia, and Fort Benning. Huddled together were a mother and three children, one asleep on a pillow across her lap, paper bags holding clothes and toys. At the baggage counter, Boy Scouts in uniform tagged duffel bags while their leader bought tickets. A relief driver, shaved and rested, sipped coffee by one of the gates. A pretty teenaged girl, guarding new luggage, tried to ignore a buckskinned troubador strumming his guitar.

Promptly at five-forty, a sonorous voice announced the arrival of the bus from New Orleans and a dozen other points south and west including Hattiesburg. When Sonny heard the bus rumbling and stood to see it amble into the terminal, rolling gently and belching blue diesel smoke, he stepped outside beneath the yellow lights of the depot. First off was the driver, his gray uniform wrinkled from the all-night run, and right behind him came Jake in the same outfit he had worn at Piney Woods: the chartreuse slacks, fake snakeskin cowboy boots, Poole Truck Line cap, Graddick & Sons windbreaker.

Gesticulating with one hand, rolling an unlit cigar in his mouth with the other, Jake hit the pavement in the middle of a story as the driver opened the baggage hatch on the side of the bus. ". . . and when I said, 'Alabama Highway Express votes Hell No,' this damned Eye-talian from New Jersey leaned across the table and said, 'Well, we can't be responsible' and when I said, 'For what?' he said, 'You'll see.' "

"Teamsters play rough, all right," the driver said as he stooped to begin unloading baggage. The other passengers were queuing up around them.

"They got me, too."

"That so?"

"Brickbat right through the windshield. And me still in the truck."

"Change your thinking any?"

"Why, hell no. I didn't need nobody to help me do my job. It ain't 'dues' they wanted, anyway. It was protection money."

The other passengers were grumbling now, impatient for their baggage. "Which one's yours, Jake?" the driver said.

"One with the Hawaii stickers on it."

"You sure?"

"I ought to know my own bag."

"Pink Samsonite?"

"Well, I was in a hurry when I left home."

Jake didn't acknowledge Sonny until he grabbed the bag and wheeled away from the knot of fellow travelers. For an instant they awkwardly faced each other, not ten feet apart, neither knowing exactly what was supposed to happen next. Sonny's loyalties had been shifting for more than a week, on the side of good sense one day and to the side of his father the next, and he tried to discern Jake's posture. What would it be: outrage or contrition?

Jake put down the suitcase and, in one movement, raked a match across the pavement and lit his cigar. "Ain't actually smoked the damned thing since the last stop, in Tuscaloosa," he said.

"They're getting pretty strict these days."

"Always were. ICC won't let you do nothing."

"I presume you brought it up with the driver."

"Company man all the way. Nice fellow, though."

"I heard him first-name you."

"Yeah," Jake said, "he didn't want me talking to him at first. Some more damned regulations. By the time we hit Laurel we'd got right neighborly, though. Turns out he used to drive long-haul himself for Baggett, right here in Birmingham, but then when his wife started in on him about being gone all the time and not having a fancy house and all that crap he lost his nerve. Biggest mistake he ever made. Says he hates it."

"Just goes to show you," Sonny said.

"Just goes to show you."

Sonny had nodded toward the car, parked across the street from the taxi stand in the gathering daylight, and was bending over to pick up the suitcase when Jake took him by the shoulders. Only then did the old man, eyes bleary from the long night's ride and a longer week in limbo, wrap his arms around his son. "I ain't exactly used to sneaking back into town before sunup like a damned convict that just got let out. I'm much obliged you came, son."

Jake took the keys to the car and, once he had cranked it, made much ado of adjusting the seat and the mirrors to his liking while coddling the engine and checking out the dials. In spite of a year of relative confinement to the retirement home and Evelyn's inability to pack up and go on an hour's notice, he had managed to put 72,000 miles on the car in the four years he had owned it. Big chunks of the mileage had been rolled up on several trips to the West Coast, pre-Mimosa days, wherein he would drive across the country to inspect and bid on lots of surplus tires for Charley Graddick and then receive his payment: cruises for him and his wife to Alaska and Hawaii and Mexico. They had thoroughly enjoyed the cruises, filling the house with made-in-Taiwan tusks and leis and sombreros, but what Jake Hawkins enjoyed the most was the fact that Internal Revenue couldn't lay hands on a penny because there was no penny.

"Runs good, don't she?" Jake said as he eased away from the curb.

"Don't call it the 'touring car' for nothing."

"Mama wanted a Buick, you know."

"General Motors Corporation, right?"

"GMC. General Mess o' Crap."

Downtown Birmingham had always struck Sonny as looking more Midwestern than Southern, laid out as it was in grids (avenues running east-west, streets north-south), with broad streets and undistinguished two- to five-story buildings (except for the twenty-story "skyscraper" Calder Building) the only street with any charm being brick-paved Morris Avenue, a sort of alleyway for delivery trucks until it was converted into a dank touristy stretch of "speakeasies" resembling Printer's Alley in Nashville. Birmingham was more Midwestern than Southern at heart, too, given its industrial background, a place where things had always been made rather than merely processed, as in Atlanta, an overgrown town, rather than a bona fide city, where substance meant a great deal more than style.

But the chamber of commerce was trying to change all of that, Sonny noticed as Jake turned right onto Twentieth Street at Woodrow Wilson Park. The eight-block stretch that lay before them, the widest downtown main drag south of Dayton, Ohio, had been renamed Birmingham Green and was actually pleasant to look at now: trees, brick sidewalks, gaslights, a leafy island right down the middle of the boulevard, and a plethora of cozy restaurants and bars and boutiques and high-fashion clothing stores. There was now a handful of concrete and glass buildings more than twenty stories high, the cut-rate places of Sonny's youth, the pawnshops and jewelers and dime stores and dress shops, having been driven to the side streets with the band-instrument suppliers and sporting goods stores and the sewing centers. And, yes, there was the old Ritz Theater where Jake and Evelyn Hawkins had been married during the Depression, the movie palace, like the newlyweds, beginning to fade but hanging in there. And there was the grand old Alabama Theater, where at least fifty Miss Alabamas had been coronated and millions of kids had necked in the balcony while singing along with Stanley Malotte and (so the joke went) his rising organ, with serious block letters on the marquee: SAVE THE ALABAMA. The developers had already gotten the gargoyled Tutwiler Hotel, to mention one edifice worth saving, but the new people of

Birmingham weren't going to let them take Birmingham's answer to the ornate Fox Theater in Atlanta without a fight.

Street sweepers were noisily working both sides of Birmingham Green, rushing to finish before cars began to file in from the distant suburbs, and Jake angrily honked the horn at them. "They fixing it up for a damn parade or something?" he said.

"You've got to admit it looks pretty," said Sonny.

"Pretty for what?"

"Well, hell, *pretty*. Like a real city. At least you can see it now that the smoke's gone."

Jake, disgusted, twisted his cigar and made an illegal left turn onto First Avenue, headed east toward Roebuck Hills. "Like I always said. The day there ain't no smoke in Birmingham is the day folks start starving."

"Come on, Pop, that was another Birmingham."

"It's that damned Ralph Nader that done it."

"He was just trying to save Monk Strickland's lungs."

"Hell, he don't even know Monk. Nader and them put him out of work and didn't even ask him what he thought about it."

"Monk retired, Pop. And he's almost deaf."

"Just look at that, would you." Jake had zipped up onto the First Avenue Viaduct, a broad half-mile-long concrete bridge spanning a maze of railroad tracks and loading docks, and suddenly he stopped the car and turned on the emergency blinkers. Rising up above the viaduct were the hulking remains of the giant Sloss Furnace. One of Sonny's sharper memories of his earliest years, after Jake had bought the family's first car, was when they capped off an evening at the old Temple Theater downtown (movie, magicians, hoofers, live band) by slowing the car on the viaduct to gawk at the fireworks display below: great showers of sparks splaying in the blue Southern sky, rivers of molten slag coursing beneath the mammoth steel roof, antlike men bent over with acetylene torches that breathed blue flames and turned I-beams orange, other men in hard hats and asbestos gloves guiding the freshly forged beams that swung from cables, great gray clouds of acrid smoke belching from a half-dozen smokestacks, the sights and smells and sounds of men like Monk Strickland making steel for America. The Pittsburgh of the South doing its job.

Jake got out of the car, Sonny following, and they went to the railing. Nothing stirred. They could look down and see that the place had been turned into a museum now, rusty but somehow noble, with guided tours and exhibits telling of how steel once was made. There was a small amphitheater and a billboard, visible from the viaduct, announcing that the Magic City Players would be performing Shakespeare's *Much Ado about Nothing* over the weekend.

"Of an evening after the vaudeville, providing the Barons weren't in town playing the Atlanta Crackers, right here was the best show in town," Jake said.

"Scared the hell out of me, I can tell you. I can remember Phyllis and me trying to pick out Monk working."

"He didn't work here. He was at TCI."

"They were all the same to us."

"Truth is, Monk probably felt the same way." Jake buttoned his windbreaker against the morning chill. "Times was good then. Had me the seventy-eighth new Dodge automobile sold in Birmingham after the war."

"The green four-door."

"Paid cash for it, too. Hauling tires to Akron."

Sonny laughed. "Those trips. You remember the time we had to run over to Pittsburgh?"

"Looking for a return load, most likely."

"Probably. Boy, I was finally gonna get to see Pittsburgh. All my life I'd heard about Birmingham being 'The Pittsburgh of the South,' you know? What a letdown. I thought you'd pulled my leg and gone to Allentown instead."

"Remember what I told you, don't you?"

"No, I don't."

"In the café, in front of a bunch of Yankees."

"Oh, hell, and there was almost a fight."

"All I said was, 'Naw, son, it's Pittsburgh, all right. Birmingham of the North.' "

"I remember now."

"What really got 'em going, though, was when I said they talked funny."

They moved away from the railing and got back into the car. "Remind me when we get home to tell Monk that Shakespeare's showing at the old Sloss Furnace," said Jake. "He might want to make a special effort to attend." Soon they were off of the First Avenue Viaduct, riding into the sun as it rose above the clear air of Jones Valley.

Sonny had envisioned a scenario of Jake's return from Piney Woods, and the old man didn't disappoint. The minute Jake entered the house, he went straight for the thermostat in the hallway and turned the setting up to ninety degrees while delivering a diatribe about air conditioning and the Alabama Power Company. He continued to the master bedroom at the end of the hall, where he tossed his jacket and Mama's pink suitcase on the bed and checked the windows to be sure there hadn't been a break-in during his absence. Next he went to the family room, where Sonny sat stiffly on the sofa flipping through a *Reader's Digest* that he had nearly memorized, and turned on the television set to Channel 6 and the "Country Boy Eddie Show." Finally, having stood in front of the set until Country Boy returned after a used-car commercial, Jake moved across the room to sit at the old Baldwin upright and, cigar between his teeth, hammer away on "Your Cheatin' Heart" for a few minutes. Then he abruptly threw back the piano bench and lurched to the basement.

Sounds drifted up the rickety steps: desk drawers being

jerked open and slammed shut, cursing, paint buckets being kicked, the cap of a liquor bottle being unscrewed, the wheeze of the discarded Naugahyde recliner, Jake talking to himself. Finally, Sonny heard the dialing of the old rotary phone and a muffled conversation that lasted no more than three minutes. He got up from the sofa to turn down the volume on the television set and raise some windows, since Jake's return meant the end of air conditioning for a while, and was making a pot of coffee when his father came up from the basement.

"Coffee soon," Sonny said.

"Much obliged, but I coffeed out on the trip."

"Y'all must have stopped at every crossing."

"Felt like it. Mostly, it was niggers headed for Chicago." Jake went back down the hall to the bedroom and returned in a moment with a record album for Sonny. It was Jolene's, "From the Bottom of My Heart," with an airbrushed photograph of her, Jolene Blondell, and an inscription: "To Sonny, who's Daddy taught me more in one week that I've learned in a lifetime." Jake returned to the piano bench and said, "At least we got *something* to show from that place."

Jake began to play, rocking back and forth to the awkward clunking of the left-hand keys, fluttering his right hand to give the tune a honky-tonk effect, riding right through the missed notes as though they hadn't happened. The song was "Lazybones," taken from a gray-covered Hoagy Carmichael Song Book that had been bought for fifty cents in 1943 and rested atop the piano ever since, and Jake aimlessly tried to sing along in a bray that would have startled a mule while Sonny poured some coffee for himself and returned to the sofa. Country Boy Eddie had been replaced by "The Today Show" from New York, which mattered not a whit to Jake anymore. He played on, from "Georgia on My Mind" to "Rockin' Chair," rolling the cigar butt in his mouth, a man at his only leisure.

"How'd you leave Piney Woods?" Sonny said.

"Fast as I could."

"No, hell, I mean the others. Jolene and them."

Jake stopped playing and reached for a box of Diamond kitchen matches on top of the piano. "I was telling her just the other day about how come I ain't so good with my left hand. You heard it, ain't you?"

"Oh, Christ, go ahead." Sonny watched as Jake this time struck the match with his thumbnail.

"See," Jake said, "my left-handed lessons was coming in from Chicago when the Pony Express rider got shot by the Indians. Jolene said she never heard tell of such. I told her that was because we lived so far back in the hills that Tuesday was always a day late."

"Come on, Pop. Piney Woods."

"Why, hell, son, they were happy for me. Bastards that run the place tried to keep 'em in meetings so they wouldn't see me go. That boy, Reggie, he was wanting to drive me home personal, but I told him I had to hurry back to be with my wife. Jolene was crying when I walked out the door."

"Was that Mama you just called?"

"When?"

"In the basement. I thought I heard you dialing."

"Oh," Jake said. "Poor thing. Woke her up."

"Did you tell her you're home?"

"Never got that far. Took me ten minutes to tell her it was me. She thought it was that bastard Collier." Jake shoved away the bench and headed for the basement again. "Almost plumb forgot something. I'll be right back."

Sonny said, "Pop, why don't you just bring the shit upstairs?"

"There's some important papers down there."

"Papers, my ass."

"They're in my suitcase. The blue one."

"You've been playing this charade for forty years, Pop."

" 'Charade.' That's a new one."

"It's a wonder you haven't mistaken weed-killer for bourbon down there in the dark. Who do you think you're fooling, anyway? Mama's not here."

"I just didn't want to tempt you, that's all."

"I'll be okay."

"Won't bother you none?"

"I told you. I quit."

"All right, then," Jake said, ducking his head to go back down the stairs. "But it ain't gonna taste near as good this way."

Jake was going to celebrate his freedom, and Sonny didn't want to be a party to it. He poured another cup of coffee and then stepped outside into the first full blaze of morning sun over Roebuck Hills, just in time to see a jet rocketing over the chimneys, and as he walked through the high dewy grass he saw Beulah Strickland weeding her flower bed across the street and they waved to each other without speaking. Soon he was sitting at the picnic table in the backyard, alone except for bluejays squawking in the sweetgums and the mute presence of Dixie Redball IV, crouched sullenly in the gravel beneath its jerry-built shed. Through the windows of the family room came the sounds of Jake thumping the piano.

It had been a happy childhood, he reflected, a great place for a kid to ramble: children in every house, working fathers and clucking mothers, no divorces or scandals of any sort. Roebuck Hills around the time of the Second World War had meant pies cooling on kitchen window ledges, radio soap operas filling the afternoon air, urchins roaming the shady streets to play games in season, neighborhood barbecue and watermelon parties, American flags hoisted on the Fourth and on Armistice Day, front porches and backyard toolsheds, and, from Air Corps trainers during the war and commercial planes after, the incessant reminder of the airport.

Laughing aloud, Sonny looked to see if Beulah was sneaking around the house again with, say, hot biscuits and jam. He knew that Lee Riddle had moved back since his parents' deaths, but where were the others, those merry pranksters of his youth: Bobby Joe Cook, who on Halloween torched a bag of shit on old Mr. Hood's porch before ringing the doorbell and running for his life? Karl Dennard, the oldest, who shared a deck of playing cards showing a couple "doing it" fifty-two different ways, and Peggy Black, who allowed him to practice the Queen of Diamonds on her one July night (according to Karl) in a vacant garage? The summer when the Birmingham Barons' shortstop lived in the Thorns' garage apartment and the boys would manage to be outside as he left for Rickwood Field; the surge in popularity of their house, the first to have television, especially on Sundays when it was time for Ed Sullivan; the day, shameful now, when James Hudson started a rock fight by pinging the tin roofs of "Niggertown" with his Red Ryder air rifle; the afternoon when Mickey Rooney came — *Mickey Rooney!* — to add to his list of wives the pretty girl up on Fifth Terrace who had been Miss Birmingham; the day in 1946 when Jake Hawkins, flush from hauling war materiel for nearly five years without a full weekend at home, introduced that first automobile.

Until then, it now occurred to Sonny, he had seen Akron in Ohio before he had visited his Aunt Marie's house across town, had crossed the muddy Monongahela in Pittsburgh before he had stuck a toe in the pretty little green Cahaba in Birmingham. Once Evelyn Hawkins got the hang of driving, though, Sonny and Phyllis were liberated: from walking the two miles to school, from lugging grocery sacks eight blocks, from depending on the trolley to reach downtown. Not only were there now summer vacations to the Smokies and Florida, Jake proudly showing them what they had been missing, there was a broadening of Phyllis and Sonny's world. With their mother as chauffeur, they came to know the mill villages on the west side of town, the delights of teenagers' hangouts like pools and skating rinks that had been out of bicycle range before, dance recitals for Phyllis and sandlot baseball for Sonny, and, on Sunday afternoons after the roast beef and mashed potatoes, parking on a ridge overlooking the airport to marvel as DC-3s lumbered off the ground to Atlanta.

Sonny figured he had better initiate a call to Phyllis before she did the calling. It wouldn't do for Jake to answer the phone, drunk at this time of day. When he left the picnic table and went back inside the house he found Jake curled up on the sofa in the fetal position, snoring loudly with his mouth open, a half-empty bottle of Old Crow on the table beside him, the television turned to the "Nashville Network," where Ralph Emery was interviewing a singer who looked remarkably like Jolene Blondell. He had no idea how much of the bourbon had been drunk that morning, only that it wouldn't take much to embalm a man who had been on a bus all night and had missed breakfast and hadn't had a drink in a couple of weeks.

Sitting on his parents' bed, using Mama's pink Princess phone, he dialed the Bradfords' number. He was about to give up when Phyllis finally answered, groggily.

"Lord," she said, "what time is it?"

"About nine. You've usually done toilets and a load of wash by now."

"It was a long night, Sonny. Collier was furious, and I couldn't sleep."

"You know, then."

"Do we ever. Brother Boggs called last night after it all happened."

"Well, the eagle has landed."

"Is he all right?"

"Sleeping it off."

"I just knew it. I told Collier he was going to get drunk on that old bus."

"He's tired, Phyl, that's all. It was a long ride, and he didn't have any breakfast. But tell me. What does Boggs say?"

"It's simple. Daddy can't live at Mimosa Towers anymore. I told you that's what would happen if he didn't stay for the whole month. That was the deal, Sonny, and Daddy didn't do his part. Mama stays, but he doesn't."

"Can't the esteemed Collier put in a word? I mean, if not with the Lord maybe Fenster P. Boggs."

"Collier's finished. He says that makes three strikes, and Daddy's 'out' as far as he's concerned. He doesn't even want to talk to him anymore."

"Pop'll be relieved to hear it, I'm sure."

"Maybe *you* could talk to him."

"Boggs? Forget it, Phyl. I'm not his type."

"Well, he knows about how *you* stopped drinking."

"Yeah, but I fessed-up. Pop isn't about to."

Phyllis brightened. "Let's just suppose for a minute, Sonny. Suppose you stayed here for a little while longer, and you and Daddy started going to AA meetings *together*. There's this nice little AA club that meets near the airport every night. The Pilot Club? I was thinking if you could kind of *guide* him, you know, if y'all could maybe — "

"That's sweet, Sis, right out of an Al-Anon pamphlet, but you know what happened in Mississippi. The sonofabitch turned it into Abbott and Costello."

"Well, I didn't ask Brother Boggs. It was just a thought."

"He's never joined a group in his life, and AA is no place to start."

"I guess you're right. I *s'wanee*? What're we going to do? What's going to happen now?"

"First, I thought I'd tidy up the yard."

"Oh, you know what I mean."

"We've got to get something to eat, too. Pop's probably got a hankering for some barbecue."

"*Really*, Sonny."

"Then, of course, there'll be his triumphant return to see Mama. We ought to sell tickets."

"Please stop pulling my leg, Sonny. I mean what about the rest of Daddy's *life?*"

"That's the point. All we can do is play 'em one day at a time."

Throughout the morning and on into the balmy afternoon, pausing only to snack from a cache of peanut butter and saltines and canned soup he had bought at Robinette's Superette before the trip to Mississippi, Sonny worked off nervous energy by piddling around the house: washing his pickup and the Dodge sedan, mowing the lawn, pulling weeds, doing laundry in the basement, even going through his parents' medicine cabinet to trash the oldest of Mama's prescription medicines. Now and then, walking through the family room, he would see that Jake had risen from his stupor long enough to swig from the bottle. On such occasions they didn't speak, only nodded like strangers passing on the street, and then Jake would ease back onto the sofa to resume snoring.

It was during one of those sweeps through the house, around five in the afternoon, when Sonny was in the kitchen boiling water for tea, that Jake suddenly bolted up from the sofa and said, "Mail come yet?" The sound of a voice startled Sonny at first.

"Mail? I thought it went to Mimosa now."

"I ain't letting that damn Boggs read my mail."

"Jesus. A conspiracy at every corner."

"I've already missed one social security check, son. No telling what else they've stole."

"You're imagining things, Pop."

"The hell I am. I don't miss nothing."

"Did you notify the Feds about the check?"

"Why, hell, no. Wouldn't do no good. They're all in it together.

Boggs, Phyllis, the government, all of the bastards. Wouldn't be surprised if that damned Collier bought himself some new golf clubs with my check."

The mailbox at the curb was overflowing. When Sonny brought the mail into the house and dumped it on the round dinette table, Jake brought his bottle to the kitchen. The advertising circulars went into one pile, bills into another, and there was a third pile where Jake placed the church bulletins addressed to Evelyn Hawkins and a series of missives for J. E. Hawkins Sr. from a law firm out of Miami.

Jake tore open one of those and hooted. "Got these bastards right where I want 'em."

"Who?"

"That place in Florida. Rio Rancho."

"The trailer camp."

"It's a mobile home retirement park, son."

"Whatever. How come lawyers are writing you? I thought you paid cash for it."

"They want us out of there."

"You haven't been there in three years, Pop. The way I remember it, you hated the place. They wouldn't let you in the bingo hall anymore, and about the only friend you had was the alligator down at the dock."

"Well, it's the principle of the thing. I got an old boat and parked it in the yard. Turns out, that's against regulations. By God, that's my boat and I can do anything I damned well please with it. Them lawyers are just wasting stamps."

"What do you want the place for, anyway, Pop? You've said it yourself: 'Ain't nothin' but mosquitoes and Yankees in Florida.' "

"Jews, too. Don't know which is worse."

"Why keep it, then?"

Jake uncapped the bottle and took a long draw from it, gargling before he swallowed. "Man never knows when he might need a hideout, boy."

It had been Sonny's hope that the two of them could wash up and ride into East Lake for a feast at Andrews Barbecue, Jake's favorite eating place since the day it opened in the early fifties, but it was obvious that the old man wasn't finished with his drinking yet. Sonny went through the drive-in window at Andrews instead and rushed home with two of the pork specials with baked beans and cole slaw and garlic bread, and Jake swallowed his with the efficiency of a trash compacter before washing it down with more bourbon straight from the bottle. Then he groaned and lay back on the sofa, inert, snoring, hallucinating.

9

FORCED FROM THE SOFA by seniority, Sonny had moved into the bedroom of his boyhood that night for the first time since his return to Birmingham, and it had taken him forever to fall asleep. The snores, farts, and shufflings that sporadically emanated from the family room had been only partially responsible. The rest was bittersweet déjà vu: the baseball bedspread, the crinkled sports photographs papering one wall, the hatrack holding caps of teams like the St. Louis Browns that were no more. At one point he found a cracked bat in the closet and practiced a few swings in front of the full-length mirror he had installed for that purpose alone, and at midnight he had tried to pick up KMOX out of St. Louis, where Harry Caray had regaled him with descriptions of Stan Musial uncoiling at the plate, but found that the proliferation of radio stations since then made that impossible now.

He slept long and hard when he finally went under. And

when he awoke, to sunlight blazing through the louvered Sears shutters stained and installed by Jake around 1950, there was another reminder of his youth. From the kitchen came the smells that had always meant Sunday morning at the Hawkins house: a trucker's breakfast of sausage and fried apples and scrambled eggs and biscuits and sawmill gravy and grits.

In jeans and a T-shirt, barefooted and rumpled, Sonny followed the smells. He didn't believe what he saw. Jake, with a cigar in his mouth and the Poole cap on his head and one of Mama's frilly aprons around his waist, stood at the electric range minding four burners and humming "San Antonio Rose." Sonny turned down the television, where Ralph Emery was interviewing yet another blond singer on the "Nashville Now" show.

"Got some of that hot sausage we like, boy," Jake said. "Piggly-Wiggly had a special on, and I near 'bout broke the bank."

"I don't believe this. I thought I'd be making funeral arrangements this morning."

"Little hair of the dog and I'm ready."

"You expecting company, or what?"

"Just you and me. I figure it's been a while."

"Been a while since I've had a breakfast of any kind."

"Be different if you worked for a living."

"I'll let that pass."

"Figured you would."

There was coffee, too, and when Sonny poured himself a cup he took a chair at the dinette table. The cuckoo clock on the wall above his head showed that it was nearly nine o'clock. Another jet roared over the roof as Jake began to lay out the spread.

They ate like wild dogs, elbows on the table, saying nothing, the only sounds being their slurping and the clanking of forks on hard-plastic plates as they shoveled down the food. It was while they were sopping up gravy with biscuits that Sonny said, "Wonders never cease. So what happens next?"

"I got some things to get cleared up," Jake said, "starting with that bastard Boggs."

"You going over there this morning?"

"Me and you both. Hope Mama can tell us apart, poor thing."

"Hey, Pop, you aren't going to try to spring her."

"Tried that already."

"Phyllis told me."

"Naw, I mean the time I hired a nurse."

"When was this? Damned if you aren't full of surprises this morning."

"Well, I found this gal from Trussville. Fat little thing, but she knew her business. White girl, too. Didn't make it to sundown, though."

"Let me guess. Interfered with your drinking."

"Naw. It was Mama that fired her."

"Mama?"

"Said she smoked, but I knew the real reason."

"Which was?"

"Hell, boy, she got jealous. She didn't want no other woman around the house."

"You scoundrel. Almost seventy years old."

"Ain't you learned nothing about women yet?"

Sonny began clearing the table. "Okay," he said, "so we go by the place this morning. What do you mean by 'things to get cleared up'?"

"First, I want to be sure they're gonna treat Mama right."

"You aren't going back yourself, then."

Jake said, "They won't let me, and that suits the hell out of me. I had plenty of time to think over there in Mississippi, son, and one thing I figured out is that it was a mistake for me to go with Mama in the first place. She belongs there, with all of them biddies and church people, but I don't. Me being there upsets her and everybody else, including me. I can see that now."

"But what if you determine that they *aren't* going to take care of her right?"

"By the time I get done with Boggs this morning," Jake said, "he's liable to name Mama the Queen of Mimosa."

Jake looked somber and downright respectable as he carefully eased the newly washed Dodge into the parking lot in front of Mimosa Towers, where less than a month before, on slow days, it had been his habit to scandalize Brother Fenster P. Boggs by brown-bagging booze out of the trunk of the car in broad daylight. He had chosen to wear the chocolate Polyester suit, bought nearly a decade earlier for pallbearer duties when his peers had begun to drop, and he reeked of after-shave and hair oil. Going along with the gag, or whatever it was to be, Sonny had worn his blazer and slacks.

They had entered the glass double doors of the retirement home and announced to a scrubbed young receptionist that they, the Hawkinses Senior and Junior, had come to visit Mrs. Evelyn Hawkins, when they heard a male voice from behind. "Well, Mr. Hawkins." They turned to see Boggs, smiling tight-lipped in the doorway marked Office, looking as though he had been born in an undertaker's uniform: midnight black suit, starched white shirt, maroon tie, black wingtips.

"Brother Boggs," said Jake. "What a pleasant surprise. Is everything going well for you today?"

Boggs was taken aback. "Well, of course. Fine, fine."

"That's good to hear. You've met mine and Evelyn's son, I presume?"

"Why, yes. We haven't seen you in a while."

"It's a long way from Tallahassee."

"Well, your dear mother's fine here," said Boggs, not proffering a handshake to either. "Just fine." He slid his rimless glasses up the bridge of his aquiline nose with delicate pink fingers. "In spite of everything."

Jake said, "Damned place does get on your nerves after a while, don't it?"

Boggs flinched and shot a glance at the receptionist behind her glass cage and asked Sonny and Jake if they would come into his office. Soon the three men sat facing each other across a large walnut desk, Sonny and Jake in red velvet wing chairs, Reverend Boggs in a black leather executive swivel chair, surrounded by potted plants and walls bedecked with framed Bible quotations and diplomas from seminaries.

The Lennon Sisters were piping over the Muzak system as Boggs clasped his hands together at his pursed lips as though to pray, spinning slowly and dramatically in his chair, momentarily observing the traffic on Airport Boulevard, before returning to face Jake. "Might we speak man to man, Mr. Hawkins?"

"Ought to be fun to try," said Jake.

Boggs said, "I keep asking myself, 'Why?' I've asked the Lord to help me understand *why* a man can't accept his fate. *Why* a man can't pass on gracefully. *Why* a man has to be so, so *intemperate*."

"We're talking about whiskey, am I right?"

"Among other things."

"What else you got? I'd like to hear the charges." Jake reached into his inside coat pocket and pulled out an envelope and a ballpoint pen.

"Well," Boggs said, "it's the running in the halls. Now we just can't have that, Mr. Hawkins."

"I was just getting my exercise, Preacher."

"And there was the piano playing."

"Put a piano out there, I'm gonna play it."

"But the *music*. It's so *inappropriate*."

"That Hank Williams was a piece of work, wasn't he?" So far, Sonny could see, Jake had scribbled "whiskey" and "exercise" and "piano" on his envelope. "I'd be much obliged if you'd take it kinda slow, Preacher, so I can keep up."

Given the opportunity, Boggs continued the litany of Jake

Hawkins's "disruptive actions" during his stay at Mimosa Towers. Sonny hadn't realized what a heller the old man had been until now: turning up the volume of the giant television set in the lobby to watch old cowboy movies on Sunday mornings while everybody else was nearby in the chapel, raising hell about the food and the service at the cafeteria, successfully hustling more than that one widower at horseshoes, once even causing a cancellation of Bingo Night when he accused the caller of cheating so only women could win, and, of course, the growing of tomatoes.

When he heard the tomatoes mentioned, Jake brightened and looked up from his notes. "Well, hell, Preacher, why didn't you tell me you wanted in on the tomatoes? All you had to do was speak up."

"No, you don't understand," Boggs said. "I'm talking about the very *existence* of the tomatoes. Right out in the open. At our Garden of Gethsemane."

"Tomatoes need sun, Preacher."

"No, no, *no*. It's the *fertilizer*."

"Sometimes the Lord needs help, Preacher. Hell, even *you* know that."

"But *human* fertilizer, Mr. Hawkins."

"Lord needs lots of help, Preacher."

The blood rose into Fenster P. Boggs's face. They had not prepared him for Jake Hawkins at the seminaries. His jaw tightened, his eyebrows scrunched together, and he began drumming his fingers on the desk. "Will you *please* quit calling me 'Preacher' like that?"

"Like what, Preacher?"

"In that mocking tone of yours."

"I was just trying to be respectable, Preacher."

"Well, it's *irritating*. It's as though you're ridiculing me."

"Now, if you ain't proud of your calling."

"I'm proud to serve the Lord, damnit."

"Get a-hold of yourself, now, Preacher."

"Yes, well. All right, then." Boggs took a deep breath and reached across the desk for a manila folder. His glasses had steamed up, and he took them off to wipe them clean. Then he began to speak to some point on the wall behind Jake as he nervously fingered papers in the folder. "There are certain formalities we will have to tend to, Mr. Hawkins, now that you have forfeited your right to remain at Mimosa Towers," he began. "It is agreed, is it not, that you will no longer reside here with your wife?"

"Agreed, and double agreed, Preacher."

"There are some personal articles in the apartment that you and Mrs. Hawkins once shared, and we ask that you remove those which your wife does not require."

"Me and the boy can take care of that, Preacher. I reckon that little mess o' crap he drives can handle the load without breaking down."

"Fine," Boggs said. He paused for a great clearing of his throat. "And then, on the advice of our legal counsel, I'm asking you to sign a waiver of any claim you might feel you have on your fifty-thousand-dollar deposit."

"Whoa, Preacher, hold up."

"It's nonrefundable, Mr. Hawkins. You signed the contract to that effect."

"That was fifty thousand for two people, Preacher. Only one of us is staying."

"Well, yes, but — "

"I figure you owe me twenty-five thousand."

"No, you see — "

"I tell you what, though, Preacher." Jake had swelled up and now was leaning back, magnanimously, in the regal wing chair. "I've figured out some ways you can keep all that money and put it to good use."

"There's no reason to make deals with you."

"If you want me out of your hair, there is."

"Are you threatening me?"

"Aw, naw, Preacher. I just wanted to warn you about my nature." Jake turned the envelope over and began to read from notes he had jotted on the other side. "Let's say I'm over here visiting my wife at lunchtime and the service ain't quite up to the hundred dollars a day that my wife's being charged to stay in this joint. Or maybe I pass by that piano and I just can't help myself. And there's some of these old gentlemen here that can't help betting on horseshoes. And you know deep down in your heart them tomato plants are gonna die if we don't keep pouring the fertilizer to 'em. Of course, now, if you don't understand my nature, I can get on Country Boy Eddie's show over at Channel 6 about any time I want to and say anything that might come to mind."

Boggs sat there aghast: mouth open, eyes dilated, knuckles white from gripping the arms of his executive's chair. He swallowed hard. "Go on."

"There's just a few things I want for Mama."

"I'm listening."

Jake read from his list. "I want fresh-cut flowers in her room every morning. I want the poor thing to sleep whenever the hell she wants to without being woke up for no shots and pills. I want her to be able to eat in bed if she feels like it. I ain't gonna have her sharing her room with some old biddy that she don't like or that's dying. And I want a permanent personal chair for her on the front row at that chapel of yours so the darling can hear the preaching and singing good."

"That's all?"

"That's all I'm asking."

"But this special treatment is expensive."

"You got my twenty-five thousand dollars to work with, Preacher."

It was as crude as bribing a state trooper with a fifth of booze, or showing the high hard one to a weak-kneed batter, and every bit as effective. Boggs was left with the feeling that he was indeed a lucky man, that life and death could now continue at Mimosa Towers Christian Retirement Home with no more ugliness, and Jake sent Sonny to wait on the balcony off the mezzanine while he went to fetch his wife.

Except for a couple of old men who sat at a table in the shade of the eaves at one end of the long balcony, engrossed in a game of dominoes, nobody was venturing into the broiling heat. Airport Boulevard was rumbling with automobiles and local delivery trucks, their drivers made testy by the heat, the noise causing Sonny to wonder that anybody would think of escaping to the balcony for relaxation. From the other side of the twin towers, less than a mile away, came the urgent sounds of eighteen-wheelers changing gears and making time on I-20. A computerized time and temperature sign atop a drive-in bank across the street showed ninety-four degrees at five minutes to eleven. Lunch would be served soon, and Sonny, cringing at the memory of the cloying lunch with Mama less than a week before, hoped that Jake would find a way to wiggle out of it.

He had staked out one of the round patio tables in the shade and was draping his blazer over the back of a chair when the glass doors opened behind him. Jake was leading Mama by her elbow, grinning and winking at Sonny, which he took to be a sign that she was having one of her more lucid days. Behind them came Phyllis: sullen, in her Ray-Ban glasses, a sweater draped loosely about her shoulders.

Sonny embraced his mother, seeing again how frail and tentative she felt in his arms, and they kissed each other lightly on the lips. Powdered and perfumed, wearing a flowery sun dress, she seemed ready to go for a spin.

"I s'wanee," she said, smiling radiantly, "*both* of my boys have come calling."

"At your service, Mama."

"Save *me* some sop-sop, now," Jake said.

"This one's for my *oldest* boy." She and Jake kissed like lovebirds. Then he eased her into a chair and took the one next to her.

There was an awkward silence while the four of them settled into their chairs, nobody quite knowing what to say or where to start. Sonny deduced that Phyllis had been visiting Mama in her room when Jake popped in, and from the looks of it she was none to happy to see him back at Mimosa, drunk or sober.

"Mama's got some news for us," Jake said.

"What's happening, Mama?" said Sonny.

"Aw, you."

"Come on," Jake said. "You tell 'em or I will."

"Well" — Evelyn Hawkins looked around before whispering — "I won at bingo."

"I bet you sweet-talked the caller," Jake said.

She giggled. "Didn't."

"How much did you win, Mama?"

"Lord, honey, I don't know. Phyllis knows."

"Twenty dollars," Phyllis snapped.

"Mama, that's just great," said Sonny. "What're you going to buy with it?"

"Buy? I don't know about" — suddenly she was flustered, coming undone again, and she turned toward Phyllis for help — "I don't know how to . . . I can't remember what I used to . . ."

"I *s'wanee*," Phyllis said, "can't y'all see she's tired?"

"What the hell, Phyl, let her talk."

"You two have got her all confused now."

"You say that like we're strangers."

"Well, you are. You don't know what's good for Mama anymore."

"Hey, come on. Lighten up."

"You're treating her like a baby."

Jake cleared his throat and cut in. "You kids cut it out now." He stroked the back of his wife's neck and pulled her toward him, kissing her on the cheek, and tried to think of something to change the subject. "It's so hot out here, Mama's liable to melt. Reckon they got waiters that bring drinks to the table like on them cruise ships?"

"Oh, Daddy, stop it."

"Just trying to make conversation. What's eating you today, anyhow?"

"All you've done now is *remind* her."

Mama said, "Lord, no, you can't drink at Mimosa."

"Honey, I was just carrying on."

"Daddy, just quit it now."

"Sis, I'm trying to talk with my wife here."

Mama looked down at her lap and began to dreamily finger the knotted ends of her sash belt. "My husband used to drink all the time, but they made him go away. I wonder if he got cured? Has anybody heard from Jake lately? He's my husband." She smiled and looked at her children and Jake. "He went to, he went somewhere, now where'd they make him go? I can't forget, I can't remember, I don't know exactly what . . . I s'wanee . . ."

"Lord," said Jake.

"Well, Daddy, what do you expect?"

"I expect my wife to remember what I look like."

"Well, she never sees you."

"Just a damned minute, daughter."

"You're off gallivanting around while she's alone in her room here. I guess you and Sonny have been having a fine old time together."

"Gallivanting?" Jake said. "Hanging out with a bunch of drunks where you and your damned husband sent me ain't exactly 'gallivanting,' girl. Where the hell's he at this morning, anyway?"

"He's in Florida, playing golf."

"With them new clubs he bought with my money?"

"What on earth are you talking about now?"

"I should have had my head examined for letting y'all have

the key to the house." Jake was livid now. The battle was pitched. Evelyn was merely smiling and talking to herself, her opaque eyes observing a low ridge of trees somewhere above the busy boulevard. "It must have give you the idea that you could steal my checks or any other damned thing of mine that you took a liking to."

"Maybe Collier's right after all," Phyllis said.

"He ain't right about nothing."

"He thinks you're crazy, Daddy. Ready for Bryce."

Jake moved so quickly that all Sonny could think to do was reach for his mother's hands, still in her lap playing with her belt, to divert her from whatever was coming. Jake had turned away from her and lurched toward Phyllis and, in a flurry, torn the sunglasses away and stripped the sweater from her shoulders. Her eyes were purplish-black. Her upper arms were the same.

"I thought so," he said.

"It was an accident," said Phyllis, fumbling with the glasses and the sweater.

"Looks like a hit-and-run job to me."

"Just leave me alone."

"How long's this been going on, daughter?"

"It's none of your business."

"I might aim to make it my business."

"Collier's been under a lot of pressure lately, Daddy. No thanks to you."

Jake produced a chewed cigar from his shirt pocket and made a ceremony out of striking a match on the underside of the wrought-iron chair. As he puffed to light it, he peeked to see that Mama, after the confusion, was back to humming to herself. "Me and your mama had some hard times ourselves," he said, "what with the Depression when y'all were babies. Had me that one-man coal mine off of the Sylacauga Highway back then. What I'd do was go down in that hole and dig all day, no matter if it was summer or winter, in hopes of finding enough coal to swap for some groceries on the way back home at the end of a day. Sometimes Mama'd be a little snappish of an evening when I'd come dragging home, and I wasn't feeling none too good myself. One thing I never did about it, though, and that was hit her. A man that hits a woman ain't nothing but a snake."

Phyllis had begun to cry softly. "Why didn't you at least *try* to stay for the whole month, Daddy?"

"Wasn't doing me a bit of good over there."

"But couldn't you pretend?"

"It's too late to start living like that."

"Just look at the problems you've caused. Collier and I had a nice life until you started acting up."

"I didn't invite no outsider to look out for my welfare."

"Somebody had to."

Jake wrapped an arm around Phyllis's shoulder. She winced, but she leaned into him and ran her fingers beneath the sunglasses to wipe away the tears. "What me and Sonny ought to do is go track him down and teach him a lesson or two."

"Don't do that, Daddy. Please don't."

"Both of you married out of your class. You and Sonny. Didn't seem to be nothing I could do about it."

"Collier's good to me, Daddy. You know that."

"He's got plenty of money, if that's what 'good' means."

"This is just temporary."

"I've heard of 'temporary insanity' in killings."

"Just don't do anything foolish, okay?"

"That 'foolish' is in the eye of the beholder," Jake said. "So's 'crazy.' I'm getting damned tired of other people telling me what's wrong with me. Now that me and that Preacher Boggs have come to an understanding about Mama, I'm taking charge of my life again. And I don't need no help."

*

Jake and Sonny managed to miss lunch at Mimosa Towers on the pretext that Boggs wanted the apartment cleaned out immediately, and after spending the afternoon carting away clothes and furniture in Sonny's pickup they found themselves seated at a torn red leatherette booth in the rear of Andrews Barbecue as dark fell upon East Lake. Dining there on Friday night had been a ritual for Jake and Evelyn Hawkins for twenty-five years — often he would get out of Redball after covering the last five hundred miles from Akron, quickly wash up, and drive her over in the car without taking time to change clothes — and it never occurred to him to try any of the fast-food places that had sprung up along First Avenue as the city spread eastward away from downtown. Andrews was a great barbecue joint, with generous servings and a country jukebox, and like Jake Hawkins himself it had changed little over the years; just begun to settle into a routine and slow down a bit was all.

"I see the old movie house has gone X-rated," Sonny said as the large Formica tables began to fill with extended families from the neighborhood.

"Ain't changed much, though," said Jake. "Lot of the businesses are still open, even if Nader did shut down the steel."

"You bought me my first suit at Morgan's Department Store across the street."

"He's still there. So's Hamby's Shoes."

"Mister Hamby must be a hundred by now."

"Ninety-nine, anyway," Jake said. He was on his second draft beer as their plates of ribs and beans and cole slaw arrived. "Couple of years back I came across a claim ticket for some shoes I'd left there about thirty years ago. Figured I'd play a joke on the old man, so I went in there and give him the ticket and he took it and went to the back. Came back in about ten minutes and said, 'Jake, them shoes ought to be ready about Tuesday.' If I'd squawked, he'd o' probably give me somebody else's."

"There's something to be said for all of this."

"Old fella that don't know when to quit?"

"That's part of it." Sonny knew he was about to open a can of worms but went ahead with it. "Sometimes I wish I hadn't left Birmingham."

"Maybe you wouldn't o' done it if you'd married different."

"Yeah, the former Beverly Mengert wasn't exactly East Lake. I can see that now. The woman nearly killed me."

"That may be closer to the truth than you think, son." Jake finished his beer and suddenly turned morose. "But maybe you don't remember."

"What're you talking about?"

"Suicide. One time you said you was thinking about doing yourself in."

"I said that?"

"You'd left her again. Didn't have a place to live or nothing. Course, me and you were drinking it up pretty good that night so maybe you forgot. But you sure told me. A man don't forget when his only son says he might kill himself."

"Jesus, Pop. I'm sorry. I was really hurting."

"Reason I happened to remember it now is because there's been a time or two lately when I thought the same thing myself."

"Has it gotten that bad?"

"It has, especially when it looks like nobody needs you no more. Today, for instance."

"That surprises me, Pop. Your generation — "

"My generation jumped off of buildings, in case you forgot."

"That was different. That was the Crash."

"Despair's despair, son. Same difference."

"Well, Pop" — Sonny never thought he would hear this conversation — "what're you saying to me?"

"I'm just trying to believe what I told you."

"What'd you say that night?"

"I just told you to hold off a day or two and see what came

up, that there wasn't nothing gonna come up except daisies if you're dead."

"Well," said Sonny, "that's what I did. I guess I'm much obliged to you for saving my life."

"Naw, you saved it yourself," Jake said. "She ain't still bothering you, is she?"

"Not since she married the lawyer and moved to Atlanta. Now she's got the credit cards she wanted."

"So's your sister."

"What's the deal with Collier, anyway, Pop?"

"It's like I said this morning. Both of y'all married out of your class. If she wants all that crap over the mountain, there's one thing she's got to know. The fleas come with the dog."

"You gonna do anything about him?"

"I've already done it."

"I must have missed it. What?"

"Damn, son, you ain't paying attention." Jake hailed a waitress for another beer to wash down the barbecue. "I told you I had some things to get cleared up. Well, you was with me when I took care of the first one: Boggs and Mama. You was there for the second one, too."

"All you did was find out for sure about Collier whipping up on Phyllis."

"Found out why, too."

"You."

"Me. See, people like Collier don't like people like me. I'm tacky, that's how they put it, but what they really mean is that they can't figure out which way I'm gonna go next. Tends to gall the hell out of 'em when I don't go by their rules."

"I'll buy that," Sonny said. "But I don't understand how you equate what you did this morning with clearing things up with Phyllis."

"Hell, son, didn't you hear me? I've just told your mama and your sister good-bye."

10

WHAT? *I've just told your mama and your sister good-bye.* Jake had insisted on stopping by a liquor store on the way home from Andrews Barbecue, and the minute they hit the door the cap was off and he was into the bourbon again. The night became long and tense for Sonny, his father's words echoing in his ears like the refrain of a bad country song, and he felt like a jailer charged with keeping his eyes peeled for sudden moves and sharp instruments. Jake didn't play the piano that night, nor did he watch "Nashville Network" on television. He drank, and he cried some, and at one point he took down the tarnished Trucker of the Year trophy from its sconce. "I'd always kinda hoped that you and me and Mama and Sis would all go together when the time come," he blubbered as he put the trophy back, giving Sonny another reason to ponder sitting up all night with him. But Jake had finally passed out around midnight, commencing to snore and talk in his sleep, and soon Sonny had gone on back to his own old bedroom down the hall.

He bolted upright, in a panic, the next morning. Lines from Hank Williams rang in his ears. *I'm so lonesome I could cry . . . I'll never get out of this world alive . . .* It was a Saturday, but this time there were no smells or sounds of Jake cooking breakfast. There was nothing to indicate life in the house, just the pounding of his own heart and the silly cuckooing of the kitchen clock striking nine. Quickly he jumped out of bed and into some jeans and a T-shirt before rushing down the hall to the family room. The only sign of Jake was the soiled pillow on the sofa, where he had passed out, and the half-empty bottle of bourbon on the kitchen counter.

He called for his father, as he ran from room to room, but heard only the thin echo of his own voice. The basement. All of the bolts and chains were undone, meaning he must be down there amid his treasures, but when Sonny had rattled down the rickety stairs he found nothing. The Dodge. Maybe he had taken off again for groceries or even to visit Mama. But no; Sonny could see, as he padded across the cold concrete floor to look through the window, the car was still there in the driveway where they had parked it the night before. He thought of the backyard, that Jake might be piddling around in the neglected flower beds, but when he unbolted the door and stepped out into the blazing sun he saw not a sign.

It was then, as he scanned the backyard, that he saw his father's legs. They were sticking out from under Dixie Redball IV, looking as forlorn as ever beneath its green Fiberglas canopy down in the kudzu bottoms. *Wait up, Pop, wait up.* Sonny froze for a moment, letting out a gasp, and then he went flying down the hill in his bare feet.

The scrawny hairless legs began to twitch as Sonny reached the truck, and before he could dare to bend over and touch them he saw the rest of Jake emerge in a sort of crab crawl in the gravel.

"That's what I get for not using Quaker State," Jake said, unlit cigar in his mouth, oil smeared on his face and running down both arms, overalls caked with years of grease.

"Jesus Christ Almighty, Pop."

"You get what you pay for, I reckon."

"You scared the living hell out of me."

"Ain't nothing to be afraid of, son."

"Yeah, but I couldn't find you and I thought — Ah, shit, forget it."

"Ain't nothing to fear but fear itself." Jake reached under the truck for an old paint bucket that sloshed with black engine oil as he slid it along the gravel. "FDR. Can't remember whether he said it before or after he married that bag Eleanor."

The flow of adrenaline had left Sonny limp, so he dragged himself to the picnic table under the trees. Jake poured the dirty oil onto the gravel and then trudged up the hill to join him. It was going to be another scorcher, with no rain in sight, and up and down the street there could be heard the faint *whup-whup-whup*-ing, like baby helicopters, of lawn sprinklers. Sonny realized he had left his cigarettes in the house, such was his haste, and settled for sharing the fumes of Jake's cigar.

"You going somewhere?" Sonny said.

"Just ain't changed the oil lately is all."

"How long's it been?"

"Probably since my last trip for Charley."

"Oh, yeah. When you almost missed the anniversary party. That makes it three years."

"Well, a man does what he's gotta do." Jake watched a pair of bluejays engaged in combat among the sweetgums, pretending to be absorbed by it all, but there was a faraway gaze in his eyes. "That was a good trip. Probably too good."

"How so, 'too good'?"

"Left too good a taste in my mouth for trucking. Hell, son, I went out there to Amarillo empty. That's how confident I was that I'd win the bid and haul 'em back. I'd gotten to be an expert on judging carcasses by then, and everybody knew it. I could just hear 'em saying, 'Uh-oh, it's all over, here comes ol' Jake Hawkins. What else y'all got?'"

"Obviously, you won the bid."

"Yeah, but that ain't the best part."

"You didn't have to take the duds."

"How'd you know about duds?"

"Charley told me," Sonny said. "One time."

Jake wiped his brow with a bandanna, thoroughly filming his face with oil. "Well, the fun came when they offered to help me load 'em, seeing as how I was this scrawny old cuss from Birmingham that didn't have no sense, and I said to this young air force boy, 'No, thanks, Cap'n, but I work alone.' He said, 'You can get killed doing that, *Grandpa*,' and that done it. I started filling that trailer so fast, it made their heads swim. Hell, pretty soon there was a crowd out there watching me. In the rain, by God, cheering me on. And directly, this photographer showed."

"You got a clipping?"

"Yeah, it's somewhere in the basement there. Anyway, the best part was about the duds."

"They didn't charge you for 'em."

"Naw, better," Jake said. "I sold 'em back. I said, 'Look here, since this is my last haul before I die, and seeing as how I ain't got hardly enough gas to get back home, I was wondering how y'all might feel about a memorial tire to mark the occasion.'"

"They went for that shit?"

"Twenty duds, dollar each. Ate steak that night."

It wasn't necessary that Jake's stories be true, or even have any basis for truth, and for anyone who chose to challenge his veracity he had a standard rejoinder: "It's my story, and I'm stickin' with it." This one was pure Jake Hawkins, the only fragment of truth about it being that he really had made a trip to Texas for Charley Graddick at that time, so they sat on the patio laughing over the very possibilities of the story as much as anything.

Sonny thought he would test the water. "Actually, Pop, Charley told me about duds last week. I was reluctant to tell you, but I went by to see him."

Jake twirled the cigar in his mouth. "That a fact."

"He was worried about you."

"Do tell."

"Nobody'd told him about Piney Woods."

"He didn't appreciate it a damned bit, neither."

"You mean you've talked to him?"

"He called the minute you left."

"Well, that's good," Sonny said. "Boy, I couldn't believe how big his business is now. He was headed for Europe on a redeye that night."

"He'll be back Monday morning."

"Maybe you could drop in on him, for old time's sake."

"Plan to. Got an appointment, first thing."

"An 'appointment'?"

"Me and Charley got some things to discuss."

Sonny had been slow to pick up on it. "Hey, Pop, wait a minute. That would've been Tuesday night when Charley called you. Wednesday was when you went over the wall at Piney Woods."

"That sounds about right to me."

"Holy Christ. Are you thinking what I think you're thinking?"

"One day at a time, son. One day at a time."

"Pop, you can't go on the road again. You're too damned old. Christ, you're on one of those senior citizen driver's licenses now. Are you crazy?"

Jake coughed and stood up and said, "You want some coffee?"

"Look, Pop, goddamnit, don't change the subject."

"Coffee and a shower ought to do me. I can't go breaking my word with Mama and Preacher Boggs."

"Damnit, sit down and let's talk," Sonny said, but it was too late. Jake disappeared into the basement of the house, whistling.

In the ten days since Phyllis had called him in Tallahassee with the news that Jake had been dispatched to Mississippi, Sonny had put his own life on hold. He had covered a lot of ground in that time — becoming reacquainted with Birmingham, visiting Hattiesburg, now sitting on the sideline while his father danced — and hadn't given much thought to his own meager career. He had thought that he would be back in Tallahassee by now, to get a firsthand report on whether he would be retained by Panhandle Community College in spite of his outburst at Dudley Lyons's soirée, but he had joined the others in waiting to see which way Jake was going to jump next.

When his father left the house around eleven o'clock that morning, buoyant and sober and dressed in his suit for lunch with Mama at Mimosa Towers, Sonny fished out his address book and dialed Leo Miranda's apartment in Tallahassee.

"Turns out that Dudley Do-Right's got a better sense of humor than we give him credit for," Leo told him. "Come home. All's forgiven."

"Christ. You can't even insult the bastard."

"You want me to say yes for you?"

"I don't know, Leo. I've got to think about it."

"Well, it'll hold. Lyons isn't exactly deluged with people begging for your job. Anyway, you might have something else to think about, pal."

"Lu-Ann misses me desperately."

"No, there was a phone call from a publisher."

"Me? Who?"

"Some place I never heard of in Oklahoma. Sallisaw. Sounds like a university press."

"What'd they say? Is it the Seminole book?"

"How many more do you have out?" Leo said. "The secretary

in Lyons's office took the message, and I told her I'd try to get word to you. She scribbled something that looks like 'Bowlegs.' I don't know if that's part of the message or an insult."

Sonny said, "Billy Bowlegs. He was a wild-ass Seminole chief."

"How does that strike you?"

"Billy was as crazy as my old man."

"Whatever it is, the guy wants you to call him. He won't be back 'til Tuesday."

When Sonny recited the short form of what had transpired since his arrival in Birmingham, Leo said it was now imperative that their beleaguered fathers meet to compare notes. His father, the old Conch in Key West, was in trouble with the local chamber of commerce.

"He's selling bumper stickers," Leo said.

"What, without a license?"

"No, it's what they say. 'Yankees Go Home.' "

"I can imagine the chamber isn't thrilled."

"He may get away with it yet," Leo said. "It seems he also printed up another batch with a different message, and he's threatening to sell those if they don't quit hassling him about the 'Yankee' ones."

"What's the other one say?"

" 'Queers Go Home.' "

By late afternoon, with the shadows growing long over Roebuck Hills, Sonny was dragging. In the hours since Jake's return from lunch with Mama, Sonny had been driven like an apprentice mechanic and general go-fer as he and Jake crawled all over Dixie Redball IV beneath its canopy at the rear of the backyard: washing the truck, cleaning out the inside of the cab, putting new linen in the sleeper, polishing the chrome inside and out, fetching beer for the old man. Jake had been busy with the more important matters: completing the oil change (Quaker State this time), scraping the fifth wheel of caked old grease, checking air hoses, replacing dead bulbs, cleaning dust and grease from the engine with kerosene-soaked rags.

They had teamed up to wax Redball by hand, Sonny laying on the Simoniz and Jake coming along behind him to grind it off in the same clockwise motion, when Monk Strickland wandered across the yard to see what was going on. He wore powder blue short sleeved overalls from Sears, his yard-working uniform.

"How much you want for that old thing?" Monk said.

"Pull up a tire and have a brew, Monk."

"If a man didn't know no better, he'd think you're going somewhere, Jake."

"Just looking out for my equipment is all."

"Sonny here decide to take up driving?"

"Be a cold day in hell. He found out a long time ago it's work. Talking's easier."

"Well," Monk said, "you managed to do 'em both."

"Reckon so. Reckon so." Jake stood back to admire the brilliant red that was beginning to shine through on the truck's long snout, pointed out a place that Sonny had missed, and decided to take a break. He and Monk opened beers for themselves and then sat on stacks of worn out tires in the shade of the canopy. Jake sniffed and said, "If you and Beulah don't hurry, you're gonna miss the show."

"Say what?" Monk cupped a hand around his ear.

"You're gonna miss the Shakespeare," Jake shouted.

"Where at?"

"Sloss Furnace. Guess you know they've turned the damned place into a theater now. Tonight they're putting on some culture for us. What's that show they're doing, son?"

Sonny said, *"Much Ado about Nothing."*

"If that don't beat all," said Monk. "After all's said and done, I reckon that's what the mill come to. Much ado about nothing."

"You don't miss it none, do you?"

"Not a bit. Wasn't exactly a career."

"Well, hell, you provided for your family."

Monk took a sip from his beer and addressed Sonny more than Jake. "Sometimes it didn't seem fair how you'd come rolling in every Friday afternoon in your truck. I'd come walking up the hill after working all day and half the night at TCI and there wouldn't nobody but dogs be here to greet me. But, hell, when ol' Jake topped that hill in Redball, with that trailer behind him and the horn a-blowing, it was like Santa Claus had come early. Every boy on the block would get himself all worked up and run out of the house just to watch you park that thing. I heard tell that Walter Riddle wouldn't let his boy Lee do that because it made him look bad, seeing as how he was just a insurance man."

Jake seemed embarrassed to hear it. "Well, I reckon trucking *is* a little different from most callings."

"It's like you was born in a truck, Jake."

"Can't say I hardly remember anything else."

"It's a wonder you never had a bad wreck."

"Three million miles without an accident chargeable to myself."

"You wouldn't happen to remember your first trip, would you?"

"Does a bird fly?" Jake stood up to stretch his legs and light his cigar. "It was about 'forty-one, I reckon. January, in fact. The war was coming on and I figured they was gonna need some stuff hauled and I might as well help 'em out. What I did was convert this old Dodge dump truck I had for hauling coal; the kind with them old crank-out windows? Found a fifth wheel in a junkyard somewhere, and I borrowed three hundred dollars to buy a flat-bed trailer. Got to sawing sideboards out of two-by-fours right here in the backyard, where we're at right now, and I was ready to roll."

"What was you loaded with?"

"Steel hatch covers. You might've had a hand in making 'em."

"Yeah, we made those. For tanks and ships."

"Well, to make a long story short, I took 'em to Oregon."

Monk was incredulous. "You went over the Rockies in January?"

"Only way to get there, ain't it? Can't go by way of Florida unless there's some roads I don't know about. What I did was take this kerosene heater and put it on the floorboards on the shotgun side, but that meant I had to keep the windows cranked out so I wouldn't suffocate to death. I took the southern route through lower New Mexico and Nevada, burning up one minute and freezing the next, and when I got to California I headed up through the San Joaquin Valley to Portland."

"That must be six thousand miles both ways."

"Speedometer was broke, so I don't know."

"How'd you come out?"

"Made the round trip in ten days."

Monk was figuring in his head. "That don't sound right, Jake."

"Well, hell, if you drive six hundred miles a day for ten days, that's six thousand, ain't it?"

"Looks like you'd o' got tired."

"Just curled up in the truck when that happened. They didn't have sleepers back then, see, and I sure didn't have no money for truck stops. Mainly, I lived off of coffee and the sandwiches Mama made before I left."

"You must've made some good money."

Jake swelled up. "Netted one thousand and ten dollars for my trouble."

"That was a lot of money in 'forty-one."

"I bought this house in three payments, Monk. I ain't had a house payment to worry about in forty years." He winked again at Sonny. "Why I'm rich today."

Monk got himself another beer and pondered all of this as the fireflies began to blink and dusk fell over the neighborhood.

What was remarkable, it seemed to Sonny as he stole glances at the two men, was how much younger and more alert his father looked than Monk. It had been his observation that long-distance truckers aged faster than most men, what with the tension of being in charge of several tons of precarious cargo being propelled through traffic at sixty miles an hour, but it didn't show in Jake's face. In their retirement, Monk Strickland resembled a swaybacked plow mule and Jake Hawkins a thoroughbred, restless at stud. Jake, in fact, looked ten years younger on this evening than a week earlier when he was being led off to the AA meeting in Hattiesburg.

"But now look here, Jake," Monk was saying, "you ain't fixing up Redball just to sell her."

"Naw, Monk. Nobody'd want her. It's diesels now."

"Just what in God's name are you doing, then? Ain't you living at the retirement home no more?"

"Reckon not. Just didn't work out."

"Evelyn okay?"

"Living like a queen without me in her hair. Y'all oughta visit more."

"And you're moving back into the house?"

"That's what it looks like, don't it?" Jake made sure the doors of the truck were locked and then made a move toward the house. "Getting a little dark out, I'd say."

"Damned if you don't beat all," Monk said.

"You talking to me?"

"I ain't talking to Sonny. You hard-headed old fool, you don't know when to quit. I know what you're up to. You're aiming to die in this truck."

"Now, Monk, you know that ain't gonna happen," said Jake, clutching his heart with both hands. "I'm too careful a driver for that."

Jake's visit with Mama at Mimosa that night was a brief one. When he returned to the house he was shining with redemption:

Reverend Boggs had personally shown her the special front-row seat reserved for her in the chapel, and she couldn't wait for the Sunday morning services. Sonny had made biscuits from scratch, one of the few culinary tricks he had learned in his four years of bachelorhood, and by ten o'clock the two of them sat at the dinette table wolfing down the biscuits and Jake's warmed-over patties of hot Tennessee sausage.

"There was fresh-cut flowers in her room, too," Jake was saying.

"I don't suppose Phyllis was there."

"Don't 'spect I'll be seeing Sis for a while."

"But Mama's doing okay."

"She's where she's supposed to be, son."

"Pop" — Sonny wasn't sure he would get a straight answer, but he figured he would try — "what's the deal with Charley? Level with me, will you?"

Jake had spent his fun for the day on Monk, it seemed, and now he was in a serious mood. "I won't really know until I go see him Monday morning, son. But I can tell you that ol' Charley was plenty put out when he called me in Mississippi, mainly because nobody'd bothered to tell him about me. He's got the notion that maybe I quit working too soon, that I ain't ready to be put to pasture yet, and he said he might be able to work something out if I was of a hankering to leave. He didn't exactly put me up to leaving the joint, but I figured he knew I would when he told me that. Charley knows me better'n most."

"By the way you started working on Redball, I assume he's not talking about a job around the yard."

"Maybe some short haul around town. I don't know. He just got me all excited is all."

"Short haul."

"He's got warehouses all over town."

"Let's say it was bigger than that, Pop. Let's say he was talking about hauling some tires a long way. He's got a whole pile of 'em headed for Nevada."

"That so?"

"C'mon, Pop, don't be coy."

"Charley didn't say nothing about that. Honest."

"Would you do it?"

Jake took a beer from the refrigerator, popped it open slowly to savor the fizz, and moved over to the piano bench. He tinkled the first bars of "Stardust" with his right hand, took a deep draw from the beer, and then said, "In a New York minute."

"That's got to be two thousand miles one way."

"Depends on where it's at in Nevada."

"You think you could still handle it?"

"Look at this." Jake stuck out his right hand, perpendicular to his body, and spread the fingers. "That hand was jumping all over the place a week ago at that looney bin. I'd be the first to admit that I've been acting like the damned old fool Monk says I am ever since my last trip. But that hand's been steady as a oak since Charley called, boy. Truth is, I'm of a mind to go on living for a while longer now. What do you mean, do you think I can handle it? Does a baby mess in his drawers?"

He finished that beer and got another, and then, with Sonny stretched out full-length on the sofa, he began playing every song he knew in his peculiar honky-tonk way. Sonny's head swam with visions from the past, of ribbony highways gleaming in the moonlight and truck stops beckoning their neon welcomes and stark little weigh stations threatening danger, and for the first time in years he heard the music of the road as he drifted off to sleep. *Six days on the road and I'm a-gonna make it home tonight . . . That's one-thousand baby chicks, folks, sex not guaranteed . . . Damned fog's so bad you gotta get out and feel the signs . . . Truckin's good enough for me, and I notice there ain't nobody starvin' . . .*

11

WITH JAKE'S APPOINTMENT to see Charley Graddick on Monday looming as ominously as the D-day invasion of Normandy, Sunday would be a day spent in limbo. Both Jake and Sonny slept as late as possible and then moved listlessly about the house looking for things to do. They finished waxing the truck. They pulled weeds. They hosed down the flagstone patio in the backyard. They washed the few dishes and clothes they had dirtied. They filled a large leaf bag with the remarkable array of outdated prescription bottles and other reminders of Mama's physical decline — hospital hot water bottles and bedpans, bottles of Maalox and Pepto-Bismol — before moving on to the basement to fill two more with dead plants and paint buckets and empty oilcans.

"Look here at what I found, son," Jake said, noon approaching, as they rummaged through the basement. He was going through the drawers of an old desk that held every logbook and expense report he had ever filled out, stopping to reminisce about several. It occurred to Sonny that those logs, tattered and filled out under all sort of conditions, would do as a diary of Jake Hawkins's life.

"Let me guess," Sonny said. "A menu from a truck stop in Maryland."

"Naw. It's your first income tax return."

As a sportswriter for the Birmingham *News* during 1958, Sonny had earned $75 a week. "Considering the times," Sonny said, "it wasn't bad pay."

"What they paying you down at that school?"

"Not a hell of a lot better, Pop, if you consider inflation. But the benefits are good."

"Benefits. Retirement and all?"

"Sure. They take out for that, too."

"Little young to be thinking about retirement, ain't you?"

"It goes with the territory."

Jake got up from the desk and went so far as to open the door of the refrigerator he kept in the basement, primarily for stowing beer, but he closed the door without taking one when he remembered that he would be visiting his wife later in the day. He sank into the ratty Naughahyde recliner where he had drunk and slept away many an afternoon in his retirement and said, after lighting his cigar, "Seems I been so busy with my own problems that I ain't bothered to ask how you're doing yourself."

"Oh, it's all right, Pop."

"Now that you got that bitch off your back, I thought maybe you'd be looking for something different besides just teaching."

"I enjoy teaching, Pop. I like to watch kids grow."

"Naw, I mean something for yourself. Wasn't you thinking about doing a book?"

"I still might." Sonny told him about the conversation with

Leo in Tallahassee the day before and about the phone call from the publisher in Oklahoma. "It takes a lot of guts to quit a job and write a book, though. It may be too late for me."

"Like I say, it ain't over 'til it's over."

"That might not apply here, Pop."

"I never did understand much about what you chose to do for a living, son, but it did seem to me like there was a time when you was on your way."

"Yeah, I was a promising young man there for a while. Harvard thought so, anyway."

"Harvard." Jake laughed. "Remember when I come up there in my truck? That must've been Redball III."

"I don't think Harvard Square was ready for Jake Hawkins. They may not be over it yet."

"Stopped and asked this old boy, 'Say, Cap'n, wonder if you can tell me where the Charles River's at?' And he took his pipe out of his mouth and said, 'My good man, here at Harvard we never end a sentence with a preposition.' So I told him, 'All right, then, lemme put it another way. Wonder if you can tell me where the Charles River's at, you sonofabitch?' Thought he was gonna swallow his pipe."

Sonny wasn't sure he wanted to talk about this with his father. From the Birmingham *News* he had gone on to papers in Charlotte and Richmond, and at the age of thirty-three he became the first sportswriter ever named as a Nieman Fellow at Harvard, free to do whatever he wished for a year in Cambridge. It had been intended as a year of growth, but the truth was he was intimidated by Harvard, this son of an Alabama trucker, and when he returned he found that he had lost his self-confidence. He scurried off to academia soon after the experience. Under the radar.

Sonny snapped from his reverie when he heard Jake say, "I don't know whether this story might make any sense to you or not, son. Found myself thinking about it, for some fool reason, while I was over there in Mississippi. You heard of my Uncle Zeb. Zebulon Kennesaw Hawkins?"

"Seems like. But I never met him."

"That's because he got killed when I was a boy."

"Wasn't he the engineer, the one who had the wreck?"

"That's him." Jake changed positions in the recliner, settling in for another story. "Provided the folks up home are taking care of the graveyard like they're supposed to, there's still a marker that makes him out to be a hero. It must have been around 'twenty or 'twenty-one when it happened. He was engineering for Norfolk and Western at the time, and one night he was blowing through the mountains, pulling about forty boxcars full of coal, when he lost it on a curve up around Hot Springs in western North Carolina. Him and about six others were killed, including a couple of hobos that was hitching a ride. Lord, there was coal slung all over the valley for five or six miles and people coming around with flour sacks to pick it up and take it home. Well, Uncle Zeb had been a hero of mine and I'd already made up my mind to grow up and be an engineer just like him. There was stories about the wreck, and a fancy tombstone for Uncle Zeb, and there was a song about it. That was before I found out what really happened."

"And?"

"It wasn't but years later when I ran into some old fella who'd been part of the investigation of the wreck, staying in a hotel where I was in Chattanooga, and he told me they should've strung him up instead of making a hero out of him. That's if he'd lived through it, of course. Turns out that Uncle Zeb lost his nerve on the curve. Rhymes, don't it? 'Lost his nerve on the curve.'"

"I don't know any more about trains than I do trucks. What was he supposed to do?"

"He was going into it all right, but right there where he was supposed to tell the fireman to start throwing on the coals he got scared and he hit the brakes. Well, any damned fool knows that it don't matter what you're driving, if it's a train or one o' them little Jap cars, when you see you might be in trouble on a curve the last thing you do is hit the brakes. You stomp it. You take that sonofabitch head-on or it'll kill you."

"Did anybody get the story straightened out?"

"Hell, no. Why should they?"

"People need heroes, I guess, even if it's wrong."

Jake said, "I got to thinking about that story one day at Piney Woods when they had us in one of them 'therapy' things where everybody sits around crying. They was talking about the need for 'lowered expectations,' and that's when I broke in and told 'em that was just another way of saying 'I quit.' A man ain't meant to go through life riding the brakes, boy, he's supposed to be pouring on the coals."

Lee Riddle's name had come up more than once in conversations with Monk and Beulah Strickland, and Sonny was puzzled to learn that he was a postman, now living alone in the family bungalow at the top of the hill since the death of his parents. Lee and Sonny were the same age and had spent their young lives together as a double-play combination, from the kids' sand-lot leagues to a summer baseball camp in Missouri, and of the two Lee was the most promising: a lithe, natural shortstop who made every play look easy. He had been heavily courted by the scouts, but nothing had come of it and Sonny didn't know why.

After Jake had left for Mimosa, Sonny decided to satisfy his curiosity. It was around three o'clock on Sunday afternoon, with little noise from the airport and hardly any movement in the neighborhood, as he walked up the hill to the Riddle house. There was a '70 Plymouth Valiant rusting in the weeded gravel driveway, paint flaking on window shutters, onion weed and dandelions choking the lawn, a thick film of pollen covering the terrazzo front porch, and parched plants wilting in concrete urns. When he knocked on the heavy door, he found Lee to be in much the same stage of neglect: robe and slippers, thinning gray hair askew, eyes heavy-lidded, face puffed. Drunk.

"It's me, Lee. Sonny."

Lee opened the door wider and peered at him. "Well, I'll be. It sure is."

"It's been a long time, pal."

"Well" — Lee scratched his head and nervously glanced over his shoulder — "come in. Come on in, if you can stand the mess."

The living room, once tidy under the hands of Edna Riddle, now resembled a seedy motel room. Styrofoam cartons of take-out food littered the coffee table, and the tables at either end of a worn sofa were covered with newspapers. A striped gray cat narrowed its yellow eyes at Sonny from the mantel above the stone fireplace, sharing space with an array of framed photographs: of Edna and Walter Riddle, of young Lee in a baseball uniform and an older Lee in a naval officer's whites, of a pretty blond woman holding a beautiful little girl. The blinds were closed, and the only light in the room came from the television screen.

"Sorry if I woke you up."

"I was just getting organized." Lee cinched the belt around his robe. "Want a drink?"

"No, thanks. Seems I abused the privilege."

"Oh." Lee shuffled to the dining room table to pour from a half gallon of vodka into a tea glass, not bothering with ice, and when he returned from the dining room he snapped off the television and opened a blind to let some sunlight seep through unwashed windows. They sat uneasily on the sofa.

Sonny said, "I was sorry to hear about your parents. What happened?"

"Mom just didn't hear the train. It was at the Seaboard crossing, where we used to leave pennies on the track."

"Beulah said your father died a year later from 'heartache.'"

"There's such a thing, you know." Lee leaned forward to peer at the antique clock on the mantel.

"Am I keeping you from something?" Sonny said.

"Oh, I've got all the time in the world these days. I was just curious about the time."

"So. You're with the post office now."

"Part-time, at the East Lake branch. I made twenty years this spring, so now I just put in some time sorting mail and taking care of things. I don't go in until midnight."

"Not married?"

"Twice," Lee said. "The second one was about the best thing that ever happened to me. That's her in that picture up there" — pointing to the framed photograph Sonny had noticed coming in — "with our little girl."

"I heard you lived alone. They at church?"

"My wife died of cancer in February, Sonny."

"Oh, my God. I'm sorry."

Lee's voice was flat. "Good things don't last very long, do they?"

"Well, what about your daughter?"

"I gave her to Rosalie's sister."

"*Gave* her?"

"I signed the papers."

"You see her, don't you?"

"When I'm up to it." He hoisted the glass and smiled weakly. "It's best for her this way."

When Lee got up to freshen his drink, Sonny strained for a way to change the subject. "I came across some pictures the other day of us at the Ozark Baseball Camp. Do you ever think about those days?"

"Not much."

"Ty Cobb. What was that, 'fifty-one?"

"'Fifty-two, I think."

"That's right. I had my sixteenth birthday there." Sonny offered a Camel to Lee, who shook his head no, then lit one for himself and laughed. "Remember how they gave us this lecture about how Mr. Cobb was a retired gentleman now and he didn't like to be asked about spiking guys when he played?"

For the first time, Lee laughed. "And that was the first question."

"Right. Some kid said, 'Mr. Cobb, is it true that you once spiked a man?' Like he'd killed somebody or something."

"And Cobb said, 'You're damned right I did, and I'd do it again. Those base paths were *mine*.'"

"God, what a week *that* turned out to be. You couldn't shut the old guy up after that. There must have been a dozen serious spikings before he left, kids trying to impress the old fart." Sonny felt he could press Lee now. "Wasn't that when the scouts started talking to you? That summer in Missouri?"

"I guess. I don't remember."

"Hey, come on, one day six of 'em showed up just for a camp game. You hit two in the Current River."

"I did okay that day."

"'Okay'? You had 'em drooling. Lee, what happened? How come you never signed? Hey, the *Yankees*, for Christ's sake."

Lee wouldn't look Sonny in the eye. "I was scared."

"What's scary about signing with the Yankees?"

"Failing." A sheepish smile belied the sorrow in his eyes. "When the papers started all of that 'hometown boy' stuff, I started asking myself what would happen if I *didn't* make it. So I just told 'em I'd rather go to college."

"Where'd you go? I lost you after that."

"Howard. Right here at home."

"Why didn't you go to 'Bama? They had great baseball back then."

"And it would've started all over again. See what I mean?"

"You went under the radar."

"Not a bad way to put it," Lee said. "Anyway, I thought I

wanted to be a navy pilot. Everything went fine until they took us out into the Pacific for carrier landings. I tried five times to land on that thing before the instructor said, 'Lemme have the stick before you get us killed.' I threw up, and then I asked for desk duty."

"Christ, Lee, I bet it happens all the time."

"Well, that was enough adventure for me."

Suddenly there was an explosion in the neighborhood, followed by a clattering roar that was enough to set windows rattling and dogs barking up and down the street, and for an instant Lee froze. There was more banging and popping, and it wasn't until they got up and opened the front door that Sonny knew what the noise was all about.

"Never fear," Sonny said as they stepped onto the porch. "The king of the road is here."

"I thought your dad was in a nursing home."

"They couldn't hold him. I've been here for a week just to see what happens next."

"I know. I saw you cutting the grass."

"Well, why didn't you holler?"

"I wasn't so sure I wanted to see you, Sonny."

"Why not, for God's sake? It's been years."

"Aw, you've been doing things."

"Believe me, it's all relative."

"To tell you the truth," Lee said, "I was always intimidated by y'all. That truck, boy, that said it all. We'd hear it start up and Dad would say, 'Wonder where Jake and Sonny are off to now?' and I'd just look through the blinds. I knew *we* weren't going anywhere."

"That was then, Lee. Things change."

"Not unless you make 'em change."

The hood was open on Redball and Jake lay on the fender, his head and shoulders buried in the engine housing, his legs thrashing wildly in the air, when Sonny walked into the backyard. "Looks like major surgery to me," Sonny said. Jake sneezed and farted, then eased himself off the truck. He was back in his overalls, already covered with grime, contented as a pig in a mud bog.

"Just changing plugs," Jake said.

"I thought you'd blown up on the launching pad."

"Timing's all messed up. I'll have to get Junior to do the rest."

"That the mechanic at Liberty Motors?"

"Junior Wages. Thought I'd run by there tomorrow after I see Charley. Let him tune 'er up."

"Christ. I thought he'd be retired by now."

"Junior kept four Redballs and thirty-five years' worth of Dodge automobiles running like clocks for me. One time he said he wasn't quitting 'til I did."

Jake took a wrench from the pocket of his overalls and mounted the truck again to tighten the fresh spark plugs he had installed. When he finished, he dismounted and slammed the hood closed and then stepped back to observe the truck from a distance as he bit off the end of a new cigar. They stood together, halfway up the sloped yard, in unspoken agreement that the old chariot looked as able now as when it had "come out of the box" more than nine years and a half-million miles earlier. Those miles had been put on since Jake's sixtieth birthday, at a time of life when most long-haul truckers were opting for pasture, and this fact made Dixie Redball IV the favorite of his trucks.

"How's about we take 'er for a spin?"

"Right now? Sunday afternoon?"

"Of course, now, if you're too embarrassed . . ."

"What the hell. Why not?"

There wasn't nearly the commotion this time when Jake settled behind the wheel, set the choke, patted the accelerator, and ceremoniously turned the ignition. There was an initial blast, and a loud backfiring — *Bbrrrrmmm-Pop-Pow-Pop-Bang-Bang-*

Bbrrrrmmm-Pop-Bbrrrmmmmm — but within two or three minutes the engine had begun to settle down as well as could be expected. Jake checked his clearances all around through the wide mirrors on either side of the cab and then clutched and nudged the gearshift into its lowest range. Dixie Redball IV, the last of Jake's proud steeds, bucked away from its stall and crept up the gravel to the street. Jake looked both ways for traffic, as though entering a freeway, and even flipped the blinkers for a right turn. As they bobtailed up the hill, bouncing in the cab like cowboys on a bronc, they grinned at each other and Jake let out a whoop. Sonny thought he saw the blinds part when the truck backfired in front of Lee Riddle's house.

12

FOR THE SAKE of ceremony, as much as anything, Jake insisted on showing up at Graddick Tire in Dixie Redball IV. He had been up since daybreak, sprucing himself and guzzling coffee and glancing to see who Country Boy Eddie's guests were, even donning the gray gabardine driver's uniform that he had seldom worn. Reeking of mothballs and cigar smoke and Mennen's After Shave, he had stalked about the house in a way reminiscent of those countless Sunday afternoons when domesticity had paled and the road was calling his name. The plan on this Monday morning was for Sonny to follow in his pickup, in case the truck didn't make it to Graddick's, and later to leave Redball with Junior Wages at Liberty Motors for a tune-up.

When they rolled through the gates of Graddick Tire, at eight o'clock, they saw that Charley's white Cadillac with its special license tag — WHEELS — was already there. The truck had bucked, backfired, and belched huge puffballs of blue smoke for the entire five-mile trip, but that didn't seem to concern Jake as he parked in the gravel between the mounds of tires and swung out of the cab like the Lone Ranger dismounting Silver. Sonny, in his jeans and T-shirt and sneakers, parked behind the truck and fell in behind Jake as he swaggered into the front door of the building.

Heads turned when Jake entered. "I'm assuming my credit's still good around this joint," he said, waggling his cigar like Groucho Marx. Somebody said, "Jake?" Another voice said, "Look what the cat drug in." The last man in the office to notice his arrival, in fact, was Charley, suit coat off to reveal yellow suspenders, engaged in a shouting match with Charles Jr. in a glass cubicle beyond the front counter. Charley waved through the glass, got off a parting shot to his son, and then came out front to shake hands and finally bear hug Jake as though he had been around the world.

"You're gonna have to return those gifts you got at the retirement party, you know," Charley said.

"Seems I drunk 'em up," Jake told him.

"That's what I hear."

"Course, now, they're refillable bottles."

"No thanks. It was bad bourbon to start with."

"Ain't no such thing, Charley, and you know it."

They followed Charley as he hobbled up the stairs on his bad leg, and soon his soundproofed office was swirling with the smoke of good Havana cigars and fine cussing and Jake's bravado. Charley told somebody downstairs to hold his calls, and as he rocked from side to side in his executive's chair he let Jake run like a marlin, feeding him straight lines, howling at his tales of Piney Woods and Mimosa Towers, commiserating over Mama's predicament, all the while, Sonny could see, trying to get a reading. At one point, noticing that Jake's eyes had focused on the row of decanters gracing a marble-topped cart beside his desk, Charley asked Jake if he'd like a drink. When he said no, not right now, Charley smiled.

"I guess you saw me chewing out Chuck when y'all came in," Charley said. "Damned kid. Almost thirty-five and he still don't know a good tire from a dud."

"Well, it takes a lot of years to know how to judge 'em."

"Tires, or sons?"

They looked at Sonny. Jake said, "Both, I reckon."

"I go to Europe for three days, and when I get back I find out he's lost a bid that could've made us twenty thousand dollars."

"Where at?"

"Amarillo. Same place you went on your last trip." Charley leaned back and let out a sigh of disgust. "Now there's a big inspection coming up in Vegas, and I don't know if I can trust him on it."

"Nellis?"

"Yeah. The air base."

"Lemme guess. Two-thousand-by-twenties. Bomber tires."

"That's the ones. Five lots. Those B-52s flat burn up the rubber, don't they?"

Jake was salivating. His eyes rolled like cherries on a slot machine, and his lips began to move as he ran figures through his head. "I can see it," he said. "There's usually close to twenty percent duds in each lot, lots run around seventy-five to ninety carcasses each, gives you maybe fifteen or twenty duds you got to ditch somewheres. Best place I know is this canyon over the line in Arizona. Ain't a hundred miles from the base, but you got to drive four or five miles of dirt so the boys don't see you."

"Whoa, Jake, hold up," Charley said. "It seems like the perfect way for you to get back in the swing of things is to *fly* out there."

"I'd sure like to bid on 'em, Charley. I know that place good."

"You already know who you'd be up against."

"McCormick from Denver is my guess."

"They always bid too high."

"Bunch of uppity sonsabitches on top of that."

"Well, how about it, then?" Charley winked at Sonny, who had been following the exchange of volleys as though it were a tennis match. "You want to be my man out there? I'll buy you a plane ticket today. First class."

"That's fine, Charley." Jake picked at an errant hair in his ear. "As far as it goes."

"You hear that?" Charley threw out both hands and addressed Sonny. "I'm rescuing your old man from the grave. The old fart's driving with a senior citizen's license. But what do I get? A first-class ticket to Vegas is 'fine'? That's not enough?"

"I want to go get 'em, too, Charley."

"Wait a minute, now, Jake. That's not what we talked about on the phone."

"We talked about me working. Flying ain't working."

"Listen to that. Just listen to him, Sonny."

"I got a deal for you, though," Jake said.

Charley feigned exasperation. "All right." He leaned back and clasped his hands behind his head.

"You let slip that you got some tires for Nevada. There ain't but one place they'd be going, and that's to that copper mine other side of Ely. Right?"

"Sly sonofabitch, aren't you?"

"Funny-named operation."

"Knudsen-Menke," Charley said. "In Sarah."

"Be right smart of you to let me haul them out for you, and then run on down the road for the inspection at Nellis. They ain't but two hundred and eighty miles apart, best I recollect. And when I win the bid, I'll bring 'em back for you."

Charley flopped forward, both elbows on the desk now, serious. "I don't know, Jake."

"I work cheap, remember? I ain't helping the damned revenuers any more than I have to."

"It's not that, Jake."

"You think I can't handle it? Is that it?"

"I'll level with you, Jake."

"Too old, huh? You gonna be like all them other bastards and say I'm too old to cut the mustard? Why, hell, over there at that damned crazy farm in Mississippi I was the only one that could — "

"Damnit, Jake, calm down."

"And I ain't retarded, neither."

"Shut up and listen for a change, will you? I never have bullshitted you before and I'm not gonna start now." Sonny thought he saw a grin flicker across Charley's face. "The facts are that you're almost seventy years old, you haven't driven a truck in three years, it took you two weeks to get over *that* trip, and you've been swimming in bourbon ever since. I've been known to take my chances, Jake, but I'm not crazy enough to put you out on the road alone with a brand-new rental rig worth a hundred and thirty thousand dollars — "

"I got Redball running again."

"Jake, that truck ought to be bronzed."

"Tune-up's all she needs."

"All right, but provided she runs there'd still be a thirty thousand dollar trailer, not to mention two dozen tires worth a thousand dollars each. I'm telling you, Jake, a man your age can't be driving a load like that all the way to Nevada alone."

"I always drove alone."

"Yeah, but now it's different. They don't call U.S. 50 the 'Loneliest Road in America' for nothing. Chamber of commerce didn't dream it up. What if you're out there in Utah, say, and you break down or you have a heart attack and you're all alone and . . ."

Alone. Sonny had been sitting back during their chat, idly enjoying the repartee and the Havana cigar Charley had given him, thinking about how he ought to take his father out to see the Birmingham Barons play before he returned to Tallahassee, when he heard the talk stop. He raised up and saw that Charley and Jake were looking at him, expectantly, as though he were an actor who had flubbed his cue. When he said nothing, they began to speak of him in the third person, like Mama sometimes did, as if he weren't there.

"He looks kinda soft to me," said Charley.

"Teachers get like that," said Jake.

"Can't drive a truck, either, can he?"

"Little ol' pickup's about all."

"He *could* put out flares if you broke down, you know."

"Well, that'd be something, I reckon."

"Wonder if he's ever been that far west."

"I do recollect that he chased a gal as far as Little Rock one time," Jake said. "Maybe we oughta ask him if he's got any plans."

Sonny could look back now and suspect that it had been a conspiracy all along, ever since the day he had told Charley about Jake, and he had to admit that he didn't mind if that were the case. He took a long draw from the cigar and leaned back to let the smoke curl toward the ceiling before pushing up from the deep chair and walking away from them, slowly, theatrically. When he turned to face them there was a wisecracker's side-of-the-mouth smile on his face. "You know me, boys," he said, waggling the cigar, trying to imitate his father. "Biscuit, shot of whiskey, little shut-eye, I'm ready to roll. Think I was born like this. I'm a traveling man myself."

In the yard, while a bare-chested teenager on a baby forklift noisily arranged piles of tires for destinations around the world, Jake sat in the cab of Redball with the door open as Charley stood in the gravel beside him striking the deal. Straight ahead of them, stacked upright on the loading dock, the earth-mover tires stood at attention: an ominous row of them, each standing more than six feet tall and nearly three feet wide, each weighing 1,000 pounds, each armed with monstrous new teeth to bite into the raw Nevada earth.

"How many we got there?" Jake said.

"Twenty-five of 'em, all told."

Jake said, "Puts me overloaded for Mississippi, Tennessee, and Arkansas."

"Never seemed to bother you much before."

"Don't reckon it will now. Can't hardly get there without going through a piece of each. Anyway, I've already worked out a route."

"All right," Charley said. "The guy to see is this old retired army sergeant, fellow by the name of Red Mathis."

"He the one that caught for the Barons?"

"How the hell would I know that?"

"Sonny got an autographed ball from him one time. Wouldn't that be something?"

Charley said, "Now look here, Jake. This trip's gonna take you up to fifteen days, total, once you've run down to Nellis for the inspection. How much gas and oil money do you figure it'll take?"

Jake's adding machine went to work. "Forty-two hundred miles, six miles to a gallon for regular, average ninety cents a gallon. Comes to six hundred and thirty dollars. Plus a little oil."

"All right, then. I want y'all staying in good motels and I want you eating right. I'm giving you five hundred in cash for your expenses, plus my American Express and three different oil cards. And I want you to use the damned things, Jake, you hear?"

"Interest is eating you alive, Charley."

"That's my problem, hoss. Not yours."

"Sonny's ex-wife didn't know that."

"Goddamn it, Jake, we're talking about hauling tires, not Sonny's personal life." Jake was listening, but again he wasn't. It was obvious to both Charley and Sonny, as Jake sat behind the wheel of Redball with his eyes glazed, that in his mind he was already on the road. "Couple of other things, too, Jake," Charley said. "Jake, are you listening to me?"

"I'm right here, good buddy."

"I'm renting you a brand-new Great Dane trailer."

"Fruehauf's better, but that's okay."

"I'm relieved to know that you approve. When do you want to leave?"

"Dawn Wednesday, I reckon. That way we can beat the heat and the women drivers."

"All right, I'll have the boys load 'er up for you tomorrow."

Jake said, "Charley, if you don't mind, I'd rather do the loading myself. Them boys of yours don't know how to load tires so they won't shift on me."

"No, damnit, no. You aren't loading. I don't want you handling these tires at the other end, either. You'll get yourself killed, Jake."

"Be a fitting way to go, wouldn't it?"

"Let's don't get poetic about it. I don't want your blood on my hands."

"I been handling tires most of my life, Charley. I know what I'm doing."

"You forget that you almost got bit by one of 'em that time. Same tire, too."

"Wasn't my fault. Some sonofabitch tried to help me and he got the damned thing wobbling."

"Jake, it's no deal unless you promise."

"All right, then, if it'll make you feel good, I promise I'll be careful."

"That isn't what I said, Jake."

"I promise I won't do it by myself, then."

"You hard-headed old fool."

Jake, victorious, squinted and rolled his cigar in his mouth. "What else you got on your mind, boss?"

"While I'm in a leasing mood," Charley said, trying to win at least one point, "how about if I get you a brand-new Freightliner with one of those big sleeper units on it? They got TV, stereo, king-sized bed, toilet, and a shower stall in those things now. All the comforts of home, Jake. Hell, do it for *Sonny's* sake. He's not used to this."

Jake swung down from the cab of Redball and gently shut the door. "If I had a rig like that, Charley, I wouldn't drive the damned thing, I'd *live* in it. If a man wants all the comforts of home, he ought to stay at home." He rubbed his hand over the fender, glistening from the new wax job like a candied apple, a cowboy soothing his horse.

Charley, who had been co-owner of Redball, legally, until Jake paid off the note, spoke of the truck almost lovingly. "She's been some places, hasn't she?"

"Thirty-eight states, half a million miles."

"She gonna make it?"

"When Junior tunes 'er up she will."

Charley toed the gravel, took a breath, and made one more try. "Another thing about a Freightliner, Jake, is air conditioning. I guess there's something to be said about the wind blowing in your face and all of that, but it's gonna be hot as hell out there. Dodge City had a hundred-and-two yesterday."

"I thank you kindly, Charley," Jake said. "I know you got my best interests in mind. But if it's all the same to you, I'd just as well dance with the one that brung me."

Jake was hailed by one of the recappers who had come into the yard for a smoke, a black fellow grown old but still sinewy in spite of the twenty-five years that had passed since Sonny's college summers of working the lot at Graddick Tire, and when Jake sauntered over to talk with him, Charley said he and Sonny would be in his office. There, Sonny sat while Charley swung open a fake painting hung on the paneled wall and began fiddling with the tumblers of his safe. "I think they call it the fastball under the chin," Charley said, "what we just threw at you."

"Yeah," said Sonny, "but it doesn't work if the hitter's looking for it."

"I was pretty sure you'd go along, or I wouldn't have done it. I'd never send him out there alone."

"It's a one-shot deal, right? Jake Hawkins's farewell tour."

"We've got to get it into his thick skull one way or another that he's too old for the road. I figure wearing him out ought to do it."

"I've only got one question, Charley."

"Let's have it."

"Suppose it's a textbook trip. He doesn't get tired, he gulls the boys, Redball runs like new, he even gets there a day early."

"Maybe you could write it up in *Trucker* magazine."

"Come on, I'm serious."

"I know you are, Sonny. But you and me know it won't happen like that."

"Maybe you do, but I don't. I see him coming back off the trip thinking he's thirty years old."

"Ain't no way." Charley had lost track of the combination and had to start all over again with the safe. "I wouldn't be sending him out there if I thought there was a chance in hell of that happening. It's gonna go the *other* way. He's gonna come back feeling a *hundred* years old, and then I'll have him right where I want him."

"Which is?"

"Right here."

"An office job? Like a mascot?"

"Naw, naw. Running tires around town, maybe hauling some up from Maxwell Air Force Base in Montgomery. I might fly him here and there now and then to look at tires."

"Sounds like you've planned it that way."

"Jake just wants to feel useful, Sonny."

"It's a gamble. He might get the idea he can go back to driving full-time."

The safe opened and Charley reached in for the cash, credit cards, and papers Jake would need. "I know that, and I hope we don't regret this. I may be a bigger fool than your daddy is."

"You're a hero, Charley, not a fool."

"Well, I'm not looking for any medals."

"It's worth an asterisk, anyway. If you'd seen him at Mimosa and at that recovery center, you'd really know what this means to him. He'd more or less been marked for death. That was his perception, anyway."

"Well, I couldn't stand to watch it."

"Me, either."

"Look here, now, Sonny" — Charley closed the safe and spread out the cash, cards and papers on his desk — "you've got to watch out for him."

" 'Am I my father's keeper?' "

"What?"

"Something Phyllis said last week."

"Well, I guess it's come around to that." Charley plopped into his swivel chair and put a Zippo lighter to his cigar. "He told me one time that the proudest day of his life was when he took you on your first trip. How long's that been? You remember?"

"Almost to the day," Sonny said, eschewing his Havana for a Camel. "It was the first week of June, in 'forty-eight. Thirty-three years ago. I was twelve and school had let out for the summer."

"Lord. I was still racing stock cars then. Where'd y'all go?"

"Cumberland, and then over to Akron for a return load."

"That was for Alabama Highway, wasn't it?"

"Took these big spools of cotton up and brought the finished tires back. Did it for eight years. He always said it was the best run he ever had." Sonny started to tell Charley about the incident in class, less than two weeks ago, when he read "Do not go gentle" to his students in Tallahassee, but instead spoke of the recurring dreams of those trips with his father when he was a boy. "There's this song, 'Six Days on the Road,' that didn't get recorded until years later, but every time I hear it I see Pop and me going somewhere in a truck. It's kind of our National Anthem."

"I know that one. Dave Dudley."

"Story of Pop's life back then."

Charley began to count out five hundred dollars in twenties and fifties. "What'd they used to say on that TV show, 'Mission: Impossible'? 'Your mission, should you choose to accept it,' is to keep an eye on him all the time. I don't worry so much about the drinking, like I told you." Charley paused. "You're okay on that score, aren't you? I mean you, yourself?"

"I think so. As long as I'm busy."

"You ought to be busy, all right, just looking after your daddy. Damnit, Sonny, don't let him push it. He can take two weeks delivering these tires, far as I'm concerned. I want y'all staying in good motels, and I want you eating right, and I don't want him acting like some damned cowboy on an all-night cattle drive out there. He doesn't have to prove anything to me or you both. Hell, get him in the mood that y'all are on a vacation if you think that'll work."

"It probably won't, but I'll try."

"And call me collect when you can. He won't."

"Every night?"

"Any time at all." Charley smoothed out a bill of lading and began to fill it out. "Jesus Christ. He didn't even ask me how much I'd pay him."

"I don't think it matters very much, Charley."

When Jake burst into the office his eyes were dilated and he was jabbering, like the drivers high on coffee, NoDoz, and amphetamines that Sonny recalled from truck stops in the middle of the night, and Sonny and Charley recognized that the patient was healthy.

"Where the hell you been?" Charley said. "I thought maybe you'd changed your mind."

"That Jo-Jo's pretty smart for a nigger."

"Ought to know a thing or two. He's been with me for thirty-two years now."

"You won't mind if he takes a day off from 'capping tomorrow, then."

"Oh, now you're going to run my business."

"Naw, I just want him to load the trailer for me if you ain't gonna let me do it myself."

"Jake, I need Jo-Jo recapping. We got a big order waiting."

"Well, me and him was just wasting time, then."

"What're you saying, Jake?"

"I've showed him how to load tires proper."

"Damnit, Jake, you promised."

"See, it's all in the leverage — "

"I guess you tumped one over to show him what happens when it's not done right."

"Of course, I did. You ain't gonna respect a rattlesnake until you've heard one get riled up and commence to rattling."

"All right, Jake. Just all right. I'll let Jo-Jo do the loading."

"I thought the boy was gonna turn white on me for a minute."

"Ah, shit," Charley said. He fished two sets of Graddick & Sons Tire Company baseball caps and windbreakers from boxes on the floor. "Here's your uniforms, boys. Wear 'em with pride. Jake, I'll call you when the trailer's loaded."

Late that night, Jake was in the basement of the house happily going through a ritual that had been the very fabric of his life for forty years: preparing to hit the road. He had left the truck at Liberty Motors with a startled Junior Wages, nursemaid to three editions of Dixie Redballs, who assured him that this one needed little more than a full-scale tune-up to make it to Nevada and back. He had called Charley to talk money and to tell him he could forget leasing a Freightliner, that Redball was fit. He had taken a nap, paid a long visit to Mama at the retirement home, and treated Sonny to another barbecue feast at Andrews.

Now Sonny sat on the edge of a rollaway bed, where Jake had spent many fitful hours passed out during his "retirement," watching as he made preparations for a trip neither had dreamed would be made. "You and Charley ever work out what he's going to pay you, Pop?"

"Ain't gonna pay *me* nothing."

"How so?"

"I got the revenuers to worry about."

"I know that, but hell, this is a big job. You ought to get *something*."

"Charley's trying to figure out a way to make a charitable gift to that damned Mimosa. One of those tax-deductible things. If he can get away with it, he'll give a thousand dollars in Mama's name."

"Well," Sonny said, "that'll relieve everybody of a little guilt."

"Exactly my thinking."

"Did you tell Mama about the trip?"

"I did."

"And?"

"Damnedest thing, son. I didn't know if I even ought to tell her about it, seeing the way she is and all, or if she'd know what the hell I was talking about if I did." Jake had been turned the other way, wiping off the old citizens' band radio he would install in the truck for the trip, and when he turned there were tears in his eyes. "I told her, I said, 'Sugar, I'm gonna be hauling a load out west and I won't be seeing you for a while.' And she said, 'Lord, I wish I could make y'all some sandwiches.' And then she said, just like she always did, 'You be careful, now, and you come back safe 'cause I love you.'"

Sonny leaned toward his father and clapped him on the shoulder. "That must have been pretty hard for you to take."

"The whole damned business is, son. It got me to wondering again about her and the church. Here she's spent her whole life talking to the 'Lord' and when she needs him he ain't nowhere around."

"I'm no closer to understanding it than you are, Pop."

"Gives her *somebody* to talk to, I reckon."

Soon, Sonny had to get off the rollaway to make room for the array of equipment Jake was beginning to assemble from all corners of the disordered basement: signal flares, flashlight, toolbox, cans of Quaker State, poncho, cleanest dirty rags he could find, the old Confederate flag that was actually a mesh bug net that would be attached to the grill of Redball when it was ready to roll. Jake whistled while he worked, a man newly returned to his element, shot at but missed, bent over as he rummaged through a lifetime's collection of the sort of odds and ends that a man never knows he might not need again.

"I guess the maps are in the truck," Sonny said.

Jake raised up and smiled. "Maps?"

"Sure. Road maps. Nevada's a damned long . . ." Sonny stopped himself and smiled back at Jake. "Real truckers don't use maps, right?"

"Name me a place in the Forty-eight, and I'll tell you how to get there. Maybe you'd want to put some money on it."

"Not me, pal."

"Come on. Supper at the first truck stop."

"No way I'm betting. That cost me a whole week's allowance one time. Your boy ain't that dumb."

Jake fumbled through a wooden apple crate crammed with old logbooks and bills of lading and various receipts until he found a tattered ten-year-old *Rand McNally Road Atlas*. He tossed it across the bed to Sonny and said, "Tourists wouldn't know what to do without 'em. Open it up to Mississippi and I'll tell you how we're gonna get there."

13

At dawn Tuesday, still uncertain about how it had come to pass that he was dressed in his blazer and dress slacks and Weejuns before he had so much as smelled a cup of coffee, Sonny rode shotgun in the Dodge sedan as Jake eased into the paved parking lot of WBRC-TV atop Red Mountain overlooking Birmingham. The first blush of orange was coming from the east to enliven the haze of the gray morning sky, the only other color being the red torch in the hands of the statue of Vulcan perched beside the station's tower.

"See where some fool went and killed himself yesterday," said Jake, dressed again in his trucker's uniform and the new Graddick Tire cap.

"Huh?"

"Vulcan's torch is red. Means a bad wreck."

"Right. I hadn't noticed."

"Personally, I always saw it as a good luck sign before I left out."

"How can a traffic fatality be good luck?"

"Means the quota's been used up for the day."

Sonny stumbled out of the car and followed Jake to the front door, painted with a garish number 6 for the station's logo, and as Jake pressed the buzzer to summon a guard Sonny continued the protest that had raged since he had been roughed awake at five o'clock. "Just forget about it if you think I'm going to be on the show."

"We'll let Country Boy be the judge on that one."

"Christ, Pop, are you crazy?"

"There's that word again. Don't tell me you think he's 'tacky,' too, like Phyllis and Mama and them."

"I'm just saying it's tacky to be up this early for a damned TV show. *Anybody's* TV show. I ought to be home watching, anyway."

"This way, when it's done with we just zip right over to Liberty Motors and get Redball so I can take 'er home. Saves me a trip."

"Well," Sonny said, "I might as well practice getting up at dawn."

"There you go," said Jake.

The security guard recognized Jake and unlocked the door not with questions but with a hearty laugh, as though still not entirely recovered from the old man's last visit, and it was the same with the other people they met as Sonny followed Jake down a corridor that suddenly opened onto the set of the "Country Boy Eddie Show." The show had already moved into overdrive, with that same steel guitar player flying away on "Steel Guitar Rag" and Country Boy braying his first *Hee-haw, Hee-haw* of the day, and when Country Boy stepped from under the lights after handing the microphone to a Ford dealer to do his own commercial he ran smack into Jake.

"You old codger, I thought you'd died but I was afraid to ask," said Country Boy. This morning he wore starched jeans, snakeskin cowboy boots, and a red and white checkerboard shirt with pearl buttons.

"Prison couldn't hold me, Country Boy."

"I knew it. And how's the wife?"

"Well as could be expected."

"That's fine, Jake. Mighty fine." Country Boy feigned a startled look and fingered the collar of Jake's driver's uniform. "What's this getup mean, hoss? Looks to me like you're ready to roll again."

"Sure am, Country Boy. Me and my boy here are heading out for Nevada first thing tomorrow morning." Jake had to introduce Sonny and Country Boy after all of these years. "Comin' out o' *retardment*, don't you know? Thought I'd come by and mention it on the show. That is, if you don't mind."

"Why, sure, Jake, anything you want to say."

"Like to talk about that damned place where my wife's at, too."

Sonny winced, and Country Boy had a pained look. "On one condition, Jake."

"Yessir?"

"You got to promise you'll play the piano for us, too. You got fans out there."

"Well, I'm a little rusty."

"You can do 'Movin' On,' can't you?"

"Maybe if you'd hum me a few bars." Jake winked at Sonny, took the cigar out of his mouth, and cleared his throat. "This old boy was pickin' and singin' in his room about three o'clock one morning when a guy next door starts bangin' on the wall and says, 'Hey, buddy, don't you know there's a sick lady over here?' And the guy says, 'Naw, but maybe if you'd hum me a few bars I could learn it.'"

"That's a good'un, Jake," Country Boy said as he turned to head for the set. "Why don't you tell it on the show? I got to go to work."

A young woman wearing a jogging outfit and headphones showed Jake and Sonny where the coffee was, and when they had helped themselves they stood behind the cameras to watch the show as it progressed. Country Boy sang "Your Cheatin' Heart," the manager of a reclaimed freight outlet in Scottsboro announced a new shipment of stuff left on planes, the band did "Orange Blossom Special," and after Country Boy read condolences "for our sick and shut-in friends" from a handful of flip cards he brought on his special guest for the day. Jake Hawkins.

The band broke into "I'm Movin' On" as Jake slinked out of the shadows and sidled up to the upright piano on the set. Unlit cigar clenched between his teeth, harsh studio lights accenting the deep ridges carved in his face, Graddick Tire cap shielding his squinty eyes, he looked like a scarecrow as he took a seat on the piano bench and tried to catch up with the band just as the music died. Country Boy, microphone in hand, sat down beside him.

"Been too long between visits, Jake."

"Might say I been tied up."

"Vacation didn't suit you?"

"Had about all of *retardment* I can stand."

"Don't let me forget to give you your fan mail before you leave now, hoss. Last time you were here with your wife you got a ton of it."

"Hope it wasn't the Infernal Revenue."

"Naw, naw. You got a regular Jake Hawkins Fan Club going. What do you think about that?"

"You can fool some of the people some of the time, is the way I look at it."

"Your wife doing okay, Jake?"

Sonny, still lurking behind the cameras in hopes that nobody would see him, held his breath. Country Boy Eddie had delivered his father a straight line, given him a blank check, and there was no telling what he would do with it. He saw Jake's jaws tighten as a camera zoomed in on him.

Jake said, "We get old, you know?"

"Tell me, pardner."

"Some get old faster than others."

"No argument there, Jake."

"That's what happened with me and Mama." Jake's face filled the screen of the monitor that Sonny was now watching in the studio. "The poor darling's doing just about as well as could be expected. They've got her over there at Mimosa Towers, that place on Airport Boulevard, the one run by the Methodists."

"Doing okay, though," said Country Boy, glancing at the studio clock while an engineer started giving him the hurry-up sign.

"It'd be my guess that Evelyn Hawkins, wife of yours truly, is getting about the best health care available in the United States of America today."

"That's fine, Jake. Mighty fine. Now, if we — "

"I ain't through yet. I wanted to announce that I'm dedicating my next trip to my wife, and me and Charley Graddick of Graddick Tire Company" — Jake looked for the camera with the red light and tipped his Graddick Tire cap toward it — "we're giving all of the proceeds to Preacher Boggs and them over at Mimosa so they can continue their fine work."

"That's touching, Jake."

"I wanted to go on record as saying it."

"Mighty fine, Jake. Now how about — "

"They better treat her right, too. I ain't likely to be this nice the next time."

Jake had done himself proud, even if it hadn't been easy, was the way Sonny looked at it. He had told the joke about "hum me a few bars," had led the band through a calamitous version of "I'm Movin' On," had collected a half-dozen cards and letters the station had received after his last appearance on Country Boy's show (only one of them taking him to task, for allowing his wife on the show "in her condition"), and had been so swept up by it all that he forgot to drag Sonny onto the set.

By eight o'clock, after breakfast at a diner near Liberty Motors, Jake parked the car around back just in time to see Junior Wages pulling on a rope to raise the wide metal door of the truck service department. A sawed-off man who had been a competitor of Charley Graddick's on the Southern stock-car racing circuit during the fifties, Junior had changed little since Sonny had seen him some twenty years earlier: jet black hair brushed back in a flattop ducktail, bandy legs, bad teeth, beady pig eyes, a chaw of tobacco pooching out his jaws to make him look like a squirrel stowing pecans. When he had cinched the rope he grinned like a jack-o'-lantern and gave Jake the thumbs-up signal.

"Same question I been asking you for thirty years, Junior," Jake said as they shook hands. "Would you drive it yourself?"

"I'd drive it to heaven if I had a map," Junior said. "Don't tell me this is Sonny, all growed up."

"The one and only. Gonna be my copilot on this little run."

"What I heard on the 'Country Boy Show.'" Junior offered a permanently grease-stained hand to Sonny.

"How'd I do?"

"You're getting old, Jake. I told my old lady when you come on, said, 'I hope I don't turn out like that.' Ain't they got no make-up over there?"

"You wouldn't want to arm wrestle, would you?"

"I ain't talkin' 'bout muscles, Jake, I'm talking about the Uglies."

The work had been finished on Dixie Redball IV at quitting time Monday and Junior had parked the truck in a lot usually reserved for new ones just off the assembly lines. Redball had looked splendid after the washing and waxing Jake and Sonny had given her, sitting alone in the backyard at the house, but when she stood beside these sleek new monsters she looked like a powdered dowager who should have stayed at home rather than venture to the ball: proud, erect, straining against age, but with wrinkles that no amount of make-up could hide. Sonny didn't take Junior to be a man given to metaphor, but the business about make-up wasn't bad. "Dance with the one that brung me," indeed.

Junior had heard about people falling into icy water but surviving because the heart and other vital organs got put in cold storage, he was saying as they reached the truck, and that was the only way he could explain Redball's condition after sitting for three years. He had replaced things like the battery, the points, the filters, and one of the air hoses, but basically he had set the tuning of the engine and lathered every joint with grease and now could proudly pronounce the truck ready to go anywhere Jake chose to take her. The men stood next to Redball, side by side, like a fighter pilot and his chief mechanic.

"Brakes okay?" said Jake.

"Little adjusting was all."

"Well, I never rode 'em is why."

"Yep, it's like your daddy always said" — Junior smiled at Sonny — "a man don't even need brakes if he knows how to work his gears."

Jake opened the door and climbed into the cab. "I don't know if he remembers it, but one time when Sonny was just a boy we were in the Blue Ridge at night, headed for Cumberland, and I was going up a switchback so slow that he'd just peed off the running board without getting wet. Anyway, he hadn't hardly put his pecker away when I saw headlights swinging around the top of the mountain about two miles off, so I moved over to make room. Thing is, he never did show up. You remember that, son?"

"I *did* pee on myself. I remember everything about that night."

"Wouldn't let you get out of the cab. Figured you was too young to see it."

Junior said, "Fella lost it, huh?"

"When we came around the last curve before the top, I saw this flashlight waving and I pulled over and made Sonny stay in the truck while I went to check things out. This fellow had blood all over him and was talking crazy. Said the driver and a young girl were under the cab and for me to come help him pull it off of 'em. Well, hell's bells, when we got to the bottom of the canyon through all them briars and trees I could see they were both crushed to death. He kept saying, 'Naw, come on, help me out, they'll be all right.' Well, they weren't all right. They were dead. I just told the fellow to get a-hold of himself and I'd go get some help."

"And for a change," Sonny said, "you stopped a trooper instead of the other way around."

"Yeah, you remember. The sonofabitch was running a speed trap in the valley, trying to catch us flying off the mountain, and I knew he always set himself up there behind this particular See Rock City sign. I told him about the wreck, and when he left I got the hell out of there. Made me some good time while he was off investigating."

"Tried to use the brakes instead of the gears," Junior said. "That it?"

"Come to find out what happened about three days later on my return. Fellow at a Pure station where I always stopped told me, yeah, the driver had forgot about how you're supposed to go down a mountain in the same gear you went up it at." Jake nodded at Sonny. "Think I told you about that the other day. How there's a damned graveyard for truckers out there at Four Corners, where all the states come together, full of fellows that forgot? I'll show you when we're coming back from Vegas next week. Any rate, the thing that scared the boy that survived more than anything was how he was gonna explain being a party to taking that little girl across state lines at her age."

Junior just shook his head. "You know the thing I miss the most about you not driving lately?"

"All the money I pay you for repairs."

"Hell. If it was that, I'd starve."

"Yeah, you do take too good o' care of her for your own good, I reckon."

"What I miss the most is the stories, Jake. If it wasn't for you, I wouldn't know nothing 'bout what's going on in the world."

"There seems to be varying opinions about that." Jake tossed the keys to the car to Sonny, adjusted the seat to suit his long legs, shut the door to the cab, set the choke, patted the accelerator, and then fired the ignition. There was no explosion this time, only a low rumble, bringing a sly smile to Jake's face. He began to test the brakes and run through the eight forward gear positions, all the while checking to see that Junior hadn't repositioned the side mirrors. "I ought to have some more good'uns to tell you when we get back, Junior." He pulled the chain to give a blast on the air horn, checked his clearances all the way around, and put Redball into its lowest gear. "Race you back to the house," he said to Sonny. The truck groaned away across the gravel and bumped off the curb and bulled its way into the traffic.

Now, with less than twenty-four hours to go before their departure, the countdown began. Sonny knew only vaguely the route Jake had chosen, the first part of it predicated by the need to see as little as possible of Mississippi, Tennessee, and Arkansas because of the weight limits in those states. The basic plan was to get beyond Memphis and on into the plains of southern Missouri as quickly as possible, perhaps all in the first long day out, where from there it would be smooth sailing on the old U.S. highways straight westward through Kansas, Colorado, and Utah until, finally, Ely in eastern Nevada. Except for the eastern portion of Utah, where U.S. 50 and Interstate 70 were one and the same, Jake intended to eschew the interstates for the simple reason that he despised their order and monotony.

The truck was ready, the trailer was being loaded, Jake had made his peace with Mama's situation, and everything seemed to be in order except for some loose ends. Sonny had so sublimated himself to the developments in his father's life, and the further drama about to unfold, that he had almost forgotten about his own: namely, the inquiry from the publisher in Oklahoma. There wouldn't be anything he could do about it for a while, in case he had finally gotten a bite on his much-traveled manuscript about the removal of the Seminoles, but after ten years and eighteen rejections he knew he would be a fool not to respond, even if this did sound like some jackleg publisher whose office was a phone booth.

Shortly before eleven o'clock, when Jake had gotten slicked up and left for a farewell lunch with Mama at Mimosa Towers, Sonny slumped to the dinette table in the kitchen and called the number in Oklahoma. As the phone rang at the other end, in the dull clatter signifying a rural exchange, he peeled back the organdy curtains and saw a neighborhood dog peeing on the left front tire of Redball as she lay at berth.

A woman with a rough country voice answered. When Sonny asked for E. J. Hardison, the name Leo had given him, the woman simply dropped the phone and yelled, "Hardy?" and never returned. If not a phone booth, Sonny thought, maybe a kitchen.

"We got a big rodeo coming up this weekend in Muskogee and I was working one of my show horses," Hardison said, in a booming Western twang. Sonny learned very quickly that he owned a thousand-acre ranch outside of Sallisaw near the Arkansas line, had every novel Louis L'Amour had ever written about the West, and ran his own publishing house: OK Press. "We like books about misfits and various scalawags" was his summation of the OK Press backlist.

"How in the world did you come across *Children of the Swamp*?" Sonny said.

"Title like that, I'm wondering myself."
"That was just a working title."
"Well, it won't work, pardner."
"But you called, anyway."
"I got me a mole at one of the houses in New York that stays on the lookout for my kind of characters," Hardison said. "What he did was make a copy of your manuscript and dog-eared all the stuff about Billy Bowlegs. He's my kind of wild-ass. Billy, not my mole."

The Seminoles were the only tribe not entirely removed to Indian Territory in the early nineteenth century, simply disappearing into the Florida swamps, and one of them had been an obscure chief named Billy Bowlegs. What John Hardison was proposing to Sonny was that he cut away Bowlegs from his novel ("like cutting a mustang out of a herd") and write a short novel about him alone. OK Press paid $1,000 to sign, another $1,000 for delivery. Hardison was thinking the book should be a juvenile novel, for boys eight to fourteen years of age, a paperback original.

"Well," Sonny said with little interest, "I don't know."
"The money or the juvenile part?"
"And paperback. Frankly, it's pretty damned depressing."
"I sell 'em at rodeos, too. Got a new breed of cowboy that can actually read."
"Holy shit."
Hardison cleared his throat. Loudly. "Mr. Hawkins," he said, "I did some checking up, and it seems you ain't doing so hot."
"Wait just a damned — "
"You wait, please-sir. There's something fishy about a fella working without an agent, even if I do despise the ten percent bastards myself. Took me some looking, too, to find out just what the hell a Panhandle Community College is. You *comprende*, pardner?"
"Sallisaw, Oklahoma, ain't exactly New York, sport."

"That's worse news for you than it is for me, I'd say."

"Well, look" — *good thing Hemingway doesn't have to hear this shit* — "I'm going out of town for maybe three weeks. On the road. Let me be thinking about it, and call you back."

E. J. Hardison stopped Sonny from hanging up. "One thing you ought to know is, I've had real good success turning around and selling these things to the big boys in New York that were too busy to pay 'em any mind the first time around. What you'd be doing if you hook up with me is working on spec, putting yourself on the line. Seems like you're a pretty spunky fella, but I don't know if you still got your fastball."

Getting to sleep hadn't been easy for Sonny, beset as he was by the notion that a jovial rancher from Oklahoma might stand between him and any dreams left for a literary career, but when he finally dozed off he had crashed. The shadows were long when he awoke in his old bedroom, and his first move was to lurch down the hallway toward the kitchen and find something to eat — anything — to make up for the lunch he had missed. He assumed Jake was somewhere about after visiting Mama, probably in the basement continuing with the final preparations, but he would think about that later. He was chasing a peanut butter and jelly sandwich with milk, thinking warmly of the chicken-fried steaks slathered with gravy that awaited him at truck stops from Alabama to Nevada, when he heard a squawking commotion rise up from the backyard.

Jake, back in his work clothes again, sat in the cab of Redball with both doors sprung open so the faint breeze would pass through. Sonny crossed the yard in bare feet and climbed into the shotgun seat with another sandwich and a glass of milk. Jake seemed to hardly notice him, so intently was he fiddling with a radio dial and cocking an ear to hear the wavering static that filled the cab.

"Opry's not until Saturday night," Sonny said.

"Sshhh." Jake was homing in on something: engine noises, bullish male voices, kittenish females making blatant sexual pitches, a chorus of other males trying to cut in. "It's my CB."

"What the hell's that racket?"

"Truck Stop Annie somewhere. Probably up on 31 North to Huntsville." Now the woman was telling a driver with the CB handle of "Bull Durham" what astonishing things she could do for him in his sleeper quicker than they could clean his windshield. Jake said, "Sounds like the fellow wants his oil changed more'n his windshield washed."

"You didn't have one of these in my time."

"They ain't much good, to tell the truth."

"The old hand signals are better, I bet."

"People get on 'em and carry on like what you're hearing. If a driver wants to know about the scale situation, he'll be in jail before he can get through to ask."

"What's your handle?"

"You'd never guess."

" 'Dixie Redball'?"

"Smart as a whip, ain't you?"

They slid from the cab, leaving the doors open so it would continue to air out, and walked up the slope to the picnic table beneath the trees where Jake had laid out the equipment he had uncovered in the basement the night before. Once the toolbox and the flares and the spare oil and the rest had been loaded, only their personal things would remain. The serious countdown had begun. Sonny felt a familiar tingle in his neck, one that visited him every time he heard a big rig changing gears, and he was as ready as he would ever be. There was a fleeting thought that they were about to embark upon something special, that maybe the ground that he and his father were going to cover on this trip would not be measurable in mere miles, that nothing was going to be the same for either of them when it was over.

"Way it turns out, I did the right thing this morning," Jake said as they lugged the heavy toolbox to the truck.

"Don't tell me Mama was watching Country Boy."

"*Somebody* did. Instead of the regular flowers in her room, there was roses."

"She's all right, then."

"Looked like a queen, son. Phyllis showed up, too, so they brought us lunch in the room."

"Phyllis?"

"Yeah, and Preacher Boggs."

"Charley must've worked something out, then."

"All right, now, heave." They slung the toolbox onto a platform between the cab and the fifth wheel, clamped it down, and walked back up the yard for more. "From the looks of everybody, I reckon he did. Boggs was carrying on about my generosity, and Mama was holding my hand, and Phyllis was wishing us a good time on the trip. I thought for a minute I might be in the wrong damned room."

"Money talks, I guess."

"Don't matter what kind of language you use."

The flares and spare oil and other necessities stowed wherever space could be found in the cab, they were stretching the mesh Confederate-flag bug screen over the grill of the truck and pinning it into place when Monk and Beulah Strickland came around the side of the house and strolled toward them. Beulah bore a picnic basket and a triumphant smile; Monk sidled along behind her, hands jammed in his pockets, grinning like he had known it all along.

"Lord," Beulah said, "I have to watch the 'Country Boy Show' to get your news, Jake."

"Saves a lot of time that way," Jake said.

"Here. I fixed y'all some traveling food." She lifted the lid of the basket to reveal cold fried chicken, makings for roast beef sandwiches, cole slaw, paper napkins, deviled eggs, and two large Mason jars of iced tea. "I figured Evelyn wouldn't mind my taking her place."

"Well, that's real kind of you, Beulah. This ought to get us through our first day. To Memphis, anyway."

Monk said, in his half shout, "Sonny, ain't you got business elsewhere?"

"It can wait," Sonny said.

"Thought maybe you didn't really want to go."

"No, I'm really looking forward to it, Monk."

"If it's just the company Jake needs, now, I was thinking maybe — "

"You're too old, Monk, and you got the garden to tend," said Beulah, turning to Jake. "The minute you told Country Boy about Nevada, he started acting like a fool. Even got out a *National Geographic* and started reading up on the place. I told him, I said, 'Sonny needs to be with his daddy on this trip, Monk, so you can just forget about it.' He came up with another idea, though. Go ahead and show 'em, hon."

Monk produced a leather pouch from his pocket and, holding it by its drawstrings, jiggled it. There was the clinking of silver. "Quarters," he said.

"Much obliged, Monk, but we got plenty of money for our gas and eats," Jake said, deadpanned.

"This is for the slot machines out there."

"You mean gambling? I don't know, Monk."

"It won't hurt nobody, Jake."

"Well, it don't sound very Christian to me."

"Damnit, Jake, how 'bout taking 'em and playing 'em for us without doing any preaching. Ain't no skin off your nose."

Jake took the cigar from his mouth and clucked and shook his head before taking the pouch. "You got to promise me you'll report your winnings to the Infernal Revenue. But don't mention my name."

"There's twenty of 'em in there. Now what I want you to do

is play the first five for Beulah, the next five for me, and the rest for Rickey and June. Try to keep the winnings in separate piles if you can, Jake, so it don't make nobody mad."

Charley Graddick called to say the trailer was loaded and to give Jake the exact weight he would be pulling. Phyllis called to say good-bye and that she would pray for them every day. Country Boy Eddie even called to say he wouldn't mind getting a postcard from along the way. And in the gloaming, with fireflies dancing around Dixie Redball IV as she glistened in the light of a quarter moon, Jake and Sonny sat at the picnic table in the backyard tearing into Beulah's fried chicken. A jet whistled directly over their heads, but they didn't bother to look up. They ate in silence, their minds on the open road that lay ahead of them like a lush black velvet carpet.

When Jake hit the sofa around ten o'clock, still in his clothes, he began snoring immediately. But Sonny, tossing and sweating on top of the covers, thought sleep would never come. His head swirled as he tried to project what might come of a journey that was looking like a good idea that had gotten out of hand. It now seemed foolish to him, in fact: rudderless, quixotic, dangerous, a no-win situation which would leave the few people remaining in Jake Hawkins's life damned if he pulled it off and damned if he didn't. Sonny envisioned neither a textbook trip nor a disaster, neither a seamless flight nor some ungainly capitulation, but something in between, and it was the in-between that worried him the most, for that would settle nothing. His father, this lion whose snoring from the den now fairly rattled the windowpanes, was about to go hand-to-hand with the world. *"Do not go gentle," my ass.*

= *Part Three* =

NEVADA

14

IN THE HOUR before dawn, moving through the house like cat burglars, Jake and Sonny went about their preparations. The only sounds were the slurping of coffee, the flushing of toilets, the rasp of a radio announcer reading news and weather, and the soft rattle of the screen door as they made trips between the house and the truck. They passed in silence, following flashlight beams across the dewy grass, rubbing sleep from their eyes, tossing bags into the cab of the truck, looking for omens in the inky sky, finally returning to the house for a last look around before unplugging the coffee pot, cutting the lights, and locking up.

Burrowing into the contoured truck seat, chewing his cigar, leaving the door of the cab open to pick up any strange nuances the engine might utter, Jake flipped the ignition. Junior Wages had done his work well. There were no fireworks this time, only the low guttural rumble of a bear coming out of hibernation, and when they shut the doors Jake, mindful of the hour, turned on the dim parking lights and found his lowest gear and slowly eased Dixie Redball IV from her nest. Only when he had bumped over the curb and turned onto the street did he bring the headlights to full beam. They caught Lee Riddle like a startled deer.

"What the hell's he doing?" Jake said, in a whisper, as though he might awaken the neighbors.

"Coming home from work."

"This time of morning? Kinda job is that?"

"There's lots to tell about Lee, Pop. Plenty of time to tell it." Jake blinked the lights, and Lee stepped back on the curb to wave halfheartedly as they passed.

Across the potholed side streets of east Birmingham, empty except for newspaper carriers and the first delivery vans and buses of the day, they jounced along in the darkest part of the day: the "dark thirty," the half-hour before daybreak. Once they reached Graddick & Sons Tire they saw Charley's white Cadillac parked in its place, the high barbed-wire gate left opened wide for them, a massive silver Great Dane trailer reflecting a single spotlight that gave the old stone building and the tire lot the appearance of a stockade. Jake drove through the gate, crunched across the gravel, and had begun to back the truck up to the trailer when Charley came out of the shadows.

"Figured you wouldn't mind doing a little free advertising for me," he said when Jake and Sonny had swung down from the cab. He held a fat roll of black electrical tape and two posters printed with the company name.

"After the 'Country Boy Show,' you ought to pay me for tooting your whistle for you."

"That was a hoot, Jake. I appreciate it."

"I'm much obliged for what you done for Evelyn."

"Where's your uniform?" Charley said, flashing a light on

Jake's khaki trousers and T-shirt. "You aren't going to go on the road representing me like that, are you?"

"That's for show, Charley. This is for work."

Charley had picked up a box of sausage biscuits, and he put it on the running board of the truck while Jake and Sonny busied themselves taping the Graddick & Sons posters on the doors. When that was done, Sonny fetched a thermos of coffee from the cab and took the biscuits and stepped aside with Charley as Jake, squinting through his wide side mirrors, lined up the fifth wheel and the trailer's hitch until they seated with a clang. Jake cut the engine, stepped on the platform between the cab and the trailer to connect the lines for lights and air brakes, and then jumped down to crank the trailer's landing struts up into its belly.

Tugging at his Graddick Tire baseball cap, flapping a T-shirt already soaked with sweat, he joined Charley and Sonny as they picnicked coffee and biscuits from the running board. "Six days on the road," he croaked.

"I hope you mean that," Charley said.

"Hell, two thousand miles oughten take but four."

"Just take it easy, Jake, that's all I ask. The inspection at Nellis isn't until next Thursday morning. You got eight days to drop these tires and get yourself to Vegas." Jake was admiring the rig, Redball, and the new Great Dane, like a boy and his Christmas bicycle. "You hear me, Jake?"

"Loud and clear."

"Turn it into a vacation. You and Sonny. Just like the old days."

"It ain't no vacation out there, Charley. Never was."

"I know that, Jake. I just want you to be careful, that's all."

" 'Careful' don't always get the job done."

"And give me a call, will you?"

"If I come across a phone booth in the middle of the desert, I'll do that, Charley. All it'll do is slow me down, though."

Charley laughed and shook his head. "Get out of here, will you?"

"Sounds like an order to me, Cap'n," Jake said, but it was to Charley's back. He was already walking away, in the first faint light of dawn, knowing that his part was finished.

Jake restarted the engine, left Sonny behind the wheel to flip the turn signals and pump the brakes, and began walking slowly around the rig with a flashlight to make his final inspection: signals, brakes, hoses, spare tires; trailer locked, twin fifty-gallon gasoline tanks secure. That accomplished, ready to roll, he motioned brusquely for Sonny to take the shotgun seat. Behind the wheel again, reorienting himself after being away from it for three years, Jake checked the play in the steering column and the positioning of the mirrors and the cant of his seat. Now changed from his cowboy boots to thin-soled moccasins, for a better feel of the pedals, he worked the clutch and the brakes and then ran through all of the gear positions. Finally satisfied, Redball rumbling at idle, he grinned at Sonny. A match flared and he bent over it, the deep lines of his face looking like a relief map of the tired old Appalachians, sucking on the cigar until it began belching smoke.

"Think you could drive this thing?" he said.

"No more now than thirty-three years ago."

"That how long it's been?"

"Almost to the day, Pop."

Jake hit the switch to turn on all of the lights, and suddenly the rig blazed like a roadhouse. "It's been a pretty good run," he said as he jammed the gearshift into low, checked his clearances, and began to ease Redball toward the gate of the lot. "I notice there still ain't nobody starving."

There was a hint of pink in the sky, a portent of rain, as Jake maneuvered the rig along the waffled streets of the bleak armpit side of the city, deftly timing it to beat every traffic light on the downtown truck route that took them past the small foundries and railroad sidings and warehouses representing Birmingham's last sad claim as a city of industry. His cigar had gone out again, as was the case ninety percent of the time, but he paid it no mind. Intense, leaning forward like a wizened jockey, squinting through the windshield, feverishly working the gears, seeing all things, immersed in a world of concrete and metal and smoke and road signs threatening danger at every turn, Jake was again in touch with all of his senses, alert to every pump of a piston, every flash of light, every jolt in the pavement, every whiff of gasoline exploding beneath the hood that shuddered before him.

It took an hour for them to hit open highway, when Jake left U.S. 78 just beyond the raw little railside town of Jasper, and even then they were on a two-lane stretch of asphalt filled with logging trucks, school buses, and farm tractors. Sonny remembered enough about that part of the ancient route connecting Birmingham and Memphis to realize that Jake was already making his first shortcut: choosing this route, with dangers of its own, over an even more perilous one with six towns strung out along a fifty-mile stretch. Jake was so bent over the wheel in concentration that Sonny didn't speak until he happened to notice, while absently pulling back the curtain of the sleeper, that the old Rita Hayworth cheesecake calendar for the year 1948 was riding with them.

"My God," Sonny said, "you been keeping that all these years?"

Jake grinned. "Come across it the other night. Mama'd made me stow it in the basement."

"Rita Hayworth. First love of my life."

"Too bad she went and married a rich A-rab on you."

"I gotta tell you, Pop, that damned thing made me nervous. Between that and the jiggling of the cab, I got my first hard-on."

"Well, then, that must've been about the time I gave you my famous advice about women."

"How can we forget? 'Always use a rubber, boy.'"

"Seems like you didn't pay a damned bit of attention, neither."

Sonny was afraid this was going to segue neatly into a preachment from Jake about his failed marriage, something he fervently hoped to avoid during the trip, but suddenly a more pressing worry came upon them. Jake had already geared down to forty miles an hour for the approach to Hamilton, the northwest Alabama town where they would meet up with U.S. 78 for the run through Mississippi to Memphis, when suddenly a logging truck crawled out of the piney woods like an old turtle that had decided to try the fast lane: sagging with pine poles, no taillights, no turn signals, no license tags; no flagman, no signs of Men at Work. With a steep blind hill straight ahead, and shoulders of only three feet on either side of the narrow country road, the only option Jake had was to stop before he hit the truck. Cursing through his teeth, chomping his cigar, furiously shifting the gears and applying the foot and air brakes, somehow letting loose a blast of the air horn through it all, Jake hung onto the steering wheel with both hands as Redball began to shimmy and burn rubber on a road still wet from morning fog. A jackknife became a very real possibility as the logging truck, its only safety measure being a red rag attached to the longest of the poles, loomed larger by the split second in the windshield of Redball. Sonny was rigid, both feet pushing through the floorboards, feeling his face contort from what felt like gravity forces. Redball shuddered and creaked, and an ominous thumping noise came from a trailer now rocking behind them under its load of jumbo tires.

The crisis was over as quickly as it had begun. Redball had nearly kissed the red flag, just somebody's dirty red bandanna, before the logging truck began to chug away from them. Jake pulled over onto the narrow shoulder and flicked on his emergency blinkers, his eyes blazing, and cut loose with a half-dozen bursts on the air horn at the logging truck as it belched smoke and wobbled to the top of the knoll. The middle finger of the driver's hand shot up in the air, just as a little yellow Toyota came zipping from the other direction at seventy miles an hour.

Jake's knuckles were white, in a death grip on the steering wheel, and for a full minute he sat staring straight ahead through the windshield. Acrid smoke drifted through the open windows from the truck's rear axles. Heat from the engine shimmered through the floorboards. There was a creaking from the trailer. Sonny leaned forward for a glance through the mirror on his side of the cab and saw ugly rubber scars stretching for at least a football field's length behind them, emitting little tails of vapor.

Finally, Jake took his hands from the wheel and shakily lit his cigar. "It may be too late for me to learn a respectable trade," he said.

"Jesus Christ, Pop. Those fucking tires could've killed us."

"Yep. Him, too."

"And then the sonofabitch gives you the finger."

"They ain't known for their manners up here."

Sonny was flustered. "What the hell is this, Pop? Two hours out, we damned near get wiped out, and you're cracking jokes."

"Truth of the matter is, son, I think I messed in my drawers."

The only real damage was to Jake's nerves. Jo-Jo had packed the tires into the trailer so tightly that when Jake unlocked the doors he found nothing out of place. "If they can survive a jolt like that," Jake said, "I won't be having to check on 'em again until it's time to take 'em off." While they waited for the brakes to cool they calmed down by walking off the adrenalin, smoking, kicking tires, and sliding down the steep embankment to relieve themselves in the bushes. On the ride through Hamilton, the courthouse clock showing eight o'clock, they found themselves scanning the side streets and the gravel lots of little diners for the battered logging truck that had nearly killed them all. Jake muttered about what he might do if he found the driver, brandishing the tire iron he kept on the floor of the cab for protection, but Sonny took it as nothing more than bravado.

A fine rain had begun to fall an hour later by the time they cleared Tupelo, in Mississippi, and spied the neon signs of Harold's Truck-O-Rama blinking through the gray mist at a busy crossroads community called Mock. The breakfast hour and the poor driving conditions had filled the huge asphalt lot with rigs of all sizes from all over America: a monstrous chrome Peterbilt from Ohio, a shabby little International from Georgia, boxy local delivery trucks, an Allied van with a sleeper as big as its cab delivering household goods from Pennsylvania, a refrigerated unit pumping away behind a sleek Freightliner hauling produce from the San Joaquin Valley of California, and, yes, skeletal logging trucks from the piney woods counties of eastern Mississippi. Far off in one corner of the lot was a hand-painted sign — Tourists Here — under which a scant dozen compact cars and station wagons were parked, leaving no questions about the pecking order at Harold's.

Jake backed Redball between a White cab-over diesel out of Virginia and a Mack from Texas with the curtains of its sleeper drawn, changed into his boots, donned his Graddick cap and windbreaker, dismounted, and locked up. He and Sonny strode across the lot, past the crowded gasoline islands, Jake pointing out a bumper sticker on a pickup truck (How's My Driving? Call 1-800-EAT-SHIT), and then opened the fogged glass door to the restaurant. What Sonny saw, once they entered the din, was the truck stop of his youth: the carousels of postcards and trinkets, the tables laden with goods ranging from gimme caps to cowboy boots, the clattering floor fans, the long Formica counter with a trucker at every stool, the dull, stainless-steel coffee urn now filmed with grease, the hubbub of the jukebox playing and men laughing and waitresses shouting orders and of forks being raked across plates. To one side of the front door, in an area marked Truckers Only, there was a bank of pay telephones beside a bulletin board with push-pinned advisories about jobs and loads and road conditions, and then a dank lounge where drivers lolled on fake leather sofas aimlessly watching others play pinball and shoot pool.

They walked across the pocked linoleum floor, beneath sputtering fluorescent lights, to take a torn red plastic booth below a framed poster of a cottonfield being harvested by slaves. The selections on the jukebox at the booth were limited to hard and pure country, from George Jones's drinking songs to Merle Haggard's "Okie from Muskogee," and when Sonny saw Dave Dudley's "Six Days on the Road" he couldn't resist.

Jake opened up the handwritten menu and moved it in and out, trying to focus. "Wonder if they got that quiche."

"I doubt if Harold approves of it," said Sonny.

"What the hell's quiche, anyway?"

"Egg pie, more or less."

Suddenly there appeared a fortyish waitress in a tight gold lamé jumpsuit, the name Loretta on a laminated tag above her left breast, in one deft movement pouring coffee into chipped earthenware cups and producing a pencil from her orange beehive hairdo. "What'll it be, fellas, breakfast or lunch?"

"I need to gas up," Jake said, poker-faced.

Loretta knew the game. "High octane or low?"

"Whatever'll get me to Missouri before dark."

"Pinto beans oughta do fine," she said, howling so that she almost lost her wad of gum.

"Beans, beans, the musical fruit . . ."

". . . the more you eat 'em, the more you toot."

Jake said, "Might need me a lube job, too."

"Honey, we've got enough grease to service a whole fleet of Peterbilts."

They settled for the $2.95 Trucker's Special Breakfast of ham and eggs and grits and biscuits, attacking their platters like wolves, paying little attention to the cacophony around them.

By the time they had finished, the mist outside had turned to a driving rain, sheets of it rattling the plate glass windows, and drivers who had decided to wait it out kept Loretta flying from booth to booth refilling cups with steaming black coffee. When Jake overheard the driver at the table nearest their booth mention to Loretta that he had begun the day in Memphis, he turned and asked about the weigh-station situation.

"We might be a tad heavy," Jake said.

"They were open around Holly Springs about an hour ago," the trucker told them. He was barely past thirty, clean-shaven and trim, wearing the pressed uniform of AstroFreight out of Wichita.

"Where it goes four-lane?"

"That's correct, yessir" — the "sir" made Jake twitch — "between the second and third exits."

"Didn't give you no trouble, did they?"

"Oh, nosir. I'm legal."

"Well," Jake said, lighting his cigar, "I reckon we'll have to run around 'em, then. You say it's this side of the Red Banks exit?"

"That's right. Yessir."

"Sonofabitch. That means we got to take fifteen miles of back roads just to get around the scales. Be Victoria before we can get back on."

"Maybe the rain drove 'em in. Maybe not."

"It's the maybe not that's worrisome," Jake said. "But look here, how's Arkansas? You must o' come through there yesterday."

"I did, yessir."

"The boys out?"

"Frankly, I didn't pay much attention. I'm legal everywhere."

Jake dripped sarcasm. "You don't say."

The driver ignored it. Looking directly at Sonny, he said, "If you don't mind my asking, how heavy are you?"

Sonny went blank, looked at Jake, and started to answer. Jake headed him off. "He weighs about a hundred-and-fifty, soaking wet. Me, I'm twenty-five goddamn thousand."

"Oh."

"It's all he can do to drive a little pickup."

"It's just that for a minute I thought — "

"You think I'm too damned old or something?"

"Well, nosir. No offense." The young driver seemed genuinely embarrassed, even muttering an apology, and when Jake told him about this load and Redball IV and the preceding forty years and three million miles he was flabbergasted. "You mean to say you're driving an old gas Dodge all the way to Nevada?"

"What's a few more thousand miles?"

"I just turned my first million, and I'm worn out already."

"What you got to do is pace yourself, son," Jake said, suddenly paternalistic. Sonny thought for an instant that he was going to reach over and pat the driver's hand. "Take 'em one day at a time. It ain't over 'til it's over. And all o' that."

"Well, old-timer," the driver said, reaching for his check and standing to go, then pausing. "You don't mind if I call you that, do you?"

"I've been called worse, son."

"Hell's bells." He broke into a broad grin and offered a handshake to Jake. "My name's Bobby McNeese, out of Wichita."

"Jake Hawkins. Birmingham, Alabama."

The driver sucked on his toothpick and tugged at the shiny bill of his uniform cap. "Keep 'er in the road, old-timer," he said.

"Much obliged, son," said Jake, watching to see if he would wince when they shook hands. "I fully intend to do exactly that."

This was not exactly starting out as a trip for the family album, nor for a trucker's manual. It took them more than two hours to cover the seventy-five miles from Harold's Truck-O-Rama to the Mississippi River bridge at Memphis. Jake was taking no chances with the Mississippi Highway Patrol, rain or no rain, so he had left U.S. 78 at the Holly Springs exit and for fifteen miles chugged along a potholed county road, busy with pickups and tractors, in order to avoid the scales that Bobby McNeese had told him about. As soon as he returned to the main highway at Byhalia, still smarting from being called "Pops" by Harold himself when he paid for breakfast, Jake promptly encountered traffic backed up for the last ten miles into Memphis by a rig that had jackknifed while trying to avoid a fender-bender involving two women in Toyotas.

Not until they had cleared Memphis, bumping over the old steel bridge that took them across the roiling Mississippi, could Jake finally drop Redball into high gear and start to roll. They had picked up U.S. 63, a "scenic route" according to the road signs, that would take them for 100 miles through the scrawny rolling Ozarks of northeastern Arkansas to the safety of southern Missouri, and only now was Jake able to sit back and enjoy the ride. It was two o'clock in the afternoon. In eight hours, including the stop for breakfast, they had covered only 280 miles.

The rain had stopped as they raced along the flat macadam highway, past roadside settlements with names like Gilmore and Tyronza and Marked Tree, and to the east Sonny could see the incongruity of a cluster of ante-bellum homes rising from cottonfields that spread along the sandy delta all the way back to the river. He had expected the first day out to be uncomfortable for both of them, unaccustomed as they were to the whole business, but the sun and the whistling wind on his pale skin lifted his spirits. Jake seemed better, too, as though the roughest part of the trip were now behind them. He had pushed his seat back as far as it could go, to stretch his legs for a while, and had donned his wrap-around aviator glasses.

"How's it going, old-timer?" Sonny said, having to shout above the steady noise.

Jake accommodated two barefooted boys standing beside the road, yelling and pumping their arms in the air, with a tug of the chain that delivered a blast of the air horn. He said, "You, too, huh?"

"I think that young driver was pretty impressed, once it sank in."

"Seems like I keep setting records everywhere I go. First, I was the oldest human being ever committed to that place in Mississippi. Now I'm the old man of the road. Might turn out to be a legend in my own time."

Among the many things Sonny was already recalling about life on the road, before they had even put in a full day, was the pace of conversation. Maybe it was different in an air-conditioned rig, without having to shout above the rush of the wind and the steady roar of the engine, but he doubted it. On the road, especially on a haul of this magnitude, there was plenty of time to talk. He would ask a question, or just try to make conversation, and it might be five minutes of Jake's shifting gears or struggling to light his cigar in the face of the wind or simply mulling it over before there would be a response.

So it took a while for him to find out, in more detail, the itinerary that Jake had laid out. His plan was to reach southern Missouri on this first day out, freeing him of any more worries about his weight, then heading almost due west for the remaining 1,600 miles or so. This night they should be up on the shelf of the Missouri plains and then would make a beeline on the old U.S. highways, the ones in red on the *Rand McNally Road Atlas* that Sonny had brought along for his own edification, riding across the wheat plains of lower Kansas until they met up at Dodge City with U.S. 50 — the Loneliest Road in America — for the drive across the high plains and the Rockies and, finally, the stark moonscape that was Utah and Nevada. If all went well, they would make the copper mine in Sarah, Nevada, in time to unload the tires on Monday, the sixth day out. Then they would hustle down to Nellis Air Force Base, near Las

Vegas, to bid on the lots of tires for Charley Graddick and, if successful, load them up and return to Birmingham over a more southerly route through New Mexico and Texas.

Sonny noticed an increasing number of big semis on this stretch of 63, many of them serious Freightliners and Peterbilts, the cross-country lords of the road in those days, some running so heavy that Jake was able to pass one now and then as they struck into the undulating foothills of the Ozarks. The highway was not exactly a trucker's dream, narrow, forested, and with blind rises every mile or so, and yet the eighteen-wheelers seemed to be seeking it out, entering the flow of traffic from obscure county roads from all directions. It had become a virtual caravan.

"Looks like they'd have scales along here," Sonny said. "The boys could have a field day."

"Yep," Jake said, "everybody here's overweight. Never thought I'd see the day I passed a Peterbilt."

"I haven't seen you use the CB to check things out."

"Don't have to." They had just passed another, groaning up a long steep grade around a cluster of state parks near the town of Black Rock, and Jake had burped the air horn to acknowledge the driver's moving over on the shoulder to let him pass. "These boys are running from the scales on both sides of us. I ain't got to call anybody up to see that."

Sonny got out the *Rand McNally*. He saw U.S. 167 about twenty-five miles to the west and Interstate 55, connecting Memphis and St. Louis, a full seventy-five miles to the east. He saw a lot of squiggly little gray lines, connoting poorly paved mountain roads, leading them to the road they now were on. "Jesus Christ," he said, "they must be *really* overloaded to do that."

"You've seen 'em busting their guts," said Jake.

"Some of 'em must be going hours out of the way."

"You can see I ain't been making up stories all these years, then."

"Well, how do they know the scales aren't here?"

"Truck stop talk. CB radios. Mainly, it's instincts. A real trucker can *smell* scales."

The sanctity of tourism might have played a part, too, in the state patrol's leaving northeastern Arkansas to its own devices. Soon after Jake had passed the first runaway-truck escape ramp they had seen on the trip, rumble strips announcing it with a *thrump-thrump-thrump* on a harrowing roller-coaster stretch of road south of Hardy, the hills came alive with billboards playing on the hillbilly theme: a Hatfield-McCoy drama at a summer stock playhouse, Hooten's Holler Motel, Dogpatch Yard Ornaments, Ozark Antiques, Arky Vittles diner, The Still liquor store. Driving the last fifteen miles to the Missouri line meant joining the flow of vans and campers and station wagons, loaded with kids and dogs and parents who had pretty much had it with driving, all turning off into motel parking lots in the late afternoon to call it a day.

Jake was ready to call it quits, too, from the look of him. It had been a hard day's work, nearly 400 miles in eleven hours, with only the one stop, exacerbated by the near crash with the logging truck in Alabama, the rain in Mississippi, and the twisting roadway of the scruffy Ozarks, and he was showing the tension of his return to the road: rubbing his eyes, wiggling his cramped toes, shaking out fingers that had gripped the steering wheel for too long, massaging his neck. He decided to stop at the first motel that hadn't already turned on its neon No Vacancy sign.

The Li'l Abner Inn, plopped right on the Arkansas-Missouri line, in Mammoth Spring, was available. When Jake saw that one of the Peterbilts they had seen earlier was already parked in the gravel out back, on a bluff overlooking the Spring River, he shifted down and wheeled in beside it. "If it's good enough for this old boy, I reckon it'll do for us," Jake said, sending

Sonny with Charley's American Express card and his own senior citizen's discount card from the American Association of Retired Persons to check them in while he battened down Redball: kicking tires, checking the oil, again opening the trailer doors for assurance that the load was okay, fetching their suitcases.

"Forty-eight damned dollars just to sleep?" Jake said when they had entered their room: cinder-block walls painted bilious green, rickety floor lamps, dank moldy carpeting, hillbilly spreads on the twin beds, fake paneled partitions separating them from rooms on either side, roaches in the shower stall.

"It was their last room."

"I'm of a mind to sleep in the truck."

"Choose your poison, Pop."

They ate the $10.95 fried mountain trout dinner at a touristy diner across the road, walked to The Still so Jake could buy a fifth of Old Crow bourbon, and at dusk settled in for the evening. It was a night without end: Jake collapsing early from the strain and the bourbon, snoring and hallucinating about the near miss with the logging truck, Sonny aimlessly watching the flickering black and white TV while sounds of children crying and parents shouting reverberated through the thin walls past midnight; water pipes clanging from toilets being flushed up and down the line; jalousied windows rattling from big rigs rolling by, making time, not thirty feet from where they lay. Four hundred miles down, sixteen hundred to go.

15

LIKE MOST of the shenanigans engineered by Jake Hawkins in a lifetime of marching to a drummer just a millisecond off the prescribed beat, the Critter Caper began with what was perceived as a mild affront, a queasy feeling that he was being screwed, but quickly got out of hand, escalating into a crusade, all in the name of consumer protection, that might have kept the Ozark Board of Tourism busy for a while had Jake not prevailed. Although he would refuse to see the connection when it was pointed out by Sonny later in the day, while they were rolling on toward Kansas and the owners of the Li'l Abner Inn were still trying to figure out what had hit them, Jake's blood enemy Ralph Nader would have been proud.

The first indication that something was afoot came when Sonny, his head pounding and his body aching from a restless night, awoke to daylight and a commotion coming from the bathroom.

"Pop?"

"Goddamned little boogers. Come here."

"You all right in there?"

"Gotcha, you little sonofabitch."

"Hey, Pop, what's happening?"

Jake emerged, already dressed for the road, but flushed and triumphant. One hand held a plastic tumbler, and the other was clapped over its mouth to keep the creatures from escaping. He held it to the window and inventoried his catch. "Three roaches, two crickets, some kind of spider," he said.

"You getting into entomology in your old age, or what?"

"What the hell's that?"

"Studying bugs."

"You might say so. Don't move." Jake lurched across Sonny's bed toward the lamp on the nightstand and in one movement trapped a moth. "That makes seven of the little bastards."

By the time Sonny had showered and dressed and they had taken their bags to the truck, Jake had stretched a cellophane wrapper taut across the tumbler and punched pinholes in it so his collection of creepy-crawlies, now grown to a teeming community of thirty-one, could live for yet a while longer. Then he sauntered into the lobby.

It was checkout time, seven-thirty, and a dozen sleepy travelers were milling around waiting for their bills to be toted up when Jake bulled his way past them and plopped the tumbler on the counter.

"My Lord," gasped the blue-haired old woman at the desk. "What's *that?*"

"It got kinda crowded in my room last night," said Jake.

"Eeuughhh" — she was sputtering — "*bugs*."

"Thirty-one of 'em, if they ain't started eating each other yet."

There was some giggling, whispering, and pointing from the other travelers. The proprietress nervously glanced at them and then said, "Those exterminators. I swear. If you'll give me your room number, sir, I'll have them come back today."

"Well, ma'am, that ain't gonna help me much."

"I'm *terribly* sorry, sir."

"I could be sweet-talked into forgetting about the whole thing, though."

"Sir?"

Jake turned so he could address her and the crowd at the same time. "Forty-eight dollars seemed like a lot of money to pay for just the two of us. Come to find out this morning that I was actually paying rent for thirty-three of us. Me and my boy here, plus thirty-one critters."

"Oh, this is ridiculous."

"Let 'em pay their own freight, I always say."

"Why, I never."

"Like I told you, ma'am, I could make a deal."

"What are you doing to me?"

"Take off a dollar a critter. That ought to put my bill in line. Seventeen dollars sounds more like it. And don't forget the ten percent I get off for being old."

Safely in Missouri and its softly rolling plains, where they would soon pick up U.S. 60 and be westbound for the rest of the way, Jake and Sonny figured the laughs of the morning justified the discomfort of the night. Jake's scam had worked, resulting in a room charge of only $12.20 at the Li'l Abner, once his AARP discount had been computed, and the appearance of more rain as they took the by-pass around West Plains failed to dampen his glee.

"No kidding, Pop, Nader would've loved it."

"Little liberal pissant like that?"

"Damn, you're stubborn," Sonny said. "You're the same way about Roosevelt. If it hadn't been for TVA, you would've been thirty before you saw a light bulb."

"I don't like being lumped in with neither one of 'em. All I was trying to do was teach the bastards a lesson."

"That's the fabric of Ralph Nader's life, Pop."

"Well, he talks funny."

At Cabool, rather than hold onto his cash by using one of Charley Graddick's credit cards, Jake opted for a muddy little independent no-frills service station where he could save three cents a gallon. The savings would come to less than four dollars, once the two fifty-gallon tanks and the main tank were replenished, but Sonny knew better than to bring it up. Instead, while Jake was working one pump and the scrawny young bones-and-hair station manager was pumping from the other, he went inside to use the restroom. Those places still had the usual array of condom machines, he noticed, displaying French Ticklers and Ribbed Passions, except that now a sign proclaimed a Family Planning Center and the wares were behind a hinged mirror with a warning: "If you find this material offensive, don't lift cover." *Always use a rubber, boy.* He got a Coke and a pack of Camels out of machines, and when he returned to the truck Jake was already revving her up, ready to head west.

"Ol' boy says he ain't sure, but I might be overweight for Missouri," Jake said as they pulled away. "Weight limit keeps changing."

"I thought we were safe now."

"He probably don't much know what he's talking about. We'll just to have to keep our eyes open."

"Hey, look" — Sonny saw a sign pointing north to Montauk State Park — "I wonder if Ozark Baseball Camp's still there. I didn't know we were that close."

"Fella told me about that, too, when I asked. Says they flooded the ball fields. Turned it into a Waste Stabilization Lagoon."

"What's that? Fancy name for a cesspool?"

"Says they call it 'Turd Pond' these days."

That was an ignominious end for such a place, they agreed, as Jake got Redball up to a steady sixty miles an hour on the crowded four-lane that would take them to Springfield and Joplin and ultimately into Kansas. This was proving to be the smoothest part of the trip so far, in spite of the rain, dense traffic, and the threat of an unannounced weigh station, and over the roar of the engine and the slapping of the windshield wipers they reminisced about baseball and the summer of Ty Cobb and, after a while, Lee Riddle.

"I used to dream about y'all making double plays together in the big leagues."

"Lee, maybe. Not me."

"Any rate, he was the sweetest shortstop these old eyes ever saw."

"Magic," Sonny said. "Pure magic."

"You mean he's just quit?"

"Given up on everything, Pop. I think he's in the process of killing himself the slow way."

Jake rolled the cigar in his mouth. "It must have scared you to see it."

"Well, sure. I mean, hell, he was my best friend. What do you expect?"

"What I mean is" — Jake cleared his throat and narrowed his eyes — "aw, hell, son, I don't know what I mean. Forget I said anything. Why don't you see what you can rustle up on the radio."

"No, Pop. Let's talk about it."

"We're close enough to St. Louis for KMOX."

The rain had abated to the point that Sonny could roll the window down all the way to feel the cool wind blowing into his face and hear the singing of the tires and the rhythmic *whump-whump-whump* of the telephone poles zipping by. "If you wanted to know if it was like looking in a mirror, the answer is yes," he said. "There's a funny thing about it, though. Lee didn't exactly come out and say it, but I got the idea that he thinks he would've come out better if he'd had a father like you to look up to. You know: somebody a little more exciting than a life insurance salesman."

"Walter did the best he knew how, I reckon."

"Maybe. All I know is the reverse side."

"I ain't sure I follow you."

"Well, shit, Pop. You can be overwhelming, you know? I mean, I was ready to run and hide back there at the motel this morning. Who would even think of some crazy-assed stunt like that, much less *do* it? You're a pretty goddamn exotic fellow if you don't know it."

"Some folks don't appreciate it. Your sister, for one."

"That's another matter. What I'm getting at is, you're a hard act to follow. Maybe Lee's got it all confused and turned around. Maybe he would've never even played ball in the first place if he'd had you around to keep reminding him about losing his nerve."

"Losing nerve."

"It seems to be a recurring theme."

"That so?"

"Jesus." Sonny slapped both hands on his thighs in exasperation. "In the last two weeks I've heard about a half-dozen morality tales dealing with the lack of nerve. The Greyhound driver, Uncle Zeb, truckers at Four Corners, Lee Riddle. Now it's me."

"That's right." Jake began tapping the brakes, checking the mirrors, gearing down. "Even you."

"Hey. What're you doing?"

"Truck stop's coming up. We got to eat sometime."

"Oh," Sonny said. "For a minute I thought we were gonna stop and have a heart-to-heart."

"Won't be none of those from me, son."

"Too late, anyway, seeing how I'm forty-five."

"Never believed in 'em much, myself."

"What, a sign of weakness?"

Jake hit the turn signal and took the wide gravel shoulder, then neatly wheeled into the parking area of a seedy little truck stop a half-hour east of Springfield. "You're the teacher, son, not me. You tell 'em. I show 'em."

The place, near a town named Seymour, might have had its moments as a full-fledged truck stop, but those days had passed with the construction of Interstate 44 out of St. Louis as the primary truck route through southern Missouri. When they had walked in at eleven o'clock in the morning, there was only a smattering of locals seated in the booths: farmers and local delivery truck drivers, mostly, sipping coffee and talking about fishing and the weather. Jake and Sonny, caught between breakfast and lunch, had loaded up on chicken-fried steak, beets, cornbread, and sweet iced tea. They had eaten quickly and in silence, the air between them grown foggy, and gotten back into Redball and rejoined the flow of traffic headed for Springfield and Joplin before noon.

Jake had told Sonny how the serious trucker's fascination with citizens' band radio had been short-lived, worth a couple of country songs and a bad movie before its demise, and now he could see why. In the early afternoon, when the rain had picked up again as Jake maneuvered his way around Joplin, he was fiddling with the CB and found that it had virtually gone public. It might not be of much use anymore to a trucker wanting to find out directions or weather conditions or about the scales, he could see, but it certainly had its place in popular American culture. In one ten-mile stretch of road, as Jake worked Redball on county roads north of Joplin to avoid the known permanent weigh stations, he listened while two truckers fought for the services of a hooker speaking from her van at a big truck stop on the Interstate, a fellow with the handle of "Chicago Willie" delivered an outraged monologue about his marriage, and a self-proclaimed country songwriter auditioned his latest composition, "Yellowbird Blues," which had to do with various amphetamines. Another voice was trying to break in, to say a few words about Jesus, when Jake suddenly hit the brakes.

"My, my," he said, frantically shifting down.

"What's happening?"

"The boys. Out in the middle of nowhere."

A half mile ahead, on a county road that shot like an arrow to the Kansas line not four miles away, portable scales had been set up on the broad shoulder. A semi was already there, backing up to be weighed on scales the size and configuration of baseball bases, under the eyes of two state troopers wearing wrap-around sunglasses and ponchos that billowed in the breeze. The lights atop their patrol cars were flashing madly, and a portable sign was blinking All Trucks Stop, the lights glistening off the rain-slickened roadway.

Jake muttered, kept braking with his gears, and began working his cigar in earnest. "Get up in the sleeper fast," he yelled to Sonny.

"What?"

"Get the hell behind the curtain. You're drunk."

"This is the eighties, Pop. This shit won't fly anymore."

"We'll just see about that. Now get up there fast, before they see you. I want you dead drunk. Put your experience to work."

Sonny crawled up into the narrow sleeper of the cab, wriggling like the snake he felt he was becoming, and pulled the curtain tight behind him. From the stultifying little cocoon he now shared with Rita Hayworth, smiling somewhere in the dark in her satiny negligee, he held his breath and strained to hear the play unfold. There was the sound of the other rig revving up and easing away, of Jake edging Redball forward, of the air brakes wheezing, and of the gears being set in neutral and the emergency blinkers beginning to click as the rig came to a full halt.

"Boy, am I glad to see y'all," Sonny heard Jake say.

"Need to see your paperwork, please-sir."

"Paperwork."

"License, permits, bill of lading, logbook."

"I got my senior citizen's pass if that'll do you."

"Come on, old-timer, we ain't got all day."

"I'd help you out, Cap'n, if I knew where it was at."

"You can't be running around the country without papers, old man."

"He didn't tell me about no papers."

"Who, this Graddick you're driving for?"

"Naw, the driver of this damned thing."

"What're you talking about?"

"All I wanted to do was see the Rockies before I die," Jake said. "See, my boy's the trucker. I'm just a retired plumber from Birmingham. Ain't never been west of the Mississippi. Well, when the doctors told me I might not make it to Labor Day he got himself this little ol' load o' tires just so I could ride along and see the Rockies."

"I'm sorry to hear about that, grandpa, but we've got our job to do. The driver sleeping? Is that it?"

"What I was going to tell you about, Cap'n."

"Come on, let's go. Wake him up."

"Play hell doing that. He's passed out drunk. Commenced to drinking around breakfast, and that's when I took over. Didn't have no idea he was taking my death so hard. Last thing he did before he crawled up in the sleeper and passed out was show me some gears."

"All right, all right," the trooper said. "Back it up onto the scales. We might as well weigh you while you try to wake him up and find the papers."

"Well, that's gonna be a problem, Cap'n."

"You overran the scales. Back her up."

"Naw, see, he didn't show me reverse."

Curled up in the sleeper, trying to keep his composure, Sonny heard the two troopers converse. He heard that other rigs had been caught in their trap and were lined up behind Redball, impatiently awaiting their turn at the scales, and he gathered that the troopers weren't too keen on moving the four portable scales in the rain just to weigh one truck loaded with old tires and driven by some old codger who wouldn't shut up.

The trooper who had done the talking said, "We know what you're up to. You're trying to avoid the scales on the Interstate like all the others."

"No, sir," Jake said. "I'm looking for it."

"The Interstate? Toll booth *and* scales? That's a new one." Both troopers laughed.

"My thinking is, there ought to be a big enough lot there so I can park this damned thing and let the boy sleep it off."

"All right, then, goddamnit. We'll let Kansas worry about you. What you do is drive straight ahead about five miles 'til you get to Galena, then head south. That means turn left, to you. You got it?"

"Left at Galena. South, in other words."

"Stay on that road for six miles and you'll run right into the Travel Plaza."

"Probably will, Cap'n, if I don't get the hang of the brakes."

"Get the fuck out of here."

Two successful scams in one day had made a new man out of Jake. When he rolled away from the troopers he gave them several blasts on the air horn and did some fancy double-clutching just to give them something to remember him by, and when he hit the Kansas line he rumbled through Galena like a runaway train. He didn't want anything to do with I-44, which became the Will Rogers Turnpike to Tulsa when it entered Oklahoma, not with its toll fees, weigh stations, and Travel Plazas crawling with the station wagon crowd. He wanted the barren little two-lane country roads that would take him through the sparsely settled land along the Kansas-Oklahoma border that only a wheat farmer could love.

Kansas. It seemed fitting that the clouds would evaporate in the infinite cobalt sky as soon as they struck across the undulating plains, moving toward the heartland of the wheat country past wild roadside growths of giant sunflowers and rolling fields dotted with the specks of Herefords and Angus and the stark silhouettes of lonely irrigation windmills laboriously pumping away. They had enjoyed their laughs about the Missouri troopers, slowing only for caution lights in the little farming communities with names like Edna and Tyro and Peru, stopping only in Coffeyville to observe the monument jutting into the street that marked the spot where the Dalton Gang tried to rob its last bank, Sonny nestling into the shotgun seat and Jake puffing his cigar and squinting into the blazing afternoon sun through his aviator glasses. And now, for the first time, they were running flat-out: past golden wheat shimmering in the hot breeze, skunks and possums dead on the road, skeletal bleachers at a county rodeo, gnarled tire carcasses flung from other rigs littering the highway, vultures fleeing from Jake Hawkins's growling approach, butterflies giving their lives on the windshield, farmers paying them no mind from their glass, air-conditioned tractor cabs. Movin' on.

Jake began to flag a bit around six o'clock, as they approached the Kansas Turnpike south of Wichita, blinking his eyes, rubbing his neck, slapping himself in the face. Once, using the old trick from the first trip he had taken more than thirty years before, Sonny reached up and pulled the air horn chain to jolt Jake from his reverie. The sun was dead ahead of them now, an orange ball descending quickly toward a horizon shimmering with heat waves, and Sonny noticed that the old man was getting a trucker's sunburn on his left arm and the left side of his face after having been exposed to prolonged sunlight for the first time in three years.

"I could eat a dead cow about now," Jake said as they passed a billboard welcoming them to Sumner County, "Wheat Capital of the World."

"From the looks of the cattle we've been passing, the steaks ought to be great, all right."

"You never can tell. They might import 'em."

"How so?"

"One time I was broke down in the middle of Iowa," Jake said. "Told myself, 'Boy, howdy, I'm gonna eat me some real pig now.' Hell's bells. For three days I ate that processed ham that comes in a can. Same thing with their corn, too. Turns out they send their pigs and corn off to Chicago or Kansas City, and when it comes back they don't even recognize it."

"Sounds a lot like kids who leave the farm for the city. They come back different, too."

"Not near as good as the original?"

"Totally unrecognizable form. Packaged and processed."

"That's pretty good, son. You got a way with words, you know that?"

"I've been told. A time or two."

"Reckon where you learned it at?" Jake said, suspending his cigar in the air, expectantly. "School?"

"Looking at the world through a windshield," Sonny told him.

"What I figured you'd say."

After the experience in Arkansas the night before at the Li'l Abner Inn, Jake decided to take a chance at a Travel Plaza on the Kansas Turnpike where the odds were better that the truckers would outnumber the tourists. They hadn't passed a place that even resembled a real truck stop since Harold's Truck-O-Rama, and both he and Sonny had their hopes up as Jake, refusing to drive as far as fifteen miles on a toll road, took instead a rocky county farm road to reach the plaza more or less through the back door. Spirits high, another 400-mile day behind him, Jake briskly parked Redball between a pair of towering Freightliners and strode across the newly paved parking lot to the main desk of the motel-restaurant.

*

"Pop, you won't be worth a damn tomorrow if you sleep in the truck."

"The hell I won't. I been doing it all my life, even before I had the sleeper."

"Yeah, but you were younger. Look, it's just for one night."

"Naw, much obliged. You go ahead, though, seeing as how we already paid the bastards. Look over there, would you? Don't they see the damned sign that says Truckers Only?"

"I guess you could go tell 'em, if it bothers you that much."

"Anybody that'll come in here and pay good money for this crap ain't got sense enough to listen. Eighteen dollars for a damned frozen steak. I should o' known something was wrong when I saw that trucker walking back across the road with a box of Colonel Sanders."

"Well, look. Why don't you get another beer and we'll go shoot some pool. You'll feel better then."

"They call it 'billiards' here."

"Come on, Pop. Pool's pool."

"Not on orange tables, it ain't."

"Okay, how about some pinball in the game room?"

"It ain't pinball, it's them video games. And you gotta get in line behind them kids to play. And on top of that, they won't let you smoke."

"Ah, shit. Promise me you'll at least come by and use the shower in the morning."

"If you'll clear the critters out first, I will."

Jake's spirits had come crashing to the earth the minute he saw the phone-booth room for which he had paid fifty-two dollars. This was the new American motel, a flimsy chain-operated eyesore of prefabricated aluminum, frozen food, and Muzak that bore no kinship to the quaint caravansaries of his memory, and he was having nothing to do with it. Only Sonny's insistent pleading that they both needed to eat and sleep kept him from demanding his money back and stalking out to the truck and driving into the blue Kansas night only to find, as Sonny argued, more of the same. They didn't make truck stops like they used to, Sonny mused as he walked down the long corridor, past identical drapes drawn to reveal identical rooms in which the same people watched the same television show. Nor truckers, either.

With Jake bedding down in Redball for the night, and thus out of earshot, it was a perfect time for Sonny to give Charley a progress report. Charley sounded agitated at first, having just sat down to the dinner table at home in Birmingham, but when the operator said where the call was from he couldn't accept the charges fast enough.

"Kansas? Godamitey, he's trying to set a record."
"It's been a hell of a show, Charley."
"You mean Redball hasn't broken down?"
"Running like a sewing machine."
"He's not tired?"
"Charley, the old man's having the time of his life."

It took a while for Sonny to finish telling of the near miss with the logging truck and the great Critter Caper at the motel and the shenanigans with the Missouri troopers, because Charley was in hysterics. Sonny thought Charley had laughed himself dry, that there were no more tears left, but when he reported that Jake was spending the evening in the sleeper of the truck rather than bed down in an overpriced haven for tourists Charley came unhinged again.

"Well," Charley said, "there's still the rest of Kansas. That ought to slow him down."
"It's gonna be a scorcher."
"How about you? You okay?"
"To tell you the truth, Charley, there were times before we left that I thought this whole thing was sheer folly. I just figured it was something he had to get out of his system, you know?"

"I wouldn't exactly call twenty-five thousand dollars' worth of my tires a folly."

"You know what I mean, Charley."

"We discussed that, all right." Somebody was calling Charley back to the table. "Well, look here, Sonny. I still think my original thinking was right. Your daddy's gonna wear out in due time. If Kansas don't get him, Utah will."

"I suppose you're right. But after these first two days — "

"Aw, hell, he's had three years to rest up. He'll break."

"That's something I forgot to ask you about, Charley. If he does break, I mean *really* break, starts acting crazy, what the hell am I supposed to do? Make him abort?"

"Wouldn't be the first time a trucker quit. But don't use that word around Jake."

"I'm not that dumb. But what happens? Do I make him park the trailer, or what?"

Charley went silent for the first time, as though he hadn't thought about such a possibility. "Damned if I haven't put you in a pickle, son."

"You're telling me."

"Nobody's gonna *make* Jake Hawkins do anything."

"Especially his son."

"Well, look here, Sonny" — Charley cleared his throat and somebody said something about dinner getting cold — "do the best you can. Keep your eyes on him, and keep calling me."

"Thanks a bunch, Charley."

16

IN THE GIFT SHOP of the restaurant, Sonny discovered a rack holding a score of original paperbacks published by OK Press. The books were fanciful little dramas, half fact and half fiction, about a bountiful array of masculine heroes connected with the South and the Southwest: Davy Crockett, Geronimo, Sam Houston, John Wayne, even Louis L'Amour himself. Sonny bought a dozen of them, including slick photographic albums on rodeo cowboys and truckers, and spent the evening hours perusing them in his room after the call to Charley. He had to admit they were no more and no less than E. J. Hardison had advertised, loose on facts but high on drama, and he figured he might be able to produce a 50,000-worder on Billy Bowlegs over the rest of the summer were he so inclined. OK Press's authors, so far as he could discern, were the dime novelists of their time.

When he awoke at seven o'clock the next morning, to the

wailing of children, the slamming of doors, and the cranking of station wagons, he slipped into his jeans and a T-shirt and sneakers, not knowing whether Jake had tried the door during the night, and stepped outside into the broiling sun to track him down. More than half of the rigs of the night before were gone, including the Freightliners sandwiching Redball, and those that remained were being tended to by their drivers as Sonny walked across the hot pavement. When he reached Redball he slapped his palm on the cab and shouted for Jake through the half-opened window.

Jake was a wreck: eyes bleary, hair askew, T-shirt sopping wet. He literally rolled out of the sleeper, becoming entangled with the curtains as he descended and the gear shift when he landed, and he swung open the door gasping for air. A pile of crushed beer cans littered the floorboards. "I thought it was Truck Stop Annie again," he rasped, sitting sideways on the wide truck seat, blinking and cradling his head in his hands.

"At your age?"

"Them gals ain't particular, far as I can tell."

"I wouldn't go home bragging if I were you."

"Nothing to brag about. We just talked."

He had persuaded one of them to join him in the cab around midnight after her business slowed, he said, simply because it had been a while. She was a waif from Tulsa, eighteen years old, already with a vivid tale of abandonment, wandering, drugs, and various degradations. They had sat up in the cab for an hour, swapping life stories, drinking beer, and listening to the all-night truckers' show over WWL in New Orleans, "The Road Gang," about the only place on the dial where one could hear the country music of the forties and fifties anymore.

"Name of Darlene," Jake said. "She was a right spunky little thing."

"I can imagine. Christ, Pop, you should've come and gotten me."

"You ain't *that* horny."

"Call it research. Americana."

"Then that'd make two of us with the wobblies this morning. Now's when I wish I'd taught you how to drive a truck. Don't know how far I'm gonna get today."

Jake took his time preening himself and the truck, and it took forever for them to get breakfast in the motel cafeteria, something Jake reluctantly agreed to only because the "only way a body can screw up grits and eggs is out of meanness," so it was nearly nine o'clock before they got on the road that day. It was a Friday, and it was going to be a scorcher as they headed for the high plains of western Kansas in hopes of making it to the cooler air of Colorado before they fried. They would pass the halfway point of the trip in the early afternoon, about the time they picked up U.S. 50 at Dodge City, putting them on schedule to reach the mine in Nevada on Monday afternoon. His bursting head aside, Jake's only concern seemed to be how Redball would take the heat that was in store for them that day.

Jackrabbits and black racer snakes, not as quick as their reputations, replaced skunks and turtles as the prevailing dead-on-the-roads once Jake had wiggled back onto U.S. 160. They were on the pure Kansas plain now, imperceptibly gaining altitude as the telephone and power poles clicked off the miles, rocking through tiny crossroads farming communities with their flat Midwestern names of Milan and Danville and Harper painted on silver water tanks gleaming in the blistering sun of early summer. The view through the windshield was a split screen, an artist's rendering, of golden wheat on the bottom and endless blue sky on the top, with a horizon broken only by windmill-operated water pumps, stark white grain elevators known as Kansas Skyscrapers, and skeletal praying mantislike contraptions on wheels, spraying the fields with water so precious that men kill for it out there. And that is precisely what the country was called, Out There, by those who had been overwhelmed by its sheer breadth and emptiness. Counties named Comanche and Kiowa. Ruts meandering over the horizon, the Chisholm and the Santa Fe trails, just as the lumbering Conestogas had left them one hundred years earlier. Alfalfa, wheat, corn, soybeans. A lone farmer aboard an air-conditioned thresher, raising eddies of dust, seen from three miles off. A little yellow biplane crop duster, looping the loop and coming in at ten feet off the ground, trying to beat the grasshoppers to the wheat. The words Keep Out whitewashed on tires affixed to a barbed-wire fence surrounding a spread the size of a whole county in, say, Georgia. And the heat, the relentless breath-sucking heat, ninety-seven degrees according to a digital bank sign at midmorning as Jake and Sonny cruised through Medicine Lodge.

Sonny had never experienced such heat. In Tallahassee there was the breeze coming up from the Gulf, swimming pools everywhere, and the air conditioning at both his apartment and the college, but here there was no escape. He had tried to tame the hot wind rushing into the cab of the truck, first by cracking the window an inch or so and then by rolling it all the way down, but either way it was like sitting beside a blast furnace. He had begun to strip, one article of clothing at a time, until soon he was down to his jeans and a bandanna tied around his forehead to keep the sweat out of his eyes, with his bare feet propped on the dashboard to escape the heat pounding up from the engine well. Since they had found nothing of interest on the radio at this time of day, and the CB frequency seemed to have been discovered by kids, housewives, and jackleg preachers, he absently watched Kansas roll by and skimmed through the stack of OK Press paperbacks he had placed beneath his seat.

Sweating, himself, but preoccupied with staying alert for stray livestock and the occasional eastbound cattle rig coming at him on the narrow highway, Jake seemed to want to talk. "Geronimo," he said. "That got something to do with your teaching?"

"It's just an interest of mine."

"Saw a movie on him one time. Kirk Douglas did him, I think it was."

"Jeff Chandler."

"Believe you're right." Like a one-armed juggler, steering with his elbows and guessing where his cigar was, Jake lit up. "Who wrote the book?"

"It says Jesse Dalton, but that's got to be a *nom de plume*."

"'Nahm-day-ploom.' That's a good'un. Saw it in a crossword one time. Means 'pen name,' don't it?"

"You got it."

Sonny told Jake all about E. J. Hardison and OK Press and the proposal that he crank out an original paperback on Billy Bowlegs. Jake seemed astonished that Sonny would hesitate. "It ain't exactly like writing for the *Reader's Digest*, you understand, but it beats being on somebody's payroll."

"You might be right, Pop. I don't know."

"Don't know? Hell, coming back, we could run right through Sallisaw and make the deal."

"This guy sounds like a Hadacol salesman on the phone. Which reminds me. I owe you for a phone call."

"Might turn out to be the call that makes you a free man, son. Since that bitch is off your back and your kids are growed up, looks like you can do anything you want to now."

"I want it to be right, though."

"Hell, one thing leads to another. Take me and the coal, now — "

"This is different, Pop."

"Ain't that much difference."

"It sounds degrading, a book like this."

"You want to hear about 'degrading'? During the Depression, I had my choice: I could go off and work on one of them damned CCC camps that Roosevelt dreamed up, or I could dig my own coal out of my own hole in the ground and deliver it in my own truck. Wasn't near the money I could've made, working for that rich sonofabitch Roosevelt, but by God it was mine. And then, because I had me a truck when the war came, here I am. There's plenty to be said for being your own boss."

"I appreciate your sentiments, Pop."

"It takes a lot of guts to try it now."

"Right. The old nerve again. Uncle Zeb and the bus driver and them."

"Might be a little off to say it, son, but you could be running the risk of turning into another Lee Riddle."

"Wait a minute, Pop."

"Like I said" — Jake waggled his cigar in a manner that had begun to unnerve Sonny — "we can do Sallisaw coming back."

"Goddamn you." Sonny muttered it, bit it off, but he had spoken loud enough to make himself heard over the rush of wind and the roar of the engine.

Jake looked stunned, as though he had been slapped in the face. The cigar was poised, like a question mark. "Say what?"

"You heard me. I said god*damn* you."

"What's eating on you?"

"You're a fucking cowboy, just like Phyllis said."

"Doubt if she said it like that." Jake cackled in falsetto: "Yippy-ti-ki-yo, I'm a lonesome — "

"Cut out the bullshit and listen to me for a change, Pop. I'm not some guy you ran into at a loading dock. I'm your son. I've already heard your stories."

"That mean you don't want to better yourself?"

"See there? That's what I'm talking about. 'Better yourself.' 'Where's your nerve?' "

"Well, hell's bells, son — "

"You think life's a country song, don't you? No grays, just black and white. Good guys, bad guys, simple solutions to everything. 'If you can't stand the heat, just get out of the kitchen.' Damned if you don't have a homily for everything."

" 'Homily.' Got a nice ring to it."

"Damnit, Pop, stop the clowning and listen to me." Sonny wondered why this had taken forty-five years. "Phyllis wasn't that far wrong when she said cowboys are fine on the movie screen but they're hell to live with. She and Mama have sure paid the price, cleaning up your messes. But, by God, so have I."

"I don't know what you mean by 'messes.' "

"It's been a psychic thing for me, Pop, and I may have suffered as much as anybody."

"That mean I ain't been a good father?"

"Ah, shit" — *how do you say it?* — "yes and no. You're honest and hardworking and a hell of a truck driver and all of that."

"Looks to me like that'd be enough."

"No, it's not, damnit. I told you yesterday after you'd pulled that crap at the motel with the bugs that you're a tough act to follow. You think there's just one way to live, and that's your way. 'Everybody off the streets, Jake Hawkins has arrived.' " Jake kept trying to cut in, but Sonny wouldn't let him. "I'm talking now, Pop, and I'm going to finish. The mess you've left *me* to clean up is one you can't see. What you're doing is asking me to live my life, which turns out to be words and ideas, like it was just another load of tires. You're trying to tell me that it don't amount to shit if you can't weigh it, load it, haul it, and unload it."

"It's been good enough for me — "

"Yeah, yeah, and there ain't nobody starving."

"Well, it's the truth. If you'd been a trucker, you'd o' — "

"I'm not a trucker, Pop. Maybe my life would've been simpler that way."

"You might've been a good'un."

"We'll never know. All I'm asking is for you to quit equating earth-mover tires with Shakespeare."

Jake cleared his throat and finally stuck the cigar in his mouth. "Like I said, we can do Sallisaw coming back."

"Let's see how it goes. I got plenty of time to think about it."

Sonny tucked the book beneath the seat with the others and looked up in time to see them being welcomed to Coldwater, elevation 2,100 feet, where the highway abruptly made a ninety-degree turn to take them through Greensburg en route to Dodge and U.S. 50. "Jesus Christ," he said, changing the subject, "this must be what it was like, working at the Sloss Furnace."

"I usually did Kansas at night," Jake said, rolling his shoulders and flexing his hands, still trying to straighten out the kinks from spending his night in the cab. "It ain't so bad when the sun's gone down. Gets downright airish, in fact."

"How long since you've been out here?"

"Western Kansas? Maybe ten years. Redball IV was brand-new."

"Looks to me like you would've paid a little more and gotten air conditioning," Sonny said.

"Too damned expensive. I didn't come out here that much, anyway, after I bought this one. You just got to tough it out."

"Well, air conditioning would be nice."

"A lot of things would be nice."

Jake, even while they talked, had been keeping a close eye on his gauges, frowning and muttering to himself during lulls, and when Sonny leaned over for a glance at the dials he saw that they hadn't been making fifty miles an hour, not even on the flat stretch of forty miles that had run from Medicine Lodge to Coldwater without a single town between the two.

"Trouble?"

"Hard to tell," said Jake.

"From the way the wheat's bending, it's windy out."

"We've been running right into a twenty-mile-an-hour headwind. It's always like this."

"We seem to be climbing, too."

"Seems I heard you climb about five feet a mile out here. It adds up." Jake double-clutched and grabbed the next lower gear, but nothing happened. "Come on, damnit," he said.

"Redball okay?"

"Probably needs some looking into. I'm hoping to make Minnie-Lou's without stopping."

"Who's Minnie-Lou?"

"It stands for Minnie and Lou Dahmer."

"A truck stop, then."

"Minnie-Lou's is more than that," Jake said. "They're about two of the best people I ever met. Back when I was running refrigerated to California, I was known to drive all the way across Kansas without stopping just so I could make it in time for supper."

"I hope it's coming up soon."

"It's still four more hours if Redball don't act up. Right near the Colorado line."

"Please tell me," Sonny said. "Air conditioning."

"Got them big floor fans, anyway."

"The kind that sound like jets taking off?"

"Same ones," said Jake. "Steaks as thick as your arm, and Lefty Frizzell on the jukebox. And ol' Lou knows his trucks about as good as Junior Wages does."

The prevailing rule of thumb about gaining five feet in elevation for every mile of roadway headed west was holding true. At Greensburg, where the water still came from a 109-foot-deep well dug by hand in the 1880s, the town limits sign gave the elevation as 2,240 feet. Steadily rising, pushing toward the sky, seeing more traffic now as they neared Dodge City, they began to pass giant feed yards where as many as 4,000 cattle were being fattened for slaughter in mucky corrals that could be smelled from five miles away. More wheatfields, more grain elevators, more jackrabbits; now running beside the Arkansas River and the railroad tracks. Dodge City: old Fort Dodge barracks, major railyard teeming with cattle cars, tourists in Bermuda shorts swarming all over Boot Hill and a tacky "restoration" of Dodge with their cameras and credit cards, El. 2,500. And, finally, at Dodge City, they rolled onto U.S. 50.

It was around three o'clock in the afternoon, now Mountain Daylight Time, the sun at its hottest, when Jake spied the rusted old blue and white Pure Oil sign being buffeted by the wind of the high plains less than ten miles from the Colorado line: Minnie-Lou's Truck Rest. Those signs were collector's items now, Pure Oil having become Union 76 some years earlier, but he knew Minnie and Lou Dahmer to be cantankerous enough not to change it for the very reason that some corporation said to. Clucking and smiling at the sight, still a mile ahead of him, Jake checked the mirrors and began the process of bringing Dixie Redball IV to heel: hitting the turn signals, tapping the brakes, gearing down, flipping on the air brakes, blasting the air horn in case there were any doubts as to his intentions, finally easing off the highway onto the shoulder and then rolling into the empty gravel parking lot that once had held as many as twenty big rigs at a time.

Puzzled by the stillness, changing into his cowboy boots and a pearl-buttoned long-sleeved shirt, Jake slid from the cab and surveyed the place. Where once there had been four gasoline islands, each sheltered by its own corrugated tin roof, now only two pumps sat mutely in the searing heat. The Pure Oil sign rocked and squeaked in the wind whistling down from the distant foothills of the Rockies. Nestled in a grove of trees, like a slain dinosaur, there was the low-slung white adobe building that since the early fifties had beckoned truckers like an oasis, no matter the time nor the weather: steaming coffee, great gobs of heavy food, loud country music, sassy waitresses, telephones, bunkhouses out back, Minnie and Lou Dahmer themselves.

Jake tugged the bill of his Graddick Tire cap, motioned for Sonny to follow, and slumped across the gravel to the twin plate-glass doors. They, like the picture windows that stretched all across the front of the place and wrapped around the sides, were caked with dust. Wiping a circle clean with his shirt-sleeve, Jake peered inside to find a sea of white bedsheets covering the long counter, the tables, the jukebox, the coffee urn, the cash register, and the floor fans in every corner of the place. Beside the doors was a hand-printed note, "Restaurant Closed — Ring for Gas Beer — M. Dahmer." Jake pressed the buzzer and stepped back, lighting the stub of his cigar, turning to watch a Kenworth diesel smoke past on the highway with a reefer rocking in tow. Sonny toed the gravel with his moccasins and squinted into the sun to see a hawk soaring on the thermals.

"What'll it be, boys?" They were startled to hear a voice in the stillness of the plains, and when they spun they saw a woman in tight jeans and a man's blue work shirt and cowboy boots. Her face burned and freckled from the incessant wind and sun, her steel gray hair secured in a ponytail by a bandanna, she had come around the west side of the building and was heading toward them. With her was a German shepherd on a leash strapped to her wrist.

Jake took the cigar from his mouth and stared at the woman, a cockeyed smile playing on his face. "We was hoping for the works," he said.

"About all I got these days is beer, ice, and gas."

"Won't your Wurlitzer play no more?"

She paused. "Lord, no. Can't you see we're closed up now?"

"Be damned. And here I've come all the way from Alabama."

She gasped. "I don't see no banjo on your knee."

"Well, you wouldn't happen to have none of them big El Productos, would you?"

She came toward them now, the German shepherd growling and straining at the leash, and when she got close enough to Jake she stopped and cocked her head and looked directly into his eyes. "Jake?"

"Me and Dixie Redball are thirsty, both."

"It *is* you. You old rascal."

"I come a thousand miles to see y'all, Minnie."

"Lou would appreciate that, Jake. He sure would."

"Well, where's he at?"

"Out back, Jake. What was left of him."

Over the next hour, Sonny felt like an outsider, a friend of a friend of a friend who had been invited to a family reunion. Stories of people and places and events flew back and forth between Jake and Minnie Dahmer as the three of them sat in the darkened living room of her adobe bungalow, cooled by a window air-conditioning unit, sipping iced tea, stuck back under the trees behind what once had been Minnie-Lou's Truck Rest. From the way they carried on, touching and eying each other long after their laughter had run its course, Sonny had a fleeting thought that perhaps there had been more than just a highway friendship between his father and this tough woman of the plains, one whose life was a world away from that of Evelyn Hawkins, "the only woman this old man ever loved," with her churches and sewing circles and begrudging acceptance of his life as a man of the road.

Later, beneath sycamores behind the house, they sat on stone benches around a grotto whose centerpiece was a stone cross marking the grave of Louis Grist Dahmer. Grasshoppers and locusts played in the trees and the tall brown weeds as Minnie told of what had transpired in the ten years since Jake's last stop. They had closed the truck stop soon after, when the serious long-haul truckers began favoring I-70, which crossed Kansas some one hundred miles north of U.S. 50, and at the age of fifty-five Lou had bought his own rig and taken to the road as he had always wanted to do. He died five years later, at the bottom of a canyon at Four Corners on U.S. 160, leaving Minnie to get by on insurance, her own social security checks, and what income came from dispensing gas and beer from what remained of Minnie-Lou's Truck Rest. She was now sixty-six years old, alone, her children long ago established in Kansas City and Denver.

Using Lou Dahmer's tools, stored in one of the six motel units affixed to the rear of the place, Jake spent the afternoon under the trees tinkering with Redball. Fine-tuning was about all it had needed, he said, making adjustments on the carburetor and the water pump, changing a fan belt and replacing the air and oil filters while he was at it. Sonny sat in the relative cool of the grotto, aimlessly watching the grasshoppers and reading about Geronimo, as Minnie kept Jake company or fetched iced tea for them or waited on the random customer who rang the bell out front.

"So tell me about yourself, Sonny." Minnie had just sold some gas to a local in a pickup, and now she sat on one of the benches near Lou Dahmer's grave. "Married? Kids? What do you *do*? All I know is that one time he told me and Lou that he'd raised an educated fool."

"Sumbitch said that about me?"

She smiled. "When he quit bragging on you."

Sonny filled her in about himself and about Jake's adventures in retirement. "I feel more like an enforcer than anything else."

"I can't say I'm surprised," Minnie said. "These fools get the road in their blood and there's no stopping 'em. I ought to know something about that. I knew the minute Lou got a truck that it was gonna be his coffin."

"So here you are."

"Here I am. The Widow Dahmer."

"Couldn't you have stopped him?"

"Why, Lord no." Minnie seemed surprised that anyone would ask such a question. "Why would I want to?"

"So you wouldn't be left alone like this, for one thing."

"That would've been selfish for me to try and stop him."

"It seems like he was the selfish one."

Minnie said, "Let me tell you about these boys, Sonny. They *are* selfish, the good ones. They have to be to do what they do. Seems like I read where fifty thousand people get killed in traffic every year, and I never saw a trucker yet who thought he was gonna be one of 'em. They aren't much different from test pilots and these tightrope people at the circus. They work alone, and they can get killed doing it, and in their mind that makes 'em special. They've got to be selfish to survive. That's why no trucker ever walked into my place after driving all day across Kansas and said, 'If it's not too much trouble, could I please have a little coffee?' "

"Well," Sonny said, "I thought maybe you could help me."

"Help you do what?"

"I was going to ask you to reason with him."

"Reason with Jake Hawkins? Hah."

"He's causing an awful lot of trouble back home. I told you about the alcoholic place and about Mama. My sister gets slapped around by her husband every time the old man acts up, and I'm still not convinced that he won't do something that'll get Mama kicked out of the retirement home, even in her condition. Me, I've got ambivalent feelings about the whole thing. On the one hand, I understand how he feels about trucking and I hate like hell to see him dry up like he's been doing. But on the other hand, I wish he'd start thinking about other people for a change."

"Well, it's too late for that."

"He's already had his career. It's time to quit."

"Truckers don't quit, Sonny. They just die."

"But he's almost seventy years old, Minnie. He can't even see to read a menu anymore. We didn't cover three hundred miles today, but he's a wreck. There's all that trouble he's left back home. Can't you say something to him?"

"About all I can do is make today a good one for him." Minnie arose from the stone bench, tugged the knot of the bandanna that held her hair in a ponytail and sidled over to where Jake was humming and working on the truck. She said, "Jake? I was thinking about reopening the place. What do you think?"

Jake raised up from the opened hood of Redball and said, "You won't even be able to pay your power bill, Minnie. Nobody stops here anymore."

"I'm talking about for one night only."

"What do you mean?"

"For old times' sake, Jake. Please."

"I don't know. Me and Sonny ought to be moving on. We could make good time and it'll be cool."

"You got plenty of time, Jake. You need rest. Come on, I'll cook up some steaks and clean up a couple of rooms for you to stay the night. Look at Sonny. He's no more used to this than you are. Not lately, anyway."

Around nine o'clock at night, with the blinds closed and an improvised sign saying "Private Party" taped to the front door, the three of them sat in the middle of the restaurant finishing off a dinner of chicken-fried steak, mashed potatoes, and sawmill gravy, and biscuits. Jake and Sonny had showered and changed in the tiny rooms, last rented in the spring to a crew of highway construction workers, and Minnie had dressed up in a cowgirl skirt and pearl-buttoned blouse. While the two men were lifting the bedsheets from a table, the jukebox, and the floor fans, Minnie had done the cooking in the kitchen at her house. Now, with the fluorescent lights and the fans causing the white sheets to billow and glare, they dined as though on a cloud.

"Kinda pie you got, Minnie?"

"Sliced."

"Still sassy as ever, I see."

"Among friends, Jake. Among friends."

The Wurlitzer, rigged especially for the evening, required no quarters as it ran through Bob Wills, Lefty Frizzell and Webb Pierce, music of another time, another place: "San Antonio Rose," "Mom and Dad's Waltz," and "There Stands the Glass." Plates pushed aside, cold six-packs of beer on the red Formica table, cigar smoke clouding the stark lights, jukebox pounding, Jake glowed like a man furloughed from prison. Sonny, full and content himself, chanced a beer as he silently watched Jake and Minnie parry like lovers reunited.

On the jukebox, "Faded Love," Bob Wills and the Texas Playboys. "Jake," Minnie said, "dance with me."

"Lord, Minnie, I can't dance."

"Anybody that can drive an eighteen-wheeler can dance."

"What would my wife think?"

"Promise I won't tell her if you won't."

"How 'bout Lou, then?"

"This is for Evelyn and Lou and every trucker that ever came through that door, Jake."

While the fiddles played, Minnie took Jake by the hand and led him to the jukebox. She in her denim skirt, he in cowboy boots and polyester slacks of hideous green, they held each other close and danced. Across the road, the new moon and the stars high in the Kansas sky glistened on the lazy Arkansas River. On the road itself, the loneliest road in America, big rigs thundered into the night, rattling the windows as they passed.

17

THE OVERNIGHT STOP at Minnie's had come at a propitious time. The first two days of the trip had been hard 400-milers, not without their tense moments, and the strain had begun to show on Jake before they had gotten halfway through Kansas. There had been the near miss with the logging truck in Alabama, the rain through much of the first two days, the night of sleeping in the cab, followed by the crawl across the plains when, against the relentless wind, in searing heat, with Redball acting up, they had made less than 300 miles. So the unplanned visit with Minnie had given them both exactly what they needed: relaxation, food, conversation, a good bed, some music, a respite from what the truckers and country singers called White Line Fever. More important, it seemed that they had put aside their spat, if, indeed, that was the word for a conversation beginning with the son saying "goddamn you" to the father.

Minnie had sent them on their way with a big breakfast and a hug the next morning, a Saturday, and when they were welcomed to Colorado around nine o'clock they were in high spirits. Rested, not a cloud in the sky, Redball running like a fresh mount, sun at his back, elevations approaching a cooler 4,000 feet, Jake was humming the tunes of the night before as he exchanged horn blasts and raced with a serpentine Santa Fe freight highballing across the sparse high country of eastern Colorado. He was talking of making nearly 500 miles that day, to the great stockyards of Grand Junction, which would enable them to reach Ely on Sunday night so he could unload on Monday. That would give them two full days to fool around before the tire inspection on Thursday in Las Vegas.

"It ain't what you might think about Minnie," Jake said, cruising at sixty miles an hour after clearing Lamar.

Sonny felt it was okay to be jovial for the time being. "I knew it all along," he said. "A girl in every port."

"A lot of truckers do that, you know."

"That explains the husband and wife driving teams these days, I guess."

"A man does get lonely. The trucking outfits know all about that."

"Probably what Mama was afraid of."

"Don't hurt to keep a woman guessing a little, I reckon." Jake went through the routine of lighting his cigar with the wind whipping through the cab. "Naw. Wasn't never any of that stuff with me. Mama was about all I could handle."

"Damned if you and Minnie didn't carry on like lovers back there, though."

"In a way, I guess we did."

"She's a tough old bird," Sonny said. "A lot different from Mama."

"That's what always made this life interesting, son." Sonny felt a soliloquy coming on. "You get out on the road and it seems like there's something new every time you top a hill. There's wrecks, weather, the boys, a damned cow stepping in front of you when you're doing seventy. Hell, I bet you could write a book about every trip I ever made and not a one of 'em would read the same. By the time you get in off a run, you're all tied up in knots. That may be where Phyllis and Mama and that damned Collier got the idea that I was in need of that treatment place in Mississippi. I didn't do much drinking when I was on the road, except at the end of a day, but when I got home I felt I was by-God entitled."

"That's what Charley thinks. And he says you probably took to drinking out of loneliness when you retired."

"Well, I'd say he's right. I knew when I quit, when I *retarded* myself, that it wasn't going to be no picnic. Reckon it wasn't."

"But how about the loneliness out here?"

"People like Minnie take care of that."

"So there *is* a girl in every port."

"That's what the waitresses are for," Jake said. "Just somebody to talk to. You've seen these old boys come into a truck stop. They've been driving for ten hours and they ain't talked to a soul unless you want to count the CB and talking back at the radio. They're ready to kill for somebody to talk to by the time they park the rig and walk in. Then they start loading up on coffee with lots of sugar in it, or maybe start popping pills, and pretty soon you can't shut 'em up. Then they can't sleep, so they get back in the truck and try to make another five hundred miles. I've seen a lot of bad wrecks start that way."

"It must have been a pretty abrupt change to come home. I mean, I remember how Mama always kept a list of things to be done when you got back. You'd be worn out, and she'd want a room painted."

"Truth is, son, I always felt like I was living two lives. One of 'em was represented by Minnie and the other one by Mama, you might say."

"What if you'd had to decide between them?"

"Minnie and Mama? It never came to that."

"No," Sonny said. "The road and home."

Jake said, "That beer you drank last night's got you thinking funny."

"I didn't have but three or four, Pop."

"Whatever it was, you ought to know better than to ask a question like that," Jake said. "I told you back at Piney Woods that time you came to visit. I wouldn't be nothing without my truck. That ought to be right clear by now."

Ever since they had cleared La Junta and Rocky Ford around eleven o'clock, with the pitch of the road becoming steeper and beginning to twist a bit now, they had seen the face of the Rockies loom larger with each passing mile. Through the windshield, again splattered with the juices of butterflies and grasshoppers a tad too slow for Redball, the mountains had presented themselves as a formidable wall that seemed to cast a spell over Pueblo even though it was fifty miles away. The highway had been four-laned into and around and out of Pueblo, busy with lunch hour traffic as they passed through, but they found out soon enough that Kansas had been a mere spin in the country compared to what lay ahead.

The real test of Jake's skill began when they reached a mile in elevation around Canon City. It was there that the four-lane ran out and U.S. 50 became a mean adversary for a trucker pulling a load in a swaying aluminum trailer: a twisting, steeply banked roller coaster jammed with other rigs and tourists and awkward trucks delivering rubber rafts to points of portage on the dancing Arkansas River. The Arkansas at this point, having built up a head of steam since bubbling out of the ground at Leadville some 100 miles north and west, was now a frothing bull that madly tossed canoes and kayaks and rafts full of screaming white-water adventurers dangerously close to the rocky shoals. Holding tight in the shotgun seat, Sonny glimpsed a roadside marker, with the international symbol of a stick figure mounting a forty-five-degree incline: "In Case of Flash Flood, Climb." Working every bit as madly as the paddlers, but for survival rather than thrills, Jake was arms and legs and eyeballs: grabbing gears, pumping brakes, hitting horns, checking mirrors and gauges, chewing the cigar, cursing campers and station wagons crammed with oglers, smiling like a stock-car driver running through a caution flag.

It went like that for sixty miles, until they reached the town of Salida, advertising itself as the "Heart of the Rockies," surrounded by peaks of 14,000 feet. The run had taken nearly two hours to negotiate. Sweating profusely, chewing furiously on the cigar, rubbing his eyes from the relentless tension of the ride, Jake turned on the blinkers and brought Redball to a halt on wide shoulders where the road had flattened out between Salida and Poncha Springs. When he cut the engine there were the pops of hot metal cooling, the simmering of tires, the hissing of steam from the radiator, the acrid smoking of oil, the sloshing of gasoline. To the north, whence the Arkansas River had come, they could see the sparkling snow on the bald granite pate of Mount Shavano that formed the wings of the "Angel of Shavano." Straight ahead, not twenty miles away, lay Jake's one last challenge: Monarch Pass. The Continental Divide.

"Like taking one of them rides at the Alabama State Fair, ain't it?" Jake and Sonny were standing in the shade and the privacy afforded by the trailer, relieving themselves in the gravel as cars whizzed past on the other side.

"Now I see why you insisted on Redball instead of a rental."

"It helps to know your truck on road like that."

"She doing all right?"

"I don't hear anything I ain't supposed to hear," Jake said. "Soon's I get her up to the top of the hill, we'll all take a rest. I'm plumb wore out."

The twenty miles to the huge paved parking area of Monarch Pass, a groaning pull that saw them gain 250 feet for every mile traveled forward, put them squarely on the Continental Divide at shortly before four in the afternoon. In seven hours, they had covered only 280 miles. That wasn't bad, considering what they had just been through, but from the looks of Jake they wouldn't be bedding down that night in Grand Junction.

It looked as though a truckers' convention were taking place when Jake wheeled Redball into the parking lot. Monarch Pass, at 11,312 feet, was a natural pit stop for long-haulers, and a dozen rigs of all sizes and from all over the country were cooling in the thin air of the Rockies. Their drivers were checking oil levels, kicking tires, filling radiators, cleaning windshields, using the pay telephones, snoozing, or simply walking around to work out the kinks. When Sonny jumped to the asphalt, his legs rubbery, he noticed a husband and wife team standing near a gleaming Peterbilt with one of the king-sized $25,000 sleeper units attached: he gazing eastward toward the 14,000-foot Collegiate Peaks, she imploring a leashed white poodle to do its business in the grass of a picnic area. There was also a cluster of vans and station wagons, but the tourists tended to stay to themselves, sneaking inquisitive glances at the truckers.

Jake and Sonny did some housekeeping of their own, shaking out the Rebel flag bug-catcher, washing the windshields, cleaning out the cab, and filling the radiator with water from a drinking fountain before drifting over to a cluster of redwood picnic tables. There, Jake opened up the large grocery bag that Minnie had packed and found a six-pack of beer and some fried chicken and sausage biscuits. Sonny hesitated for a moment, but took the beer Jake offered him. They began sipping from the warm cans, trying to keep straight faces while the married drivers snapped at each other about whose turn it was to drive or whether to take a motel for the night.

"All in all," Jake whispered, "I'm kinda glad Mama chose to stay home all them years."

"The poodle, too. Can you imagine that?"

"From what I've seen, I'd take the dog and leave her at home where she ought to be."

Sonny washed down a drumstick with a second beer. "You want another one, Pop?"

"Naw. I got a little more driving to do. You go ahead, though. Good to see that you ain't an alcoholic after all."

"Well, I don't know."

"Didn't seem to bother you none last night."

"It tasted good, all right."

"How come you quit in the first place? Don't think I ever asked you about that."

"The divorce got to me, I guess. Beverly was keeping the kids from me. Turned out I wasn't Ernest Hemingway. I don't know. Lots of things."

"Sounds like you had your own kind of lonely."

"It was the pits, Pop."

Jake searched Sonny's eyes. "Well, I'll help you out when we get to Gunnison. It'll be good to have somebody to drink with again."

"That where we'll spend the night?"

"I reckon. It's another hundred and eighty miles to Grand Junction, and I'm afraid I ain't up to that. Gunnison's just an hour down the hill. The way I remember it, they got pretty good vittles there."

Sipping on his beer, enjoying the thin air, Sonny watched with bemusement as the couple coaxed their poodle into the Peterbilt and cranked up and eased away from the parking area on the eastbound ramp. When the rig had dropped out of sight, he turned to find Jake flattening out and perusing an array of crumpled envelopes and scraps of paper on the redwood table.

"What you got, treasure maps?" Sonny said.

"Might be. Just might be."

"Don't tell me you're actually gonna keep a log book."

Jake held up a crinkled envelope and made out his own penciled handwriting. "Bentrup. Carl Bentrup. Deerfield, Kansas. Sheep."

"What're you talking about, Pop?"

"Fella's always needing sheep hauled to Colby."

"That's his problem."

"Minnie says he can't hardly find no drivers since Lou died."

"So?"

"Well, that's one load I can count on when I get stuck in Kansas." Jake reached for other scraps of paper, sorting them in piles. "I must've come up with a dozen leads that night I stayed in the truck. Hell, I'll never run out of work as long as Redball holds up. Only problem is making too much money and losing my social security."

When Sonny realized what Jake was saying, what he probably had been planning all along, he exploded. "Goddamnit, let's stop this nonsense right here and now." Their truce hadn't lasted very long. Sonny jumped to his feet, hurled the beer can toward a row of garbage barrels, and glowered at Jake.

"I don't hear no nonsense."

"Let's go. Let's park it."

"What do you mean, park it?"

"I mean drop the struts and unhitch the truck."

"Be a cold day in hell when I walk away from a load."

"Well, the day just came. Come on. This trip's over."

Jake twirled the cigar and leveled his eyes at Sonny. "It ain't over 'til I deliver my tires."

"That's it, Pop. Get unhitched. Let's go."

"Well, now, if it's getting to be too much for you, I reckon the nearest airport's at Grand Junction. Or you can always flag a Greyhound right here on U.S. 50 if you ain't got too fancy to ride a bus."

"Look, they got pay phones over there. Let's go call Charley and straighten this shit out right now."

"Charley can't stop me, and you know it."

Sonny said, "Don't you understand that we've been humoring you all along? Can't you get it through your head that this is your last ride?"

"That's for me to decide."

"I'll call Charley and tell him you're too sick to talk, and that we're parking the trailer and bobtailing back down the mountain to the hospital in Salida."

"I don't care what you tell him. In ten minutes I'm cranking Redball and heading down to Gunnison for a steak and some shut-eye before I take 'er on into Nevada. Whether you go along is your business. I don't give a damn."

"You don't give a damn about anybody but yourself anymore, you old fart. Minnie was right."

"I told you before we left, I'm making decisions about my life. Last time I let somebody do it for me, I wound up in a looney bin with a bunch of drunks. That ain't gonna happen no more."

"I'll tell you one thing," Sonny said. "You can scratch Charley from your list. He gave you this load because he felt sorry for you. But that's all you'll get from him."

"That's why I got this list going. After forty years on the road, I got friends everywhere."

"Most of 'em are dead, Pop, and you know it."

"Just the drivers are gone, that's all. The ones that done good has got businesses now, just like Charley."

"So you're just gonna ride away, huh? Leave Mama and everybody hanging. Is that it?"

"Might sell the house, might not. I ain't worked out the details yet."

"Holy shit. I can't believe this."

"You might as well start believing it. You and Phyllis and Charley and that sonofabitch Collier, in case it's any of his damned business what I do. Everybody can just stand back and get out of my way, 'cause I ain't slowing down for nobody." Jake gathered up the scraps of paper, stuffed them into his pockets, and began walking toward the truck. "Me, I'm headed for Gunnison. Alone, or with somebody, it don't matter."

Although the run from Monarch Pass to Gunnison was less than fifty miles, it was like a parachute jump off the western slope of the Rockies: a twisting, hurtling free fall of nearly 4,000 feet. Mindful of the old rule of thumb about going down a hill "in the same gear you went up it at," Jake took it easy and felt vindicated when he pointed out a runaway-truck escape ramp where highway department workers were still raking the gravel churned up by a rig that hadn't made it. This was breathtaking ski country, signs along the roadway pointing to the ski resorts. In some places the temperature was known to hit fifty below zero in January.

It was a pleasant eighty degrees, though, when they eased into Gunnison at six o'clock, the little town quiet now except for the fishermen who had come in from the nearby reservoir campgrounds for supplies or a Saturday-night restaurant meal, and they could have their pick of motels lining the long, wide boulevard. In keeping with the skiing motif, most of the restaurants and motels had worked "lodge" or "alpine" into their names and adopted Bavarian architecture. Jake passed on all of those, however, quickly wheeling into the Rockies Tourist Court, a cluster of ancient stone cottages with fireplaces and no air conditioning, when he saw the sign saying "Couples $17" and noticed plenty of room in the empty gravel parking lot.

When they had settled into the room and staked out a place up the street that promised thick steaks and a live country band, Sonny pleaded with Jake to call Charley Graddick, his hope being that Charley would reiterate what he had said at Monarch Pass. Jake wouldn't hear of it, saying he had better things to do and didn't need anybody checking up on him. So when Jake left the room, having talked the owner of the place into letting him hose down the truck in the parking lot, Sonny placed a collect call to Charley at his home.

It was seven-thirty in Birmingham, and Charley was being dragged to the opera that night by his wife. "What the hell time of day is it out there?" he shouted, as though they were a continent apart, which, Sonny had to remember, was very nearly the case.

"Six-thirty," Sonny said. "We don't go Pacific time until Nevada."

"I was afraid you'd already made it."

"We'll get there Monday afternoon. We've still got Utah and parts of Colorado and Nevada to go."

"Sounds to me like he's slowing down."

"We haven't made six hundred miles, total, these last two days."

"Good, good. See there? Just the way we — "

"This thing's backfired on us, Charley."

"What do you mean, 'backfired'?"

"We made a serious mistake at the very beginning," Sonny said. "You should have come right out and told him that this was going to be his last run. Seems like everybody knows that but him."

When Charley heard about the plans Jake had sprung on him, he exploded as he had when he first learned about the Piney Woods experiment. "Get his skinny ass to the phone," he shouted.

"Hell, Charley, he won't — "

"Put the receiver down and go get him, Sonny. Right now."

"What're you going to do?"

"Tell it to him straight. Now fetch him."

Sonny dropped the receiver and left the room, trotting across the gravel to where Jake stood, bare-chested, noisily hosing down the trailer. Jake hadn't been exactly cordial since their spat, and when he saw Sonny holding an imaginary telephone receiver at his ear and pointing to indicate a call, he spat tobacco juice in disgust. "That mean you made your plane reservation?" he shouted.

"It's Charley. He wants to talk to you."

"Tell him I'm busy. Take a message."

"Pop, you can't treat Charley like this. He's the best friend you've got left. Come on, talk to him."

"Tell him I'll call him from Vegas. Soon's I get these tires off and get on down there."

"He wants to talk to you right now."

"You just tell him it's too damned late to stop me if that's what he's got on his mind. If there's been a change in the inspection at Nellis, write it down." Livid, Jake turned the hose toward Sonny and peppered the gravel in front of him. "Now go on, before you get hosed down yourself."

Back on the phone with Charley, about all Sonny could do was express his helplessness. "For a while there," he said, "I had some noble ideas about how I was going to save my father from himself. But I don't know how you do that when you can't agree on what 'save' means. The sumbitch won't budge."

"Well, now, look here, Sonny" — there was a great clearing of the throat — "we'll just have to take 'em one at a time. We'll worry about this new career of his later. What we got to watch out for right now is when he gets to the mine. I don't want him unloading those tires, you hear?"

"Maybe he knows better than that, Charley."

"The hell he does."

"He let Jo-Jo load 'em, didn't he?"

"The way Jake looks at it, there ain't no glory in loading. That's grunt work. 'Nigger work' is how he'd put it."

"What's the difference between loading and unloading? A tire's a tire."

"Unloading means mission by-God accomplished. It's like

being able to trot around the bases real slow after you've hit a home run. He'll try to leave 'em with something to talk about."

"He ought to be tired by then."

"Don't count on it. Sonofabitch thinks he's immortal."

"We sure contributed to that."

"I don't even want to think about it," Charley said. "Lord, I've got to be getting on. I don't know which end is up on these damned cummerbunds. But look here, now. You don't let him get near those tires. Y'all go play the slots or something. Get him drunk if you have to. *Comprende?*"

"I'll do the best I can, Charley."

"He's your daddy. I'm holding you responsible."

At twilight, having showered, dressed, and drunk the rest of Minnie's beer, they walked up the road to the restaurant-lounge and feasted on steaks as thick and as good as promised. The place was called AspenLodge, done up in fake Bavarian architecture, and the live country band turned out to be a muscular ski bum on a keyboard synthesizer who accompanied his blond, guitar-strumming girlfriend. Their idea of country music was "Rocky Mountain High" and other John Denver hits, which their friends and the tourists in the audience wildly applauded. AspenLodge was, at best, a sad little café, made sadder still, for Sonny, when he caught his father's face in the harsh overhead light and realized that four days on the road had taken a fierce toll. Suddenly Jake appeared to be a very tired old man, not the indomitable hustler who had danced away only the night before with Minnie in his arms, now with a full-blown sunburn on his wrinkled arms and hollow black pits holding dazed opaque eyes. Sonny chose not to burden his father with that observation, so when they had heard about all the music they could stand they arose, tipsily, and wandered back to the motel.

"What's your thinking for tomorrow?" Sonny said when they were in the room. It was only ten o'clock, but Jake had already stripped to his boxer shorts and was fluffing up the pillows.

"There was a time when I'd go all the way in."
"How far's Ely?"
"Not quite six hundred miles."
"Hard driving?"
"It's all downhill once you get to Utah." Jake turned on the television set and stood in front of it for a moment, watching a car chase, before getting into bed and pulling the cover to his neck. "Course, technically, it's all downhill from Monarch Pass."

"Hot as hell, too, I bet," Sonny said. Instead of an answer from Jake, Sonny heard a snort and, shortly, the troubled snoring of a man who had run out of gas.

First, Sonny turned off the television, fished one of the OK Press paperbacks from his overnight bag, and tried to read by the pale yellow lamp on the table by his bed. Then he tried taking a long, hot shower, his second one of the evening, to relax. Finally, putting on some jeans and his thin Graddick Tire windbreaker, he pocketed the room key and locked the door behind him to take in the bracing chill of the Colorado night. He contemplated the white moon, now illuminating the peaks of the Rockies all around, and reckoned that it would be full by the time they hit Ely. They were still going strong at AspenLodge, he noticed, but that wouldn't do it, not John Denver, thanks. Then he saw it, a discreet neon sign up the road beyond AspenLodge, and he began to walk.

18

Sonny couldn't remember how long it had been since he had hit the hard stuff. Maybe between Christmas and New Year's, he guessed, when neither of his kids could make themselves available for the holidays. Whatever. It had been long enough for his body to have grown unaccustomed to taking on nearly a fifth of vodka in one sitting, which is what he had downed in the gauzy two or three hours after trotting back to the motel from the liquor store. Now, with sunlight flooding through the drapes, he lay paralyzed, covers pulled to his chin, surveying the musty little room. There was no sign of Jake, but on the table beside the bed was the bottle with about three inches left. And under the bottle, scrawled on Rockies Tourist Court stationery, there was a note: "Bringing breakfast. Sorry I missed the party."

Jake had apparently put him to bed during the night or at

least covered him in the morning when he awoke. Sonny blinked and tried to get his bearings. Kansas? Colorado? Utah, already? Eyes burning, tongue bloated, stomach roiling, he lurched from the bed and careened toward the bathroom. He was still on his knees, retching, when he heard Jake come into the room. Back on his feet, bare skin on cold tile, not daring to look into the mirror as he toweled off with a wet washrag, he smelled coffee and biscuits.

"About all you can do is try," Jake said when Sonny emerged from the bathroom. Dressed, smelling of after-shave, ready to go, he gestured toward the dresser, where he had placed a full breakfast in a Styrofoam plate from a fast-food place. "Eggs, ham, biscuits, home fries, tomato juice, the works."

"Holy Christ. I don't know."

"We can use your eyes for road maps today."

"Not funny."

"Good thing you brought an expert along," Jake said. "I'd recommend some hair-of-the-dog first."

Sonny poured equal portions of tomato juice and vodka in a plastic motel tumbler, fell into the room's lone chair, and knocked back what would have to pass as a Bloody Mary. Jake, leaving him to his misery, closed his suitcase and stepped outside again.

It was ten-thirty before they rolled away from Gunnison, the latest start for them on the whole trip, meaning there would be no monster mileage on this day. It was a Sunday, hot and bright, and now they were truly entering the wide-open spaces of the West. Unlike Kansas and eastern Colorado, where there was a town or at least a settlement every ten miles or so, they were faced with stretches where the only other humans they might see for fifty miles or more would be fellow travelers.

They were both too preoccupied with their own problems to converse during the first hour. The last rugged leg of U.S. 50 dipped and rolled for seventy miles, most of it downhill through a wide, heavily trafficked canyon choked with tents and campers, and Jake was using nearly every gear Redball had to negotiate the run to Montrose. Sonny had allayed the shakes with the rest of the vodka, and managed to keep some of the breakfast on his stomach, but a ride like this wasn't exactly what he needed to start the day. He was hanging on to the handle on the dashboard, leaning his head out the window to catch the rush of air, pushing his feet hard against the floorboards, as goggle-eyed as a kid on his first Ferris wheel.

Only after they had cleared Montrose at noon and the roadway leveled out into a four-lane that would send them on their way to Grand Junction did Jake speak. Even then he was tentative, prodding, much like the time he had awkwardly advised Sonny to "always use a rubber" and let that stand as the sum total of the sexual counsel he had to offer his adolescent son. This time, as before, he lit his cigar and cleared his throat before glancing at him sideways.

"Looks like you're gonna live to see Nevada after all," he said.

"I wouldn't bet on it."

"I don't know if they sell beer on Sunday in these parts. I could check on it at Delta, coming up. Might perk you up some."

"Oh, God, no. Forget it."

Jake was tight-lipped, nervous, confused. "It wasn't nothing I said, was it, son?"

"What the hell do you think?"

"You got me boxed in pretty good back there."

"It was about time, I'd say."

"Didn't think it was gonna do this to you. All I was doing was trying to protect myself."

Sonny said, "All it takes is something like that to touch it off. Then I'm off and running. I just can't drink, that's all."

"You mean you can't stop yourself?"

"Not once I get started."

"What I was afraid of."

"I told you that."

"Reckon I didn't want to believe it." Suddenly Jake's eyes opened wide. He had been so busy thinking of what he would say next to Sonny that he had slowed to fifty on a straightaway. Now, too late, he saw in the mirror a Freightliner, gleaming like a diamond in the sun, preparing to blow past him at seventy miles an hour. Jake blinked his headlights out of courtesy to let the Freightliner know the trailer had cleared, but he didn't smile when he did it.

Sonny said, "I can't just have one, that's all."

"Well, I won't be tempting you no more, then."

"What, no more talk about going back to driving full-time?"

"No more drinking while we're out here."

"Suit yourself. It's just *me*."

"Naw, naw. I promise. No more beer, no more nothing." Jake slowed again, foot off the gas this time, as though the world could pass him for all he cared. "It's about time I started paying you back for the last couple of weeks."

"Aw, hell. Let's don't get maudlin."

"I was ready to die, son, 'til you came along."

"You ought to credit Charley."

"That's different," Jake said. "Charley's business. You're family. I know I ain't gonna live forever, but by God now I know I'm gonna go out with a smile on my face. And it's how you go out that counts."

The CB radio had clearly been an impulse buy for Jake during the seventies, when it had been popularized more by Hollywood and Nashville than by the truckers themselves, and he had used it very little on this trip except for idle entertainment. The frequency seemed to belong to everybody but truckers now, as he had told Sonny, and he had learned the hard way that it had become passé to use the term "good buddy" anymore, like they did in the movies, because that meant something else these days.

Burly truckers, weary of the road and armed with pistols and tire irons, were not likely to be amused.

It was for use in the barrens of the Far West that Jake had brought along the CB, anyway, and as they groaned toward Grand Junction he turned it on just in time to hear somebody in a falsetto voice saying "good buddy" within earshot of a trucker who was coming in from the northeast on I-70.

"You little faggot sonofabitch," the trucker growled, "how'd you like a Freightliner driven right up your asshole? Over."

"*Ooooohh.* Over, good buddy."

"Goddamn little shitass. Where you at? Over."

Jake took the receiver from the dashboard and cut in. "Breaker-breaker. This is Dixie Redball coming in from the east on Big Lonesome. Need some information about Utah. You read me? Over."

"Dixie Redball, this is Big Shakey. What can I do for you? Over."

"Where you at, Big Shakey? Over."

"Coming at you, Dixie Redball. Just cleared Grand Junction, headed east with lettuce out of Sacramento. I say if the Mormons want Utah, let 'em have it. Over."

"Big Shakey, Dixie Redball." Jake was loving it. "Don't sound like it's changed much since I was out here. What's on the other side of Green River? Over."

"Scales are open, but they're passing everybody through that ain't hauling food, seeing it's Sunday. Past that, there ain't a damned thing but Indians selling Jap stuff at the rest stops. That do you? Over."

"That you coming up in the white Mack, Big Shakey? Over."

"Blinking my eyes, Redball. That's me. Over."

"I got you. What I need to know is, I can either stop for the night at Green River or go on. My horse is tired and I got a sick rider. Over."

"Ain't nothing for a hundred miles after that, hoss. Beds and eats at the river. Over."

"Reckon I'll try it, then." Before Jake could sign off, Big Shakey himself came rocketing toward them, blasting his air horn and blinking his lights, and Jake acknowledged him when he had passed. "Much obliged, Big Shakey."

Jake was reaching over to turn off the CB and hang up the speaker when what sounded like the voice of God, breathing heavy, boomed through the cab of the truck: "If you haven't been saved yet, brother, it's not too late. God loves everybody, and he's sent me on the road to talk to you on this glorious day of reckoning." Jake and Sonny looked at each other, amazed, and then a squawky female voice came on. "This is Sister Millie and Brother Frank, traveling east on I-70, bringing tangerines and the word of the Lord to you all from Bakersfield, California. Over."

Angry truckers came from everywhere. "Get off the air, you goddamn freaks," one of them shouted. "This ain't no church. This is Long Gone, from Lincoln. Over."

"The Lord's riding with us today. Over."

"Well, you better let him out before you kill him. Over."

"Bless you, Long Gone. This is Sister Millie. Have you been saved? Over."

"Saved from what? Over."

"Saved from a life of sin. Over."

"Naw, sister, but I could use some tempting. Why don't you try me? Over."

Sister Millie and Brother Frank had no direct response to that, but they had plenty to say about the Lord as they and their captive parishioners rolled their separate ways across the sparse land. Once they had the air, they weren't about to relinquish it, and after five minutes of listening to their harangues Jake turned off the CB and lit a fresh cigar.

"Makes Preacher Boggs seem kind of tame, don't it?" Jake said as he settled into his seat and began to gear down for the interchanges coming up at Grand Junction.

"Enough to make a Methodist out of me."

"You don't really mean that."

"Of course not."

"Something I always wondered is how come all this church stuff." Jake turned on the washer and wiper to clean the windshield of bugs, but it only made things worse. "You missed most of it when you moved away, but I never saw anything like it. Mama and Sis might as well live at the church. Lately, the older she got, the more Mama started asking me what was gonna happen to my soul when I die."

"Well?"

"What?"

"What'd you tell her?"

"To myself I'm saying, 'What the hell kind o' question is that?' For Mama's sake, I just said we'd meet again somewhere up yonder."

"Don't suppose that satisfied her," Sonny said.

"Reckon not. But I didn't know what else to say to the poor thing. Wouldn't do no good to tell her what I think Heaven looks like."

Here we go. "I'm all ears."

"Got a sign off in one corner that says Truckers Only."

"That a fact?"

"That's to keep the riffraff out."

"I think you've got a country song going."

Jake waggled the cigar again. "Already got the words and the lyrics, both. I was thinking Merle Haggard."

The landscape abruptly changed the moment they reached the Utah line. Now, rather than the breathtaking sweep of the Colorado Rockies, they were looking at an eroded magenta moonscape that was still being fashioned by the wind. The highway moved slower now, through narrow wind-swept canyons, and on both sides of them they could see odd, striated mesas sprouting from the scrubby desert bottoms into the hot, blue cloudless sky. To the north was Desolation Canyon and a

300-square-mile Indian reservation, and to the south were the eerie Canyonlands and Arches National Monument of many a cowboy movie. They stopped at a "View Area," where extended families of Indians, up from their reservation in Arizona for the weekend, lolled beneath colorful cabanas and beach umbrellas while Midwestern tourists piled out of their Winnebagos to haggle over silver and turquoise trinkets spread out in the sun on striped Navajo blankets. Sonny came out of the putrid septic-tank restroom just in time to see a sinewy lone bicyclist, sunburned and loaded with gear for a cross-country trek, get blown against a station wagon by a sudden twister of wind.

Jake, to Sonny's great relief, had decided to heed the caution of "Big Shakey" and stop for the night at Green River. The alternative was to travel on in the broiling heat of midafternoon for another hundred miles into the belly of Utah, an empty stretch where not even a gas station could be found, and it didn't seem to be worth the gamble in a truck the vintage of Dixie Redball IV. He began the process of gearing down for the Green River exit when he crossed the river itself, nearly dry at this time of year, and saw an ominous highway marker: Next Services I-70 100 Miles.

"I don't know if you ever noticed," Jake said, "but when I talk about the three million miles without an accident I always tack on 'chargeable to myself.' "

"I just thought it was a figure of speech."

"Wouldn't have to say it if it wasn't for Utah."

"You had a wreck out here, then."

"Only one I ever had that didn't involve livestock," Jake said. It was around 1965, he said, and he was pulling a reefer eastward from the San Joaquin Valley at night to avoid the heat and the troopers. He was also driving a spanking-new White cab-over diesel, the only truck he had ever bought that wasn't a Dodge. "Cured me of driving Utah at night, and cured me of driving anything but Dodges."

"Maybe it was the new truck. Maiden voyage, all of that. You'd never driven a diesel before."

"Naw," Jake said. "The damned road just run out on me. I must've been doing sixty-five when I saw this little sign that said 'Detour.' Like a whisper. 'Detour.' Too damned late for me to catch it. Plowed right into the sand and then the whole rig rolled over, trailer and all. I damned near got killed on that one."

"Christ, Pop, you never told me."

"Wasn't particularly proud of it."

"Doesn't sound like it was your fault."

Jake said, "It took me five years to convince the damned insurance people of that. First, they tried to make it out that I was drunk, which I wasn't. Then they tried to say I didn't know how to drive a truck, which any damned fool can tell you ain't so. Then they finally got around to blaming it on the sonsabitches that didn't know how to mark their roads right. My problem was, I didn't have no witnesses."

"Back up a minute," Sonny said. "How'd you get out of there? How bad were you hurt?"

"I was knocked out for a few minutes, but mainly I just got some scratches and bumps. Lost the whole load of strawberries, though."

"Who found you? And when?"

Jake laughed. "State troopers, of all people. Think it was them that put it in the insurance company's head that I'd been drinking."

"How so?"

"Well, hell, I'd been sitting out there more'n an hour. It was getting chilly and I could hear what I figured to be coyotes crying out there in the dark. Come to find that the whiskey I had in my suitcase had survived the wreck better than I did. So I put my flares out on the road and went back to the truck to wait for help. I was just sitting there, having me a drink or two to calm down, when their spotlight found me."

"Like Charley said, 'You don't drink 'til your work's done.' "

"Yeah, well, they didn't see it that way," Jake said. "It's like this old boy that stole some fancy hubcaps off a Rolls-Royce. When he couldn't find nobody to buy 'em he took 'em back to the Rolls, and that's how the boys found him. Wasn't no way they were gonna believe he was putting 'em back on."

This would be their last overnighter before the final run across Utah and into eastern Nevada to deliver the load of tires, and although they had covered only 250 miles that day they were both bushed and in need of exactly what the big truck stop at Green River had to offer: adequate rooms, air conditioning, a decent restaurant with pinball machines and a jukebox, even a swimming pool. During the late afternoon hours, as the sun began to turn into a fiery ball settling on the horizon, like an orange sinking in a sandbox, Jake fiddled around with Redball in the football-field-sized truck parking yard while Sonny lazed around the pool. Green River was truly an oasis in the desert; there were no other highway services available for 100 miles around, and most of Utah's scant population was clustered 200 miles to the north around the Great Salt Lake.

At sunset, scrubbed and famished, Jake and Sonny took a booth next to the picture windows that wrapped all the way around the dining room. It was a large room, capable of seating as many as 200 people at a time, but no more than two dozen travelers were in the place. Jake said that was because I-70 was a road to nowhere, ending two hours west in the middle of Utah, that most east-west traffic was 200 miles north and south of there on the Interstates 40 and 80. Although there was no section reserved for truckers in the dining room, the tourists had drawn themselves in a circle at one end while a half-dozen truckers had gravitated to the other. A third group was gathered around the pinball machines and video games, and there was no escaping their presence: eight tattooed and bearded thugs, in boots and leather, drinking beer from bottles and cursing loudly as they played the games.

"Sunday in Utah," Jake said as he squinted at the menu and stirred the iced tea that a waitress had already brought. "Wonder what the Mormons got to say about that."

"Not exactly what they had in mind, that's for sure," said Sonny.

"Sonsabitching hippies. Lucky for them that they got the truckers outnumbered."

A new voice said, "The West is still full of outlaws, ain't it?" Jake and Sonny turned to see that the voice belonged to a trucker, in the uniform of an outfit out of Kansas City, seated alone at the booth behind them. He was in his fifties, ruddy and stout, with a smile that said he had seen it all.

"Been a while since I been out here," Jake said.

"Here and Nevada's where bikers come to die. End of the line for 'em, I guess."

"Seems fittin', out here with the vultures."

The trucker said, "They didn't give you any trouble, coming in, did they?"

"Naw. First I've seen of 'em. You?"

"Some." They were bikers, he said, and earlier in the day as he drove eastward on a two-lane stretch of I-70 they had harassed him by passing and then slowing down, passing and slowing for half an hour, until finally he had revved up his Freightliner in an attempt to plow them under. "Thing is, those bikes they ride must do a hundred when they want 'em to."

"What are they, them Hell's Angels you hear about?"

"Bunch of bikers is all I know. Got 'em parked over there in the truck lot." The driver pointed through the window, and they could see them: eight giant Harley-Davidsons, glowing in the sunset, parked in a neat military row like dominoes.

Jake said, "Looks like they would've caused you some trouble after what you tried to do to 'em."

"That's why me and my partner are eating in shifts. So they don't mess with the rig."

"Y'all staying the night here?"

"No. We're gonna run on home. He already ate."

The trucker had finished his meal and was having pie with coffee as Jake and Sonny piled into their platters of pork chops and mashed potatoes. For the next half-hour they forgot about the bikers, in spite of their ruckus, and spoke of trucks and roads and country music and truck stops. Marvin Bandy was the trucker's name, and although he had forsaken the life of the independent for the security of a big outfit, Jake didn't hold it against him. The man, clearly, had paid more than his union dues.

"Tell you when I miss running independent the most," he said. "That's every time I got to park the rig and call in to the office."

"How often's that?" Jake said.

"At least twice a day, sometimes three."

"Lord. What for?"

"Company policy is what they say. Guess it gives their executives something to do. Tried to tell 'em the reason I got divorced was so I wouldn't have to check in with anybody."

"I was lucky there, I guess," Jake said.

"You manage to stay married?"

"My wife always knew I'd be home when I got there. My boy here can tell you that."

"Well, trucking wrecked mine. Guess I'll spend the rest of my life on the road. You ought to know something about that." The trucker looked closely at Jake for the first time. "How old *are* you, anyway? If you don't mind my asking."

"Sixty-nine and holding," Jake said. "Old enough to know better."

"Hauling tires two thousand miles?"

"If the creek don't rise. And that ain't likely out here, from what I've seen."

"Well, old-timer, I'd say that gives me something to shoot for. It sure does."

The waitress came with the check and a paper cup of coffee, and when Bandy had left a tip he headed for the cash register. From the goosing and nodding that was going on among them, the bikers had apparently determined that this was the trucker they had toyed with earlier in the day. One of them reached the cash register at the same time, and when Bandy took a sip from his cup and set it down on the counter to pay his bill the biker dropped a lighted cigarette into the cup. The biker, egged on by his friends, was staring at the trucker. The waitress, the cook, and the tourists froze.

Marvin Bandy did nothing. He smiled at the biker, paid his bill, asked for a receipt, thanked the waitress, and turned and walked out the door into the gloaming, finally disappearing around the corner of the truck stop on his way to the line of rigs in the big parking lot. The bikers were stunned at first, then surly, but soon they returned to horsing around at the pinballs and the video games. Diners who had seen the drama began to laugh nervously among themselves, quietly, but they soon forgot about it and hunched over their food again. It had become a piece of history, a brief threatening moment, a little slice of life to tell the folks about back home in Des Moines.

About ten minutes later, though, the people in the dining room were startled by a mighty roar from the truck parking lot. The driver of one of the rigs was revving his engine like a jumbo jet preparing for takeoff. He began to blast repeatedly on his air horn, like a runaway train headed for a sure disaster. He flipped on every light at his disposal, fog lights and overhead searchlights included, lighting up even the interior of the restaurant. Everybody in the place, astonished bikers first, rushed to the windows to see what was going on. They got there just in time to see Marvin Bandy's Freightliner flatten the eight bikes.

19

THE NUMBER OF RIGS overnighting at the truck stop had swelled to a dozen before the full moon reached its apex in the infinite Utah sky, but not a single driver spent the night in his room. Instead, guarding against possible retaliation by the bikers, they catnapped in their sleepers, tinkered with their rigs, and milled around under the sputtering arc lights of the parking lot. It was as though a truckers' convention were taking place, much boasting and strutting the order of the evening, with special entertainment provided by the sullen bikers. All through the night, under taunts and parries from the assembled drivers, they had frantically cannibalized parts until they were able to get four of the eight Harleys in good enough shape to roar away at dawn. The mangled remains of the other four bikes lay in a heap in front of the truck stop, glistening in the hot morning sun, mute testimony of the truckers' victory.

In the restaurant, after the bikers had gone, there was great jubilation. The truckers, social activists in their own right, figured they had won one for blue-collar America, and they were celebrating it by repeatedly punching "Okie from Muskogee" on the jukebox, recounting the night with much bravado, as they shoveled in the free Trucker's Breakfast being offered by the truck stop's grateful manager.

"I need me another coffee bump, Irma," Jake said to the waitress when he had shoved his plate aside. He, like the others, had barely slept during the night, and Sonny was concerned about how he would fare on the final run into Ely that day.

"Best thing about it," Sonny said, "they rode east toward Grand Junction when they left."

"Yeah," Jake said, "the boys headed that way are putting together a convoy. Be my guess it ain't over yet."

Irma was refilling Jake's cup with coffee. "Who was that driver, anyway?" she said.

"Name of Marvin. Out of Kansas City."

"I seen you talking with him before it happened."

"All I know is," Jake said, "he's about the worst damned driver I ever saw."

"Pshaw."

"Couldn't see eight motorbikes parked right in front of him. Even had 'em in his lights."

Irma began howling and spilled the coffee she was trying to pour. "Ain't that the truth."

"Fella like that ain't likely to win no courteous driver awards, now, is he?"

Interstate 70 and U.S. 50 had been one and the same road since Grand Junction, and it would be like that until the interstate came to its end at a town called Salina in the middle of southern Utah. Now came the dullest part of the entire trip, Jake advised Sonny as they pulled away from Green River around nine o'clock in the morning for the 340-mile leg to Ely. During the long night, between naps in the sleeper, he had filled all of the gas tanks, tightened the belts, and topped off the oil to enhance the chances of making it through the last long hot day without any trouble or so much as a stop. He looked very tired to Sonny, but his spirits were still high from the escapade with the bikers.

"About the only way you can die out here is from boredom," Jake said when they were unable to find anything of interest on the radio or the CB.

"Or the road can run out on you."

"That's right. The wreck. I'd show you the place, but they've probably fixed it by now."

Sonny, observing the forlorn landscape through his window, had a thought. Anything to beat the boredom.

"Whatever happened to the old Burma Shave signs? I don't think I've seen one on the whole trip."

"Hell, I don't even know if they still sell Burma Shave anymore. Say you remember those?"

"Some. Let's see. 'Don't take a curve at sixty per . . .'"

Jake finished. "'We hate to lose a customer.'"

"Right. Hey, I got another one. 'Henry the Eighth, Prince of Friskers, lost five wives but kept his whiskers.'"

"Always liked that one. How 'bout, 'Does your husband misbehave? Grunt and grumble, rant and rave? Shoot the brute some Burma Shave.' That was Mama's favorite."

"There was one about birds crapping on the signs," Sonny said.

"Oh, hell, yeah. 'Listen, birds, those signs cost money. So roost a while, but don't get funny.'"

It beat counting jackrabbits and vultures, which became the principal signs of life as they struck deeper into Utah. So desolate had the country become that there were not even any telephone poles or power lines visible for miles around, only copper-colored, mile-high mesas in the hazy distance, signs saying "Ranch Exit" that led onto dirt roads apparently going nowhere, and high, lonesome cumulus clouds floating in the blue. There was the feeling that one was in the middle of a sad and forgotten country where one morning everyone would wake up and find they were lost in a desert with no way out. It was absolutely lifeless, except for the big rig they would occasionally see chugging toward them from three miles off on a six percent grade, or a rancher who had stopped his pickup on the shoulder to gun away in disgust at a writhing six-foot rattlesnake, or signs that a Truck Escape Ramp had recently been put to use. Sonny couldn't fathom how his father had made these trips alone.

Sonny had been absently watching a pickup truck disappear into the foothills of a mountain range to the north, bobbing along in a puff of smoke, perhaps two miles away. "One thing I can't figure," he said over the roar of the engine, "is who would live out here on purpose."

"Not many, from the looks of it," Jake said. "Mormons, ranchers, miners. Reckon that's about it."

"It's so damned lonely out here. Nobody's home."

"Takes a certain kind. Me, for example."

"You?"

"I always fancied myself cowboying. That's probably how I'd o' wound up if it wasn't for trucking."

"Well, I can see the connection between the two. But out here? Look at this country. For one thing, who would you tell your stories to?"

"Always be a saloon somewhere."

"Right, and John Wayne hanging out. Come on."

"I'd be my own boss, anyway."

"I wonder if anybody's his own boss, Pop. I mean, ultimately there's always somebody you've got to answer to."

"Not if you don't want to, there ain't."

"How about on this trip you're on right now?"

"Name me who I'm answering to."

"Well, there's Charley. You're pulling his trailer and his tires.

This fellow Mathis, at the mine, he's gonna tell you where he wants the tires stacked. When we get to the air base at Vegas, they'll have some rules to follow for the inspection. And you've gone to a little trouble avoiding the weigh stations, too."

"Doing it my way, though, if you ain't noticed."

Sonny said, "It just seems like most of the time you go out of your way to be different. It's become a way of life."

"Aw, me and you come from a long line of loners, son. You don't have to live out West for that." Jake went through the ritual of relighting his cigar with wind rushing through the cab of Redball. "You never met your grandpa or your great-grandpa, but they both brought their own drummers with 'em."

"Wasn't Grandpa the Seventh-Day Adventist?"

"Probably the only damned one in east Tennessee."

"How'd that happen?"

"Because there wasn't no more in east Tennessee, far as I can figure."

Sonny said, "Hell, that must've made him an outcast."

"He paid the price for it, all right. He ran the biggest store in the county. Of a Saturday morning, everybody'd ride their buggies into town and buy what they needed. 'course Paw, being a Seventh-Day, he'd be closed up tight. But then, come a Sunday, he'd open up and be ready to do some business, but that was the day them Baptists and Holy Rollers up there wouldn't leave the house except to go to church and do their shouting."

"How'd he manage to stay in business?"

"Hitched a mule to a wagon and took it to 'em during the week, that's how. Goes to show there's a way to get around almost anything."

"And Great-Grandpa?"

"Only man in the county that fought for the Yankees."

"Jesus." Sonny laughed. "It's a wonder you didn't get *run* out of east Tennessee when you left for Birmingham."

"I'll admit there wasn't much love lost on the Hawkinses,"

Jake said. "Paw died when I was eight, and they played hell getting six pallbearers for him. Probably gonna be the same with me when I go."

"Oh, hell, Pop, you've got plenty of friends."

"Name me a few. When you get past Charley and Monk, there ain't nobody. Most of my friends are people that ain't got last names. People I know from truck stops and loading docks."

Once they had eased through the town of Delta, around one o'clock in the afternoon, they found out why U.S. 50 was called the Loneliest Road in America. Between there and Ely, a distance of 150 miles, there was not a single black dot signifying a town or community on the *Rand McNally Road Atlas* that Sonny now held in his lap. All he saw were deserts, isolated little Indian reservations, dry lake beds, and off-limits "experiment stations" that he took to be bombing ranges. They rode in silence in the insufferable heat, down to their bare chests again, as the view through the windshield of Dixie Redball became that of a lunar landscape: eroded cliffs, baked desert valleys, hazy 10,000-foot mountain ranges ten miles distant with names like Confusion and Wah Wah, occasional little twisters spiraling up from the rocky floor of the Great Basin, now and then a hawk or a buzzard floating above all this desolation in search of a meal. During one stretch they drove for thirty minutes before seeing another vehicle, a Kenworth laboring up from a five-mile-wide desert bottom with a reefer in tow, and both Jake and the other trucker were so delighted to see each other that they playfully blasted their air horns like explorers passing in the wilderness.

Finally, after two hours of emptiness, during which few words had passed between them, a mirage began to take shape in the distance. Sonny blinked his eyes at first, thinking he had seen a windshield glinting in the sun, but soon he could see that it was the flash of metal from some sort of building. As they rolled on down the highway, closer and closer, the objects became clearer to him and real: gas pumps, power lines, a weathervane, a pickup truck, a cable television dish.

"Nevada?"

"If it ain't, I missed a turn somewhere," Jake said, reaching for a lower gear, checking his mirrors, squinting, chewing his cigar. Then they saw the first of a series of hand-painted signs coming up, staggered like Burma Shave signs: State Line Slots.

"You're not going on in?"

"It ain't but two o'clock, Pacific Time."

"How far's Ely?"

"No more'n an hour. Figured we could use a break. I'm about to bust a bladder."

"I take it you're not going to try to unload today, then."

"Naw," Jake said. "That's liable to take a couple of hours, and I'm too tired to think about it. Figure that can wait 'til tomorrow."

"Well, that's a relief. I won't have to call Charley to tell on you."

"Charley who?" Jake said. He was turning on the blinkers now, making his turn into the crushed-gravel lot in front of the place, a flat-roofed, concrete-block building tattooed with advertisements for beer and cigarettes and warnings about Nevada gambling laws. "You still got them quarters?"

"Quarters."

"Ones Monk give us, for him and Beulah."

"Oh, hell, I'd forgotten."

"Better flush 'em out. We're about to make Monk rich in his old age."

"Who're you kidding? This guy probably pays all of his bills with one bandit."

"That what they call 'em? Bandits? This is gonna be like robbing Wells Fargo. Ride in, take the money, and ride out."

"These are machines, Pop. Not people."

"People made 'em, didn't they?"

The quarters were gone before Jake and Sonny could finish their Nehi orange sodas, but they didn't mind. It was enough just to get in out of the sun, away from the constant jarring of the truck, and bathe in air conditioning. The owner of the place was a man of about sixty, with a face as coppery and eroded as the hills they had been seeing all day. He stood beside the cash register in boots and straw cowboy hat, oiling the parts of a high-powered rifle that he had broken down and laid out on the long counter, while his Indian wife sat in a metal lawn chair rapt over a soap opera on a jumbo color television set.

"You boys want some more change?" the owner said when Jake shook the pouch that once had held Monk Strickland's twenty quarters.

"Might need a dime to call my friend with the news that he just lost his life's savings," said Jake.

"I could've swore you were gon' win on that machine there. Bunch of hippies primed it for you yesterday."

"They weren't riding motorbikes, were they?"

"Yeah. You must of seen 'em over in Utah."

Jake told him about the incident with the bikers at the Green River truck stop. "Them boys could use every quarter they lost about now."

"Sure you don't want to try some more?"

"We'll do some high rolling when we get to Vegas."

"That where you headed?"

"Got a load for Sarah first."

"Must be for Knudsen-Menke. The mine."

"Yeah. Got a load of earth-mover tires."

"When you get there, tell 'em J.D. said go to hell. That's me, J. D. Lawson." He had driven the big earth-movers at the mine for five years, he said, after retiring from the army, and the only good thing about the experience had been the big money he had made. "Especially that goddamn Red Mathis."

"Mathis? You wouldn't happen to know if he was ever a catcher for the Birmingham Barons, would you?"

"Hell, no. Too damned mean for playing ball."

"Well, what's the deal with him?"

"The sonofabitch thinks the war's still on. He was a sergeant in Korea. Won all kinds of medals, according to what he says, and maybe he's right. All I know is, he's the workingest, drinkingest, gamblingest sonofabitch I ever had the displeasure of working for."

"He's the one I'm supposed to turn over the tires to. Red Mathis."

"Watch the fucker," said J. D. Lawson. "He'll try to make out like you work for him, when all you're doing is delivering tires."

"I don't work for nobody," Jake said. "Never have, never will."

"It's gon' be an interesting match, my friend."

Jake had talked about calling Mama once they had reached Ely, just like in the old days, to let her know that he had made it to the other end of the road alive, but about all he managed to accomplish before he was ready to crash was to take a steaming bath and find a thick steak. They had found a grim little fifteen-dollar motel on the main drag of town, the Desert Pines Resort, its concrete blocks painted pink, and by nine o'clock that night as the hot sun finally gave way to a full and brilliant moon over the Great Basin they cut the lights and called it a day. They had been exactly six days on the road.

20

By eight o'clock in the morning they had checked out of the motel and were finishing breakfast at a seedy little diner on the west side of town, not ten miles from the copper mine. The only others in the place were an old Navajo woman with two toddlers, a hard-hatted miner, and a waif in long hair and beads and sandals who seemed to have missed the last bus leaving the sixties. Jake ate voraciously, paying no mind to anything that wasn't on his plate, while Sonny sipped coffee and perused the weekly tabloid newspaper that covered eastern Nevada. Redball was parked at curbside, like a patient pack mule, waiting up.

"Listen to this," Sonny said. He folded the newspaper to an entire page billed as Police Blotter. "Vehicle versus sheep. U.S. 50 near Eureka."

"It's them damned open range laws."

" 'Vehicle versus two cattle.' In Elko."

"Looks like we're outnumbered."

"Christ, it reads like a sports story. 'Rams versus Jets.'"

"You'll think sports when you hit one doing sixty miles a goddamn hour," Jake said.

The unloading at the mine should take only two or three hours, Jake had said, and then they would be on their way to Las Vegas to await the inspection of tires at Nellis on Thursday morning. They had a long day's drive ahead of them, 280 miles of treacherous highway that wound south out of Ely through the very heart of the forbidding Great Basin, with very few settlements in between, so it was imperative that they get rid of the tires by noon.

Sonny put the paper aside and sipped the last of his coffee. "What's the time difference between here and Birmingham, Pop? Two hours?"

"Unless they changed it."

"This would've been a good time to call Mama. Between breakfast and lunch."

"I don't know."

"She would've gotten a kick out of it."

"Naw," Jake said. "It would've just got her confused."

"Well, you'll never know now."

"It don't seem to matter no more. I've already said my good-byes to Mama as we knew her."

"Not 'good-bye.' 'Hello.'"

"What the hell's the difference?"

Sonny said, "Why so morose this morning? You've done it, Pop. You made it. Six days on the road."

"It ain't ending up right."

"'Getting there's half the fun.' That it?"

"Naw, it's the tires. It'd be different if I could unload 'em."

"I guess I understand," Sonny said. "Charley says it's like being able to trot around the bases after hitting a homer."

"Didn't know Charley was that smart."

"Come on, Pop. He's smarter than you and me put together. You know that."

"Damn him, anyway. This is gonna be about the first time something like this ever happened. It ain't right." Jake was on his feet, digging for a tip. "Let's get the hell out of here. I want to see how tough this fella Mathis is."

As soon as they pulled away from the diner, they began to pass the last of everything: last slots, last eats, last gas, last toilet. Over the next 330 miles of U.S. 50 there would be only three towns of any size before Carson City and Reno, and the Pine Mountain County Chamber of Commerce was trying to make the most of a bleak situation by heavily promoting the Loneliest Road in America with billboards and highway markers, businesses in Ely joining in by selling T-shirts, bumper stickers, key chains, and even "exit visas" celebrating the theme "I Survived the Loneliest Road." When they had passed the last of these signs, Redball groaning under the strain, they suddenly entered a twilight zone: lifeless, parched, rocky, layered with dust, uninviting, apparently unforgiving.

Within ten minutes they saw the mine on the south side of the road, to their left, marked by a dusty sign with an arrow pointing to Knudsen-Menke Mining Corporation. Jake, who had never left his lowest range of gears that morning, slowed almost to a halt and hit the turn signal. For six days and nearly 2,000 miles they had rolled through canopied piney woods and coasted over undulating plains and chugged over jagged mountains, through the heat, rain, and boredom of the open road, and now it had come to this: a huge open wound in the earth, everything the color of copper, the roar of machinery, giant earth-movers scooping dirt like feral dogs digging for bones, the horizon dotted with abandoned open pit mines that now resembled dormant volcanoes, not even the contrails of a jet breaking the limitless cerulean sky.

They bounced along the crushed gravel road for a quarter mile and then took the wide concrete bridge that spanned an intricate switching yard choked with small-gauge railroad cars loaded with ore. Coming into view was a cluster of double-wide trailers, surrounded by high barbed wire fencing, which appeared to be the mining company's offices and storage area. Beyond that, through a windshield already beginning to film with dust, they could see a yellow earth-mover crawling up the side of one of the pit mines by switchbacks. And at the base of that man-made mesa, next to a row of monstrous machines like the one now crawling up its face, there was a sight that made Jake grin and gnaw his cigar: a mound of discarded tire carcasses, perhaps two dozen of them, the tires he had come two thirds of the way across America to replace.

Jake stopped the truck when he saw a young man angrily slam the door of one of the double-wides behind him and come striding their way. He was burnished and strong, dressed in the heavy work boots, hard hat, long-sleeved khakis, and sunglasses that seemed to be the uniform around the mine, and he held a clipboard and a black lunch pail.

"Looks like your troubles are over, son." Jake had leaned out the window and was smiling broadly, cigar still clenched in his mouth.

Preoccupied, the worker stopped in his tracks. "Say what?"

"You drive one o' them things, don't you?" Jake pointed to the line of earth-movers.

"Not good enough, to hear the old man talk."

"Well, I brought you some new rubber. Maybe it'll dig in for you now."

The young man stepped closer, and he smiled when he read the Graddick & Sons poster on the door of the truck. "Birmingham, huh?"

"Prettiest city in Alabam'."

"Well, I'm from Arkansas."

"That a fact. Where 'bouts?"

"Up above Memphis? Little town called Trumann?"

"Hell," Jake said, "we was through there, wasn't a week ago. Passed right by the Baldwin piano place."

"That's where my daddy works."

"He don't make 'em, does he?"

"Nah. Runs a forklift in shipping."

"I'd o' stopped to play 'em a tune or two if I hadn't been in a hurry."

"Well, look," the young man said, "I got to get on top of my mule. Guess you're looking for Mathis."

"That's the one. From what I been hearing, he'll be the one breathing fire."

"You can see for yourself if you go through that first door over there."

"Much obliged, son."

"Watch the sonofabitch," the young man said, nodding to Jake, then trudging with his head down toward the line of yellow earth-movers. Little puffs of dust kicked up and whirled every time his boots hit the ground.

Jake changed into his cowboy boots and fished the wrinkled bill of lading from the small toolbox stashed beneath his seat, then jumped from the truck and motioned for Sonny to follow. He had blocked a dozen pickups that were parked at the fence, but he figured he would be there for only a few minutes. With Sonny meandering behind to gawk at the sheer scope of the landscape and the operation, Jake pushed open the door of the trailer office and heard a stream of cussing. The cussing came from a man with a barrel chest, an orange burr haircut, a coppery face wrought from leather, and a khaki work uniform drenched with coffee from the crotch right up to the sewn name tag spelling out MATHIS.

"Goddamned motherfuckin' sonofabitch, when are you assholes gonna start knockin' first?"

"Reckon I could've sat out front and blowed the horn for you," Jake said.

"Who the hell are you?"

"Then we could've called it curb service."

"We ain't got time for games, old-timer."

"I got something you need, *sarge*."

Mathis slammed the empty paper cup into a trash bin and then put his hands on his hips and seethed at the scrawny apparition who stood before him. Jake had already gone into his slow dance of discovering that his cigar had gone out, of fumbling through his pockets for a kitchen match, of looking around for a handy place to strike it, and now, after raking it sharply across the metal door he had just entered, he was puffing with great vigor as great billows of blue smoke began encircling his face. He shook the match and flipped it at Mathis's boots.

"I get it now," Mathis said, looking at Jake's Graddick Tire cap. He began to blot the coffee on his khakis with a bandanna and walked slowly to a swivel chair beside a window air-conditioning unit and behind a metal desk. "You're the hotshot that won't unload his own tires. What's that, some more union shit?"

"What're you talking about?"

"Had your boss call in sick for you, huh?"

"Charley Graddick called you?"

"Yesterday morning. Said you were too old to be unloading. Sounds like a note from mama."

"Now look here, you sonofabitch —"

"Your buddy also said it's on the bill of lading that you can't unload. That puts my ass in a crack on the insurance."

"Damn that Charley." Jake muttered and unrolled the bill of lading. He saw that Charley had, indeed, typed out a codicil: Under No Circumstances Is Driver To Unload. He tossed the papers on the desk, looking as though he could bite the cigar in half. "Well, let's get 'em off, then. We want to make Vegas before dark."

Mathis said, "Can't do it today, old-timer."

"What do you mean, you can't do it today?"

"Tomorrow. The forklift's tied up and I ain't got enough men available for fucking around with no tires."

"Hell, it don't take but one man."

"Shit. Three men and a forklift, at least."

"Not the way I do it, sarge."

"Yeah, but there ain't no way you're gonna do it, Pops. Maybe if your partner there wants to give it a try — "

"This is my boy. He's just along for the ride."

"Don't look like much of a prize, anyway."

Jake stepped backward and groped for the doorknob, leveling his eyes on Mathis as he opened the door. A blast of heat and the clatter of heavy machinery tumbled in. "I ain't even got to look at the bill of lading to tell you it don't say a goddamn thing in there about how these tires get unloaded. It just says they get delivered. Unless you come up with a way to get all twenty-five of 'em off by noon, I'm gonna open the trailer door right out front here where you got your pickups parked and then I'm gonna gun my rig and be long gone. It won't take ten seconds."

"Nobody talks to me like that, you old fart."

"You got a minute to make up your mind, sarge."

Sonny thought he saw a glimmer of a smile on Mathis's thin lips as he put on his hard hat and brushed past them into the morning sun. Without a word he pointed at the pile of discarded tires they had seen coming in, and he strode off in the direction of a large flat-roofed shed made of prefabricated steel. Jake cranked Redball and slowly rolled the rig past the shed, marked Maintenance Depot, and when he saw two newly recapped earth-mover tires standing together on their treads against a chain-link fence he began to back the trailer into place. "They're down to two," he told Sonny. "I figure the sonofabitch needs 'em pretty bad. We'll get rid of 'em, one way or the other."

Jake had made sure the trailer was on level ground. He was beginning to unlock the doors when Mathis came toward him with a giant Indian in tow. Bronze, with unkempt salt-and-pepper hair, almost as tall and wide as an earth-mover tire himself, he wore jeans, a T-shirt, work boots and an air of utter stoicism.

Mathis saw Jake and Sonny staring at the Indian. "My human forklift," he said.

"Looks to me like he could eat the tires for breakfast," said Jake.

"Me and Cochise go back to army days. I'd start fights, he'd finish 'em."

"He ever unloaded tires?"

"He'll learn. This fucker can hold up the back end of a pickup while you change tires."

"There's an art to unloading these things, sarge."

"That's what you and the Teamsters say, Pops."

Jake bristled. "I ain't no union man. Never was."

Mathis was impatient. "Come on, old man, open up. Let's get these damned things off." Jake swung open the doors and battened them to the sides of the trailer. The tires, packed like sardines, stood five abreast and five rows deep: seventy-eight inches tall, twenty-seven inches wide, one thousand pounds each. Mathis turned to the Indian and said, "Okay, Cochise, what I want you to do is take 'em off and roll 'em over there against the fence where them other two are at."

Jake said, "Don't you think I oughta — "

"He'll take care of it, Pops."

"If the damned things start to wobble — "

"Go sit in the shade, old man," said Mathis. He waved his hand at the front row of tires, the newly teethed treads grinning menacingly, and said, "Okay, Chief, go get 'em."

The Indian heaved himself up onto the narrow apron of the trailer, four feet off the ground, and began to rock one of the tires until he could get it moving toward the ledge. Jake, clucking and trying to contain himself, motioned for Sonny to back off to safety. With the tire teetering on the brink, the Indian gave it one final nudge and leaped from the trailer. Indian and tire hit the ground at the same instant, in a great whumping billow of dust, and vainly he struggled to control the wobble with hands as large as baseball gloves. The tire seemed to have a mind of its own, though, and the more the Indian tried to contain the wobble the worse it got. The tire began to pick up speed as it careened toward the fence twenty feet away, like a runaway top, and soon it went into a spin and began to run in widening concentric circles until finally it crashed to the hard-baked copper earth with a deafening thud, taking the other two tires with it.

Mathis came running up to the shaken Indian, cursing and punching him on the shoulder with the heel of his hand. "Okay, let's go, pick it up. We ain't got all day."

"Forklift," the Indian said.

"Hey, Cochise, you're my goddamn forklift."

"Fuck you, Mathis."

"Come on, now, Chief. Pick it up."

"Tomorrow, when you get the forklift."

"All right, goddamnit," Mathis said. "But by God you ain't dropping no more of 'em. Shit, if we want every damn one of 'em on their sides, the driver here says he can do that in about ten seconds. Now let's straighten up, Chief."

When the Indian looked toward Jake, pleading for help, he seized the moment. "Let me show him."

"Oh, no, Pop," Sonny said.

"Just one, son. That's all it'll take."

Mathis said, "Hold it. I can't let you do that."

"It ain't unloading," Jake said. "It's teaching."

"Just one?"

"Just one. I'll take him through it step by step."

"This I got to see," Mathis said.

Sonny had never seen it himself. Jake went to the cab of the truck for his leather work gloves, and when he had returned to the open end of the trailer and swung up into it he stood theatrically on the apron like a professor preparing to deliver an important lecture. "It's like making love proper to a woman," he said, working his fingers deep into the gloves, his cheekbones clenching as he chewed the unlit cigar. "You can't be in a hurry. You take 'er one step at a time. If you think about her and not yourself, everything'll work out fine for everybody." He took the cigar from his mouth and spat off the edge of the trailer, the tobacco juice kicking up a spurt of dust when it hit the ground. "I ain't gonna have no time to talk, Chief, so you just watch what I do."

Mathis said, "I don't know about this."

"You want the tires unloaded proper or not?"

"You old jackrabbit. I just don't want your blood on my hands."

"I understand you're a betting man, Mathis."

"I been known to put some dollars down."

"Twenty dollars says I'll have this tire standing at attention against that fence over there in less than ten minutes. You too chickenshit to bet? Come on, general."

"Twenty dollars," Mathis said.

It took only five minutes. The analogy with lovemaking wasn't bad, Sonny thought, as he watched the show. Jake didn't muscle the tire, as the Indian had; he played it, like a safecracker picking up vibrations or a lover probing for tender folds of pink skin. Imperceptibly, the thousand-pound tire was suddenly balanced on the very edge of the trailer, so precariously that a gust of wind might send it crashing to the ground. Jake then eased off the trailer, holding his breath, and positioned himself directly beneath the tire with his legs spread-eagled. Next, as though he were handling a bubble that might burst, he gently drew forward on both sides of the tire. Only he could see that it was moving until suddenly, like a thunderclap, it fell to the ground with a loud thunk. Jake had moved as one with the tire, and when the dust cleared they saw him slowly pulling his hands away and stepping back like a matador who now owned his bull.

The easy part was rolling the tire to the fence, and when Jake came back to the trailer he peered at a speechless Mathis while he lit his cigar. "I'm getting paid five hundred dollars for this leg of the trip," he said. "At twenty dollars a tire, this unloading could be more profitable than the driving."

"You made your point." Mathis gave Jake a twenty-dollar bill. He turned to the Indian and said, "You got that, Cochise? You see how he did it?"

"Slow and easy."

"That's real good, Chief, real good."

"No sweat, sarge."

"Go get 'em, boy."

The Indian could have gotten crushed by the next tire he tried. His problem was, he was *too* strong, a man who had always been able to use his brute strength to solve any problem. Sonny was remembering the story of the gorilla, trained to drive a golf ball five hundred yards straight up the fairway, who addressed a two-foot putt and cleanly drove the ball five hundred yards. Everything had gone fine until the Indian chose to jerk the tire off the lip of the trailer, rather than gently nudge it, but at least he had developed the good sense to jump clear as the tire rocketed off the trailer and rumbled past him like a galloping grizzly, not wobbling this time, but shooting straight for the fence to knock down Jake's tire. Now there were five of them sprawled on their sides at the fence.

"Look here," Jake said, "we can work it out."

"I told you, Pops, I can't let you do it."

"He just can't get 'em off the trailer. That's where my experience comes in."

"I don't know."

"He'll bring 'em up to the edge of the trailer, I'll get 'em on the ground, he'll roll 'em to the fence. There's twenty-two to go. I figure two hours. What do you say?"

Sonny stepped in. "Damnit, Pop, you promised."

"Things have changed," said Jake.

"Shit. You're sixty-nine years old. You've just driven two thousand miles. It's going to hit a hundred degrees today."

"I didn't drive all the way out here to see my load wind up on the ground."

"It's not your load. It's Mathis's load."

"Not until I get it off my trailer, it ain't."

Mathis took off his hard hat and raked his hand through his burr haircut, slinging sweat. He looked at Sonny and said, "I want it to be known that I told your old man I didn't want him unloading these tires. You heard me say that, didn't you?"

"Yeah, I heard you *say* it."

"All right, then."

"Hey, look, Mathis — "

"Now, I've been fucking around long enough with this shit this morning. I'm the foreman around here, not some damned referee."

"He's too old for this kind of work."

"He don't look too old to me, pardner." Mathis plopped the hard hat back on his head and winked at Jake. "Before you get away, old-timer, maybe you'll buy me a drink out of that twenty. And don't let Cochise kill himself."

"You sonsabitches." Jake and Mathis weren't squared off anymore but turned their attention to Sonny. They were smirking, winking at each other, clearing their throats in a smug conspiracy, waiting to see if the boy had anything else to say before the men got back to work. Sonny felt trapped. He heard Charley Graddick's last words: *He's your daddy. I'm holding you responsible.* Well, Charley, that's fine, he thought as he stood between the two men, but what was left to do? The cops had no dog in this fight; the union local had better things to do than mess with a nonunion trucker from Alabama; Charley was 2,000 miles away; Mama was more or less gone from this world. For a moment Sonny had a vision of his lying on the ground at the rear of the trailer, like a sixties sit-in protestor, but it seemed more ludicrous than workable. Finally, when he knew his options had run out, he jammed his thumbs in the pockets of his jeans and said, again, "You sonsabitches."

All through the morning, as the sun rose higher in the limitless sky, Sonny stayed close by as Jake unloaded the tires. Once he went to fetch soft drinks; another time he walked up to the office to look at a map of the sprawling mine he had glimpsed earlier, but mainly he sat on one of the overturned tires and watched the unloading as it proceeded. The Indian, either by his own design or Jake's orders, wasn't doing much besides carefully rolling the tires against the fence. As soon as he had trudged back to the trailer, Jake would already be coaxing another one of them to the ground.

They wouldn't finish by noon, due to the time lost haggling with Mathis, but they wouldn't miss by much. Around eleven-thirty, Sonny got off the tire where he had been sitting and walked to where Jake stood bare-chested, wiping the sweat from his face with a bandanna. The sun stood straight overhead, leaving him no place to hide.

"How-*dee*," Jake yelped like Minnie Pearl, "I'm just so glad to be *hyar*."

"How many more to go, Pop?"

"Believe there's five of 'em back there."

"Look, Pop, you're pushing your luck. The guy's got to bring a forklift tomorrow to pick up those first ones, anyway. Why don't you dump these and let's go?"

"I've come this far. Might as well finish."

"Well, at least take a break. It must be ninety-five, at least. Only protection you've got is your cap."

"I'm all right. It's the Indian that's about to drop." He motioned toward Cochise, who now sat on the tire that Sonny had just vacated, and lowered his voice. "See, they put 'em on these reservations and throw welfare money at 'em and pretty soon they forget about work."

"I bet he'd work if you'd let him."

"Naw, he just don't know how to do it, and I ain't got time to show him."

Sonny said, "Come on. Knock off for a while. We could go sit under the roof at the maintenance shed and drink some water. You could smoke a cigar."

"Afraid to break my rhythm. I'm on a roll."

"Tell you what. I saw a bucket and a ladle up there. I'll bring you back some water. You can have a drink, and then pour the rest over your head."

"Sounds right civilized to me."

"Okay, then. I'll be right back. Wait up."

"I ain't planning to go nowhere, son. Not when there's still some work to do." Jake swung up into the trailer again, this time not so jauntily, and his boots clunked across the floor as he disappeared into the semidarkness where the remaining tires awaited.

Sonny trudged up the slight incline leading to the maintenance shed, about half a football field's length from Redball and the trailer, fanning himself with his Graddick cap, wiping the sweat from his neck, glad for a respite from the sun. Three old mechanics who had been working on a bulldozer all morning sat at a picnic table in the shade, talking low and eating from lunch pails, and they nodded toward Sonny as he passed them on his way to the water pail.

"How do y'all stand this heat?" Sonny said as he dipped the ladle into the pail.

"By stayin' out of it," one of the men said.

"Must be a hundred degrees already."

"Be a hundred-and-eight before it's over." The one who spoke this time was a squat Chicano, brown and ageless. "The tires about off?"

"Another thirty minutes, maybe."

"That old fella doing it all by himself?"

"Yeah." Sonny took a long draught of water from the ladle. "He sure is."

"I been watching. How old is he, anyway?"

"He'll be seventy in August."

"Damnedest thing I ever saw, the way he does it."

"It's all in knowing how, he says."

"Looks like he'd know when to quit."

"It does, doesn't it?" Sonny found a small bucket. "Would it be okay if I fill this up and take it to him? He's about to burn up."

Before he could get an answer, Sonny heard shouts coming up the hill from the trailer. When he spun, ladle frozen halfway to his mouth, he saw the Indian yelling wildly and running from the fence to the trailer, arms flapping, boots kicking up spurts of dust. When Sonny focused on the trailer, across the barren stretch of copper earth shimmering with heat waves, he saw that his father was embraced in a life-or-death struggle with one of the tires. Sonny dropped the ladle and felt his heart jump into his throat. "Run, Pop, *run*," he shouted as he began to run madly, himself, and what he saw as he flew down the hill he would always remember in slow motion: Jake fighting off the tire like a man wrestling a bear, Jake grimacing and dancing and flailing and cursing, the tire beginning to move in a circle now, the battle intensifying, the Indian rushing up from the other direction, a swirl of dust enveloping Jake and the tire locked in their dance of death. "Jump, Pop, *jump*," Sonny yelled, not twenty feet away now, "let go of the sonofabitch." When Jake finally did let go, with the startled yowl of a man who had just been struck by a rattlesnake, he looked about wildly and then jumped. In a great whumping cloud of dust, right in front of his son's eyes, he was flattened by the tire. He had jumped the wrong way.

It was a broken neck, instant death, and there was nothing to say when the Indian managed to lift the tire enough for Sonny to grab Jake's boots and drag the body clear. The men came down from the maintenance shed to gawk, toe the dirt, and mumble about freak accidents they had seen. Sonny was covering his father's face with the Graddick Tire windbreaker, the neck bent grotesquely and the face bearing a look of genuine surprise, when an ambulance came careening through the dust and fishtailed to a halt. Somebody had raised Mathis over a walkie-talkie, and when he leaped from his jeep he seemed to treat Jake as one who had fallen in battle, telling, in a flat voice, of an old army sergeant in Korea who had foolishly led a fatal charge for the simple reason that he knew there would be no more wars for him to fight. Mathis invited Sonny to come to his office and drink some bourbon, but Sonny said he had to use the phone.

EPILOGUE

CHARLEY GRADDICK knew how to get things done. It was in the middle of the afternoon that day, Alabama time, when Sonny got him on the phone at the tire place, and within twenty-four hours Sonny and the body were arriving at the Birmingham airport on a chartered jet. Charley and Phyllis were waiting. Burial would be Friday morning, Phyllis said, and she wasn't sure whether Mama understood what had happened. They would worry about Dixie Redball IV later, Charley said, but he knew some drivers who would be damned proud to own Jake Hawkins's last truck.

Jake had been wrong about not being able to summon up a full complement of pallbearers for his funeral. He could have had forty, all of them from Graddick Tire, most of whom were being given the morning off to attend the burial. Picking the pallbearers was the one detail that Sonny insisted on handling. He settled on Charley Graddick and Monk Strickland, of course, and Country Boy Eddie; Leo Miranda, for himself as much as for his father, and, from Graddick Tire, an accountant whose name had been drawn from a hat, and Jo-Jo, who had loaded the trailer for Jake's last ride.

Leo had flown up from Tallahassee around dark on Thursday, in time to join a wake at Andrews Barbecue, where a dozen of the old-timers from Graddick Tire drank beer and told Jake Hawkins stories until closing time. At the Hawkins house on Friday morning, the day of the burial, Sonny and Leo were having coffee when Country Boy told his television audience of Jake's death and then led his band with a mawkish slow version of "Six Days on the Road."

"He'd like that," Sonny said.

"How about you?"

"I feel okay, Leo. I really do. He died with his boots on."

"You gonna try 'em on for size, or what?"

"Think I'll just get 'em bronzed and be on my way, pardner."

"Meaning?"

"For starters, I thought I'd try to teach the dean's wife the difference between a novel and a hardcover book."

Leo was seated on the piano bench. He aimlessly ran his fingers over the keys and said, "What was that business last night at the funeral home, with your sister and her husband?"

"Ah, shit. I was just trying to make small talk, looking for a way to break away and meet y'all at Andrews, and I said something like I always figured Pop was going to live to see the twenty-first century. This asshole brother-in-law said, 'Well, he probably wouldn't like it any more than he liked the twentieth century.' I told him that the reason Pop got up before daybreak every day of his life was so he could get a leg up on fuckers like him. That's when my sister stepped in and said, 'Just don't *do* anything at the cemetery tomorrow.'"

"Well?"

"What?"

"You didn't write out the poem for practice."

"I'll see how it goes, Leo."

Forest Hill Cemetery was no longer the idyllic place it had been when Jake Hawkins paid cash for a family plot in the fifties. Now it stood directly beside the busy cloverleaf interchange of Interstates 20 and 59. It was there, at eleven o'clock on a steamy morning in late June of his seventieth year, that Jake would be put into the ground. The preacher was Brother Fenster P. Boggs, of Mimosa Towers Christian Retirement Home.

Sonny and Phyllis sat on either side of their mother beneath the forest green canopy that sheltered the casket, now closed and blanketed with sprays of flowers, and across from them were the six pallbearers and the four grandchildren and perhaps forty friends and relatives. An additional forty, the rough-hewn men of Graddick Tire, nervously huddled together in their only suits.

There wasn't much Brother Boggs could say, and he had to almost shout to be heard above the roar of traffic on the highway interchange not more than 400 yards away. In his black suit, clearly uncomfortable, he cleared his throat and tried. "As you all know, Brother Hawkins was a resident at Mimosa Towers, along with his beloved wife, Evelyn." Boggs shot a glance at Phyllis, holding her mother's hand and smiling gravely, as though pleading for forgiveness. "I'm sorry to say that I didn't know him very well, because he wasn't always there. At Mimosa." Sonny caught the eyes of Charley Graddick, who stood directly across the casket from him, and saw that Charley was smiling.

Up from the highway interchange came the sounds of vehicles on the move. Boggs waited, as though the noise would abate until he had finished, then plowed ahead. "Mr. Hawkins was an accomplished piano player, and I remember one day joining him at the beautiful piano we have in the lobby at Mimosa

Towers and conversing with him. I said, 'Mr. Hawkins, where did you learn to play the piano so beautifully? Surely, you took lessons.' And I shall never forget his response. He told me, 'Reverend, I'm just using the talents that my master gave me.' " Sonny saw Charley's face twitch and his hand fly up to his mouth, and when he squeezed his mother's hand she squeezed back. "And do you know the name of the song he was playing that day? It was an old favorite that we all know and love so well. Mr. Hawkins was playing 'Amazing Grace.' "

Sonny rolled his eyes, and when he saw Charley break into a broad grin he reached into his coat pocket. During the night he had written out the entire poem, 'Do not go gentle into that good night,' on the back of an envelope, not sure what he might do with it, and now he felt a fire in his belly and an urge to rise up out of that metal folding chair and push the preacher aside and do this one last thing for his father. He could see it as clearly as a scene in a movie: the impassioned son, now with a full understanding of his father's life, rising dramatically to defend that life, cutting through the preacher's well-meaning revisionist benediction, friends and neighbors aghast, Charley Graddick and his men and Country Boy Eddie and maybe even old half-deaf Monk Strickland about to raise their fists in triumph, his clear voice ringing through the hills: *Rage, rage against the dying of the light* . . .

But it wasn't necessary. Sonny still had his hand on the envelope in his jacket pocket, still had time to make his move before the preacher found the passage he had marked in the Bible to end the ceremony, when time stopped. Suddenly, up from the highway interchange, there came the singing of tires, the grinding of gears, and the wailing of air horns as two Freightliners pulling glistening aluminum trailers jockeyed for position on the tricky interchange that would propel them westward across the plains and the mountains and the deserts and ultimately to the Pacific Ocean. When Sonny's hand came from his pocket, empty, he saw Charley wink.